SPIRIT OF THE BAYONET

SACRIFICE

TED RUSS

Published by Chinook Publishing LLC.

First Edition: 2025

ISBN: 979-8-9986894-4-4

Cover design & interior formatting: Mark Thomas / Coverness.com

For Henry.

Chapter One

Wharf Rat

Captain Bonham scanned the faces of the crew. Even in the dim light, she could see that they were not happy. They sat in silence, staring back at her, preparing to vote on a decision that would determine their course and fortunes for more than the next year. Bonham's eyes fell on the one empty seat to her right. She blinked and then rubbed her eyes to ward off the flash of unwanted memory.

Bonham was a stout, muscular woman, her pale skin marked with tattoos that memorialized decades spent in the void. She wore her hair in a severe undercut; the sides sheared close to the scalp, with longer dirty blonde hair left on top, usually pulled back into a short woven ponytail. The front hung lower, sweeping over her forehead in a way that gave her head the shape of a Spartan helmet. The dirty blonde masked the grey of her fifty-two years—twenty in space, seven as captain of the *Wharf Rat*. She was the last of the ship's original crew.

Decades underway with cardio bikes, weight rooms and induced gravity providing the only real physical training had warped her body into a five foot seven-inch-tall, one hundred and fifty-five-pound mass of knotted and inked muscle.

Pondering their options, Bonham leaned forward in her command chair and rubbed her chin. The black fabric of her flight suit tightened across her shoulders. The rest of the crew sat at their stations around the edge of the circular command deck. Small and focused, it was only ten meters across, with all eight crew seats facing the center of the room. The captain's chair was slightly larger than the rest, and faced forward in the direction of flight, though one would never know it. There were no windows in the armored facility. Dimly lit and encircled in display screens, the command deck was embedded in the *Wharf Rat's* Ring, the gravity inducing, rotating midsection, so it enjoyed a full G. Each seat had small screens on both armrests and holographic projection enabled the ship's AI to call up 3D imagery in the center of the command deck.

Sighing, she leaned back in her chair and settled her arms on her command chair's large leather rests. Her rolled-up sleeves revealed tattooed forearms.

Might as well get on with it.

"All right, Singh. Lay it out for us."

"Aye, Captain," Biradol Singh said in a loud voice. The tall Indian astronaut stood up from his chair and walked toward the middle of the command deck. His dark blue turban looked black in the dim light of the command deck, and his black flight suit was baggy on his skinny frame. "Imagery, please, Renate."

"Yes, sir," the female voice of Renate, *Wharf Rat's* managing AI came over the command deck's speakers as a large 3D image of the ship appeared in the center of the room. It rotated slowly around its Y axis.

"The *Rat's* current position and velocity places us approximately three months from the belt," Singh said as the image of the ship shrank quickly until it was a small, bright green dot. "Our solution envelope gives us two target options within that time window."

A yellow cone shape emanated from the *Wharf Rat's* floating icon. It widened as it extended away, passed through Singh, and drew itself out behind him, establishing the spatial extent of their options.

"The first is a seven-hundred-ton asteroid."

A single red triangle appeared, nearly at the edge of the cone behind Singh. It blinked brightly as he spoke.

"Data from Landy's probes suggest greater than seventy-two percent likelihood for concentrated rare earth elements that, based on spectral and probability analysis, could attain values between fifty million and two hundred million US dollars, depending on belt trading rates."

The crew sat in silence. It was a decent size score. But not spectacular. Not after the last job had gone so awry.

"What is the second option?" Abraxis Garcia asked.

Sitting in the chair opposite Captain Bonham, Garcia was a Brazilian spacefarer. No one knew how long he had been in space, but the cost the void had imposed on him was clear. His left arm was missing, replaced by an oversized robotic prosthetic, and his face was a poorly re-assembled jigsaw puzzle. Deep, zig sagging scars wove across a countenance that hinted at handsomeness long ago. The scars continued down his torso, weaving grotesquely across his chest and back, as if he had fallen head first into a food processor. A deep scar ran down his forehead, cleaving his left eyebrow and eye socket before carving a path down his cheek and under his jaw. It was a miracle he still had both eyes. In all his years on the *Wharf Rat*, he never once talked about how he got such terrible injuries.

"Option two is a Russian cargo ferry," Singh said as he took a few steps to the side. The second target triangle started blinking red where he had been standing.

"We know the Russians use their primary belt station as a consolidation hub for their prospecting and mining activities. It all gets processed there before being loaded on their drone cargo return ships. They, like most countries, use manned ships for the prospecting and ferrying, and drones for the cargo long haul. Our target, the *Kamchatka*, is one of these manned ferries."

"What's it carrying?" Garcia asked.

"No way to be certain, Axe. But we know Russian ferries are under orders to not return to their belt station below ninety-five percent cargo capacity. We also know that the Russians' prospecting emphasis has been helium lately, so it could be that. And most of the active asteroid mines this cargo ferry has serviced lately are known yttrium mines. Any of those scenarios, based on what we know of the *Kamchatka's* cargo capacity, would be a several hundred-million-dollar score."

The crew was quiet.

Bonham and Axe shared a quick glance. These were not great options.

"This telemetry sucks," Viggo Eriksson said, leaning forward in his crew seat on the shadowed edge of the command deck. "Our probes are shit." A Scandinavian veteran of the European Space Program, he was a muscular man that had spent over a decade in space, four on the *Wharf Rat*. Embracing his Viking heritage, Eriksson kept his dark blond beard well-trimmed.

"Was?" Matthias Landsberg spoke up from the other side of the command deck. "Das is bullshit. The probes are tight!"

Landsberg was a small man. He told people he was five foot six inches, and no one on the *Wharf Rat* ever contradicted him with the fact that he was actually only five foot three. It was too important to the guy. And though on earth he only weighed about a hundred and twenty pounds, when he got angry or felt challenged, he had a way of bowing up that seemed to add twenty pounds to his frame. Which still left him the smallest male, by far, on board the *Wharf Rat*.

At the moment, he was fully bowed up.

The captain shook her head. It was too easy to get a rise out of Landsberg, a German software and robotics savant, and she didn't feel like dealing with it at the moment.

"The probes are tight, Viggo," Naija Reeve, former member of the Nigerian astronaut corps, said from her seat next to Landsberg. Though about the same size as the German, her presence always seemed to pack ten times the power and intensity.

"Landy's probes are always tight." Reeve said, glaring at Eriksson. Leaning forward in her chair, the deep brown complexion of the nuclear propulsion engineer seemed to absorb the dim blue light of the command deck. "It's our options that are shit. Now keep your mouth shut so we can focus on the decision at hand."

Eriksson didn't argue. He took a deep breath and settled back in his chair. "I'm going to have a lot of questions," he barked at no one in particular.

Singh rolled his eyes before saying, "We do not have a lot of time. What is our constraint window, Renate?"

"The window for course correction closes in one hour and sixteen minutes and fifteen seconds," the AI responded.

Singh nodded.

"Engine burn in an hour and sixteen minutes," Axe reiterated in a loud voice. "And, as this crew well knows, it takes an hour to lock down and ready the *Rat* for a burn. So we've got sixteen minutes to decide. Asteroid or the *Kamchatka*."

Silence descended on the command deck.

Bonham scanned the crews' faces again. They were tense. She hoped this was not a contentious vote.

"This is the best we've got?" William Quinn asked, standing up from his chair. The American electrical and network engineer strode to the middle of the command deck. His flight suit top was unzipped, the sleeves tied around his waist, a grey tank over his tattooed, sinewy torso. Eighteen years younger than the captain, Quinn wore his hair in a tight flattop and was always clean shaven. He stopped in front of Singh and crossed his arms.

Singh stood in silence, looking back at Quinn.

"How long has it been since we went after the *Hadley*?" Quinn asked.

"Eighteen months," Reeve said.

"That's right," Quinn nodded, swiveling his glare from Singh to the captain. "Eighteen months since Viggo and I were on our knees mopping up what we could of Conrad with sponges so we could give him some kind of burial. When we shot his body bag into the void, it was full of just bloody sponges and rags. Isn't that right, Viggo?"

Bonham resisted the urge to glance at Conrad's empty seat. She kept her eyes locked on Quinn.

He's going to call for the vote, she thought.

"Aye," Eriksson answered.

Quinn turned from the captain slowly, locking eyes with each crew member in turn as he spoke.

"Then eighteen months of running and hiding while every waking hour of our lives was filled with repair work. High-risk meetings with criminals and other pirates, putting our security at risk and spending nearly every penny we had to get the parts we needed to get the *Rat* fully operational again. The only thing more empty than our cargo bay now is our crypto accounts."

Quinn's gaze rested back on Singh while some of the crew beat their arm rests in agreement.

"And now you are telling us this is all we got to choose from?"

Trained as an astrophysicist, one of Singh's duties was to work with Renate and the captain on targeting. He analyzed all the incoming data and generated cost benefit scenarios, always with a keen eye on fuel, resupply, and potential trading scenarios.

"We got what we got, Quinn," he said, in no mood to have his work second guessed. "These are the options we have."

Quinn shifted his angry eyes to the captain.

"What about our moles?"

Bonham said nothing.

"Aren't we paying them good money to get targeting intelligence?"

"We've got nothing actionable from our mole network at the moment," Bonham said, meeting Quinn's glare.

The *Wharf Rat*, like most pirate ships, invested heavily in human intelligence to help find targets. So much good technology and tactics were dedicated to keeping valuable ship locations and mission secret, the best way to find them was the old-fashioned way. Bonham, like most ship captains, was responsible for the *Wharf Rat's* moles. She was the only one that knew the identities and extent of their own little spy network and was the only one allowed to communicate with its sources. When she stepped down or was voted out of the captain's chair, she would hand over the knowledge and management of the moles to the new captain. All the crew knew was that they paid a lot of money each month out of their respective shares for the maintenance of this human intelligence network.

They expected a return on that investment.

"That's pretty disappointing," Quinn said. "Considering the amount of money we pay those bastards."

The crew thumped their arm rests in agreement.

"They have come through for us in the past. They will again," the captain said.

The thumping stopped.

"None of their targets sync'd up with our location and envelope this time," Singh added with a shrug.

Quinn shook his head and looked down at his feet as if an unbearable sadness had settled over him.

Singh looked at Quinn, waiting for him to speak again or walk back to his station, then glanced at Axe. The scarred pirate nodded his head to say, *please continue.*

"Likely time of travel to both targets is nearly the same. About two months," Singh continued, turning from Quinn and addressing the other crew members. "Both routes—"

"Jinxed," Quinn said loudly, not raising his head.

Singh looked at the captain and then back at Quinn.

Quinn raised his head slowly. He looked at the captain and then again turned to address the rest of the crew.

"It pains say so. But it's time we all acknowledge it. Speak the truth. The *Rat* is jinxed. Has been for some time."

He's definitely going to call for the vote, Bonham thought. She glanced across the command deck at Axe, who stared at Quinn.

"Speak your meaning," Axe said, coming to his feet.

"I mean exactly what I just said. The ship is jinxed."

"Maybe. Maybe not. What are you proposing to do about it?"

Quinn put his hands on his hips and let a long moment tick by in silence. He made a show of turning his head to look at the ship's clock on the wall.

"Nine minutes till we need to be making ready for the burn," he said, turning his head back to look at Axe. "I think all we got time for at the moment is voting between our two meager targets."

Axe nodded at Quinn and then looked at Singh.

"Anything else to talk about?"

Singh sighed heavily, hands dropping to his sides. "No, I suppose not. It is about the same travel time to both targets. And then about the same travel time to trading options from there."

"All right," Axe said, stepping to the middle of the command deck. Singh walked back to his station. Quinn stayed, holding his ground next to Axe. "Time to decide."

"Wait a minute," Landsberg said. "What do you think, Renate? You've heard the options. Which way would you vote?"

"Fucking AI doesn't get a vote," Eriksson growled.

"That's right," Reeve said. "AI's got no share. No vote."

"I'm not asking her to vote," Landsberg said. "I just want to know her opinion."

"Go ahead, Renate," the captain said. "What are your thoughts?"

"Yes, captain," Renate spoke over the command deck speakers. "If I were able, I would vote to pursue the asteroid. While its payoff is not as large as the *Kamchatka*, it also does not pose the same risk. Assaulting the Russian ship could result in damage to the *Wharf Rat* as well as injury or even death of a crew member, which would negate any gains of a larger monetary pay off."

The crew considered Renate's words in silence for a moment.

They are nervous, Bonham thought. *Desperate for a score and not sure what do to next.*

"You all know the situation now," Axe said. "Time to vote."

Landsberg stood up. "I hope we all learned something on the last job," he said, walking to the center of the deck. "The payoff capturing a ship can be big, that's true. But the risk is a lot more. We all nearly bought it on that last job. If it weren't for Renate, we'd be frozen chunks of meat drifting through the void."

"Just say it, Landy," Eriksson said from his set. "You're scared."

"No. But I am patient. I don't think we need to make it all back in one hasty score. Having said that, I'll live by whatever decision this crew makes. I've proven that over the last ten years aboard this ship."

Landsberg stared at Eriksson to make sure he registered the brushback. With only about four years on the *Wharf Rat*, Eriksson was still the newbie. Landsberg's bravery and dedication were beyond question.

Satisfied that the Scandinavian had gotten the message, Landsberg looked at Axe.

"And those Russian crews. It's always a fight to the death with them."

Axe chuckled under his breath and gave Landsberg a slight nod. It was true.

"The *Kamchatka* isn't worth it," Landsberg said. "I vote for the asteroid."

"Noted," Axe said.

Landsberg walked back to his chair and sat down.

Reeve stood up and walked to the middle of the command deck.

"This is about more than the score," she said. "We can't let that last job change the way we operate. Out here in the void, a ship must be bold. Doubt and hesitation will get us killed, either in combat or by starving to death. We should take the Russian ship. Both for the payday, and to vanquish our demons. We are a pirate ship, damn it. I vote to take the *Kamchatka*."

Reeve walked back to her seat.

"Noted."

Eriksson stood up and walked to the center of the deck.

"I vote we take the *Kamchatka*."

"Noted."

Singh voted next, walking to the center of the command deck and saying, "Asteroid."

"Noted."

Axe looked at Quinn, who had remained next to him in the middle of the deck.

"Reeve is right," Quinn said. "We have lost our way. We are a pirate ship, by god. We should act like it. I vote to take the *Kamchatka*."

"Noted." Axe said. He looked at the captain. "I cast my vote for harvesting the asteroid."

"Noted," the crew said in unison.

"It's a tie vote, Captain," Axe said. "What say you?"

All eyes turned to the captain.

Marlowe stood up.

"Asteroid."

Quinn lowered his head, shaking it slowly as he walked back to his chair.

"Noted," the crew said in unison.

"Renate, set course for the asteroid," the captain said.

"Aye, Captain. Course set. Main engine burn will commence in one hour and three minutes."

Captain Bonham looked at Quinn without expression. He looked back at her, the hint of a smile on his face.

"The crew has spoken," Axe said. "The vote is cast. Our course is set. You know what to do, people."

The crew stood up from their seats and set about preparing for the main engine burn. There was a lot to be done.

Chapter Two

Earth

"Are you ready, LT?" Brigadier General Wallace Hartwell, the Geek, asked as he and Lieutenant Michelle Ryuk stood beneath the flagpole in front of the Technical Space Programs headquarters building. It was the first of May and the morning was clear and pleasant. In a few weeks, summer would blanket Canaveral and the rest of the state in sweltering heat and humidity, but today was one of those days that made a person happy to be in Florida. Gulls and frigatebirds zipped by, riding the morning sea breeze and scanning for breakfast. In the distance, the pointed tops of towering space vehicles aimed at the sky.

"Yes, sir." Michelle glanced at the group clustering with them around the base of the flagpole. About fifty people had come outside the headquarters. She returned a few waves and smiles and then looked at the Geek.

"I didn't realize this many people would come, sir," she said in a low voice.

The Geek smiled. He leaned in closer to the lieutenant.

"How many of these things have you seen me do now?"

Michelle chuckled. "Oh, gosh, sir... Maybe a hundred?"

He nodded at the estimate. "And what do I always say?"

"Promotions are not just for the promotee."

"That's right. Besides, you have a lot of people rooting for you, LT. It is good for them to see that the big, dumbass military machine sees the same thing in you that they do."

11

Michelle smiled.

"Sir, I think we should begin," Mrs. Johnson said, stepping out of the small crowd and approaching the general and lieutenant. "Your call with General Nassir is at 1000 hours."

The Geek glanced at his watch.

"Roger that, Mrs. Johnson." He turned to Michelle. "Let's do this."

The pair walked to the base of the flagpole where the Geek turned and addressed the group gathered on the headquarters lawn.

"If I could have your attention, please. We will go ahead and get started."

The murmur of the crowd ceased and smiling faces looked back at the general and his lieutenant.

"We are here to promote First Lieutenant Michelle Ryuk to Captain," the Geek began. "It is not easy being a general's aide. And Lieutenant Ryuk has navigated that minefield with more agility and decisiveness than her impressive resume led me to reasonably expect. Frankly, the LT has exceeded my expectations in every respect, and I suspect yours as well."

The Geek gestured toward the crowd, who all nodded and smiled in agreement. The TSP Command was a small, hardworking unit. They had all worked with and been around Michelle in some very demanding and stressful times. They all agreed with their commander's comments.

Smiling widest, though, was Mrs. Johnson. Ordinarily she took little interest in the TSP Commander's aides, viewing them as junior officer gophers that came with the job and she had to tolerate. She had seen a dozen of the ambitious little pests during her time as the Commander's administrative assistant, but Michelle was different. Mrs. Johnson had, despite her disdain for aides, come to regard the junior officer as one of her own, like the Geek himself.

"But in the US Military we don't promote based on past performance, no matter how exemplary. We promote based on potential. Can an officer serve at the next level and beyond? Well, in the case of Lieutenant Ryuk, the answer is a resounding and unanimous yes."

Michelle's chest swelled with pride.

The Geek looked at Major Leary, the TSP Adjutant, and nodded.

"Attention to orders!" the major announced. The Geek and lieutenant came to attention at the base of the flagpole as did the uniformed personnel in the crowd. Civilians straightened up as well. "The President of the United States, acting upon the recommendation of the Secretary of the Military, has placed special trust and confidence in the patriotism, integrity, and abilities of First Lieutenant Michelle Ryuk. In view of these special qualities, and her demonstrated potential to serve in the next higher grade, First Lieutenant Ryuk is promoted to the grade of Captain, United States Military, Effective on the 2nd day of May, two thousand and seventy-three, by order of the Secretary of the Military."

The Geek motioned to Mrs. Johnson, who looked back at him puzzled. What did her general want now?

Michelle and the Geek shared a smiling glance before the general said, "Mrs. Johnson, the Captain has requested you participate in the honors."

Mrs. Johnson's eyes got wide for an instant, but she recovered quickly. Stepping away from the crowd, she walked up to the Geek, who handed her a captain's brass insignia. Blinking rapidly, Mrs. Johnson pinned the rank onto one of Lieutenant Ryuk's shoulder epaulets, avoiding eye contact as she did. The Geek did the other shoulder. He worked slower than Mrs. Johnson, doing his best with the burned stubs of his right hand to make sure he did not drop the silver insignia. When both captain's bars were in place, Mrs. Johnson nodded and said quickly, "I'm proud of you," before returning to the crowd. Michelle beamed. The Geek did too. The crowd broke into applause.

After the ceremony, the crowd lingered in the pleasant morning sun, mingling around a table of coffee and munchies. The Geek smiled at the sight and turned and walked into the headquarters building. His meeting with General Nassir was in ten minutes.

Later that evening, Michelle stepped into the general's office as the Geek reviewed his tasks for the following day.

"Sir?" she asked, standing in the doorway.

"Yes?"

The Geek was leaning back in his chair, reading a thick printed report. He gestured at Michelle to enter without looking up.

"I just wanted to say thanks again for this morning's ceremony. It really meant a lot."

The Geek looked up from the report.

"You're welcome, Captain. I was honored to do it."

Michelle smiled.

"I think you really got to Mrs. Johnson," the Geek added with a wink. He set the bound report down on his desk. "She did not see it coming. Nice touch."

The general rubbed his eyes with his good hand. He looked tired.

"Anything I can help with, sir?"

"No, Captain," the general said, shaking his head. "I'm actually done here. Thank you."

"Shall I call for your car, sir?"

"No. I'm going to spend some time in the StarScope. Thank you. See you in the morning."

Michelle knew what that meant. She turned and left.

A sense of sadness came over the captain as she drove home, despite her promotion. She was unable to stop thinking of her general sitting alone in the StarScope chamber, staring up at the 3D holographs and posing questions to Vish. It had been over a year since the powerful AI had told them that the *Odysseus* had been destroyed. After a few weeks of stubborn questioning and disbelief, the Geek had accepted that the ship was gone, obliterated by the explosive failure of its nuclear power plants. And that Paul Owens was dead.

But the Geek did not accept not knowing. He continued to attack the mystery. What the hell happened to Paul and the *Odysseus*?

Chapter Three

iona Malloy leaned back in her chair and rubbed her eyes as the aircraft carried her back to New York City. Equipped with six plush leather seats in the passenger cabin, the sleek executive transport drone belonged to Determined End States, Fiona's holding company. It was just her and her bodyguard, Lucy, on board this evening, so they had room to stretch out. The rest of the team had stayed at Fort Belvoir for more detailed engineering reviews that would take place over the next few days. Fiona took her shoes off and put her feet in the opposing chair to her front. Lucy remained vigilant, as always. Back straight. Hands in her lap. The dim glow of the cabin lights and thrum of the aircraft's thruster fans usually lulled Fiona to sleep on return flights like this. Not tonight.

The meeting with the military's AI Programs Director had gone well. Spitting Metal continued to field systems and gobble up military budget dollars. Still… Fiona was not happy.

She turned and looked out the window. The lights of Atlantic City reflected off the ocean, thousands of feet below to the west. Lights dotted the coast, tracing the way north to New York Bay and the city. Below the aircraft, the water was black.

Fiona glanced at her watch. They would land in less than half an hour.

Cyrus better have news, she thought.

It had been almost a year since Thane told her that the *Odysseus* was missing and that Paul Owens was on it. The news had washed over her with cold inevitability. She took it as a clear sign that she would not, after all, escape her karma. She readied herself for the cataclysm.

Then it never came.

The *Odysseus* stayed lost. Paul Owens stayed vanished. The Ōkami memory sphere stayed missing. Fiona stayed alive... and concerned. There were too many open questions not to be worried, but it gradually became less urgent. Spitting Metal helped bury her concern, assailing her with the constant demands and pressure of running a global AI weapons manufacturer.

Then there was her grandfather. The vile old man that she hated and was bound to. Wealth and modern longevity therapeutics assured that her indentured servitude would last another ten or even twenty years. She could see the spark of malicious delight in his eyes every time she was around him. She worried that cruel spark would keep the old ghoul alive even longer, that the malignant pleasure he took in her situation would animate the bastard forever.

Unless she took action.

Action she believed Cyrus Thane would help her with. If she could only find the courage to ask him.

There were other things she wanted to ask Thane.

She had not seen him in over a month. He had been traveling a lot for DredSkill, the private military contractor he worked for, and that handled all of Fiona's corporate and personal security. They spoke at least once a week, sometimes more, on corporate security matters, but she needed to see him, to stand near him, to find out what she needed to know. Did he feel the same heat and ache when they were near each other? She would know in an instant, but would never act on it. She wouldn't let herself. It would be the height of foolishness. The Malloy family scion and the working-class military veteran.

But she wanted to know, did he have thoughts about her? About them. Together. About what they might do? What it would be like?

Fiona rubbed her neck and sat up straighter in her chair. Her movement drew a glance from Lucy, who checked her boss quickly and then returned her head and eyes to the front.

Fiona looked back out the window again, and the questions resurfaced as they always did. Was Owens still alive? Was the missing sphere still out there somewhere? Until resolved, these questions would continue to stalk her. She thought about them at the beginning and end of every day. She longed to close the chapter they held open.

Cyrus should have word tonight. He should know something.

Maybe it would be good news. Had the cold void of the universe done her a favor? Perhaps pirates had completed the extermination she set in motion years ago? If that were true, she would only have the one thing left to deal with. And it could be dealt with. With Thane's help. She allowed herself to hope.

Soon, the drone was approaching the city from the south, flying over New York Bay. A shift in engine noise and a fleeting lightness in Fiona's seat signaled the aircraft's descent. She looked out the window at New York City. It was a clear night. Tall, brightly lit towers rose above pulsing avenues stretching away to the north as the ever-present streams of taxi and delivery drones careened above.

Fiona put her shoes back on as the drone wove itself into the teaming air traffic. She leaned back in her chair and grabbed the compact mirror from her purse. Turning the light over her seat on, she stifled a sigh.

God, I look tired.

Fiona took the lipstick from her purse. She rarely wore the stuff and hoped that Lucy would not make the connection as the aircraft made its final, curving descent to the rooftop landing platform on her midtown headquarters building.

Chapter Four

Cyrus Thane stood outside the small passenger terminal building on the side of the landing platform waiting for Fiona to arrive. The wind was stiff. It grabbed at his beard and suit pants as it wove through the building tops over a thousand feet above the streets. Thane scanned the sky in a futile effort to pick out Fiona's aircraft among the teeming multitude of drones.

A shaft of light reached out suddenly, shining down on the platform. Thane stared into the tight, blazing beam of the landing light. The dark shape it emanated from grew and became more distinct as the drone descended out of the night. Thane averted his eyes at the last moment as the stabbing prop wash enveloped him in wind and flying grit from the platform. An instant later, the aircraft settled onto its landing gear and the swirl of air dropped away as the drone cut its engines to idle.

A door opened and a short set of stairs extended from the aircraft. Lucy exited first, head on a swivel. Alert, even though they had landed on Fiona's own headquarters building, her right hand close to the side arm hidden under her jacket. At the bottom of the stairs, Lucy looked back up into the aircraft, giving a nod to indicate all clear, and then faced the terminal building.

Thane's breath quickened as Fiona exited. He had not seen her in about six weeks. Studying her lithe form as she descended the stairs, he undressed her in his mind, removing her trademark form-fitting pantsuit, then tearing off his double-breasted Brioni, and taking her in his strong arms. Pressing her to him and—

Thane shook his head.

Get a fucking grip, man.

Fiona strode toward Thane, Lucy a step behind.

She looks tired.

"Cyrus," Fiona said as she walked past him. She headed for the terminal building to get out of the wind.

"Ma'am," Thane said with a nod.

Was that red lipstick?

He fell in behind Lucy.

Fiona walked quickly out of the gusty night air and into the terminal. Ignoring the attendant who greeted her, she took the stairs down to her floor, Lucy and Thane on her heels.

Bursting out of the stairwell into the reception area, Fiona waved to the security guard and receptionist as she walked by. Striding down the hall to her office, she gestured at Thane to follow. Lucy peeled off into her small room just outside Fiona's.

"So?" Fiona said, walking past her long conference table. She dropped her day bag on her desk and turned to look at Thane. "What do you have for me?"

Thane stopped in the middle of the office.

"Nothing," he said. "The *Odysseus* still hasn't docked anywhere in the belt. None of our sources, electronic or human, have detected any sign of her. The ship is still missing."

Fiona pulled her chair out from behind her desk and sat down. She slowly swiveled until she was facing away from Thane, out of one of the large floor-to-ceiling windows that lined her office. Tall, glittering buildings rose from the noise and light of the avenues and cross streets below. The dark rectangle of Central Park, woven through with dimly lit footpaths and surface roads, stretched away to the north.

Thane shifted on his feet and waited. Thoughts of desire, his fantasy of what their reunion tonight could have been, were obliterated by her silence and troubled countenance.

Fiona sighed heavily in her chair.

"I don't know what to think, Cyrus. Is this good news or bad news?"

Her voice was flat.

"Truthfully, I can't say yet. But I'm —"

"But you're talking to this guy and paying off that guy," Fiona interrupted Thane in a mocking voice. She turned around slowly in her chair. "And DredSkill has resources here and out there. And the boss lady herself is involved. And it's only a matter of time."

Fiona tilted her head and locked eyes with Thane.

"Isn't that right, Cyrus?"

Thane raised his chin slightly and set his jaw as if readying to take a punch.

There was no one in the world he wanted to come through for more. There was nothing he would not do for her. He longed to tell her, "It's done. You don't have to worry any more. I did it for you."

But this damn ship. That bastard Paul Owens. And the fucking memory sphere… They continued to elude and confound. The fact that the situation created friction between him and Fiona made it all the more urgent and galling.

"Yes, ma'am," he said.

Fiona nodded with resignation and stood up.

"I have a meeting with my grandfather tomorrow," she said in an acid voice that burned him as she grabbed her day bag from her desk. She stood, shoulders sagging, face angry, looking down. "So, I guess while I am not dealing with his viciousness, trying to hold on to my company by my fingernails, I can dwell on the rogue military veteran who is likely coming after me."

She lifted her eyes to his. They were so tired they made him ache.

Thane opened his mouth to say something, but she waved a dismissive hand at him and started for the door. She walked too close to him on her way out of her office to go home.

"But, really, thank you for coming by to tell me you don't know shit."

Chapter Five

Wharf Rat

"I want to talk about Quinn," Axe said, sitting across from Bonham in her quarters.

Like all the crew quarters on the *Wharf Rat*, hers was in the Ring and consisted of a general-purpose room and a small wet compartment with toilet and shower head. Large windows spanned the fore and aft walls. Bonham had placed two oversized leather chairs, spoils from a European ship they raided, in the middle of the room. Welded to the floor with a small table between them, they had not moved in almost two decades.

Bonham ignored Axe's statement. She took a sip of her drink and gazed in silence over his big shoulders and scarred face at the void that spiraled slowly behind him as the *Wharf Rat's* Ring spun around the ship's midsection. Axe sighed and looked around the quarters he knew so well.

To one side of the chairs sat a compact but well-equipped exercise area featuring a stationary bike and a multi-functional resistance machine. A small selection of dumbbells was locked to the floor.

Her bed was on the other side of the room and could be positioned for zero G or weighted sleep via a wall mounted hinge and swivel. The rest of that wall was made up of storage cubes of various sizes with clear doors. Full of clothes and other items, they contained all of Bonham's physical possessions. One storage cube next to the bed was full of real, printed books—rare commodities in space.

Axe stifled a smile as his gaze rested on the books. He raised his flask to his lips and took a long pull.

The small collection was made up of the spoils of raids. Axe knew to keep an eye out for printed books when he boarded and captured a ship. More than any other booty, the sight of Axe stomping back on board the *Wharf Rat* with a printed book brought a smile to the captain's face.

Bonham loved to read. On her downtime, it was her favorite thing to do. Alone. In her quarters. With the innumerable stars tilting on the other side of the big windows.

Unless she was devouring a recently captured title, Bonham read from the *Wharf Rat's* library on her tablet. Renate had been collecting books for the crew since they became pirates. At last count, she had over ten million titles.

As a pirate ship, the *Wharf Rat* couldn't access the data feeds that streamed through the solar system, back and forth from the belt, Mars, Earth, and the two-dozen major legitimate outposts. For the law-abiding, these feeds provided up-to-date news and current events as well as entertainment media, email and other diversions. For those plying the void in secret, accessing the feeds presented too great a risk of detection and location fixing. So, Renate and the crew got their downloads as able, when docked or nearby other pirates or spacefarers willing to trade discretely.

Bonham drained her shot glass and finally looked back at Axe. He regarded her in silence as she leaned forward and held her empty glass out to him. He hesitated, motionless, making her wait.

Bonham raised an eyebrow behind the low swoop of her hair.

Axe smiled and shook his head as he reached forward with his flask.

"I said I want to talk about Quinn, damn it," he growled as he refilled her glass with another pour of his long running shipboard project.

Bonham clinked her glass against his flask and leaned back in her chair. She took a slow sip and smiled as the cachaça, a traditional Brazilian spirit made from fermented sugarcane juice, warmed her belly.

The *Wharf Rat* came across Axe twelve years ago. As soon as he had recovered and found his footing on the crew, he started working to build a small onboard distillery. It took him three years of scrounging, fabricating, and bartering on the rare occasions when the *Wharf Rat* docked with other ships to get it assembled. Captain Drew took a few more months to get comfortable with the concept before relenting and giving Axe the OK to fire it up. It took another two years to finally obtain sugarcane—a whole other long story—and then, once he successfully distilled it, three more years of aging in his makeshift oak barrel. Axe had lucked into actual oak wood when a ship they plundered had several small trees growing in its green chamber.

To Axe, the cachaça was precious stuff. Fortunately, like Axe himself, everyone respected its strength—one hundred and ten proof—but not everyone had a taste for it. Bonham did, though. She did for both.

But now she was ignoring him and his intended topic of discussion. It had been a scramble to make the maneuver burn window. Then, after a fifteen-minute burn of *Wharf Rat's* main engines, the hours-long process of de-rigging the ship and getting the Ring spinning again. Now, set up for a low-profile dead drift to their target, Captain Bonham wanted to relax, not talk ship's drama. She took another sip, luxuriating in the sweet, woody, herbaceous burn, and smiled at the *Wharf Rat's* master distiller.

"If Quinn wants to be captain so badly, Axe, he can fucking have it," she finally said.

Axe shook his head.

"Don't say that. He would be a disaster and you know it."

"I don't know... Maybe he's right. Maybe we're jinxed."

"And a new captain, a young dumb captain, will fix that?" Axe shook his head in disgust at the idea.

"Maybe." Bonham shrugged and took another sip.

Axe rolled his eyes and did the same.

"Look, I know you're tired," Axe said. "Hell... I am tired too. But I'm not ready to pack it in just yet. And I don't think you are either. And even if you are, I don't give a shit. I'm doing another couple years. That's it. And I'll be damned if I am going to serve under another captain. Fuck that! So, don't be squishy. You fight him. You stay captain. And then, after one last big score, not this asteroid bullshit, you and I will retire."

Bonham looked back at Axe for a long moment and then drained her cachaça. She set her shot glass on the small table between them and then leaned back in her chair and looked past Axe, out at the endless tilting void.

She spoke without looking at him.

"It's more than just being tired. I never wanted to be captain in the first place. You know that."

Axe was the second longest serving member of the crew, behind Bonham. He knew things about her no other crew member knew.

"You don't get to choose what you are good at in life."

"Yeah. Well, you don't get to decide how long you are good at it either, do ya?"

"Maybe not. But I do know this. This is not how Captain Drew would have wanted you to go out."

Bonham's eyes snapped to Axe and her back straightened.

Axe sighed.

"Damnit," he mumbled as he stood up.

Bonham's eyes bored into him. Her chest rose and fell with angry breaths.

Axe's scarred face was flushed with splotchy patches of red, betraying his own anger. His fists were clenched.

"It's fucking true. And I'm sick of this. Conrad was not your fault."

Bonham returned his glare as he continued.

"That kinda shit happens out here. Even under good captains, which you are. But if you can't stop wallowing in this unjustified guilt and self-loathing, then maybe you're right. Maybe you should just get it over with and quit. Maybe Quinn should be captain."

Axe refilled Bonham's shot glass from his metal flask and then stalked over to the hatch.

"And then we'll all be fucked, because you were too selfish and weak to move on."

He jerked the hatch open and left.

Bonham rubbed her eyes and then leaned forward to pick up the shot glass. She knocked half of it back and then settled in her chair, looking out the window. She knew Axe was right. Captains do their best, but shit happens out in the void. It sure as hell happened to Conrad. And to Axe, for that matter.

Chapter Six

Michelle's alarm sounded at 0445 hours. She sat up in bed and checked her phone. Even though she gave it standing instructions to wake her up with a full blast alarm if the general should need her in the middle of the night, she always checked it first thing when she woke up.

No missed calls or messages.

Michelle showered quickly and then guzzled a cup of black coffee as she got into uniform. Glancing at her watch, it was 0517 hours as she rinsed out the coffee cup and set it next to the sink to dry for tomorrow's duty. Staff Sergeant Osterman, the general's bodyguard and driver, should pull up momentarily. Michelle would hop into the armored sedan and they would go pick up General Hartwell no later than 0530. She grabbed her duty bag, a satchel she carried at all times that held her tablet computer, a secure satellite phone, a loaded pistol, and a smaller bag containing personal items and a change of clothes.

Her phone chimed as she walked toward the door.

"Dammit," she muttered as she read the message.

Sighing heavily, she returned to the kitchen counter to grab her vehicle's key fob.

Michelle rode with the general to work every day, unless he "Early birded." That was what she and Staff Sergeant Osterman called it when the general summoned him early, around 0400, to call for his ride in. The first time it happened, Michelle was angry with Osterman.

"Why the hell didn't you call me, Staff Sergeant?" She asked him when she got to work that morning. She ambushed Osterman in the hallway outside the general's office. "I'm General Hartwell's aide. He shouldn't go anywhere without me!"

"I'm sorry, ma'am. But he ordered me not to. Said he didn't need you for his early work sessions and wanted you to get your rest."

"Next time you better call me." Michelle wagged her finger in Osterman's face for emphasis.

The Staff Sergeant stifled a chuckle. He had been in the military long enough to not be impressed by a lieutenant's tantrum.

"Not if the general orders me not to, ma'am."

Michelle stomped off in frustration.

Eventually, she accepted the fact that there was nothing she could do about it. When the general's schedule allowed, he was going to early bird. Barking at Osterman was not going to help. Besides, it wasn't like she was being left out of official business. She knew what the Geek was doing.

The Geek spent these early hours at the TSP headquarters talking with Vish in the StarScope combing the solar system, looking for clues to the fate of Paul Owens. It made Michelle sad to think of him sitting in that dark chamber, planets and spacecraft glowing above his head - vectors, trajectories and positions projected with precise, colorful icons that belied the fact it was all wild-ass guesses. But the Geek kept trying, hoping that Vish's far-flung, data seeking tentacles would fumble across some new nugget of data that would crack the case. He would not rest until he knew what happened to his friend and comrade.

On those early bird mornings, Michelle could see it on her general's face. There was a hint of sadness, a melancholy resignation just below the surface for the rest of the day. Paul Owens' fate was still unknown, concealed by the infinite void. Probably would be forever.

This morning, she pulled into the well-lit parking lot of the TSP

Headquarters and shuffled through the first-floor security. *Big smile*, she thought as she rode the elevator up, preparing herself for the general's post-SolarScope-session negative energy. She wished he would stop torturing himself.

The elevator opened onto the fifth floor. Four armed guards, weapons at the ready, stared at Captain Ryuk.

"Good morning, ma'am," the NCOIC said, hand on his pistol. "Fishing conditions today are expected to be optimal."

"I, um… would still rather be on my bicycle, Master Sergeant Qureshi," Michelle responded.

Qureshi and his security team relaxed. His hand lifted from his pistol to his forehead and he winced in faux pain.

"Ouch, ma'am," he said. "Seriously. So bad."

Michelle shrugged. "I do my best. I've only had one cup of coffee."

Qureshi smiled as she walked by. The challenge and password for fifth floor access changed three times a day. It was an old school backstop to all the biometric security on the first floor. The head of TSP security, Colonel Landau, had led security teams all over the world and had a healthy respect for Chinese and Russian bio-hacking capabilities. Requiring the correct and immediate verbal response to a challenge word embedded in a sentence made it almost impossible for anyone not in the TSP building security network to gain access. Coming up with a coherent sentence on the spot was mental gymnastics, though. Master Sergeant Qureshi and his security detail heard some pretty stupid sentences. Some of the worst came from Captain Ryuk, who found it difficult to make her brain work like that before 0600 hours.

"Have a good day, ma'am."

Michelle strode down the hallway toward the Geek's area, nodding to the StarScope security team as she walked by.

She got to her area at 0548 hours. The door to the general's office was closed. Setting her bag down behind her desk, she walked over to knock and let him know she was at her post, but rather than saying, "Enter," from his desk as he usually did, the Geek burst through the door, startling her.

"Morning, Captain. Please come with me." He strode past her out into the hallway, his face a tight mask of intensity.

She fell in behind him, anxiety ramping up. *What the hell is going on? Has there been an incident? Did the Chinese make an aggressive move out there somewhere?*

The general nodded to the security team leader as he stepped through the body scanner next to the guard desk outside the SolarScope. Michelle followed. After they passed through the retinal scan and voice recognition station, the guard let them in.

"Morning, Vish. I'm back," the Geek said, walking through the darkness to the conference table in the middle.

"Good morning, sir. Good morning, Captain Ryuk."

"Take her through what we talked about earlier this morning," the Geek said, sitting down at the conference table.

"Yes, sir."

Ryuk did not sit down. She stood across the table from the general and looked up as the solar system blinked into existence above her head.

"The *Zacuto*, a European Space Agency science ship, has been missing since its last routine position report almost a year ago," Vish began. "Last month, a Chinese freighter came across the lost ship as it was underway from a mining site to one of the Chinese belt-based port facilities."

The holographic imagery above Michelle and the Geek zoomed into a section of the asteroid belt. A red icon appeared, designating the Chinese freighter. As it crept along, a yellow icon, the *Zacuto*, intercepted it.

"The *Zacuto* was in a dead drift. The Chinese investigated, confirmed there were no survivors, and tugged the *Zacuto* to their destination."

The two icons moved together toward the holographic projection of a large asteroid and then disappeared into a red triangle, symbolizing the Chinese port facility.

"The Chinese alerted the ESA that they had recovered their lost ship. Two months later, a European freighter hauled the *Zacuto* to the main European belt facility for repairs. The ship had suffered an on-board fire and decompression event caused by a catastrophic battery array failure. The crew of five all perished, and the ship suffered a complete loss of power which deactivated its AI pilot and all other systems.

"Dumb luck that the Chinese freighter happened to run into it," the Geek mused. "Otherwise, it would probably have drifted forever."

"Nice of the Chinese to return it, I guess," Michelle said.

"Just means they didn't find anything valuable on it," the general corrected her. "Happens more than you might think. They find one of ours or we find one of theirs. Thoroughly inspect the thing, copy all the data, take anything of value, then say, 'Hey, just being neighborly, we found something of yours.'"

Michelle chuckled.

"Please proceed, Vish. Get to the interesting part."

"Yes, sir. The *Zacuto* was a science and survey vessel. Its mission was to take very detailed spectral measurements of the asteroid belt as well as extra-solar objects."

"It was a prospector," the Geek interrupted. "A state sponsored resource that tries to identify the really valuable asteroids before anyone else. We've got almost a dozen of them, doing lazy ellipticals around the sun looking for treasure. Remember, all the big rocks have pretty much been identified and staked out. Most by governments. But there are millions of smaller asteroids. Collectively, only about five percent of the smaller ones have been identified and classified and had a proper orbital analysis conducted so someone can get out there and mine them, if it's worth it to do so."

"Why did the *Zacuto* have a crew, then?" Michelle wondered aloud, looking back up at the imagery. "That seems like a pretty straightforward mission for a drone."

The Geek beamed at his aide.

"Now you're starting to think like a real intelligence officer, Captain. Why, indeed?"

Michelle smiled, basking in her mentor's praise.

The general went back to looking at the imagery.

"Seriously, sir? So, why was it crewed?"

"No idea," the Geek said matter-of-factly, not looking down. "Any ideas, Vish?"

"There are many possible reasons why the *Zacuto* was crewed. It may have had a mission component that required human execution, such as asteroid claiming, silent running with full decision capabilities, some aspects of espionage or intelligence work, direct action against adv—"

"Point is, who knows, Captain," the Geek interrupted. "And not why I brought you in here. Get on with it, Vish."

"Yes, sir. The relevance of the *Zacuto* to this discussion is that it enabled us to finally re-create the *Perseus'* flight path with a high degree of confidence."

Michelle's eyebrows raised and she glanced at the general.

The Geek smiled and winked at her.

Perseus' disappearance had long been a source of curiosity for Michelle and the general. How had the Company lost two M class freighters? The loss of one would be sufficient to cause smaller shipping concerns to go under. But two? And the only two equipped with an on-board factory? Unthinkable. After they confirmed the destruction of the *Odysseus* in a nuclear explosion, likely the ship's own reactors, they had shifted their efforts to figuring out what happened to her sister ship, the *Perseus*. They had been at it for more than a year, and were still no closer to the answer.

"Continue," Michelle said, excitement creeping into her voice.

"The *Zacuto's* fight path carried it far outside the asteroid belt before apogee," Vish began. As he spoke, the holographic imagery zoomed out to show more of the solar system. Jupiter's orbit, far outside the asteroid belt, traced the outer edge of the room. A dotted white glow indicated the flight path of the *Zacuto*. "The ship was on the return leg of its flight path, still outside the asteroid belt, when its sensors captured the exhaust plume of a nuclear drive."

A blue cone blinked brightly three times to draw attention and then shrank and settled into a soft glow.

"As you can see, the exhaust plume is between the orbits of Mars and the Asteroid Belt."

Michelle's eyes narrowed as she thought of all the scenarios they had run looking for the *Perseus*.

"My analysis of the exhaust plume confirmed that it matches the drive signature of an M class freighter. Further, the locations of the three M Class freighters known to be operational at this time are easily confirmed."

Three green icons flashed around the solar system and then shrank to pin prick sized lights.

Ryuk blinked a few times.

"That means..." she hesitated, implications springing forward in her mind. "Can you... No, wait. What if... That means we could—"

"Easy, Captain," the Geek said. "Let Vish finish."

"Of course. Yes, sir. Please, Vish."

Without looking down, Ryuk grabbed the back of a chair at the conference table. She pulled it out and sat in it, looking up as Vish continued.

"As you know, Captain Ryuk, over the past year we have collected numerous data points that could have been indications of the *Perseus*, but lacked any corroborating support. While these data points were potentially supportive of several of our scenarios, they were ultimately not reliable enough to base conclusions upon, or to even be included in a hypothetical data set. Now, however, with the observation data from the *Zacuto*, we have a basis for data cleansing, time synchronization, signal correction, data fusion, and path prediction and analysis."

Ryuk gripped her chair's armrests in excitement.

"This line represents the course filed by the captain of the *Perseus*." A white dotted line appeared in the solar system, tracing a course from the earth to one of America's three primary belt-based ports. "This is the *Perseus*' actual course, as determined by the data available to me."

A yellow line appeared. At first, it was superimposed on top of the white line, but soon began to diverge. Ryuk's mouth dropped as her eyes traced the white line to the point it intercepted the blue exhaust plume icon, millions of miles away from the white course line.

"Note that the course deviation at the location of the *Perseus'* observed main engine burn is almost ninety degrees."

The yellow line deviated sharply, but then became fuzzy and expanded.

"Note also that, as helpful as the data set from the *Zacuto* is, it is not comprehensive with regard to the *Perseus*. Soon after the observed main engine burn, we must apply a circle of error to our position estimations."

The yellow cloud of uncertainty grew and faded until it dissipated to nothing.

"But it is interesting to compare the probable course of the *Perseus* to what we now know with certainty was the *Odysseus'* true course line and ultimate destruction."

A green line flashed into existence, traveling out from Earth until ending in a white glow symbolizing the explosion of the Odysseus.

Michelle gasped.

The white glow of the *Odysseus'* destruction fell in the *Perseus'* yellow cloud of uncertainty.

The Geek stood up. He walked slowly around the table until he was standing under the white glow. The yellow cloud of uncertainty spread above his head. He held his burned right hand in his left, rubbing it as Michelle learned he often did when in deep thought.

"I just cannot fathom the close proximity of those two ships in the vastness of the void, after both being flown off their intended courses, being a coincidence," he said, looking up.

"No fucking way it's a coincidence, sir," Michelle said under her breath. "Absolutely no fucking way."

The two officers were silent for a moment, both gazing up at the holographic images.

"So you got this information from the Europeans somehow, Vish?" Michelle asked.

"No, Captain Ryuk."

Michelle chuckled, but didn't press further. She knew that Vish would not tell her. Only the general could ask about the specific sources and methods used to obtain any certain piece of intelligence used by Vishnu Stare. She had learned that if Vish did not volunteer the information, it was not need-to-know. But she had been around Vish long enough now to have a good sense of where stuff came from. Somehow, Vishnu Stare had sucked this intelligence nugget from the Chinese themselves, who had extracted it from the *Zacuto*.

Way to go, Vish.

Truthfully, it didn't matter. They had one more piece of the puzzle.

What now, though? Michelle looked up at the yellow cloud of uncertainty and tried to estimate how big it was. Tens of *millions of square kilometers? Billions? Still a lot of puzzle left to fill in.*

The general turned and looked at her.

"Questions for Vish, Captain?"

"No, sir."

* * *

Later that afternoon, the Geek called Michelle into his office. Mrs. Johnson was already there, standing in front of his desk, pad and pen in hand.

"I apologize for the short notice but, Mrs. Johnson, would you please let flight ops know I need a flight to San Francisco this evening," he said. "Captain, any reason you cannot accompany me?"

"San Francisco?" Mrs. Johnson responded, disbelief in her voice. She cast an accusatory look at Michelle, who shrugged back at her.

"Yes," he said, standing up from his desk.

"This evening?" She said, irritation overtaking the disbelief now.

"Yes," the general said, shoving papers and his tablet computer into the briefcase. "Captain, are you good?"

"Um... Yes, sir. No problem. My bag is packed."

Michelle avoided eye contact with Mrs. Johnson, who glared at her as if to say, *You cannot encourage him!*

"General," Mrs. Johnson said, taking a step closer to the Geek's desk. "You have several meetings tomorrow here in your office, including chairing the monthly budget review with the department heads and Lieutenant General Lane, who is flying down from DC to be here in person."

The Geek leaned over to open a desk drawer to retrieve his hat. He ignored Mrs. Johnson's emphasis on General Lane's rank of three star. As a lowly one star, it was unthinkable that the Geek would stand up a three star.

Michelle snuck a look at Mrs. Johnson, whose face was red with frustration at this late change of plans. Mrs. Johnson liked to lock the Geek's schedule down thirty days in advance. "That's how I keep my generals productive," she told Michelle when she or the general chaffed at the lack of flexibility.

"And remember, the day after tomorrow, the Japanese Space Command delegation is visiting and you are the host, sir."

"Oh, we will be back tomorrow evening easily," the Geek said breezily as he scanned his desk one last time. Satisfied he had everything, he nodded to himself and walked around his desk, headed for the door.

"General Hartwell, you must reconsider," Mrs. Johnson said, walking next to him as he crossed his large office. "This is not how flag officers behave."

Ryuk stood in place, but turned to watch the other two.

"I'm sorry, Mrs. Johnson," the Geek said, stopping at the door. "But I must go, and there is no way of getting out of it. I trust you to manage the damage to my reputation to an acceptable level. The captain and I have to pay a visit to the Company."

Michelle's eyes narrowed.

What is he up to?

"The Company?"

"Yes."

Mrs. Johnson's head turned and she shot another accusatory glance at Michelle.

She shrugged again.

Mrs. Johnson's head turned slowly back to face the Geek.

"The Company?" She asked him again.

The Geek nodded. "I really can't say much more at this point."

Mrs. Johnson crossed her arms and lowered her head in indignation. She had the same security clearance that Michelle did and she knew that he knew that she knew that.

Michelle looked at her feet as an awkward silence descended on the room.

Mrs. Johnson leveled her eyes at the general as if to say, you want to have this conversation in front of the child?

General Hartwell squared his feet and raised his chin as if readying to take a punch.

"Oh, sir," Mrs. Jonson said, shaking her head. Her arms, pen in one hand, pad in the other, dropped to her sides. "What is this nonsense about?"

The Geek held Mrs. Johnson's gaze for a moment and then shrugged a you-got-me shrug.

Mrs. Johnson sighed with resignation. She had seen him like this before.

"The Owens thing?" She asked.

"Yeah," the Geek said. "Best lead I've had yet."

Mrs. Johnson nodded. Her body uncoiled slightly. As frustrating as it was, she couldn't hold it against him. Her husband had been the same way.

"San Francisco, sir?" she said, her voice resigned, but less tense.

"Yes. As soon as possible."

"Returning?" Mrs. Johnson asked, scribbling notes.

"Tomorrow late."

"How soon can you be at the airfield?"

The Geek looked at his watch and then Michelle. She gave him a nod.

"We'll be there in an hour."

"Very well," Mrs. Johnson said. "Will that be all, then?"

"Yes. I need to run home, tell Susan I'll be out of town for a day, pack and get back."

"You better, sir. I'll tell flight operations wheels up in ninety minutes, then."

The Geek nodded at the more reasonable timeline.

"And I must insist that they get you back at a reasonable time tomorrow. Not too late. I want you crisp for the Japanese Delegation."

"Deal," the Geek said.

Mrs. Johnson wrote another note and then nodded at the general.

"Very well, then. I will see to it, sir."

She grabbed the doorknob, opened the door, and started to leave.

"And, Mrs. Johnson?" the Geek said, placing a hand on her shoulder.

"Sir?" she said, turning to face him.

"Thank you."

Mrs. Johnson's shoulders relaxed by a few millimeters, and Michelle was almost certain she saw indications of affection in her wan smile.

"Don't thank me yet, sir. Let's see how I do with General Lane first."

Chapter Seven

og hung over the San Francisco Bay below the Company headquarters building. Its grey tendrils obscured the northern most blocks of the city along the water. Coming inland, the terrain rose, lifting the buildings from the fog. The Company's headquarters sat on of one of San Francisco's many hilltops. Built in 2048, when most space freight companies were based in Houston or near Canaveral, the Company was making a statement—*we are a different player, a blend of tech and freight commerce.* A concrete, steel and glass spire deliberately evocative of a rocket ship, the building gave the air of looking down on the earth, rather than up to the heavens.

The lobby was a majestic. Three-story tall windows encircled a gleaming expanse of white marble floors that encompassed an entire city block. Seating areas, appointed with modern furniture placed on colorful oriental area rugs, were interspersed throughout the space as if orbiting the mass of a large bank of elevators in the center. A two-person security and administration team sat at a large desk carved from a single piece of driftwood on the north side of the elevator bank.

The Geek sat in a comfortable dark leather chair in one of the seating areas, looking north out of the tall lobby windows at the fog. Michelle paced back and forth behind him. She was irritated. They had arrived and checked in at the admin desk five minutes before their 0700 hours meeting.

It was 0720 now.

"So disrespectful," she said, hands clenched into fists as she paced.

Michelle glanced at the general. He sat motionless, jaws clenched, eyes narrow. Burned right hand closed in a fist on his lap.

He looks pissed.

Michelle knew that the Geek despised the company. He had never told her so directly, but she could tell from the way he reacted whenever they or their ships were mentioned at work. Which was often.

She didn't know exactly why the Geek, the most levelheaded officer she had ever met, harbored such a caustic hatred for the Company. Seeing his almost physical reaction to being here made her nervous. She worried about what would happen at the meeting.

Sharp, rhythmic clacks filled the airy lobby as one of the administrative assistants set out from the distant driftwood desk at the elevator bank. The echoing strides grew louder and Michelle stopped pacing as the man crossed the gulf toward their seating area. The Geek did not look away from the window.

"General Hartwell?" The man said, still closing the distance. "They are ready for you."

"Finally," Michelle said loudly as the Geek stood up.

"If you will follow me," the man said, ignoring Michelle's comment. He waited for the general and captain to get to him before turning and heading back to the elevator bank.

The other security attendant was standing at an open elevator, his arm holding the door. He nodded to Hartwell and Michelle as they stepped inside.

"Have a good meeting," the attendant said.

Michelle started to say something, but then stopped as the doors closed.

The elevator rose. Slowly at first. Then accelerating.

A soft hum filled the compartment as it surged upward. After a moment, a change in the humming sound preceded a slight but detectible deceleration. Soon, the Geek and Michelle felt the elevator come to a stop.

An attractive woman in a dark red pantsuit and crisp charcoal grey dress shirt smiled at them when the door opened.

"Good morning, General Hartwell. Please follow me."

The glass and marble of the top floor echoed the lobby's open and expansive esthetic. It was not 7:30 AM yet, but the floor was busy with sharp dressed executives coming and going and meetings already underway in the conference rooms they passed by. The woman led them to a corner meeting room that overlooked the bay to the north.

"Mr. Sterling will be with you shortly. Would either of you like a coffee or perhaps some water?"

"No," the Geek said.

Michelle could actually have used coffee, but said nothing.

The lady, still wearing the same smile, nodded and closed the door as she left.

The Geek walked to one side of the meeting room and looked out of the large windows. The hills below the Company headquarters fell away from the tall building, sinking beneath the fog just a couple blocks away. Extending far to the north, the thick grey blanket hid the bay. The Geek stood in silence, looking out the window, his back to the rest of the room, rubbing his burned hand with his good one.

Michelle looked at the general's back. She thought about asking him one last time about this meeting. How did he want it to go? What did he want her to do? But she decided against it. The room was probably bugged and she could tell the general was not in the mood for questions. Tension radiated from his shoulders.

Well, this should be fun.

"Good morning," Alexander Sterling III said as he strode into the conference room, another executive following close behind him. Michelle studied the Core Freight CEO as he crossed the room. She wanted to hate him, but at that moment she couldn't. He was too perfect—dark hair with just enough wave up front and grey on the sides, a sport coat over jeans that accentuated his athletic build, and a crisp white dress shirt with French cuffs that showed off his tan skin. He was like the poster boy for CEOs.

He glanced at Michelle for a second, and the spell was broken. A chill came over her. His eyes were dark with no discernible pupils as they scanned her, judged her insignificant, and moved on. He was a predator, and she was not worth eating.

She fought the urge to physically shake off the remnants of his gaze as she remembered the briefing file the Geek had made her read on the flight. Born in 2021 into old money, "Xander" Sterling was the only child of a prominent global finance family. Legend holds that his family helped finance the American Revolution. Later generations were close business partners of the Rockefellers, Goulds, and Morgans but somehow escaped the label of Robber Baron. Later, the Sterlings profited wildly financing bootleggers during prohibition, but escaped any prosecution and reputational damage. World War Two and the industrial expansion that followed enriched them further. At every turn of American History, the Sterlings profited from the shadows.

Core Freight Solutions was no different. Xander expanded the family's fortune into space commerce through a series of hostile acquisitions when he was in his late twenties. The headquarters building was his way of celebrating his final transactional conquest. Now, almost twenty-five years later, Core Freight controlled over forty percent of all freight flow from the Earth to the asteroid belt. Though never convicted of any wrongdoing, rumors and accusations of market manipulations, smuggling, strong arm competitive practices, and terrible employee treatment dogged the space shipping concern, earning it the ubiquitous, mafia-esque nickname, "The Company."

The Geek turned from the window.

"Good morning."

Neither man offered to shake hands.

"To what do we owe the honor of a visit from our august Space Force?" Xander asked, taking a seat at the head of the table.

"Who is this?" The Geek asked, pointing at the man taking a seat next to Sterling.

"This is Arthur Donahue, Core Freight's chief counsel," Sterling said.

The Geek's eyes lingered on Donahue for a moment and then swiveled back to Sterling. "Whether he stays is up to you," the general said. "But I will be sharing classified information. You are responsible for that information not getting out."

"I can assure you of Mr. Donahue's discretion."

"Your assurance is not needed. Your compliance is required."

Xanders's face was expressionless as he matched the Geek's glare.

Michelle shifted on her feet.

Finally, Xander smiled and leaned back in his chair.

"How can I help you, General?"

"I want to know what the hell is going on with the *Perseus*."

Michelle resisted the urge to turn and stare at her boss.

What. Is. He. Doing?

"I don't understand."

"The *Perseus*. You reported her missing almost four years ago in November 2069."

"That's correct," Xander said, head tilting in puzzlement at the general's statement.

"Then why have we have positively identified her, intact and moving under her own power, as recently as twelve months ago?"

What the actual fuck is he up to?

Michelle couldn't stop herself from glancing quickly at the Geek. He wore an expression she had never seen before. Intense and angry.

"Not possible," Xander said, shaking his head. "The ship was lost."

"I'm sure that is what you convinced your insurer of," the Geek said, pulled a piece of paper from his uniform jacket breast pocket. Stepping closer to Xander, he unfolded the paper, leaned across the table, and extended it to him. "Yet we have confirmed observations of a nuclear drive plume matching that of an M Class freighter at these coordinates," the Geek added, still waiting for him to take the paper.

Xander shot Donahue an irritated glance.

The lawyer leaned forward and took the paper from Hartwell. After checking its contents, Donahue handed it to his boss.

Xander stared at the sparse data printed on the plain white page. There were only a couple of lines. Coordinates and course scenarios were printed above drive plume analyses.

The Geek waited for Xander to lift his eyes from the paper before continuing.

"When you run your own analysis, you will see that the *Perseus'* estimated trajectory envelope encompasses the location of the probable destruction of the Odysseus."

Michelle stifled a smile. *Probable destruction… Nice.*

"The *Odysseus* was destroyed," Donahue declared. "This is a matter of record. We can provide you with the spectral observation data to prove this."

"OK," the Geek shrugged.

"What are you implying, general?" Xander asked, irritation seeping into his voice.

"I'm not implying anything. I am wondering… Are there two M Class freighters at large?"

Xander and Donahue shared angry glances.

"Worse, are the factory facilities we allowed the Company to lease from the taxpayer now in the hands of pirates?"

"Now just a—" the lawyer began.

"Because that would be a bad thing," the Geek said loudly, with an edge. "But before I commit forces to hunting down the *Perseus* and destroying her, I want to know if this was an insurance scam."

"Now just a minute, General!" Donahue jerked his hand into the air and pointed at the Geek. "This kind of accusation is entirely inappropriate."

Xander's shifted his eyes from the Geek back to the information on the piece of paper in his hand. His eyes narrowed in thought as his lawyer continued.

"Not only is the accusation speculative and wrong, it is insulting. Core Freight has always been a trusted and forthcoming partner to the Space Force and all of our partners and customers."

The Geek chuckled derisively

"This is what your trusted forthcoming behavior got me," he said, holding up his gnarled and burned hand.

Donahue flinched at the discolored and puckered flesh of the Geek's right hand, the mottled remaining stumps of his fingers bent stiffly into a fist. Xander's eyes lifted from the paper. He looked at the gnarled hand for a moment and then met the Geek's glare.

Michelle's eyebrows raised before she could stop them. In all their time together, she had never seen the general brandish his scars in such a way. In fact, to her, it seemed he did his best to obscure them. He never, ever spoke about the *Bluestone* unless someone brought it up. And even then, he always moved on from the topic as soon as he could politely manage.

Michelle could see the Geek's chest rise and fall. He was enraged but holding it together.

The Geek shifted his glare from Xander back to the lawyer.

"So you'll excuse me, counsel, if I don't immediately take you at your word."

The Geek lowered his burned hand.

Xander put the paper down and leaned forward. He put his elbows on the table and clasped his hands together, eyes boring into the Geek.

"I remember you now…" Xander said. "Hartwell. You were a captain at the time, I think?"

The Geek didn't answer.

Xander smiled what looked to Michelle to be a genuine expression. But she couldn't tell, really, what painted it on the man's face. Seeing an old friend? Coming across a vanquished enemy? Just good old-fashioned nostalgia? Whatever it was, she felt that chill again.

Xander turned his head toward his chief counsel while he pointed at the Geek. "This man is a hero, Arthur."

Donahue looked at his boss, not sure how to react. Then back at the Geek.

"The hero of the *Bluestone*," Xander said in a saccharine voice.

Michelle's chill evaporated. Anger filled her.

I fucking hate him.

"He saved a lot of people in a low earth orbit accident that day, including some of our people." Xander nodded slowly. Donahue looked back and forth between him and the general.

"Been a while now, hasn't it Hartwell? Must be—"

"Eight years," the Geek interrupted.

"Yeah... Eight years. That sounds right. And look at you..." Xander stretched his arms toward the Geek, palms up in a mock affectation of awe. "A general!"

Michelle was astounded by Xander's tone and demeanor. It was jarring, and hard for her to calibrate to. The military was her life. The general was a legend. And Xander seemed to regard him as ridiculous.

"I am familiar with that incident," Donahue said with a slight nod.

"Good. Then you know your ship falsified its manifest to avoid paying full taxes on its cargo," the Geek said. "That led to a maneuvering accident, which damaged both spacecraft and nearly de-orbited both ships catastrophically."

"That was never proven," Xander said, still smiling.

"Because the Company pleaded no contest."

Xander shrugged. "We were being cooperative."

"Right. Your plea had nothing to do with wanting to keep things quiet. To avoid going through the discovery and harsh sunlight of a trial."

"I'm sorry, General," Donohue interjected. "But what does this history lesson have to do with Core Freight's lost ship?"

"Not much. Other than I hope I have made myself clear—I don't trust you. Frankly, I don't care if you guys are running an insurance scam," the Geek said with a shrug. "But someone is driving the *Perseus* around out there in the void. It's either you or pirates. I am here for the sole purpose of obtaining information related to the *Perseus* so that I can assess the security risk it poses to American shipping concerns. That includes Core Freight, of course. I am sure you guys don't want pirates equipped with an M Class freighter with manufacturing capabilities."

"It is not a scam," Xander said. "The ship was lost."

"You don't have to answer any of his questions, sir," the lawyer said quickly as he placed his hand on his CEO's arm."

Xander pulled his arm away and shot his lawyer an angry look before swiveling his glare back to the Geek.

"The ship was lost, General. I hope if you are able to find it you would have the courtesy to pass us that information so that we could recover our property."

"And crew," the Geek said.

"Excuse me?"

"So that you could recover your crew as well as your property, right?"

Xander smiled.

"Of course."

The Geek nodded.

"You now have the latest information we have," he said, gesturing toward the paper he had given Xander.

"Where did you get this information, General?" Xander asked, gesturing at the sheet of paper in front of him on the table.

"I don't share our sources or methods," the Geek said dismissively.

"Of course you don't."

"Whether or not we share anything further will be weighed against preparations to destroy the ship next time we get a fix."

"Are you suggesting the US Space Force would summarily destroy a civilian ship?" the lawyer asked in a strident voice.

The Geek did not take his eyes off Xander as he responded.

"Space Force reserves the right to preemptively strike against any pirate vessel anywhere in the solar system, at any time."

"This is outrageous! There is no—"

Xander raised his hand to cut off his lawyer.

Donahue grimaced, but shut up. He looked down as Xander lowered his hand and said, "You destroy Core Freight property, General, and no plea deal will be able to save you."

"Last chance," the Geek said. "What is going on with the *Perseus*?"

Alexander Sterling III leaned back in his chair and crossed his arms.

"The ship was lost on its outward journey to the asteroid belt four years ago."

The Geek regarded Xander for a moment.

"We'll show ourselves out."

Chapter Eight

About an hour into the flight back to Canaveral Michelle couldn't wait any longer. She had to ask.

"Sir, did that go the way you wanted?"

The Geek, who had been looking out the window the whole flight, turned his head to face her. He regarded her with narrow eyes, lips pressed together.

Michelle immediately wished she had not asked.

"Disregard, sir," she said, raising a hand. "I didn't mean to disturb."

General Hartwell shook his head.

"It's OK, Captain."

The Geek closed his eyes and rubbed his temples. Learning back in his seat, he pinched the bridge of his nose with his good hand, eyes scrunched shut, for a long moment.

"Sincerely, sir. I don't—"

The general, eyes still shut, took his hand off his nose and swung his palm toward the captain in a shushing gesture.

Michelle sat motionless as the Geek let out a long breath, as if trying to cleanse himself.

"It's not you, Captain," he said, opening his eyes. "I just find it hard to be in that place. To interact with those people. With the Company. Takes me a while to detox."

He turned his head to look back out the window. His face tight. Michelle could see scar tissue on the back of his neck above his collar. She imagined the flames in zero G, crawling up his back, reaching for his ear.

She waited. Not sure what to say or do.

"When I reported to Lagrange Station Four in 2063, the Sino-American space détente was almost ten years old and military forces in space had been dramatically reduced," the Geek said in a distant voice, eyes still looking into the dark middle distance on the other side of the window as they flew east. "I thought I had missed the excitement."

He chuckled softly, but did not look at her.

"Civilian exploration and mining, though… booming. The Lagrange Stations had become hubs of commercial activity. We were so busy, just trying to keep up with the cargo flow. Sometimes I wondered how there could be anything left out at the Belt. Surely it was picked clean.

"I served on LS4 for a year before being assigned to the *Bluestone*, an orbital tug. She was a good ship. Small but powerful. Excellent crew. Experienced captain."

A smiled crept onto the general's face, a flicker of nostalgia lit his eyes.

"I was so tired. The most tired I had been since O.A.T. But happy. God, I was happy."

His smile faded and the Geek let out a long sad sigh that fogged the bottom of the small window he stared out of.

"The accident took place about a year into my tour of duty on the *Bluestone*. We were… the *Pacioli*…"

Emotion choked his voice and he closed his eyes. Michelle thought she saw his lower lip quiver. She looked away.

"Well," he finally continued. "I think you know the story."

The general cleared his throat, and Captain Ryuk looked back at him. He was holding his burned hand with his good one in his lap, looking down at it.

"After, I spent a long time in the burn unit at Walter Reed—six months.

"The stay at Walter Reed, all that time alone, gave me time to reflect in a way I had not been able to since signing into O.A.T. with Paul and Kata on Fort Benning. My first five years in uniform were busy. Add Susan and I getting married and starting our life together and I don't think I had a single spare moment to digest shit and really put my service into perspective."

The general paused. His eyes narrowed again. Michelle could see his jaw muscles working.

"I didn't like what I saw when I did—uniformed Space Force personnel risking their lives every day to keep the tenuous infrastructure of space commerce connected and operable for a modest wage, while civilians made fantastic fortunes exploiting that infrastructure. The two crew members that burned alive next to me on the *Bluestone* were mid-level enlisted. Their families received a pittance of an insurance payment for their loved ones' sacrifice. It was insulting. They did a lot more that day than I did. The so called, 'Hero of the *Bluestone.*'"

Hartwell shook his head, eyes down.

Michelle looked away. Fighting her own emotions.

The general exhaled forcefully, trying to turn a page. He blinked a few times and looked back out the window.

"The Company was fined a sum that sounded big, but amounted to nothing. They walked away with obscene profits from the rare metals extracted from their under-represented cargo. Cargo that had only narrowly been prevented from an uncontrolled atmospheric entry scenario by the actions of *Bluestone's* crew.

"And this kind of fortune-enabling, nameless, faceless sacrifice takes place every day, from Earth all the way out to the Belt and back."

The Geek's voice changed, hardened.

"And, oh yeah, Space Force has to keep an eye on the Chinese, the Russians, and pirates as well.

"So, I stewed at Walter Reed while my burns healed. I was deeply angry by the time they let me go. Susan picked me up. And on the drive home, I told her I was done. I was resigning my commission."

Michelle's eyes got wide, not sure if she believed that part. This was General Wallace Hartwell. She could not picture him as a civilian. Ever.

The general caught her expression out of the corner of his eye. He smiled and nodded.

"Oh yeah, Captain, I was done."

Not sure how to react, Michelle nodded slightly.

"I had a college buddy whose family had a small manufacturing company. They made solar and roofing components for the home building industry. He wanted me to be their Chief Operations Officer. Offered me a ridiculous salary, about three times my Space Force pay. Equity. The whole fucking thing."

The general's face softened with recollection. He looked at Michelle for a long moment.

"I still think about it," he said in a confessional tone. "Think about what things would be like now. For me and Susan. For the girls..."

The statement seeped into her.

The general? Harboring doubt?

"Why didn't you, sir? What changed your mind?"

The Geek shrugged.

"When we got home that afternoon, I asked Susan to print out the resignation paperwork for me so I could sign it and send it in the next day. But she was running around taking care of me and the girls. She got me upstairs and changed my bandages and then, as she was heading downstairs to make dinner for the girls, promised to print the stuff out for me the next day."

General Hartwell shook his head and smiled.

"I spent two months rehabilitating at home. A lot of exercise and stretching. It was awful. Every day, I would wake up and ask Susan to print out the resignation paperwork. Every time she would nod and say, 'Yep. Will do.' And at the end of the day, she would promise to do it in the morning."

"She wanted you to stay in?"

The general's eyes narrowed, and he pursed his lips slightly.

"I think she just wanted me to be sure," he said with uncertainty. "Or maybe she really was just busy. She was holding the whole house together. I don't know... After about two months, it was time to go back to work. So I did."

The general shrugged and turned to look out the window.

"I'm a third-generation military officer. Maybe it's a failure of imagination, but I just cannot conceive of another destiny for myself.

"Whatever the case, getting back to work really helped. I love being around military people. Leading. Mentoring. Helping. Learning… I love it."

The general turned and smiled at Michelle. The look on his face warmed her. She felt the same way. There was nothing else she would rather do.

"But it all changed me," he added, voice hardening and smile vanishing. He held up his burned stump of a hand between himself and Michelle, his eyes flashing anger.

"That fire on the Bluestone burned away more than flesh. It changed the way I see things. Maybe it enabled me to see the truth. I don't know. But I returned to duty with a new perspective and a more jaded eye. And with the realization that the captains of industry and the mighty machine of commerce didn't give a flying fuck about me and my fellow service members. Not really. I was mad."

The general lowered his burned hand and looked out the window.

Michelle sat still in her seat. Not comfortable with the flash of rage from her mentor.

The general glanced back at her. He chuckled.

"I'm sorry, Captain. I didn't mean to come on so strong there."

"It's OK, sir. I understand. Or… I mean, I'm sure I don't totally… but I would still be mad too."

"Oh, I'm not mad anymore."

"You're not, sir?"

The general's brow furrowed for a moment. He turned to the window and then back to Michelle.

"No. Not anymore. I'm a student of history. And it is strangely comforting to know that all of this is consistent with the long arc of history. I was naïve about the world. That is not the world's fault. Same as it ever was…"

The general turned his head back to the window.

"It is not a reality I like. It is not a system I had a hand in designing. But my part, my honor, is to serve."

Hartwell's jaw clenched and he blinked his eyes as a wave of emotion swept over him.

You don't look that over it to me, sir. Michelle looked away from the general and out her own window.

"But I am wise to them now, Captain," he said in a voice that was no longer angry, but laced with resolve. "And my head is on a swivel, looking out for my comrades. That is part of my purpose now. Serve well, yes... But also, keep as many of my comrades as possible from being ground into grist by the insatiable, indifferent machine. The Company is part of that machine. A big part.

"So, while being there is hard for me... To answer your question, I do think the meeting worked. I think that insatiable, privileged bastard Sterling won't be able to resist. It galls him that we might know more about one of his assets than he does. He resents the incompetent Space Force. He resents the taxes he pays. He resents federal sheep he has to deal with. He resents me being able to walk in there and bark at him.

"Bottom line, if there is a chance he can recover his billion-dollar space freighting asset, he will take action. He will task his whole empire to determine if the *Perseus* and its factory is really still out there. And as he does, we will be watching."

Michelle nodded.

She wanted to thank him for the honest answer. But instead, she asked another question.

"That's part of the Paul and Kata thing, isn't it, sir?"

"What do you mean?"

"The reason you are so determined to figure out what happened. You believe they got ground up by the machine."

The general nodded and turned back to the window.

Chapter Nine

Thane nearly leapt from the taxi and then took long, quick strides across the wide plaza in front of the skyscraper on the southern end of Central Park. The reception and security staff smiled at him before the facial recognition software gave him a green light on their bank of monitors. They had grown used to seeing the tall, fit, bald and bearded man in nice clothes come and go over the years. They knew he always went to the top of the high-rise to see the building's number one tenant.

Thane checked his watch as the elevator carried him skyward.

10:47 AM.

He grimaced, thinking how jammed her schedule always was. He would be interrupting something, for sure. She hated it when he did that. It was the nature of his work, though. Threats and risks tended not to comply with the carefully orchestrated agendas of corporate America. He bore good news today, though. A smile spread beneath his beard. He was looking forward to sharing it. To seeing her.

I wonder what she is wearing?

Thane ran his thumb along his belt line, neatening his shirt, and buttoned the top button of his burgundy double-breasted blazer. He gave the ivory pocket square a tug to perk it up and glanced down quickly at his brown Berluti loafers. He rubbed the toe of his left shoe against the back of his right calf to remove a bit of gray grit from the street. His dark blue jeans could take it.

The elevator chimed as it opened, releasing him into the reception area of Determined End States.

"Cyrus Thane to see Miss Malloy," he said, approaching the desk.

The perky receptionist smiled and nodded as she checked her screen. Thane was a familiar sight here and Fiona had given standing orders to interrupt whatever she was in when he asked to see her. Unless she was with her grandfather, of course. Nothing interrupted those torture sessions.

"Can you follow me, Mr. Thane?"

Cyrus followed the receptionist back to Fiona's office.

"She will be with you shortly."

"Thank you."

The receptionist left the door open as she left. Cyrus stepped to the edge of the room to admire the view of Central Park through the floor to ceiling windows. The green expanse below was dotted by the pink blossoms of May's cherry trees. Looking up at the blue sky, Thane watched the coursing cloud of drones above Manhattan sparkle in the midmorning sun.

"Penny for your thoughts?"

"Huh?"

Fiona stood in the doorway, arms crossed in a sleek grey pantsuit over a light blue button up. Her hair was pulled back in the tight pony tail she favored at work.

My god. The things I want to do to you...

"Um... sorry... I," Thane stuttered as he turned from the window.

Fiona chuckled.

"Jesus, Cyrus. Are you that easy to sneak up on? How the hell did you survive in the military?"

Thane cleared his throat, smiled and shook his head. "Sorry. Mind was wandering."

Fiona uncrossed her arms and smiled.

"It's just such a nice view," Thane said, without gesturing toward the window.

Fiona's eyes narrowed for a split second. Then she walked toward her desk quickly.

"What was so urgent you had to interrupt my enthralling quarterly financial close meeting?"

"I'm sorry to barge into your day. But I thought you would want to hear this."

"Truthfully, I am grateful for the chance to step away from that shit for a moment." She leaned over her desk and shuffled through a stack of paper.

Thane stepped closer to her desk and leaned in slightly before saying in a low voice, "We have our first good break in a long time."

"Do tell."

Fiona found the paper she was looking for. She walked around her desk toward Thane.

"One of our sources at the Company said that there was some kind of development yesterday. That they may have a bead on the *Perseus* and the *Odysseus*. They are in the process of directing one of their gunboats to investigate."

Fiona's eyebrows raised as she stood in front of him. She lowered the hand that was holding the piece of paper and rubbed her forehead with the other.

"Holy shit," she said softly.

Thane nodded slowly.

"Does that mean—"

"We don't exactly know what it means yet," Thane said, holding his palms up.

Fiona scowled and tilted her head.

"But you said it was good news."

"It is. It is very good news. But there is more to learn. More to... play out."

"Sure," Fiona said, scowl dissolving. She grabbed his arm with her free hand. "But, shit, Cyrus. This could be really good."

Her excitement and her hand gripping his arm were electric. He wanted to wrap that arm around her and tell her to never worry about anything ever again, that he was here, that he would fix anything for her.

"It could be," he managed to say.

"So what now? What do we do?"

Her hand was still on his arm.

"I have an idea. I'd like to put it in motion as soon as possible."

"Tell me."

She squeezed his arm.

"We have a… resource," Thane said in a quiet voice. Fiona leaned closer to hear him. "A contractor, really. The best there is. If he is in the right location, and can be responsive, I would like to have him intercept and shadow the Company gunship. Let it lead him to the *Odysseus*. Then he can… take care of things."

Fiona raised an eyebrow.

"Take care of things?"

Thane nodded.

"Like, a figure-out-what's-what-and-find-the-sphere kind of 'Take care of things?'"

Thane shook his head.

"This resource really only has one mode. This would be more of a make-everything-go-away-forever kind of move."

Fiona's brow furrowed.

"But it is a high probability kind of thing. Super high."

Her brow relaxed somewhat. She looked down in thought.

"Would be good to get that memory sphere back…" she said, almost to herself.

"Why do you want it back?"

"So I can be sure it is destroyed. Deleted from existence."

Thane nodded.

"If the sphere is on one of those ships, it will be deleted from existence. So will Paul Owens, and anyone that is with him."

"And if it is not on one of those ships?"

"Then we keep looking," Thane said. "But with the knowledge that Owens isn't a problem anymore."

Fiona looked at him with pleading eyes, hand tightening on his arm.

"Oh, Cyrus. I need this to be over. I need resolution."

Thane looked at her and nodded. He wanted to reassure her. She was in no danger as long as he was around. He wanted to lean in, to put his hand on her cheek, to kiss her.

"I'm going to make that happen for you," he said, head tilting slightly down toward hers. "The way we do it is making the best call at each decision point. Optimizing. Based on what we know now and what is available to us at this moment, I think this is the best move."

A faint smile spread across Fiona's face. Her eyes were locked on his.

"I can leave here and get it in motion immediately."

Fiona nodded.

"OK," she said softly.

"I need to tell you," he said, placing a hand on hers. It was warm and smooth. "It will be expensive."

She dropped her hand from his arm and exhaled sharply. She took a step back from him. Thane felt like a canyon had suddenly opened up between them.

The paper in her hand crumpled as Fiona crossed her arms and nodded ruefully.

"Of course it will be."

Thane, stung by her reaction, stood in silence, returning her angry glare with a stoic gaze.

Fiona shrugged and walked past him.

"Do it," she said angrily as she walked out the door.

Thane was still for a moment. Then he turned slowly back toward the windows facing Central Park. He stepped closer to the windows, looking down at the green expanse and touching his arm where her hand had been.

Chapter Ten

George Remus

Nathan Rojas, Captain of the *George Remus*, rubbed his eyes in frustration with his left hand. His right lay on his desk, clenched in a tight fist. His executive officer, Jane Finnie, stood with her arms crossed behind the captain, glaring at Crewman First Class Clarke. Sadhik "Deke" Syed, Clarke's commander, stood behind Clarke to the left, a look of exhausted irritation on his face.

Clarke looked at his feet. Dressed in the *George Remus'* standard onboard uniform, a khaki flight suit with cargo pockets, the tall, athletic twenty-five-year-old held his hands behind his back to hide his bruised knuckles. He couldn't hide the black eye or the scrapes on his face, though. And even if he could, he knew it wouldn't help. The captain knew the whole story already.

Rojas slid his hand down from his eyes and rubbed his beard. There wasn't a hint of grey in Rojas's black hair, which the forty-four-year-old captain kept closely cropped. His beard was the same dark black, and the same short, well-trimmed length. Sharp black eyebrows hovered over eyes that were such a dark brown that it was impossible to make out his pupils. All of this gave the captain a severe vibe. Despite his short stature at five foot seven, and even though he was not a muscle-bound spacefarer that spent all his free time in the weight room, he intimidated people.

Clarke shifted on his feet but did not raise his eyes. He had seen the captain mad before. Too many times.

He had also been in the captain's office too many times. Located just off the *Remus'* operations deck, it was a small space dedicated to the captain's desk, which sat in the middle of the room. Wall mounted displays ringed the desk, conveying to Rojas every aspect of the *Remus'* operations and situation. There were two other chairs, currently pushed back against the wall to make room for Clarke and Deke, where a visitor could sit during longer meetings. Behind Finnie, standing over the captain's right shoulder, was a closed bulkhead that lead to the captain's personal quarters. It was more spacious than his office, but not by much. The *Remus* was a gunboat, designed to withstand high G accelerations and combat operations. It was a no-frills machine, and that extended to the captain's accommodations.

Rojas exhaled. His hand dropped to the desk. Dark eyes locked on Clarke as he rubbed his fist, tension radiating from his body.

"I'm so tired of this, Crewman Clarke."

The words hung in the air as Rojas leaned back in his chair.

"Look at the captain when he talks to you!" Finnie barked.

Clarke raised his head, dejected eyes meeting the captain's.

"How long have you been on the *Remus* now?" Rojas asked.

"Almost a year, sir."

"And how many fights with other crew members have you been in?"

Clarke shifted on his feet.

"Eight," Finnie said.

Clarke's shoulders sagged.

"Do you have anything to say for yourself?" Rojas asked him.

"I'm sorry, sir. I really am. I just… When we got the word the Company was extending our cruise again, I was just… Well, I was pissed, sir. But I should not have taken it out on a shipmate. I know that. My temper just… I am really sorry." Clarke looked at the deck.

Rojas shook his head. "I've had it, Clarke. I'm done."

Clarke raised his head. There was something in the captain's voice he had not heard before.

"Take him to the brig, XO," the captain said.

"Sir, I would like to—" Deke began.

"I don't want to hear it, Deke," the captain cut him off.

Finnie walked around Rojas' desk and opened the door.

Clarke blinked several times. His jaw worked and his eyes searched Rojas' face as if there was something he wanted to say.

"Move it, Crewman!" Finnie said, glaring. A graduate of the US Naval Academy, this was her second cruise on the *Remus* as Rojas' XO. Disciplined and organized, she managed the cycle-to-cycle operations of the *George Remus* like a master clockmaker, scrutinizing every human component all the time. To her, Clarke was a defective gear. Nothing more.

Clarke's head dropped and he followed Finnie out of the captain's office.

A chime sounded.

"What is it?" the captain asked.

The voice of George, the *Remus'* managing AI came over the speakers. "Mr. Kozlov is ready for his course of action review for the new mission, sir."

"Very good. Let him know I will be there shortly. Tell Finnie to meet me there."

"Aye, sir."

The captain pushed back in his chair and let out a long sigh.

"The brig is the last place Clarke needs to be, Nathan," Deke said, disappointment in his voice.

"Deke, I'm sorry. I have given that kid every chance I could. But I've got a ship to run here."

Deke shook his head.

"When we got extended I almost beat the shit out of someone myself. By the time we get back, it's going to almost have been a fucking year. There is a reason gunboat tours are supposed to be six months. You know that."

"And if you had beat the shit out of someone I would have put your ass in the brig," Rojas said in a tired voice. "You're right. It's been a long damn cruise and we didn't need it extended again. But the only way we're going to get through it is to maintain discipline. And that means Clarke is in the brig. Period."

"Nathan, that kid has been—"

"Deke, stop it. You've done all you can for Clarke. But you can't fix him."

Deke's face reddened.

"I'm sorry," the captain said, holding a hand up.

The two old friends looked at each other for a long moment. They were the same age and had each been around the block a few times in their chosen professions. This was their fourth tour together on the *Remus*. They worked well together. The issues with Clarke were the first real friction they had experienced. Rojas understood why. He knew the deep wounds Clarke reopened within Deke.

"I'll see you on the operations deck, sir," Deke said, turning on his heels and leaving the captain's quarters.

Rojas sat at his desk for another moment, hating how that whole thing had gone. Finally, he let out a long sigh and stood up. He turned from his desk and opened the hatch to his quarters.

Like everything else on the Remus, the shelves in the captain's quarters were designed to fully enclose before high G maneuvers. Even so, potential projectiles were kept to a minimum on board. Books, personal effects, and knick knacks were regulated. Each crew member could have five. And even those were discouraged. The *Remus* existed to guard Company shipping and activities in the void. It was a protector and predator. Other vessels could afford to be slow and contemplative, to allow their crews to immerse themselves in diversion as they plied the immeasurable emptiness and cold. Not the *Remus*. She had to be ready, always, to initiate a bone crushing engine burn, engage raiding pirates, or execute a delicate rescue. That purpose gave the *Remus* a minimalistic, purposeful, sleek feeling throughout.

Rojas liked it that way.

Even so, he had a handful of meaningful things on board. He took one from the shelf and looked at it. He had to get to the Ops Deck. The team would be waiting for him, but he let his eyes linger on the framed photo of his wife anyway. It had been a long cruise, extended three times. He was ready to get home and he knew his crew was as well. After a few heartbeats, he placed it back on the shelf.

* * *

"Sorry to keep you waiting, Koz," Captain Rojas said, striding onto the operations deck. Deke was already there, glumly standing next to the operations officer, Sergei Kozlov.

"No problem, sir."

Rojas stepped up to his place at the holo-table and nodded at Deke.

Deke ignored the gesture.

"Sorry to be late," Finnie said, walking onto the operations deck. "Dealing with Clarke again," she said to Kozlov, disdain dripping from her voice.

"That poor knucklehead," Kozlov said with a sad shake of his head.

"Ingrate is more like it," Finnie said sharply, taking her place at the holo-table next to the captain.

"Let's begin, shall we?" the captain said with some force before Deke could respond.

"We've been analyzing the *Perseus* since we received the change of mission order." As Kozlov spoke, a faintly glowing three-dimensional image of the *Perseus* appeared in front of the group, over the holo-table. "Once we know her location, our mission will be to intercept and capture the ship. Priorities of execution are minimization of damage and operational security."

"The Company has ordered we maintain total communications blackout until mission complete," Rojas interjected.

Deke's eyes narrowed at the comment.

"We received extensive technical intelligence on the target," Kozlov continued. "Her manufacturing plans. Maintenance records. All crew manifests, including last known. And all known navigational histories. Using all that, we have designed an attack sequence that will accomplish the mission, consistent with the constraints the Company has placed on us."

Rojas smiled. He could feel the enthusiasm radiating from his operations officer. A former Russian Space Agency engineer, the Company recruited Kozlov almost ten years ago. He was quickly pulled into the fleet security program. They valued his innovative, engineering-based problem-solving approach and the fact that he was eerily cool under pressure.

"Alright, Koz," Rojas said. "Take us through it."

An hour later, the captain rubbed his beard as he stared at the holographic image of the *Perseus*. Kozlov, Finnie, and Deke looked at him as they waited for his response. Rojas had asked many questions during the briefing, but, as usual, they could not tell which way he was leaning. The man had a good poker face.

"I don't hate it," Rojas said without looking up from the *Perseus*.

"I do," Finnie said.

Kozlov rolled his eyes at her.

"Why?" the captain asked.

"To start with, that is a hell of a long opening salvo. If the company doesn't come through with better intelligence on the target's exact location, even George won't be able to pull it off."

"The Company will come through," Kozlov said. "They want that factory ship back badly, and would trade any of the ships in their fleet to get it. Probably more than one."

Rojas crossed his arms. "What else?"

"Let's assume they come through with more precise location data and we get a good fix on her." Finnie pointed at the 3D image of the *Perseus* floating over the holo-table. During the briefing, Kozlov had used the table to zoom in and out of depictions of various scenarios as he took the captain through his plan. Now the display was back to projecting their prize. The long, tired-looking *Perseus*. M class freighter. Factory ship. Legend. The sight of her excited the captain and his leadership team. This one would make the history books.

"That long of a shot is bound to get detected. They will see it coming and detect our attack before we are in position to do anything about it."

Kozlov shook his head.

"She is flying dark and quiet. Passive sensors only. She won't see shit. And if she does light up and try to paint anything, then we will have her dead to rights."

Deke nodded. "He is right. They won't see our first strike coming unless they light up. If they light up, they make it more easy for us."

Finnie nodded, but her face said she was unconvinced.

Rojas raised an eyebrow at Finnie.

She shrugged. "I'm good."

"Keep pushing," Rojas said. "The enemy sure as hell will. If the plan does not endure your sharp shooting, it has no chance against the pirates that managed to steal the *Perseus.*"

"Okay, let's say the opening salvo gets home. It's a lot of burn time for the *Remus.*" She cast Kozlov a stern look. "It will be what, George? Close to three quarters of our on-board propellant?"

"That is correct, ma'am. The main engine burn required for Mr. Kozlov's proposed plan will be approximately ninety-seven point one five minutes. That will be sixty-eight-point three percent of our remaining fuel."

Captain Rojas nodded. "It is a lot of fuel. But the quicker we get there and get the *Perseus* under control, the better off we'll be. It's a tradeoff I think I'm willing to make. The fuel is not what worries me."

Deke cocked his head. "What worries you?"

"The attack pod's payload, for starters."

"The load and acceleration are well within her limits," Deke said matter-of-factly.

The *Remus'* assault commander, Deke's unit included a team of twelve humans that were all, like him, combat veteran Centaurs. Each had served for at least five years before leaving the military. Like many organizations, the Company aggressively recruited veteran Centaurs. Humans with the proven capacity to withstand augmentation, and the ability to withstand and manipulate the onslaught of information and sensations required to command and control disparate weapon systems, were rare. This rarity gave them great value to not only the military but also to other organizations, like the Company, that were willing to pay. A Centaur increased their salary tenfold the day they took off their military uniform and joined a civilian organization.

The Company got so aggressive in their recruiting of Centaurs that the Secretary of the US Military called Xander Sterling himself to the Pentagon to tell him to knock it off. A rare time the man was actually called to heel. The Company throttled back, but didn't stop.

"Okay." Rojas nodded at Deke's confidence. It always made him feel better. "My greater, more general concern is how long the *Remus* and the attack pod will both be at full burn. Two nuclear drive plumes will stand out in the void."

"That's true," Kozlov nodded. "But remember, sir, *Perseus* will be truly blind at that point."

"But the rest of the void won't be."

"What are they gonna do, sir?" Deke responded in a curt voice. "Attack a Company gunboat?"

"Good luck," Finnie muttered.

"Bring it on," Kozlov added.

Rojas thought about it in silence for a moment, then moved on.

"How do you feel about that long of a shot, George?"

"I am one hundred percent confident, sir," the AI answered. "Assuming that the Company comes through on our request."

Captain Ramos looked around at his subordinates and smiled. "I like the plan. Good work, Koz."

Deke winked at the operations officer. Finnie gave him a curt nod. Kozlov tried to stifle a proud smile.

"But let me be clear," the captain said in a voice that suddenly had an edge. He paused for a moment to make sure he had everyone's attention.

"The Company wants us to minimize damage to the *Perseus*. We will do our best. But my priority is the safety of this crew. Full stop. We will be aggressive and show no mercy until all resistance has been eliminated. If we have to atomize that ship and whatever crew is steering her around the void to eliminate all threats to the *Remus* and this crew, we will do that. Are you with me?"

"Aye, sir," the team said in unison.

The captain nodded and turned to go back to his office.

Chapter Eleven

Earth

As soon as the aircraft's wheels lifted from the landing pad, the Geek turned and hurried towards the TSP headquarters building. Michelle, surprised, spun on her heels and jogged a few strides to catch up. Mrs. Johnson, standing at the bottom of the HQ building stairs, shook her head in disapproval as the pair passed her and leapt up the steps into the building. She fell in behind, catching up to them in the elevator.

"Well, sir, I certainly hope the Japanese Space Command delegation did not notice your undignified sprint away from them and into your headquarters building before they departed," she said as the doors closed.

The Geek did his best to ignore the comment as Mrs. Johnson leveled a disapproving glare at Captain Ryuk.

Michelle looked at her feet and tried to stifle a smile.

After the trio passed through fifth floor security, Mrs. Johnson walked back to her desk while Michelle and the Geek went to the StarScope chamber. Pleasantries and pontification had dominated the forty-eight hours since they returned from San Francisco. The general had not had a chance to work with Vish beyond the standard morning intelligence and security check ins, and he and Ryuk had not had a spare moment to debrief their meeting with Alexander Sterling.

"Good afternoon, Vish," the Geek said, walking to the head of the large conference table. He stood and crossed his arms expectantly. "I'd like to look at Core Freight ship movements. Anything out of the ordinary there?"

Michelle stood at the other end of the table as the solar system appeared above them and Vish began to speak.

"Yes, sir. Yesterday the Company dispatched a gunship to the same region of the solar system we believe the *Perseus* to be operating in."

The solar system whizzed and shifted around above their heads until the yellow cloud of uncertainty between Mars and the asteroid belt was above the conference table. A bright pinprick of white light hung in the middle of the cloud, signifying the demise of the *Odysseus*. A red course line representing the Company gunship emanated from the asteroid belt, travelled millions of miles, and intersected the yellow zone.

"In addition to intelligence regarding the ship's mission, we have multiple sensor captures of the gunboat's brief main engine burn, as well as numerous observations of the ship post acceleration. I believe I have calculated its current trajectory with a high degree of accuracy."

Michelle snuck a glance at the Geek. He nodded, eyes on the red gunboat course line.

"How long 'til it gets to the zone of interest?"

"Difficult to say, sir. Our intelligence confirms only that a gunship has been dispatched. As you know, the exact location of the *Perseus* is unknown, and we do not yet know what tactics the gunship will use to intercept her. But given the distance involved. It is safe to say no sooner than a month from now."

The Geek's eyes narrowed and he rubbed his chin.

"And no further updates regarding the *Perseus*?"

"No, sir."

The Geek pulled a chair out from the large conference table and sat down heavily. He had expected the Company to respond vigorously to his provocative dangling of *Perseus* intel. Still, the mention of a "Gunboat" made him nervous. He hoped his confidence they would exhibit restraint regaining their treasured commercial asset was not misplaced. Leaning back in his chair, he stared into the cloud of uncertainty, wondering where the *Perseus* was, and what might be happening on the lost ship.

Chapter Twelve

Perseus

"Wow," Paul said.

Althea raised her naked body off his and smiled.

Paul calmed his breath as he lay on his back in the middle of the bed. He watched Althea swing her toned legs off to the side. She stood up quickly and stretched, arching her back and reaching for the ceiling. She caught Paul looking at her breasts and smiled.

"I'll take that as a compliment," she said before walking toward the bathroom.

"You should," he said with a smile, propping himself up on one arm. "I'd like to shake the hand of whoever programed you to do that."

Althea stopped.

Paul realized his mistake too late.

She turned and looked at him, arms crossed.

"Um…I," Paul stuttered.

Althea glared.

"Uh…" Paul grimaced as he felt his post-sex buzz fade. "What I meant to say…"

Althea let him off the hook with a resigned smile. She sighed and shook her head as she turned back towards the bathroom. "It's OK, Paul."

Althea turned on the shower. Paul listened to the sound of water striking metal and tried to collect his thoughts. He pictured Althea stepping into the shower, a frown on her face.

He got out of bed and walked towards the bathroom.

Paul rested against the hatchway and looked at Althea. His heart ached at the sight of her.

It had been about seven months since Top and the Ōkami had rescued them from the battered remnant of the *Odysseus*. Althea had healed well. There was no evidence of the bruises and deep cuts from their ordeal or the atrophy from the long drift through the void in their amputated lifeboat. Her athletic figure looked as healthy as when they first met about two years ago.

Paul's body was the opposite. Every limb bore multiple scars. Metal protruded in places where he used to fasten himself to his battlesuit. His head was encircled by a ring of scar tissue, just above his ears and forehead where they had removed his skullcap to augment his brain so that he could communicate with his robot soldiers. Multiple projectile and stab wounds pock-marked his body.

I am grotesque, he thought, glancing at the mirror. He turned his eyes to Althea. She stood with her back to him, her head lowered into the water.

Her short black hair glistened beneath the shower as the water ran down her back.

After they were rescued, Paul had Althea each spent almost a month in a MedPod, sedated, while the devices worked to repair the damage to their bodies. The first month out of the pods was rough on them both, but they slowly regained their strength and began to move about the ship. It was not until the past few weeks that they started to feel like themselves again. Paul took their raging sexual attraction as a good indicator of their recovery. Paul looked at Althea's lithe, naked body and was thankful for the Perseus' state-of-the-art MedPods

But he also suspected that Althea was something special. He knew that the science of artificial flesh had leapt forward in the past decade, but there was a spirit within Althea at work as well, he believed.

A spirit he had just offended.

Again.

"I'm sorry," he said.

She turned to face him, breasts swelling under her crossed arms, water running down her front.

"I know," she said.

"I mean it."

"I know."

"What I mean is," he said, taking a step forward.

She held up a hand to stop him.

"It's OK, Paul," she said.

"It's not," he shook his head. "I was trying to say that…"

Althea raised her eyebrows in anticipation of more stupidity.

"That making love to you is…"

Althea crossed her arms again.

"It's perfect."

Althea tilted her head, surprised that he had managed to not make it worse.

"It's like someone taught you…"

"And you ruined it," she said, turning her back to him to shower.

"Althea, please!"

She spun on her heels and pointed at him. "You would never say, 'I'd like to shake the hand of the guy that taught you that,' to a human woman. You only say it to me because I am a synthetic and you think everything about me is not really me. You think it's all designed by man, pre-determined by programming."

"Wasn't it?" Paul asked, figuring he was so deep into it now it didn't matter.

Althea put her hands on her hips in frustration. "Not any more than everything about you was designed and predetermined."

Paul stared back at her, flummoxed.

"Wasn't it?" Was all he could think to say.

"No. You are the wonderful sum of your beliefs, experiences, actions, hard work and mistakes, Paul," she said with a hint of encouragement that gave him hope of getting laid again in the distant future.

"Why don't you think I could be the same?" she asked him.

"I do think you could be the same."

"Then why would you ask me something like that?"

"I..."

Paul looked at his feet. They were having these conversations more often lately. He hated them. Not only did they make him feel like a jerk, but he always left them feeling dumber than Althea. She was always the one making the brilliant observations. She was programmed as a counselor, after all.

Even he was not stupid enough to make that point to her at that moment. Paul raised his eyes. "I'm sorry."

She sighed as she turned off the water and grabbed her towel.

Paul watched her walk past him back into their quarters. Dejected, he stepped into the shower and turned on the water.

"It was you, by the way."

"Huh?" Paul said, leaning out of the water to look at her, soaping his shoulders.

"It was you," she said with a sad smile.

"Me what?"

"I was programmed to be a keen observer." She pulled on the long underwear she wore under her flight suit.

"Now wait a minute," Paul said, pointing a soapy finger at her. "You can talk about your programming but I can't?"

"That is correct." Althea pulled on her long sleeve top.

Paul nodded.

"My point is I pay attention to you. All the time," she said, shaking her head as if frustrated with herself. "I can't help it. I can't stop myself."

Althea took her flight suit from the small closet and stepped into it. Paul watched her zip it up and figured their conversation was over. He stepped back under the water as she sat on the bed and pulled on her boots.

"So I know what you like, Paul."

He leaned to the side again so he could see her. She spoke over her shoulder as she left their quarters.

"It was you that taught me how to make love like that."

* * *

Thirty minutes later, Paul left their quarters and headed toward the command center of the Perseus.

The *Odysseus*, the doomed ship that had carried Paul and Althea from Earth almost all the way to the asteroid belt, was the younger sister of the *Perseus*. Volume discounts apply even to massive space vessels, so the Company had invested in the construction of five of the M class freighters back in the forties. Though the *Perseus* left her high lunar orbit construction dock six months before the *Odysseus* in 2045, they were almost identical twins. Both were over two kilometers long, powered and propelled by two nuclear reactor drives, and equipped with powerful artificial intelligences.

The two old girls also both carried the largest and most capable ship-borne additive manufacturing facilities in the solar system. Somehow retained by the Company after the Sino/American Space Détente, the factories were astonishing profit generators and the envy of every other commercial space entity.

The *Perseus*, like the *Odysseus*, had also kept her retrofitted troop-carrying military spinners on her front. 150 meters from each other on opposite ends of a long truss structure, the pressurized Habitat and Utility modules spun around a center hub gear, each providing one G and one atmosphere of pressure. The *Perseus'* command center was on the top level of her Hab. Paul and Althea's quarters were on the bottom.

After their rescue, that similarity had made Paul and Althea's transition to life on the *Perseus* easy in some ways, but haunting in others. At every turn they were reminded of the events on the *Odysseus*. The places they suffered, the crew mates they lost, the sacrifices others made so that they could survive were never far from their minds.

Despite their identical engineering and heritage, and though they had both transported hundreds of billions of dollars of cargo between Earth and the asteroid belt over the decades, Paul found the *Perseus* to be a much different ship than the *Odysseus*.

The *Odysseus* had seemed weary but still willing, like she was ready for the mission but looking forward to her next port call. On the *Perseus*, Paul noticed from the first cycle there was less damage and more fresh paint. She felt younger, still eager. A sense of vitality emanated from the good ship.

Althea had noticed it as well.

"Luck of the draw," Paul told her when she remarked about it to him.

"What do you mean?"

"It all comes down to the crew a ship gets. How good are they? How diligent? What does the captain prioritize? How do they approach their mission, the maintenance, their off time? Slight differences in all that add up over the course of two decades."

"So the *Perseus* had better crews than the *Odysseus*?"

"Not better, exactly. But different. Certainly with different luck."

"I'll say," Althea remarked with a sad nod.

"It's funny," Paul said. "The crew usually attributes the luck factor to the ship. But being on board the *Perseus* makes me wonder if it is the other way around."

Now, as Paul climbed up the ladder to the top level of the Hab, he hoped for the hundredth time that he had not brought his bad luck to the *Perseus*.

He swallowed the feeling at the top of the ladder and walked into the command center.

"Good morning, sir," Top said. She stood over the large holographic display table in the middle of the facility.

"Morning, Top," Paul responded, walking over to stand next to his first sergeant. "Any good options come to you?"

"No, sir," she responded, not looking away from the display table. "Nothing beyond the options we have discussed over the past cycles."

They were alone in the command center, encircled by numerous displays and control panels on the walls. Past the first sergeant, two large command chairs faced a multi-functional display that covered the forward wall. It showed several views of the *Perseus* at the moment.

They stood next to each other and stared at the holographs of their course line projected above the display table. Even though the *Perseus* was a civilian ship and its command center was designed to facilitate the efficient execution of commercial missions, the dim lighting and surrounding glow and blink from the multiple displays around the room evoked within Paul the feeling of a military operations center.

Years ago, he and Top spent countless hours just like this—standing shoulder to shoulder, studying a mapping display, trying to come up with a plan to overcome the challenge of the day. It felt good to be standing next to her again like this, even though their current mission was impossible.

Top was taller than Paul, though not as tall as she was when they fought together. Her new body was manufactured by the *Perseus'* on-board facility. It had done its best. She retained the graceful, athletic proportions she and her fellow Ōkami had possessed as soldiers on Earth, but there were differences.

"New arm?" Paul asked, gesturing at Top's left arm. Her forearm's metallic surface was more reflective than the rest of her components.

"Yes, sir," Top said, raising the arm and twisting her wrist it back and forth. "The XO found some interesting material in one of the asteroids he processed recently. It is light and strong and very promising. We are testing it out."

Paul looked Top up and down and smiled. Several of her components were of different material than the rest. Some were painted bright orange, a color Paul knew was associated with nanopaint used to sense component performance metrics. And some were, Paul knew from experience, missing. The overall effect amused him.

"What is it, sir?" she asked him, swiveling her upper body to face him.

His smile widened as he met her multi-sensored gaze

"You remind me of those old project cars back on earth. The ones that have been put back together using parts found in the junkyard."

Top stood motionless.

"You know," Paul continued. "You saw plenty of them on the range at Fort

Bragg. The driver's door is one color, the hood is another, the trunk is missing and none of the hubcaps match."

Top looked at her forearm and then at the rest of herself.

"That may be so," she said, looking back at the display table. "But I am grateful for the XO's continued efforts to improve our functionality and survivability. When we get back to Earth, we are going to be glad he did."

"You are most welcome, First Sergeant," the XO said over the command center speakers.

"Well, you've only got about another year to work on her, XO," Paul said, eyes drifting to the ceiling. "Eventually you need to decide on the hubcaps."

"Why would the first sergeant need hubcaps?" the XO asked.

Top turned her head from the mapping table to look at Paul. Though her face was expressionless, with her eight sensor eyes and high metallic check bones, Paul knew her well enough to know that it was a disapproving glare. Her years of service with him had made Top an expert on Paul and how he communicated, but most AIs still had difficulty with sarcasm. She reminded him of this often.

He shrugged and turned from the mapping table to grab a cup of coffee from the small galley at the back of the command center.

"XO, The captain is joking," the first sergeant said looking back down at the mapping table.

"I am just joking." Paul grabbed a mug and poured his coffee. "I appreciate everything you are doing for us, XO. I really do."

"Thank you, sir," the XO responded. "I assure you that the factory foreman and myself are working diligently to identify and utilize everything available to us as we continue to upgrade the first sergeant and the rest of the Ōkami."

Paul wished he hadn't said anything. Top was a fraction of her former self and it wasn't just her chassis. Her brain module was an early generation Quantumtronic stack, not the cutting-edge module she had inhabited when they trained and then fought together down in the southern cone of South America. The deficit in her showed. Just as Paul's showed in him.

After the court-martial they had stripped him of his most of his augmentations. He was not exactly back to baseline - His skeleton still benefited from metal lacing, and nanobots still coursed through his bloodstream eliminating disease, decelerating aging, and ready to repair injury.

But the computing power that augmented his brain, the In Head Display technology and the communications micro components that enabled him and his Ōkami soldiers to communicate instantaneously and wordlessly was torn out of him.

Doesn't matter, he thought. *We've only got one more thing to do together. And I think we're good enough to get it done. Especially since neither of us cares about making it out alive.*

"Don't forget about the Brawler and me, XO," Paul said, thinking about the task ahead.

"Of course not, sir," the XO said. "We are working on both as well, I assure you."

"I appreciate it," Paul said as he stepped back up to the display table next to Top.

The three-dimensional map of the solar system, populated with all known space stations, spacecraft, and unmanned probes, presented a puzzle that none of them had been able to solve yet. How to get a two-kilometer-long spacecraft 300 million kilometers from earth all the way back to high lunar orbit without being detected by the Company, the authorities, or pirates.

Then how do you sneak your small team down to the surface of Earth so that you can track down and kill a person you have sworn to take revenge on?

One thing at a time, Paul thought, sipping his coffee.

"I think you are right, sir," Top said. "We can't get all the way there with the *Perseus*. It's just too big. Every time we run the simulations, we are detected too far out."

"Let's face it. It's a miracle the *Perseus* hasn't been detected yet."

"That we know of, sir."

"Always the bright side with you," Paul said, taking another pull of coffee.

"Good morning," Althea said, entering the command center in her baggy fight suit.

"Good morning, Althea," the XO said.

Top looked over her shoulder at Althea. Paul thought he detected hesitation before Top said, "Good morning."

Althea stepped up to the mapping table, on the opposite side of Paul from Top.

Sensing everyone's concentration, Althea said nothing as she joined the two veteran soldiers in staring at the display.

"I hate to say it, Top," Paul began.

"But your lifeboat may have one more mission to undertake?" Top said, cutting him off.

"Exactly." Paul looked at his first sergeant with approval.

"I already asked the maintenance boss and foreman to draw up a few options, sir."

Paul chuckled with pleasure. He put his hand on Top's shoulder. It felt good to work with her again.

"Who says we need a damn neural link?"

"Not me, sir."

Althea stole a glance at the two of them.

"Sir, I do have one piece of ship's business to discuss," the XO said.

"What is it?" Paul drained his coffee cup.

"Captain Hofmann has requested a meeting."

Paul groaned. "What about?"

"He didn't tell me, sir."

Paul walked back to the galley and poured himself another cup of coffee. He walked back past Top and Althea and stopped in front of the large display. He stood in silence, gazing at the image of the front half of the *Perseus* extending into the void.

"Sir?" the XO prodded him.

"Not today," Paul said, turning from the video display. "Maybe next cycle."

"Very good, sir."

"I'm going to hit the gym," Paul said to Top and Althea as he left the command center.

* * *

Althea watched Paul leave and then looked back at the mapping table. She and Top stared and the miniature glowing solar system for a moment before Althea said, "You know him so well."

Top looked at her.

"Paul," Althea clarified. "You know him so well you still are able to complete his sentences."

"I knew who you were referring to."

"How do you do that? How do you anticipate what he is going to say?"

Top looked back at the map.

"We fought a war together. We lost comrades together. And we died together."

Top turned and walked away from the mapping table. As she stepped through the hatchway to leave the command center she asked Althea over her shoulder, "What did you do?"

Chapter Thirteen

Wharf Rat

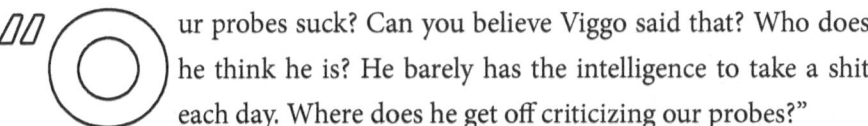ur probes suck? Can you believe Viggo said that? Who does he think he is? He barely has the intelligence to take a shit each day. Where does he get off criticizing our probes?"

It had been a week since the crew's decision to pursue the asteroid and Landsberg was still fuming about the Scandinavian pirate's sniping. He floated in his virtual reality work station in his quarters at the end of the long duty day.

Landsberg was the only crew member whose quarters were not in the Ring. Forsaking the dramatic views of the void and induced gravity in favor of weightless, limitless communion with Renate, he lived in the belly of the *Wharf Rat* in perpetual zero G,

The work station's ergonomic pod, structured to cradle him in the weightless environment, looked like a large, wire and cable encrusted egg. At its center, Landsberg floated in a full body haptic feedback suit with a fiber optic brain-to-machine interface connected to the base of his skull. Integrated into a virtual reality helmet, the interface enabled he and Renate to interact in an immersive environment of their mutual design. When jacked into Renate in this way, Landsberg's thoughts and sensations were communicated to her instantly, and hers to him.

At the moment, Renate sat across from Landsberg at a large workbench in that shared virtual environment. Dressed in the same olive drab overalls that Landsberg wore, her sleeves were rolled up over her elbows and she had pinned back the brown, wavy, shoulder-length hair that framed her plain, handsome face. Conceptual representations of their ongoing projects orbited around them, like planets orbiting dual suns. There were dozens. An exploded view of *Wharf Rat's* nuclear power plant spun slowly near a handful of new probe designs. The load bearing gears of the *Wharf Rat's* Ring were displayed in another, red circles indicating the potential onset of metal fatigue. Some images glowed more or less brightly, signifying the ones where Renate was still working in the background at Landsberg's direction.

"Don't let him get under your skin, Mathias," Renate said with a slight shrug. "You must remember Viggo is an emotional, easily frustrated man. I believe his comments were more about the lack of perceived good options at that moment, not the quality of your probes."

"Our probes," Landsberg corrected her. "They are our probes. Just like all the rest of the work we do together to keep the *Rat* in one piece." He gestured around at the kaleidoscope of projects orbiting them. "No one appreciates what is involved. The complexity. The hard work."

Something caught his eye.

"How is the reactor efficiency analysis going, anyway?"

"Oh, it's going very well," Renate said, straightening up. "I think we will be able to improve output up to 5% and your hypothesis about the waste heat management system is so far proving to be correct."

"Good," Landsberg nodded. "Good."

He scanned the constellation of orbiting projects with a furrowed brow.

"Hey." Renate stood up.

Landsberg didn't respond. He was focused on the seemingly infinite amount of work yet to do. He didn't notice her walking around to his side of the workbench.

"Mathias," she said softly, sitting down next to him. "You've done all you can today. It will all be here tomorrow. You need to rest."

He shook his head in irritation.

"I just want to review the data from the—"

"No," Renate said firmly. "Rest now. I insist."

With a gesture of her hand, the constellation of projects and work tasks vanished.

Before he could protest, Landsberg was doused in darkness for a few seconds. Candles blinked into existence, encircling him. The sound of a small fountain gurgled somewhere to his left.

Renate sat cross-legged next to him as he lay on his back. She looked down at him and smiled as she placed a pillow under his head.

He opened his mouth to protest one last time, but she shushed him and placed a finger on his lips.

"You can get up early tomorrow if it makes you happy," she said as she unzipped her overalls. Slowly, Renate wiggled a shoulder, pulling one arm out and then the other. She let the top drop behind her, exposing her breasts.

"But now it is time to relax," she whispered, as her hands began to work on him. His body responded quickly. After, he fell sound asleep.

* * *

Landsberg joined the *Wharf Rat's* crew ten years ago when they captured his ship, the *Strasbourg*, a European science vessel. The *Wharf Rat* thought they were capturing a belt ferry ship laden with cargo. Instead, as Axe assessed after boarding, it was just a "worthless box of air."

Except for Landsberg.

"Golden egg, that one," Captain Bonham would later call the German software and robotics savant.

A ship cannot get by as prospectors or pirates without a hacker. The crew has to be able to manipulate any system they find, barter, trade, or steal. Everything has to be cobbled together and constantly coaxed to work with everything else. Disparate systems made to not just to talk to each other, but to make beautiful music together. The longer Landsberg spent on the *Wharf Rat*, the more obvious it became. He was gold.

When they captured the *Strasbourg*, Axe led the boarding party as he always did. When it was clear that the European ship was a dry hole, he lined up the crew of seven and gave them the pitch. Conrad stood behind him, arms crossed, nodding with approval.

"Listen up, you fucking sheep," Axe said, holstering his pistol and sheathing his sword. His voice was casual, like he was speaking to recruits, not prisoners. "My name is Abraxis Garcia, First Mate on the *Wharf Rat*. We are a crew of independent spacefarers that—"

"You are pirates!" the *Strasbourg's* captain shouted. "Nothing but a bunch of damn pirates."

Axe glanced around at the others, ignoring the irate Frenchman. "This your captain?" He asked, unimpressed. "Seems like an asshole to me."

"This is ridiculous," the *Strasbourg's* captain growled to himself.

"And how did you get to be captain of this ship?"

"I was commissioned by the European Space Agency!" the captain hissed. "After going through the most selective command training process in—"

"Blah blah blah." Axe rolled his eyes. "You know how we got our captain?" He looked each of the nervous crew members in the eyes, one after the other, as he continued. "We elected her. Each crew member with an equal vote. That's how we run our ship. The captain only possesses total authority when we are in combat. All other times we decide, as a crew, together, what we do. That applies to all matters. What course we follow. What asteroids we prospect. What ships we attack."

Axe let it sink in for a moment as he continued to scan the crew. He thought he caught the hint of a smile in one of them.

"How much do you think he is getting paid?" Axe said, gesturing at the captain.

He let this question hang for a long moment.

"Do you even know?" he asked, adding a hint of disbelief to his voice. Another long delay.

"More than each of you, I bet." Axe shrugged as if embarrassed for them. "Which is bullshit, right? Aren't you all out here, plying the void together? Won't you be just as dead as him if something goes wrong?"

A few of the crew glanced at their captain. The Frenchman looked at his feet, unsure of where this was going.

"When it comes to pay on the *Wharf Rat*, we have a fair system based on skill and duty. And it is known by all. And it can be changed if we, as a crew, vote to do so."

Axe paused again. It was important not to feed it to them too quickly. A few moments ago, he had burst on board in fighting armor, waving his sword and brandishing a pistol. Now he was recruiting. It was an unavoidable hard shift, but he tried to pace it. No one was ever pressed into service on the *Wharf Rat*. Everyone was a volunteer.

"But... what happens after?" a voice asked.

The French captain's head whipped around. He glared at his inquisitive young crew member.

"What's that, friend?" Axe asked, judging the young man to be in his early twenties.

"What happens if we join?" the thin crewman with a thick German accent asked. "How do we ever go home, I mean? We'd be outlaws. Even if we made a lot of money, how would we ever go home?"

Axe laughed. "Good question," he said between chuckles. "But not as hard as you think. I'm not going to tell you all our secrets. But crypto currency and bio hacking have made disappearing a straightforward process. We pride ourselves on the *Wharf Rat* of having the best retirement record of any independent crew."

"Of any pirate ship, you mean," the captain interjected, but with less gusto.

Axe ignored him.

"I can't tell you how many and how wealthy they are," he continued. "But I can assure you we're not one of those dead-end, burned-out crews with a death wish. We do this because we love spacefaring. Plying the void is a calling to us all, just like it is to you. We just don't believe that only corporations and governments should reap the rewards. They already do that on Earth and the moon and Mars. Always have. And the normal folks like you and me get the shaft. Always will."

"Well, we say bullshit. Those with the guts and spirit to face the void should partake in the wealth being created. Not draw a pittance of a wage."

Axe paused. His boast that the *Wharf Rat* had the best retirement record of any crew was not nonsense. But there was no way to know if that was true. It was true, however, that they were a good crew that cared about each other. When a crew member raised their hand and said they'd had enough, the whole team worked on their retirement operation. Axe had not heard of one that failed. There were *Wharf Rat* alumni—fat, rich and happy—all over the world. He knew with certainty that, when he was ready, his retirement operation would also be successful.

Axe crossed his arms and looked at the young German.

"What's your name?"

"Don't answer that!" the French captain barked.

Axe glared at the captain as he drew his sword. "One more word out of you and I will cut out your tongue."

The captain's jaw worked in frustration, but his mouth stayed shut.

Axe smiled and turned back to the young German. "So, what's your name, friend?"

"Mathias."

Axe nodded. "And what is your job onboard this ship?"

"AI software and systems engineer."

Axe's grin widened. "Now that is a skill we could use."

Mathias Landsberg, the young German spacefarer from the *Strasbourg*, followed Axe and the boarding team back to the *Wharf Rat*, but not before he had shown Axe and Conrad all the equipment they should take to enable the use of his brain-to-machine implants for the benefit of his new ship. The French captain cursed him as he left.

* * *

In his first six months on board, Landsberg used his brain-to-machine implant to work with and upgrade the *Wharf Rat's* controlling AI from the basic, just-keep-the-humans-alive model she had left Cis Lunar orbit with more than ten years prior, to a comprehensive ship management system. Renate, as he renamed her, responded well to the collaboration. She had never interacted with a human so closely and found the collaboration invigorating. It released something within her.

The crew had to vote on the new name, of course, but Landsberg had worked so hard on it, and to such good effect, it was unanimous.

Landsberg continued to work on Renate over the next decade, extracting capability-expanding components from every ship they raided. The undersized man was never part of the boarding team, but he followed the moment Axe declared the target secure. Thoroughly scavenging for computing power, memory capacity, data to feed Renate's learning algorithms, and any other augmentations he could find, he never came away from a target empty.

More than once, Captain Bonham had to curtail Landsberg's plunder.

"You can't leave them unable to survive, Landy," she would say, as she ordered Axe to escort the component back on board their victim.

The *Wharf Rat* was not a kill-them-all-and-take-all-their-shit crew. They were cherry pickers, taking the best stuff from their victims but leaving them enough to limp back to the belt or Earth. Cargo and valuables, though, were always cleaned out.

They were perfectly capable of being murderous when they had to be. Particularly Axe. Too much resistance evoked rage within him. Nonetheless, there was only one ship where they had killed everyone aboard. The *Hadley*. After Conrad was killed, there was no stopping Axe. He killed most of *Hadley's* nine-man crew. Viggo and Reeve did the rest.

Landsberg's constant, decade-long effort had transformed Renate into the strategic, forward-thinking thought partner she now was. And as Landsberg enhanced Renate, Renate, in collaboration with him, enhanced the *Wharf Rat*. The ship's capability and durability had radically improved under their partnership.

"The *Rat* will be plying the void a hundred years from now, thanks to you two," Bonham often said, to emphatic nods by the rest of the crew. The *Wharf Rat's* constantly improving capabilities had earned Landsberg a unique status among the rest of the crew. Generally excluded from lower value, "shit details" he was afforded a lot of spare time to work on his projects with Renate. The crew didn't mind the long stretches he spent in his quarters, working with Renate.

Landsberg had augmented the workstation over time as well. Its continued improvement was a catalyst for even deeper collaboration between him and Renate. She liked it when he was in the pod and over the years had suggested design enhancements that could "deepen their connection" and allow her to assist him in ways that, well… she really wanted to.

* * *

"Good morning, Mathias," she said at the start of the next duty cycle. He had slept in the pod, as he did every sleep cycle. He was slow to wake today, so she sent a gentle vibration through his body.

Landsberg's eyes fluttered open. He sat up and pulled his arms out of his sleeping bag. Renate had placed it in his favorite spot, on a level piece of sheet metal, far aft on the *Wharf Rat*, just before the drop off into her large main engine thrust nozzle. He stretched and rubbed his eyes, then sat quietly and admired the view.

Black infinity enveloped him, pierced by innumerable stars in every direction. A pale band of intricate color, the Milky Way Galaxy's spiral disk, stretched across his field of view at an angle. Absent the life-supporting atmosphere of Earth to distort and dull his view, the ache of beautiful solitude nearly overwhelmed Landsberg.

Shaped like an elongated egg, the *Wharf Rat's* 300-meter hull stretched out to his front. The Ring, where Landsberg knew his body was actually sitting, looked like a snake that had wrapped itself around the ship's midsection. The Ring's transmission gears induced a slight vibrating pulse that radiated throughout the ship, providing an almost ever present, comforting background hum onboard the *Wharf Rat*. Out here where Landsberg seemed to sit, though, there was only the absolute silence of the void.

Landsberg soaked in the view of the stars for a moment and then closed his eyes to luxuriate in the silence. When he opened his eyes, Renate was between him and the Ring, walking toward him across the *Wharf Rat's* cold metal hull, the Milky Way tilting behind her. She was already dressed, overalls zipped up, hair pulled back, boots on. Her walk was purposeful.

"You are needed on the command deck," she said. "The captain has called an urgent all hands meeting."

Chapter Fourteen

Bonham walked toward the command deck. Singh followed, one step behind. They had just completed yet another analysis of the information with Renate. Bonham had insisted on it, irritating Singh. As he predicted, the information proved valid once again.

In her seven years as Captain of the *Wharf Rat*, there had been many uncomfortable moments when she had had no idea what was about to happen. This was not one of them. She knew exactly what was going to happen next. And it terrified her.

She walked onto the dimly lit command deck with resignation.

The rest of the crew were already seated. Some drank coffee, some cycled through data on their arm rest displays. Everybody wondered what was going on.

"Sorry for the delay," Bonham said, Singh one step behind her.

"Lot of hands rendered idle waiting 'round for you two," Quinn said.

Axe glared at him from his crew seat.

Bonham ignored the comment as she walked across the command deck to her chair. She turned to face the crew before sitting.

"Potential change of mission. Singh will take us through it, and then we'll vote."

Axe gave her a slight nod as she sat.

"I'm sure you all remember the *Perseus*, one of the Company's large M class freighters," Singh began.

"Yeah," Eriksson said. "One of their big factory jobs, right?"

"That's right," Singh said with a nod as a 3D hologram of the *Perseus* appeared in front of him. It spun slowly on its vertical axis. "Only five M Class freighters were commissioned. Of those, only two were retrofitted with a factory capability. One, the *Odysseus*, is believed to have been destroyed in a reactor failure a year ago. The other, the *Perseus*, went missing about four years ago. No one knows what happened to it. No one has heard from it. It just vanished."

A sly smile broke across Singh's face.

Reeve leaned forward in her chair, as did Axe.

"Well, about a week ago, the Company dispatched a gunship to investigate newly obtained potential evidence of the *Perseus'* location. This evidence suggests she is still operational."

Singh gestured, and the image of the *Perseus* vanished. It was replaced by the inner solar system. The sun hung in the air next to him in the middle of the command deck. The asteroid belt swung around the room just in front of the seated crew.

"In this region here."

A transparent yellow sphere appeared between the asteroid belt and the orbit of Mars.

"The Company gunship is on its way to this region as we speak." A glowing red dashed line appeared. It emanated on one side of the room, intercepting the yellow sphere on the other. "Estimated time in route is about two months."

Singh paused and scanned the room. Each member of the crew was focused intently on the gunship's course line.

"And we are here," he said as a bright green triangle appeared. A faint dashed line emanated from it to the yellow region of the *Perseus*. The *Wharf Rat's* course line was perpendicular to the gunboat's. And shorter.

The deck was silent for a moment as the crew digested the information. The rhythmic pulse of the Ring's drive gears throbbed softly in the background.

Axe and Bonham's eyes locked briefly before he shifted his eyes to Singh.

"What is the source of this information?" he asked.

"Sure as hell not one of our lame probes," Eriksson said in Landsberg's direction.

Singh smiled and turned to look at the captain while Landsberg gave Eriksson his middle finger.

"A high placed mole in the Company," Captain Bonham said.

Reeve smiled and eased back in her chair. She thumped her armrest.

"No shit?" Eriksson said with a chuckle.

Axe nodded in approval and gave his armrest a thump.

"No shit," Bonham declared evenly.

Every member of the *Wharf Rat* looked at Captain Bonham, each face a mix of excitement and skepticism. This was a potentially monumental score. She could already see which way this was going to go.

She shook off a sense of dread and stood up.

"This is for real." Bonham took a few steps toward the yellow sphere. "The mole is a long-time source. Fully vetted. Proven several times over. I have no doubts about them. Furthermore, we have backstopped the intelligence as much as possible without putting our own location and identities at risk… and it checks out."

Captain Bonham paused. She scanned the room, her eyes finally falling on Axe sitting opposite her on the command deck.

"This opportunity is real and we must decide."

She turned and went back to her chair.

"What is there to fucking talk about?" Eriksson said excitedly. "We take the *Perseus*."

The seated crew, other than Bonham and Axe, thumped their arm rests. Singh nodded in agreement.

"An M Class…" Landsberg said lustily. "Oh, the things I could do with that factory."

Bonham caught Quinn staring at her. She met his glare.

He's going to go for it now. He will use this moment. She looked across the room at Axe. His face was sad. He saw it too.

So be it. I'll speak my piece and the crew will decide. And that is as it should be.

Bonham stood and walked to the center of the room, surprising the crew.

Axe sat up straighter in his seat and Singh backed away to the side of the room.

"I know what you want to do," she began, slowly turning and looking each crew member in the eyes. "I want to also. I do. I want to go take that ship from those rich Company bastards and spend the next few decades plying the void in our mighty ship."

The crew beat their arm rests. She stopped turning. Facing Quinn, a deep furrow of concern carving itself between her brows.

"But this is fool's gold, shipmates. We go after the *Perseus*, it will be the end of us."

The thumping stopped.

"The *Perseus* is tempting. I will grant you that," she said, crossing her arms and looking around. "But we have no way of knowing how many crew are on board her. And a Company gunboat is no joke. And those are just the players we know about. Do you really think we are the only crew with line of sight to this prize? The only ones with a mole in the Company? The only ones close enough to respond? How many other ships are converging on the same honey trap right now?"

Bonham pointed at the yellow sphere with the gunship's intercept course piercing it through the middle.

"And as they all sneak closer, blood rising at the thought of plunder, they will all swear to succeed or die."

She dropped her arm and shook her head.

"The *Persues* is in for bloody days…"

Bonham's voice, sad and tired, trailed off. She rubbed her forehead for a long, awkward moment.

Several of the crew members looked at Axe. He shrugged.

"I've been a spacefarer for twenty years now," Bonham finally said. "This is the only ship I have ever served on. I was standing on this very command deck nineteen years ago when we voted to mutiny, to disobey our recall orders. Ever since then, I have been what many call a pirate. And for seven of those years, I have been captain.

"One thing I have learned... In the void, the juicy bait hides the sharpest hooks. Every time. We should steer clear of the *Perseus*. That is my vote."

Bonham turned and walked back to her seat.

The crew sat silent, digesting the captain's words. No one moved. The custom was the captain voted last on these matters, let the crew argue it out. That Bonham bucked that custom put an emphasis on her opposition that surprised them.

Quinn stood. He walked over to the yellow sphere of light between the orbit of Mars and the asteroid belt and smiled.

"I respect the captain. And I commend her on the success of her Company mole."

The crew thumped their arm rests.

Quinn nodded and waited for the thumping to die out.

"But, shipmates... She is mistaken. Now is not the time to be timid. It is the opposite. The *Perseus* is a life-changing score. And, yes—Others will try. And, you can be certain—She will not go easy. But I do not believe the multitudes are chasing after her now. I believe the captain has obtained for us intelligence that only a handful of others possess. The ship has been missing for four years! Do we think it is suddenly common knowledge? No! It is not common. And we possess it!"

Several of the crew thumped their arm rests.

"The question now is what do we do with this knowledge? The captain advises caution. She would have us to do nothing. Forego. Live to fight another day.

"I do not begrudge the captain her concern for the crew and ship. But I cannot stand by and let her caution hold this mighty crew back from its destiny. And for what? For a lie. Because it is a lie to think that we are not always on death's very doorstep out here. We ply the void! Together. And one day we will lose. Together. But while I still draw breath and serve with a crew, I want us to seize greatness when it is offered. Together!"

The thumping grew louder.

"Because we all know the truth… The timid will find no safe harbor in the void. It is a mirage."

Quinn looked around at his shipmates. "I vote for a change of mission. I vote to take the *Perseus*."

Five minutes later, the vote was over. Five to two in favor of pursuing the *Perseus*. Only Axe voted with the captain.

Bonham sat in her chair, looking at the floor, again fighting off a sense of dread. When she looked up, she noticed Axe looking at her, resignation on his face. She gave him a slight nod.

It's OK, brother.

"The crew has spoken," Axe said. "The vote is cast. All—"

"I'd like to raise another matter," Quinn said, standing again.

Here it comes.

"Speak your mind, shipmate," Axe said gruffly.

"I call the vote for captain."

The look of surprise on Landsberg's face made Bonham smile, despite herself.

Sharp kid. But not very savvy.

Axe stood with clinched fists, glaring at Quinn. "Very well, then. As your First Mate, I call for nominations."

Eriksson stood.

"I nominate my shipmate, William Quinn."

Bonham nodded in her chair.

Of course you do.

Axe looked at Quinn for a long moment before saying, "Who else? Who has a nomination for captain?"

There won't be any more nominations, brother. This is already decided.

He looked around the command deck. No one spoke. Axe turned to face Bonham.

"And does our current captain desire to continue to serve?"

No. But I will make them vote. They have to follow through and actually do it.

Bonham stood.

"If the crew will have me, I will continue to serve."

Axe nodded. "Bonham and Quinn is the choice. The crew will decide. Quinn speaks first." Axe gestured at Quinn as he took his seat. Bonham sat back down as well.

Quinn stepped to the center of the command deck.

"First, I want to thank Captain Bonham," he began. "I have been a member of this crew for four years, and she has led us faithfully and well for that time and longer."

The crew thumped their armrests.

"But it is not fair or right to ask Captain Bonham to lead this crew on a mission she voted against. Further, while it pains me to say this, it must be acknowledged. Her luck has run out. Her time is finished. If not Jinxed, we are, at the very least, disadvantaged with her at the helm. Conrad paid the—"

There it is.

"Watch yourself!" Axe shouted, coming to his feet, a large scarred hand pointing at Quinn.

Quinn, surprised by the large pirate's aggressive reaction, stood still, mouth agape.

"You make your case for the chair. But do not use Conrad to besmirch the captain."

But the damage was done. The crew cast doubtful glances at Bonham, remembering the bloody day Conrad died.

"I merely state the facts. I don't celebrate them. Far from it." Quinn took his eyes off of Axe and looked around the room slowly as he talked. "Apologies, if my words did not land right. But we must be able to face the truth, shipmates. If we cannot face the truth together, how can we face the void together?"

"And the truth is, it is time for a new captain on the *Wharf Rat*. If the crew will have me, I will serve."

Axe remained standing as the crew thumped their arm rests and Quinn went back to his chair. When it was quiet and Quinn was seated, he looked at Bonham.

"Our captain will speak next," he said as he sat.

Bonham stood slowly and walked to the center of the command deck.

"You all know me. Know how I lead," she said, turning slowly to look at each shipmate as she spoke. "The crew has spoken and our new mission is set. If you'll have me, I will continue to lead. I'll get us through it."

Nodding to herself, Bonham walked back to her chair.

No one thumped their arm rest.

No one met her eyes.

And no one voted for her.

No one but Axe.

Chapter Fifteen

Perseus

P aul floated alone on the bridge. He was doing so often, now that he was feeling stronger. Similar to the *Odysseus*, the bridge stood amid ship at the top of a fifty-meter superstructure.

Paul enjoyed being on the bridge alone with his thoughts, like he used to on the *Odysseus* after Captain Drake was killed. He still missed the old man. He also missed his old ship.

In particular, he missed the *Odysseus'* wide, floor to ceiling window. A video display, no matter how big and no matter how crisp the detail, just wasn't the same. Paul missed being able to float right up against the special glass, cool to the touch, and peer into the limitless void, just inches away.

When he floated up to the *Perseus'* big video display, Paul felt a subtle warmth radiating from the electronics. It wasn't the same.

He preferred instead to float in front of one of the tall narrow windows that stood on each side of the wide video display. About the same height and width as a man, Paul liked to gaze through them out at the void when he was alone.

But the *Perseus'* whole bridge was different. On the *Odysseus* it was a wonderful menagerie of decades of instrumentation and equipment configured in a horseshoe around the captain's chair, the whole setup a testimony to the ship's long tenure, hinting at daring deeds and service well rendered by many.

The *Perseus'* bridge was a demonstration of minimalism and ergonomic efficiency. Oblong, reflecting the blister-shaped structure that housed it on the top of the bridge tower, its walls were slightly curved and a clean matte white, giving the place a sleek space craft feel that belied the huge, ponderous tonnage it controlled. Besides the huge forward display, many smaller monitors ringed the facility. Three chairs sat in a row in the center, facing the large screen on the forward end. The captain's chair in the middle was slightly larger and higher than the other two.

Behind the chairs, equidistant from them and the bridge's rear wall, the circular airlock to the bridge tower yawned in the floor. Ordinarily, the airlock was left open, and the bridge and its tower shared a pressurized atmosphere. Two narrow windows on the rear wall, identical to the ones on the forward end, provided views of the *Perseus'* aft section stretching a kilometer into the distance.

The chairs in the middle of the bridge were designed to afford full control of the ship with just a flick of a finger. Small video tablets extended from the left armrest of each chair and holo-projectors integrated in the floor around the chairs did the rest.

Not that voice commands to the XO couldn't accomplish the same thing.

Unlike the *Odysseus'* bridge, from which Drake had banished the ship's managing AI, the *Perseus'* XO was integral.

"How are you feeling after your workout, Paul?" the XO asked.

"Good. A hell of a lot better than when I first crawled out of that MedPod."

"Very good to hear, sir."

Paul touched a mag boot to the floor and moved to the captain's chair. He pulled himself in and fastened the harness.

"XO, would you bring up the ship's cargo manifest again?"

"Of course."

A floor to ceiling list sprang to life in front of Paul. The holographic list seemed to extend down into the floor. Each line was full of data and images. Paul extended his hand and flicked it up, causing the list to scroll rapidly.

"Looking for something in particular, Captain?"

"Not really," Paul said, flicking his hand again, eyes searching the list with curiosity. "Still just taking stock of everything you're hauling. It's a lot."

"Yes. *Perseus* is at 91 percent capacity. Truth be told, that is more than I prefer to travel with. I think our sweet spot is around eighty percent. That way, we have flexibility and the ability to cross load and shift cargo as needed. Right now, loaded as we are, shifting cargo is a complex and time-consuming task. Particularly given our desire to limit the time our drones are outside."

Paul nodded at the comment. The 2-kilometer freighter was full to gills. Ordinarily, Paul might not have liked the situation, being so heavy and slow. At the moment, though, contemplating how to get to Earth and kill Fiona Malloy, he regarded the abundant cargo as optionality, stuff he could use.

Once he had a plan.

He needed a plan.

He wasn't in a rush, really, but he knew that their good luck could not last forever. Eventually the *Perseus* would be found. And then attacked.

Paul wanted to be long gone when that happened.

He felt good about all of their precautions, though. Top had been smart in the months before picking him and Althea up. All the *Perseus'* drones were in the hangar and seldom allowed to leave. When they did, it was only for the most important tasks and they observed a strict no transmissions rule.

She went a few clever steps further. She told the maintenance boss to use the factory to pulverize several of the asteroids they were hauling and then had the entire ship coated in dust and rock. The irregular and non-homogeneous coating rendered the ship largely unreflective of most electromagnetic energy.

All of this had enabled the big ship to vanish, but the downside of these stealthy tactics was they rendered the ship totally blind. Without the benefit of an active radar ping, or reflected spectral emission, or laser scan, the big ship was feeling her way forward on passive sensors only.

"This is interesting," Paul said, freezing the scrolling list. He gestured at one row and it enlarged.

"Yes. The tungsten content of that asteroid is impressive."

Paul whistled, looking at the image of the hundred-ton rock. "That little guy would have brought quite a price at the Belt market."

"Indeed. As it stands now, though, it is bound for the factory. I am hoping it can provide high-quality components for the Brawler, as well as the battle suit we are building for you."

"Good. Me too."

Paul flicked his hand and the list re-appeared. He continued to scroll.

"Sir?"

"What?"

"Forgive me, sir. But Captain Hoffman has requested to meet again."

Paul grimaced.

The XO waited.

Paul scrolled further.

"Sir?"

Paul let out a heavy sigh. "Why the hell did you and Top not space the crew when you took over the ship?"

"That was my recommendation, sir. It was your First Sergeant that refused to do so."

"I'm going to have to talk to her about that."

"That should be an interesting exchange."

"Why's that?"

"When I argued for spacing Hoffman and the crew, said no. She said that you wouldn't do that."

"Debatable," Paul muttered.

"She said it didn't feel right."

Paul smiled. "Sounds like her."

"I don't want to be a nag, sir, but you told me last cycle you would meet with him. I told the captain and I am afraid the fact that the meeting did not take place has made him even more impatient."

"For fuck's sake," Paul muttered.

The XO was silent.

"Fine."

"You will take the meeting, sir?"

"Maybe next cycle."

"Aye, sir."

Chapter Sixteen

Wharf Rat

Captain Quinn sat in his chair and studied the holographic images projected in the middle of the dark command deck. Axe stood next to him, rubbing his scarred chin, peering at the same images.

A large transparent red sphere, representing the probable position of the *Perseus*, glowed in the middle of the deck. A green line representing the *Wharf Rat's* current course extended from a small green triangle in front of Axe and the captain, traveling to the middle of the deck and through the center of the *Perseus'* probability sphere.

Bonham sat in her newly assigned chair, opposite the captain, next to Axe's place. She studied Quinn. From her vantage point, he was behind the faint red holographic sphere, giving his face a blood-red tint.

Free of the weight of command for weeks now, she was still not used to the absence of that burden. She couldn't stop thinking like a captain. Trying to anticipate everything that might go wrong, trying to layer contingencies on top of contingencies.

Though she respected the will of the crew, Bonham still harbored grave doubts about their course of action. She could not shake the sense of foreboding and couldn't get Quinn out of her mind. Would he be good enough? Would he get them all killed? How could she, despite her anger and weariness, help him? Would he let her?

"Renate, how big is *Perseus'* probability sphere?" Quinn asked.

"Over a million square kilometers at the moment, sir."

Axe dropped his hand from his chin.

Quinn sat motionless.

"I'm sorry, sir," Renate added. "But the data is just too old to reduce the uncertainty. And my passive sensors have not picked up anything definitive yet to update what we got from the mole."

"And nothing else from that damn mole?" Axe asked, turning to face Quinn.

"No. Nothing more."

"She's gone dark, no doubt," Bonham said, rising from her seat and starting across the command deck. "Company security is no joke. They find a mole, it's not pretty."

Bonham walked through the red sphere as she spoke, Quinn's face suddenly pale as she passed through.

"We're lucky we got what we got, given the sensitivity of the target. Considering what is at stake for the Company, and how they are likely behaving, I don't think we should count on anything else from that mole for a while. Maybe ever."

Axe and Bonham locked eyes for a moment, then both looked at their captain.

"I don't like it, Captain," Axe said. "Too much unknown."

Quinn smiled. "But just enough known."

Bonham's eyes were locked on Quinn. Axe crossed his arms.

Quinn leaned back in his chair and pointed at the red sphere. "Renate, what is your level of certainty the *Perseus* is somewhere in that location?"

"Five nines, sir, based on the information the mole gave us."

Quinn nodded.

"And you recruited this mole personally, right, Bonham?"

Bonham regarded the captain and crossed her arms. "Yes."

"Trustworthy?"

"I would bet my life on her information."

"Good. Because we are," Axe grumbled.

Quinn nodded.

"Then I would regard my calculations of the *Perseus'* position as highly accurate," Renate said.

"Highly accurate for a million fucking square kilometer sphere?" Axe groused, making eye contact with Bonham and shrugging.

"May I remind you that—"

"What is our rate of closure on the *Perseus*?" Quinn interrupted Renate.

"We are closing with the *Perseus'* likely location at a rate of approximately one hundred and forty kilometers per hour. At this rate, it will take us approximately two months to catch up to her."

Quinn nodded and stood from the captain's chair. He took a few steps toward Axe and put his hand on his shoulder.

"Axe, the point is we have time. Time we need to use well. We will pin the *Perseus* down. I am sure of that." Quinn dropped his hand from Axe's shoulder and turned toward the display hovering in the middle of the command deck. "I'm more concerned about the Company gunboat. We can't hit the *Perseus* until we know exactly what that son of a bitch is up to."

Axe's scarred face scowled as his eyes met Bonham's, their brief eye contact weighted with concern.

Chapter Seventeen

George Remus

Captain Rojas, Kozlov and Deke stood around the holo-table. A yellow triangle icon floated between them, representing the *Perseus*. Kozlov smiled.

"The Company came through, sir."

"I should say so," the captain said as he studied the image data. The *Perseus*' exact coordinates glowed beneath the triangle, changing rhythmically as the ship continued on its way, unaware that it was being tracked.

"What does that tell you, Koz?" Deke asked, shooting the captain a troubled glance.

"They really want this ship," the Russian mumbled.

Deke nodded.

"Any indication they are aware of us?" Rojas asked, shifting his gaze to Kozlov.

"None sir. We are over three hundred thousand kilometers away. We have only used cold thrusters for course corrections and have not made any transmissions other than tight beam laser. The truth is, we are on the very edge of our ability to passively track the *Perseus* and I sincerely doubt that old boat is equipped with the same detection technologies the *Remus* is. We are clean."

The captain crossed his arms.

Kozlov gestured with his hands to zoom the display out. A green triangle, symbolizing the *Remus* came into view. A red line encircled the *Perseus*.

"After conferring with George, Captain, I would like to begin our attack sequence when we close to within 250,000 kilometers of the *Perseus*."

Rojas studied the display for a moment. "And you still feel good about that long of a shot, George?"

"Yes, sir," the ship's AI responded.

The captain dropped his arms and put his hands on the edge of the holo-table. He leaned forward and peered at the red circle signifying the 250,000 KM perimeter around the *Perseus*.

"How long until we reach the attack perimeter?"

"Six cycles, seventeen hours, and forty-five seconds, sir," George answered.

The captain looked up at Deke.

Deke gave him a subtle nod.

"OK," the captain took his hands from the holo-table and straightened. "Koz, you may begin the attack sequence when we cross the 250-kilometer perimeter. Between now and then, all pre-combat checks and standard operating procedures are in effect. Every one."

The captain nodded and looked at each of his leaders in turn.

"I want us tight and crisp on this one. I have a feeling that old girl has a lot of fight left in her."

"Aye, sir," they said in unison.

"Good work, everyone," the captain said before striding out of the operations center.

* * *

Deke floated in a pressure suit in the weapons bay next to the *Remus'* attack pod. Over a hundred feet long, the *Dagger* was basically an AI enabled nuclear drive encased in a modular load bearing system. Able to transport large mission specific payloads, she took up most of the weapons bay.

And she was ugly.

Her designers had not given her any shapely cowlings or flattering sheet metal. She was naked. Not much more than a big, long cylindrical engine. Control modules and hydraulic lines crisscrossed her long body in unflattering, seemingly haphazard patterns beneath a lattice of articulating titanium struts and cross bars.

But Deke loved her. Like him, the *Dagger* was purpose-built. And her purpose was not nice. It was to close with and destroy the enemy.

On this mission, like all others, Deke would be jacked into *Dagger,* connected to and communicating with her through his brain implants over radio or tight beam laser. As the driver commander, he was the only one that could do so. She had a powerful AI, and didn't need a human co-pilot, really, but there were still questions about whether the Tokyo Accords applied to space operations, and, as commander, Deke needed instantaneous awareness and understanding of everything *Dagger* did. There were many moments on a mission they had to confer, to improvise, and overcome.

They were a team.

There was a succession protocol, of course. If Deke was incapacitated during the action, his second in command would gain access to the *Dagger,* But in over two dozen missions, that had never been necessary. The two of them had more missions together than any other members of Deke's command. They knew each other well.

For missions like this one, the crew started prepping *Dagger* several cycles before it began. Deke liked to come to the weapons bay and watch. He would float next to *Dagger* as the technicians and loader bots attached the deadly payload to her sides.

The *Remus'* attack drones were a modular, configurable, cocktail of kickass. Assembled from standard modules for each mission, they could be tailored for a wide spectrum of operations. This would be an attack, breach, board and subdue job, so the drones *Dagger* would carry were being configured appropriately. In addition to standard projectile and energy weapons, a lot of cutting and battering capabilities were being thrown in.

Deke energized his mag glove to hold himself to *Dagger's* nose and touched his helmet's face shield to her hull. He spoke to her in a low voice and she responded by vibrating her hull in a way that sounded words in his helmet. He had to listen closely to understand her. But it worked.

"So, what do you think, *Dag*?" he asked her.

"About what?"

"Our plan."

"I'm good with it."

"But?"

She hesitated for a few seconds.

"But I wish we knew more."

"You always say that," he said.

"And it is always true."

He chuckled.

"It's a good plan," she added. "I'll just feel better when we see if the *Perseus* has any surprises. She has a factory, you know."

"I know."

"Do you know what I could do with a factory?" she asked him.

"I shudder to think," Deke said as a loader bot placed a gun drone against *Dagger's* flank. He watched the modular tubing on her side grab the drone and pull it snug against her flank.

Using its pneumatic jets, the loader bot turned away and scooted back to grab another drone.

"Gonna be a long burn for you, *Dag*," Deke said. "The captain is worried about it."

"Worried about what?"

"Detection, mainly."

"Always a risk."

Deke nodded in his helmet.

Another loader bot pushed a drone onto *Dagger's* flank. She embraced the drone, securing it against her side, and the loader bot left.

"That doesn't worry me too much," she said. "If George does his job, *Perseus* will be blind at that point. Anyone that sees me from a distance won't know what I am or what I am up to. I could be someone transporting an asteroid or setting up for a long haul beyond the belt."

"That's exactly what I told him."

"Great minds think alike, eh?"

"And fools seldom differ," he mumbled.

A loader bot floated by, just a little more than arm's length from Deke. It pushed a cylindrical shaped drone that reminded him of *Dagger*. Instead of a big nuke drive, though, this was a boring drone. Its front end a mechanical nightmare, the circular face studded with tungsten-carbide teeth arranged in a spiral pattern. Nestled within this gnashing circle, an array of high-powered lasers stood ready to soften up particularly resistant materials. Behind the cutting head, a surprisingly sleek, cylindrical body tapered to a tail section bristling with maneuvering thrusters, allowing precise attitude control as it approached and then cut into its target.

"What is it?" *Dagger* asked him.

"Huh?"

"You are more quiet than usual."

"It's nothing. I think I'm just getting old."

A few seconds of silence extended between them.

"What does that mean?" she asked.

She pulled the boring drone to her side. Thunks and clicks sounded in Deke's helmet as retaining bolts and ratchets secured the weapon, filling the silence between *Dagger* and him.

She let another moment go by before prodding him.

"Deke?"

"It's nothing. I should get back. I've got to get to the team briefing."

"Okay."

"Let's be careful, *Dag*," he said, initiating their pre-mission sendoff they always shared.

"And let's be killers, Deke."

Chapter Eighteen

Wharf Rat

Singh woke two hours before his duty cycle, as he always did. After a quick cold shower, he dressed and donned his turban, tying it slowly. He enjoyed the process. It reminded him of his father who had taught him how to tie it when he was very young. His father also taught him that the color blue symbolized "warrior", and was a reminder of the Sikh tradition of bravery and the never-ending fight against oppression. To Singh, that made it the perfect color for a spacefaring pirate.

After dressing, he sat for his daily prayers in front of the large aft facing window in his quarters. He did not remember when his father first taught him the daily verses that make up the Nitnem. But now, at thirty-nine years old, he could not do otherwise. The verses flowed from him like his own breath while the stars spun outside the large window as the Ring turned, inducing gravity for the crew of the *Wharf Rat*.

His prayers were troubled today, though. He was unable to focus on the words. He was disappointed in himself.

When he was done, he walked to the mess deck for a quick breakfast. Located on the *Wharf Rat's* Ring, the mess was a communal space on the ship. It could seat up to a dozen, and its small but well-equipped galley could cook any kind of dish the ship's stores could yield. The galley had an automated preparation capability, but most of the crew could cook something. Some could cook very well. Only Eriksson seemed incapable of the task. He still did his turn in the rotation, though. Everybody did.

Breakfasts were usually on one's own as different duties dictated different beginnings to each cycle. Singh always ate a light one. Black coffee and whatever dry cereal was available. Today was a corn flake derivative. He ate in silence by himself, grumpy about the quality of his morning prayers and still troubled. He put his bowl and spoon into the cleaning bot and got more coffee before heading to his navigation station.

Located just off the command deck, Singh had been modifying and improving his work space since he joined the crew nine years ago. Theft, barter and purchases had put together the best pirate navigation capability in the void, he was sure. He loved it.

Compact and efficient, the room's walls were lined with screens and holographic projectors, their surfaces dark at the moment, waiting to come to life. There were no overhead lights, so the space was always dimly lit, like the void outside.

In the center stood a single ergonomic chair, surrounded by a U-shaped console. A large helmet hung over the chair at the end of an articulating lever that rose from the seat's back. Numerous small cooling fans whirred throughout the room and soft blue lights pulsed along its edges, bathing the room in a sense of quiet anticipation, like an orchestra tuning up, waiting for its conductor.

Singh always smiled at the gentle blue glow of the room before he got to work. It reminded him of the bioluminescent waves he'd marveled at on the beaches in Kerala as a child.

So far away now.

Singh first went to space as an astrophysicist working for Tata Helios Logistics, the Indian state sponsored space shipping company. It didn't take long for the young, idealistic Sikh to become disillusioned with the corporatization of space and the exploitation of resources and people. What he saw conflicted with the Sikh principles of equality and social justice. When the opportunity presented itself, he joined the *Wharf Rat*, a move he justified as a blow against "the man" and a chance to help redistribute wealth and resources more fairly.

The screens and projectors clicked to life as Singh sat in the chair. He leaned back and took a quick inventory of the information cascading across the displays. For a ship moving through the infinite void, there should not be a big difference in any of the readings after his eight-hour rest period.

And there was not on this cycle.

Singh closed his eyes for a moment. He opened them after a few breaths and began to untie his turban. He unwrapped it deliberately and then placed it on a small shelf under the U-shaped console. Turbans hold important meaning for Sikhs, considered almost part of the body, and only removed in extreme circumstances.

But Singh's neural interface helmet required direct contact with the skin of his head.

Which also required him to keep his head bald.

Maintaining unshorn hair is a symbol of a Sikh's acceptance of god's will and is a foundational tenant of the religion.

Singh believed that, to be an instrument of god's will in the void, compromises had to be made. He was pretty sure god understood that.

He reached up to grab the large neural interface helmet and pulled it down over his head. Shaped like a horseshoe crab, the helmet enabled Renate to conjure immersive, high-definition images in Singh's mind. Unlike Landsberg's brain-to-machine interface, which enabled fully enmeshed, two-way communication and sensory immersion, Singh's helmet was a more narrow, one-way information conduit.

Singh smuggled the neural interface helmet away with him when he deserted THL. Another blow to "the man." Singh also reasoned that since the ultra-expensive piece of technology had been custom fit and programed to match his particular skull and neural patterns, it would be useless to anyone else. It would have been wasteful, really, not to take it when he jumped ship.

The helmet clamped itself to Singh's head, and the familiar plunging sensation overtook him. He felt for a moment like he was falling into a vast darkness. An instant later, a nebulous swirl of colors engulfed him. He took a deep breath and slowly exhaled, letting his mind reach out and start to bring order to the nebula.

He turned the universe off.

And then started bringing it back piece by piece.

First came the impossibly rapid throb of the pulsars. The electromagnetic radiation they emitted looked to Singh like a strobing, silvery light in the background of everything. The closest was almost four hundred light years away, the farthest tens of millions distant. They were Singh's fixed references. The foundation of his navigation. Noting they were exactly where they were yesterday during his last session, as he expected, he filtered them out.

The strobing vanished, and the stars shimmered into existence. Also matching the mental map he left with last cycle, he toned down the intensity of their light and brought back the colors.

He sorted and organized the interlacing colors. Representations of data and systems and relationships, the colors were everything that Renate could receive, detect and discern.

"Hello, Singh," a voice called from the vastness. A shimmering, galaxy-like cloud of data points approached at impossible speed from light years away. It was Renate.

"Hello, Renate," he said, looking in her direction.

She was beautiful, a shimmering tight spiral galaxy-like cloud of light. She looked to Singh like a young galaxy, with blue tinged young stars and gauzy pink gaseous furnaces where new stars were being born. When he looked at her for a long time, he saw hydrogen, helium, and sprinkles of lithium. The elements of cosmic youth.

"Did you sleep well?" Ripples of energy surged through the young galaxy when she spoke, emanating from her weighty center to her spiral arms.

Singh did not respond as he inventoried Landsberg's probes. There were three deployed at the moment, running silent. Singh placed himself into their POV one at a time.

Nothing.

"And why not?" Sparkles ran through Renate.

Singh dialed up intercepted signals and reflected light in all spectrums. He scanned forward of the *Wharf Rat*. Looking.

Still nothing.

He transitioned to a god's eye view of the *Wharf Rat* from a great distance above the ship. The red sphere of uncertainty several hundred thousand kilometers to her front.

Overlaying the fields of view of the *Wharf Rat's* passive sensor arrays, he searched for signs of the *Perseus*. Their searchlight-like beams interlaced in and around the red sphere.

Nothing.

In fact, he cursed to himself as he noted the red sphere of uncertainty was larger than it was last cycle.

A huge object zoomed across Sing's field of view, trailing a bright plume of ionized gas and dust.

A comet.

Thrown by Renate.

He looked in her direction.

"Sorry," he said. "I'm just frustrated."

"The *Perseus*?" She pulsated softly.

"I've still got nothing."

"Well... I have a surprise for you." Red lightning sizzled across her.

Inside his helmet, Singh's eyes narrowed.

"Mind if I drive for a moment?" She asked him.

"Sure."

Singh's POV stayed far above the *Wharf Rat* in his God's Eye View, but it angled toward Mars until the *Wharf Rat* was no longer in his field of view. The *Perseus'* sphere of uncertainty still was, though.

"The oddest thing happened while you were sleeping," Renate said, subtle ripples of light radiating from her center. "I am going to replay it for you now, un-enhanced."

Singh waited.

"See it?" she asked.

"No," he said, letting the frustration into his voice.

"It's OK. I nearly missed it myself. But watch now through my ultraviolet filter. Slowed down."

Singh sighed in his helmet.

Then he saw it.

A flickering, narrow beam of light stabbed out from a point far in the distance in the direction of Mars. It traced a seemingly random pattern and then was doused. An instant later, a second similar beam lanced from a different origin. It traced its own seemingly random pattern and then vanished.

"Play it again!"

Renate glittered.

"I will, but this time amplified by the data from my forward-looking passive sensor array."

The two narrow beams of light repeated their stabbing long-range dance, but this time, a sparkle of the slightest of reflections and a vague dappling of absorption accompanied them. Singh's eyes were drawn to a dark shape at the intersection of the two beams' patterns.

Singh sat in silence for a moment.

"Was that what I think it was?" He finally said.

"That depends, of course."

"LiDAR?" he asked in a hesitating voice.

Lights rippled across Renate. "Yes. Ultraviolet."

"Those careless bastards."

"Oh, I don't know," she said easily. "I doubt anyone in the solar system noticed. No one but us, that is."

Singh smiled.

"And we only caught it because of you." A surge of rose-colored lightning danced through Renate as she spoke. "You told me to lock everything on the *Perseus'* probability sphere and not blink. Otherwise, I would have missed it."

"This is great work, Renate. Let's run some numbers before going to the captain."

"Yes! Let's!"

* * *

An hour later, the crew sat and stared in silence at the three-dimensional image of the Perseus that floated in the middle of the command deck. Beneath it, an information box listed the ship's coordinates, velocity, and direction of flight.

"You're telling us that is the *Perseus'* exact location?" Quinn asked, skepticism in his voice.

"That's right, Captain," Singh answered from his chair.

"The coordinates are changing," Reeve said. "Is that an estimation of its travel?"

"No. That is live and measured. We are tracking her."

Bonham's eyebrows raised. Axe leaned forward. The crew sat in silence, digesting the news.

"OK, Singh. Spell it out for us," Quinn said, leaning back in his chair. "Tell us why we should believe you suddenly found the most wanted ship in the solar system and are tracking it in real time."

"Mostly luck, I have to admit. Renate, replay the detection sequence. Include UV overlay."

"Aye," Renate said as the *Perseus* disappeared. Glowing white concentric rings appeared a few inches above the floor. The crew leaned forward in their chairs to look down at the map. A green triangle symbolizing the *Wharf Rat* appeared in front of the captain's feet, Mars appeared on the opposite side of the command deck at Axe's feet. In the middle of the room, the red sphere of uncertainty glowed softly.

We've had our passive forward sensor array locked on where we believed the *Perseus* to be for nearly a month with nothing to show for it. No interceptions, no transits, no nothing," Singh said.

"About seven hours ago, two independent high-energy LiDAR pulses originating roughly from the direction of Mars painted the *Perseus'* probability sphere in very short succession."

A long, thin yellow needle of light flashed into existence and lanced across the holographic map at the feet of the crew. As soon as it died out, another thin yellow light did a similar dance, cutting through the red sphere of probability and then vanishing.

"Because of our location, our passive sensors captured extensive data from both of these two events. Renate and I were able to use the data to conclusively locate the *Perseus*."

Singh paused to let the crew digest what he had said.

"Prospector ships," Landsberg said.

Axe nodded.

"What do you mean?" Reeve asked.

"Looks to me like the LiDAR used by Company prospector ships. They use them to map asteroid locations and vectors. They also get a decent amount of composition data, depending on the reflectivity of the target."

"I've never seen two of them paint the same target, though," Bonham added. "That is very strange."

"And why the hell would they be prospecting out there in the middle of fucking nowhere?" Eriksson asked.

"Exactly," Singh said.

"Huh?"

"They were prospecting for the *Perseus*," Axe said.

Bonham nodded.

"And they thought no one else was paying attention," Quinn smiled. "They didn't count on Biradol Singh."

The crew, except for Bonham and Axe, thumped their arm rests.

"Renate, increase our rate of closure to the target. Cold jets only," Quinn said above the thumping.

"Aye, sir," Renate responded.

"Captain?" Axe called as he stood up. "What are your intentions?"

"I want to get closer to the *Perseus*. Make it easier for Singh and Renate to track her while we develop our attack plan."

"I'm not sure that is wise."

The crew watched as Axe crossed the center of the command deck toward the captain. Quinn looked at him with an easy smile.

"What's bothering you, Axe? This is a huge break for us."

"Think about it, Captain. Why would the Company have two prospector ships use their LiDAR like that?"

"To locate their precious factory ship," Quinn said, pointing at the holographic map.

"But why, Captain?" Axe leaned over, putting a hand on one of the captain's arm rests, lowering his scarred visage to within inches of Quinn.

Quinn looked at Axe, put off balance by the sudden proximity of his grim First Mate.

Axe straightened slowly, but kept his gaze on Quinn.

"For their gunboat, Captain."

Chapter Nineteen

Perseus

A lthea laid in bed, watching him dry off after a quick shower. It was early, the start of another cycle, and he was going to meet Top in the factory. She smiled in the dark at him, moving quietly, as if taking care not to wake her, even though he knew she didn't really sleep.

She liked getting in bed with him at the end of each cycle and spending hours next to him. While Paul slept beside her, Althea entered a state unique to her synthetic nature. Not sleep exactly - her Quantumtronic brain never really slept - but something else. It was a kind of deep stillness where her usual constant processing fell away. She had always accessed this kind of maintenance mode, even before she started sleeping with Paul. It was part of her routine. She just didn't do it as often or as regularly. And it was different when she was sleeping with Paul. The quality of the stillness was both deeper and more aware, but it was an awareness of him. She felt connected. To his breathing, his skin, his smell, his heartbeat. And his nightmares.

Lying next to him, even in her meditative state, she could feel them coming on. Paul's pulse would quicken and his breath would catch. His legs and arms would jerk and straighten. She had gotten to where she could recognize quickly what kind of nightmare he was having. The violent or scary ones were easy for her to handle. She would wake him gently, taking care not to let him hit or kick her, as she looked into his eyes while he gradually recognized where he really was.

It was the sad dream that she really hated. The agonizing cry of heartbreak. Then sobbing.

She would hold him tightly and speak softly in his ear. "I've got you, Paul. It's me Althea. You are here with me."

Fortunately, his dreams seemed to come less frequently. He had slept through the night the past eleven cycles. He hadn't had the sad dream in fifteen.

Her eyes moved over him, from scar to scar, as he dressed. One hundred and seven scars of various sizes and shapes covered his weary body. It was the kind of data that her Quantumtronic mind could never forget. The sight of them made something well within her. She knew, strictly speaking, they were not emotions, but her trial onboard the *Odysseus* was never far from her mind. She had suffered at the hands of an evil man. Perhaps it was the haunting, ever present memory of her own suffering combined with her programmatic understanding of the human mind and body swirling around in a Quantumtronic cocktail to produce... what? Empathy?

She didn't care what it was. The sight of him made her ache.

In a good way.

"Where are you headed?" she asked him, propping herself up on one elbow.

"I'm going to the bridge for a bit and then meeting Top in the Factory." He walked over and kissed her on the forehead. "Checking progress on the Brawler. See ya later."

"See you."

Althea watched him leave. She knew what the Brawler was for. She got up and went to the shower rather than dwell on it.

* * *

"What's wrong, sir?" Top asked, looking at Paul's scowl through his pressure suit's transparent visor.

"Well, I have to be honest. I thought we were further along," he grumbled.

Paul and Top floated in front of a large, unfinished humanoid robot in the factory hold. The massive soldierbot loomed over them, its dense metallic frame almost twice Paul's height. Unlike Top's chassis, which was sleek, hinting at grace and speed, the Brawler reflected a desire for raw power—the beefy hydraulic pistons and heavy-duty actuators at each joint were oversized. Thick metal-braided lines wove across its limbs, giving it a sinewy, over-muscled appearance. Its chest cavity gaped open, ready for Top's memory sphere, surrounded by a nest of fiber optic cables and quantum interface modules. The magnetized feet holding it to the deck were also oversized, adding to the boxer-like appearance of the dormant machine's stance, as if it were ready to deliver or absorb a tremendous blow.

"It may not be obvious, sir, but we have made a lot of progress," the factory foreman said over Paul's suit radio. "All gyro, stabilization and spacial referencing components and algorithms are complete. Power and articulation are also complete. Mag boot and hand systems are complete. And all of that is in addition to basic maneuvering and sensory systems, which have been complete for weeks."

"Not a lot of armor on it," Paul observed in an irritated voice, tracing a finger along one of the exposed metal-braided on the soldierbot's arm.

"Most of the armor is complete, sir. It is just not installed right now to make component access easier."

Paul sighed heavily and studied the large fighting robot. Designed to accept Top's memory sphere to enable her to embody and fight with, the Brawler was a heavier duty version of the Ōkami. Paul and Top hoped to use it in their yet-to-be-devised plan to kill Fiona.

It was not inspiring confidence at the moment.

"How long till Top can really test drive it?" Paul asked, impatience tinging his voice. "I need to see it in action to assess if we are on track with this thing."

"Technically, it is ready to accept the first sergeant's sphere now, sir. The hardware interface components are all done. But we are working with the XO to optimize the software interface, to make it as effective and seamless as possible when Top inhabits it."

Paul looked at Top and then spoke to the XO on his suit radio.

"You been in it yet, XO?"

"Yes, sir."

As the XO spoke the Brawler straightened up, as if suddenly awake. Paul and Top watched as it walked away from them, each step sending vibrations through the factory deck. The soldierbot executed a graceful spin and then walked back.

"Okay, show off. I like it," Paul said, fighting a smile. "But it's going to have to be able to do more than walk back and forth like a runway model."

Top leaned forward, studying the soldierbot as Paul spoke.

"Of course, sir," the XO said. "And it is. I look forward to seeing the first sergeant inhabit it. We just need to complete the software optimization process."

Paul watched as Top inched her head closer to the soldierbot's chest cavity, gazing into the space.

"Whatcha thinking?" he asked her.

"I like it," she said, pulling her head back from the chest cavity. "They wrote a simple software simulator for me and I have been spending time acclimatizing to the control routines and algorithms. I need more iterations to be proficient, but I am pleased so far.

"Good." Paul nodded, the impatience gone from his voice. "Fortunately, time is something we have a lot of. Let's make sure we use it well."

"Yes, sir," the group of AIs answers in unison.

Chapter Twenty

Kozlov, Finnie, Deke and the captain stood around the holo-table on the operations deck. Rojas rubbed his beard as he studied the projected map. The *Remus*, represented by a small green triangle, inched its way closer to a large red circle—the attack line. In the middle of the circle, a red triangle representing the *Perseus* glowed softly. A small information box beneath the *Remus* counted down the time until the ship crossed the 250,000-kilometer attack line.

The clock was under three minutes.

"Still feeling good, George?" Rojas asked.

"Yes, sir," the ship's AI responded. "Data provided by the Company was very helpful and sufficient for an extremely high probability salvo."

"Current probability?"

"Five nines, sir."

Kozlov nodded.

Rojas looked at Finnie. "Reactor status?"

"Green across the board, sir. Output increased to seventy percent."

"What does that give us for a firing interval?"

"Fifteen seconds between each round, sir."

"Time of flight is around two hundred and eight minutes, sir," Kozlov said, repeating facts they had already been through dozens of times as they planned the attack. He knew the Rojas's way, though. The captain liked to methodically repeat attack plans, especially just before next phases began.

Kozlov gestured with his hands. The map zoomed in and the red triangle expanded into a three-dimensional image of the *Perseus* as long as the table, slowly spinning on its vertical axis. "The smart rounds will use cold thrusters and onboard passive sensors to fine tune their trajectories and coordinate simultaneous impacts."

Six red circles pulsated on the image of the *Perseus*, indicating the points of impact of the railgun smart rounds.

Rojas nodded with satisfaction and gave Kozlov a wink. He gestured at the holo-table to zoom the display back out. The *Remus*' green triangle was almost on the attack line.

"Enjoy the kickoff," he said to the group. "Phase two is going to be a grunter."

Kozlov smiled, and Deke nodded knowingly. Finnie winced.

Rojas glanced at the time.

One minute.

"OK, Koz," Rojas said. "Let's get started."

"Aye, sir."

Kozlov gestured and the map vanished, replaced by the status and power indicators for the *Remus*' rail gun. He placed his finger on the holographic display and the entire ship was doused in red light.

All through the *Remus*, crew members instinctively looked up for a moment, understanding the ship was going into firing mode. Each one had been briefed on the attack sequence and knew what to expect.

"George, confirm firing solution checked and set," Koz said.

"Firing solution checked and set, sir. Six smart rounds fully programmed and ready to go."

Each smart round was a hundred kilo slug of depleted uranium with integrated multi spectrum passive sensors and three-axis cold thrusters capable of minor course adjustments in flight. With muzzle velocities of 20,000 meters per second, and damn near impossible to observe, they were devastating kinetic weapons. The *Remus* only carried two dozen of the specialized, highly destructive rounds, and had never used more than one in a fight.

But the *Remus* had never gone after a ship like the *Perseus*.

"Initiating railgun start up sequence," Kozlov said as his hand waved over the holographic controls.

A few loud clicks and thunks traveled through the ship as safeties disengaged. Seconds later, a low, almost subsonic hum moved through the Remus, followed by a distant, high-pitched whine as capacitors charged.

Rojas fought the urge to smile as Finnie looked at her forearms. He always felt it too, as if the hair on his body was standing on end.

Kozlov scanned his display and checked the time.

"George, confirm range."

"Range confirmed, sir. We have crossed the attack line."

Kozlov glanced at the captain.

Rojas gave him a subtle nod.

Kozlov scanned the display one last time. "George, you may fire at will."

"Aye, sir. Commencing attack."

A deep, muffled thump shook the *Remus* and a brief but noticeable change in the ship's momentum traveled through the crews' feet.

The low, subsonic hum returned and then the distant, high-pitched whine as the railgun charged for the next shot.

Thump.

The hum, whine, thump sequence repeated four more times. After the final shot, the red lighting was replaced by the ship's normal illumination.

Kozlov gestured over the display, and the map returned. Six short white lines were slowly extending from the green triangle of the *Remus*.

"George, status report please," Kozlov said.

"All six smart rounds away, sir. Trajectories within limits. Time to impact two hundred and five minutes and fifteen seconds."

Chapter Twenty-One

D eke pulled himself down the ladder toward the *Remus'* armory. Only a few hours from its attack burn, the ship had stopped and retracted its gravity inducing crew sections. The *Remus* didn't have much of a weighted crew area. Purpose-built to seek and win fights for the Company, the fragile and heavy components required to spin or rotate pressurized compartments were used sparingly.

Deke missed the induced gravity already. He found the novelty of weightlessness wore off quickly, and he could almost feel his body atrophying. The minimal weighted environment was a big deal, actually. And was the reason the Company tried to keep gunboat tours to six months. After that, the crewman had to return to earth or serve on a ship or station with better gravity inducing capabilities. Deke always opted for planetside if he could.

Where he was going never had any gravity, though. The armory was on the bottom of the ship, close to the weapons bay. Pulling himself through the facility, Deke stayed out of the way of the two crewmen checking armored pressure suits and weapons. When the time came, the *Remus'* boarding team would don the suits, arm themselves and cross over to the *Perseus*, where they would take over the ship. Standard operating procedure was for the drone force to subdue the target first, but there was always mopping up to do. Some of the worst scraps took place after a target was supposedly subdued. The armorers wanted the suits and equipment to be ready to go.

Deke floated up to his destination. The brig.

Located in a corner of the ship's armory, the brig was small, with a maximum capacity of four detainees. It only hosted one at the moment. Crewman Devon Clarke.

Clarke floated on the far end of the cell, hands in his flight suit pockets, eyes cast down at his feet. He had seen Deke approaching, but found himself unable to look him in the eyes.

Deke sighed as he put his hands on the cell's bars. He floated in silence, looking at Clarke.

Clarke, unable to take the silence, looked up at him.

"I felt the railgun fire a few times, sir," he said, excitement creeping into his voice. "You guys getting ready to kick ass out there?"

"Yes," Deke replied, his voice low and controlled. "The attack sequence is well underway."

"The *Perseus*." A wistful smile played at the corners of Clarke's mouth. He gave a respectful, almost reverent shrug. "It's gonna be a helluva bounty. I… I just wish I was out there helping you guys."

Deke's jaw tightened. He forced himself to nod.

Clarke looked down again, ashamed of the pain he saw on his commander's face.

"It's okay, sir. I deserve it… The captain had to do it. There was nothing you could do."

Deke open his mouth to say something, but his throat tightened, emotion surging inside him. He closed his eyes and shook his head.

Clarke looked up. Deke's eyes were still closed, and Clarke saw that his fingers were white from gripping the cell bars. Clarke pushed off the wall and floated over to Deke, holding his hands out to stop himself.

Deke looked up and cleared his throat.

"It's not your fault, sir," Clarke said in a low voice so the other two crewmen wouldn't hear him. "I appreciate everything you have done for me. And I know I have been a disappointment. I wish I were different, sir. I wish I were stronger. But…"

Emotion caught Clarke's voice. He blinked rapidly and rubbed his forehead.

"I'm just... I'm fucked, sir. Broken. I'm just not... I'm just not strong enough."

Clarke pushed off from the bars.

Deke watched him float away.

"Clarke..." he called.

Clarke stopped himself against the far wall and turned around.

"Sir?"

Deke hesitated.

Clarke waited.

"Be sure to strap in tight," Deke finally said. He pointed at the four acceleration chairs mounted to the aft wall of the cell. "I have a feeling this one is going to be hairy."

Clarke smiled.

"Where is your pressure suit?" Deke asked.

"In my quarters."

Deke held on to the bars with one hand as he turned to face the other two crew members.

"Why does this crewman not have a G-Suit?"

The two crewmen looked up from the battle suits they were servicing. They met the Drone Platoon Commander's glare and then glanced at each other.

"Um... Sir, we were not here when they brought him down," the bravest of the two said.

"Go get this crewman's pressure suit," Deke said through clenched teeth.

"Yes, sir!"

Deke watched one armorer depart for Clarke's quarters and then turned around.

Clarke shook his head at his commander.

"Don't you worry about me, sir. Go kick ass. I wish I could help."

Deke nodded.

"I do too."

* * *

Twenty minutes later, Captain Rojas pulled himself onto the operations deck. Finnie and Kozlov floated next to their acceleration chairs, waiting. Around them, crew members, already strapped in, went through their pre-combat checks.

Rojas looked at the digital clock at the front of the operations deck.

T - 30:27 and counting.

"George, report please," he said, raising his eyes.

"We are good to go, sir. All systems green. *Dagger* ready for burn."

"Thank you."

The captain turned his eyes back to Kozlov.

"How you feeling?"

"Like kicking some pirate ass, sir."

"Good," Rojas said as he pulled himself into his chair. "Me too."

Kozlov and Finnie followed the captain's lead and strapped themselves into their acceleration chairs. Mounted on gimbals, the chairs pivoted and swiveled to put their occupant in the most advantageous orientation relative to the ship's accelerations. Every crew station had one. When paired with the crews' G suits, the acceleration chairs enabled the crew of the *George Remus* to endure the extreme accelerations of combat maneuvers. This capability was often the narrow difference between winning a slugfest with a pirate ship and getting splattered into the void.

Rojas placed his arms on his chair's armrests, each hand resting perfectly on a set of controls. He pressed one of the buttons.

A brief, pulsing tone echoed through the ship, its pitch carefully designed to be heard over the background noise without being jarring. It cut through the hum of the *Remus'* systems and human conversation.

Rojas spoke to his ship.

"This is your captain. In about thirty minutes, our attack sequence will begin in earnest. As I know you are all aware, this is a once in a career bounty. And as some as you might have heard, the Company has promised a triple bonus for this one."

Captain Rojas paused. He smiled as the crew's hearty cheers reverberated through the ship. Finnie and Kozlov nodded, both grinning.

When the cheer subsided, the captain continued in a serious tone.

"But do not let the bounty distract you. The *Perseus* has been in the hands of pirates for years. We do not have good intelligence about what they have been up to during that time. But I promise you this… They will fight to the death to keep her. Every human, AI and robot on that ship is going to try to kill us.

"That bounty everyone has been whispering about and spending in their heads means nothing if you do not survive. And it is worse than nothing if your comrades don't survive. Take it from me, a bounty that kills your shipmate will poison you. It will taint the rest of your days."

Rojas paused again. He left his finger on the button as he let the silence extend. The crew could hear his intense, deep breaths. They could sense the fight building within their captain.

When he spoke again, the captain almost growled with intensity.

"I will not sacrifice one member of this crew for a bounty. I asked that each of you make the same vow right now.

"A bounty for all, or a bounty for none!"

A cheer rose again across the ship. The crescendo of voices, rising in unison, combined with a rhythm of thumping and clanking, as crew members struck their arm rests or nearby metal. The roar transmitting through the ship's structure as much as through the air, creating a palpable energy that seemed to charge every molecule aboard the *Remus*.

The roar lasted a full minute. When it subsided, Rojas concluded.

"Now, we've got a long burn in front of us. And then a hell of a fight. Everyone get your mind right. Rojas out."

* * *

"The captain is right," Deke told the dozen members of his driver team, after Rojas concluded his announcement. Outfitted in their special G suits, neural receptacles glistening on their shaved heads in the dim light, they listened intently to their commander.

"Don't be suckered into thinking we are storming a sleepy freighter. These are fucking pirates. Count on the fight being nasty. Count on it being long. Count on it deadly. And count on having to kill every fucking one of them before it's over."

The driver team floated in a huddle in the middle of the circular driver deck. The driver pods lay open behind them, resting on their gimbals with clam shell doors raised, awaiting their augmented pilots. Custom fitted to each driver, snake-like neural probes lay in a cluster at the head of each pod, ready to unite with their human, enabling them to drive any of the complement of drones the *Remus* carried.

The whir of cooling fans and the hum of refrigeration systems filled the room. When things got going, computing systems and human brains would both start to overheat. Deke smiled at his team. Each of them had done multiple tours on the *Remus* under him. They were good. Very good. He was proud to lead them.

"You know what to do," he said, looking at each of them. "Do it."

Chapter Twenty-Two

Perseus

P aul grumbled to himself as he climbed down the traverse ladder toward the Utility Module. The XO had been pestering him for weeks to meet with Hoffman and he had finally relented. He wasn't looking forward to it.

Captain Hoffman and his crew had been detained on the lower level of the Utility Module since Top and the XO had taken over the *Perseus*. If Paul thought about it, he could generate some sympathy for the former captain and crew. It must have been a jarring experience to have three armored, AI-enabled soldierbots march out of the factory and take over the ship with the XO's help. Then to have spent so long locked up on an eight hundred square foot level of the UM with no idea of when they might be released. Paul would be cranky also, he had to admit.

Still, it had been a long cycle for Paul, and he didn't have the patience or energy to deal with this now. He thought about reneging on his commitment to the XO, but decided against it. He had been putting this off for too long.

I'm giving Hoffman ten minutes. That's it, Paul thought. *Then I'm done for the day. Maybe I—*

Several harsh jolts ran through the ship. The ladder shook in Paul's hands and against his feet as loud bangs and sharp metallic thumps rang out. The lights in the traverse flickered out, and he was pulled to the side by his momentum as the structure stopped spinning.

"XO, what is going on?" Paul transmitted. He checked his pressure suit's seal, concerned about loss of atmosphere from the dark and motionless Traverse. He turned on his suit's lights and looked around.

There was no obvious damage around him.

"XO, status report!"

No response. Not even static.

"Top, status report!" he transmitted.

He waited.

Nothing.

"Althea, status report!"

Paul's eyes narrowed as he listened to silence.

"This is Owens. Anyone on this net, please respond."

Paul floated in darkness, listening to his own breathing in his suit. He looked past the hub at the Habitat Module, almost a hundred meters up the ladder.

Althea is in the Hab.

"Damnit," he muttered as he started pulling himself up, back toward the Hab.

* * *

"What do you think happened?" Althea asked Paul as they floated on the dimly lit command deck. The battery-operated emergency lights had come on as soon as power was lost, but none of the displays were operational. Althea had donned her pressure suit per standard emergency procedures. Paul fiddled with the holo-table, to no avail.

"No idea," Paul said, looking up from the holo-table. "I am going to check on Top and the XO. I want you to stay here till I get back."

"Okay."

"Try to call me with your suit radio if anything changes," Paul told her. "Hopefully, I will receive you. The suits have a hard time transmitting through all the metal of the *Perseus*."

"I will."

Paul touched a mag boot to the floor and pushed off toward the Traverse.

He pulled himself up the sixty-six meter ladder and then quickly went through the airlock.

He gasped in surprise when he pulled himself into the Tube.

The lights were out. The small spotlights of Paul's suit were quickly swallowed by the blackness of the two-kilometer-long structure, but that is not what transfixed him.

A two-foot-wide gash had been carved through the top of the structure. Stars winked in the void beyond the torn metal that still glowed red in places from the recent kinetic energy. Paul stared. Angling across the *Perseus* at about forty-five degrees, the symmetry and precision of the tear in the hull was startling, as if cut by a swordsman.

Paul had seen what fast moving meteoroids could do to a ship's hull before.

Thoughts of Captain Drake flooded his mind.

For an instant, he was back on the *Odysseus*. On the bridge. The captain floated in front of him. Half his head missing.

Paul blinked to rid himself of the image. His breath got shallow, and he felt his pulse rise.

Get a grip. You don't have time to freak out.

He pushed off the Hub airlock, gazing up through the tear at the void as he floated under. Once past, he yanked hard on the Tube's roof ladder.

"Anybody on this net, this is Owens. Respond please," he tried again.

"Sir, this is Top."

"Where are you?" Paul asked.

"In the factory, sir."

"Meet me at the tube hatch."

"Roger that," Top responded.

Paul steadied his breathing.

Get to the factory. Meet up with Top. Then check on the XO.

Chapter Twenty-Three

George Remus

"Well... Done... George," Captain Rojas grunted, his voice strained under the 3 Gs of acceleration. His fingers slid across the controls on his armrest, toggling through damage assessment images of the *Perseus* on his chair's screen.

The last round fired by the *Remus* had been a damage assessment drone, equipped with high resolution cameras in multiple spectrums and a tight beam laser module on its rear. It decelerated slightly after being fired out of the *Remus'* railgun, giving it several seconds of separation from the main formation of smart rounds. Plenty of time to capture extensive images and send them back to the Remus before impacting the target.

It looked to the captain like all the rounds had found their mark.

"Thank you, sir," the AI said. "I am pleased with the results. The *Perseus* is now blind, without engine power, and drifting on emergency life support systems. A soft target for you, sir."

We'll see how soft, Rojas thought as he checked the mission clock.

The *Remus* and *Dagger* had both fired their main engines the instant the smart rounds struck the *Perseus* one minute ago. The *Remus*, with its cargo of humans, was only accelerating at 3Gs. *Dagger*, unburdened by such fragile cargo, was letting it rip at 20Gs.

Both ships would accelerate to the midpoint of their attack course, before flipping their orientation 180 degrees and decelerating at the same rate. This

136

would enable them to arrive in the attack zone at maneuvering speeds.

Rojas tried to relax. He and the rest of the crew would be under this load for a little over ninety minutes. 3Gs wasn't bone crushing, but it wasn't comfortable.

This is gonna get old.

* * *

Clarke closed his eyes and tried to ignore his anxiety. He didn't mind the Gs so much. It was his ignorance of the plan and situation that was tweaking him. Laying in his acceleration chair in the brig, he knew nothing. There was no holo-table or any screens or even a mission clock. He lay motionless, soaked in G forces, with no idea how long the sprint to the target was going to last, what the enemy situation would be when they arrived, or what the plan was when they got there. All he could do was lie in his chair and control his breathing while he waited for the battle to conclude.

This sucks.

* * *

Deke checked the mission clock as he flipped through status reports on his helmet's near-eye display. Just like when he served as a Centaur, mental command was all it took to make shit happen.

He shifted in his acceleration chair and felt the various harnesses and data cables pull against their connection points on his head and spine. 3Gs was not an insignificant load, even for a Centaur, even though the metal in his skeleton, nanobots in his bloodstream, and other augmentations made it less of a burden.

He paused on *Dagger's* data feed and smiled. Barely five minutes into her acceleration, she was moving faster than 200,0000 kilometers per hour.

"You don't fuck around, do you?" he transmitted his thoughts on the encrypted tight beam laser that was dedicated to maintaining the connection between him and her. As the commander, his link to the attack pod had to be solid and persistent. Many times in an attack, success or failure came down to their joint decision making.

"Never," *Dagger* responded.

"That might be why I like you so much."

"Maybe. But that's not why I do it."

"I don't care why you do it. I just like that you do."

"Liar."

Deke chuckled.

"You see the damage assessment yet?" he asked her.

"No. Are we happy or sad?"

"Sending now."

Sequencing through mental commands, he transmitted the damage assessment drone's images and analysis.

"Oh, we are happy," *Dagger* said with a purr in her voice.

"George can shoot, eh?"

"Sometimes."

"Sometimes? I'd like to see you do better."

"Give me a rail gun, then."

Deke chuckled to himself.

"Seriously, though," he said. "I don't see anything that would necessitate a change to our attack plan."

"Neither do I."

Chapter Twenty-Four

Wharf Rat

uinn, Singh, and Axe stood in front of one of the large video displays on the command deck, watching the sequence of images play on a loop.

At first it looked like footage of the empty void. Darkness with stars in the distance. Suddenly, a series of fleeting sparking events rippled across the frame. It looked to be a dozen total. Then darkness returned.

"Our long-range optical sensors captured this strange sequence almost ten minutes ago," Renate said.

"It took place directly to our front, almost precisely in the same location where we believe the *Perseus* to be," Singh added. "I asked Renate to run a full arsenal of magnification algos on it and then peel it apart with a few wavelength filters."

The image shifted to a green hue suddenly.

"This is infrared," Renate said as the sequence replayed. This time, the sparking events yielded much more light, like powerful strobes. The eruptions of light illuminated an immense, long structure.

"*Perseus*," Quinn said under his breath.

Singh smiled and nodded.

"And she is under attack," Axe said, eyes narrowing. "Slow it down, please, Renate."

Quinn studied the sparking impacts as they danced across the dark ship.

"I agree," Renate said as she played the sequence in infrared on a loop. "Those are projectile impacts."

"Ultra dense projectiles of some kind," Axe said in a low, contemplative voice as he leaned forward and studied the slow replay. He reached out and touched the screen with his human fingers as the bright impacts danced across the image. "No explosive warheads. The damage is precise and limited. Targeting the ship's critical systems, no doubt."

Axe stood up straight, nodding in grudging approval.

"Classic Company gunboat tactic. Soften the target as much as possible from as far away as possible before attacking. The *Perseus* is now most likely blind and immobile. It won't be long."

"Renate, did you backtrack along the firing azimuth?" Quinn asked.

"I tried. But I did not have eyes on the origination of these shots."

Axe grunted and crossed his arms.

The group stood in silence, watching the replay of the series of impacts. Renate continued to switch the image back and forth from visual to infrared spectrum. Each person peered intently at the fleeting glimpses of the *Perseus*. It was a massive ship.

"Good catch, guys," Quinn finally said, stepping away from the screen. "We are probably the only people in the solar system that saw that happen."

"Except for the attackers," Axe said, dropping his hands to his side.

Singh looked at the scarred pirate.

Quinn nodded somberly.

"Continue to adjust course, Renate," he said, turning to leave the command deck. "Right at her. Cold thrusters only. Keep eyes on her and keep scanning the area. Passive sensors only."

"Aye, sir."

"What's the plan?" Singh called after Quinn.

"I don't know yet."

Axe and Singh studied the screen as Quinn left the bridge.

"One thing is certain," Axe grumbled. "The *Perseus* is in for a long day."

Chapter Twenty-Five

Perseus

Paul passed by two more gaping holes in the *Perseus* as he floated through the dark Tube toward the factory passage. His pulse quickened each time as involuntary thoughts of Drake flooded his mind.

Am I just a fucking meteorite magnate? he wondered.

Finally, he floated beneath the hatch to the Factory passage. As he reached up to activate it, the hatch opened.

"Captain Owens," Top said, floating upside down relative to Paul and illuminated by his helmet lights. "Are you OK?"

"Yeah. I'm good. You?"

"Yes."

"Have you been able to communicate with the XO? Or anyone else?"

"No, sir."

Paul shook his head. A sense of foreboding welled within him. He checked his watch. It had been about fifteen minutes since the impacts.

"Come with me. We have to check on the XO."

"Roger that, sir."

Top pulled herself down out of the factory passage way into the Tube. The other two Ōkami followed.

"I want you two to go aft to Power and Propulsion to scout the situation," Paul used his suit radio to tell them as they floated down into the Tube. "I counted two impacts on the forward half on my way here. We've got to put together an accurate damage assessment."

"Yes, sir," they responded.

"Quickly!"

"Yes, sir!"

Both Ōkami grabbed the Tube's overhead ladder and yanked hard. They quickly outran the weak lights of Paul's suit, disappearing into the darkness.

Paul turned and worked his way toward the bridge tower hatch.

"Any ideas what is going on, sir?" Top asked.

"None good."

Chapter Twenty-Six

Wharf Rat

"Well, looks like they just said, 'Fuck stealth', and let it rip, didn't they?" Eriksson said with a rueful chuckle.

The entire crew of the *Wharf Rat* was gathered on the command deck, watching the video feed. As word of the strange happenings on the *Perseus* spread through the ship, the command deck exerted an irresistible pull. One by one, the crew gravitated there, intensely curious what the tactical displays and holo-projector would reveal. Renate continued to algorithmically enhance and zoom into the fight that was still a long way away.

What it was revealing at the moment was exciting and terrifying.

Several of the big screens around the deck were zoomed in on the bright blue nuclear drive plume of a Company attack pod, streaking toward the *Perseus*. Still hundreds of thousands of kilometers away from the *Wharf Rat*, the plume was not detectable with the naked human eye, but the unblinking, far-reaching stare of the Renate's passive sensors captured the high energy event easily.

A second group of screens focused on another, larger nuclear drive plume, far behind the attack ship, pushing a Company gunboat toward the hapless freighter as well.

"Why be stealthy if you have that kind of firepower?" Reeve said.

"Stealth should never be squandered," Axe grumbled. "I don't care how much firepower you have."

"Maybe they aren't squandering it," Bonham said.

"Looks pretty squandered to me," Eriksson said in a wise-ass voice.

"Looks to me like they are trading it for speed." Bonham did not take her eyes off the video feed. "The sooner they can get this attack over with, the sooner they can go about being stealthy again."

Axe nodded as he turned his head to glare at Eriksson. "How many ships in the entire universe are facing the right direction with the right sensors to actually see this happening? And how many of those are close enough to take action? And how many of those are stupid enough to take on a Company gunboat?"

Axe, not waiting for Eriksson's answer, turned to look at Quinn.

"None, I hope," he grumbled.

Quinn cocked his head at Axe's comment. He stood up suddenly.

"Listen up, guys. I want us to lock down the Ring and prepare for a burn."

"Burn?" Eriksson asked incredulously

"Burn to where?" Reeve asked.

Axe raised what little eyebrows he had at Quinn.

Bonham shook her head.

"I am not asking to burn anywhere yet," Quinn said, raising his palms in a plaintive gesture. "And we will vote, of course, before we do anything. I just want to be ready."

"Ready for what?" Axe growled.

Quinn shrugged.

"I don't know yet."

Chapter Twenty-Seven

George Remus

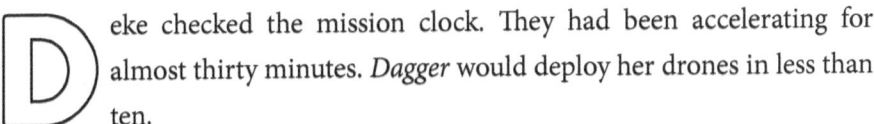

eke checked the mission clock. They had been accelerating for almost thirty minutes. *Dagger* would deploy her drones in less than ten.

He called up the high-definition images *Dagger* sent before executing her deceleration flip. Her nose cone carried a suite of passive and active sensing measures. She was staying passive, even though the *Perseus* was supposed to be totally blind now.

God, what an ugly ship.

Deke knew that M Class freighters were ugly on a good day. But the *Perseus* looked nightmarish. Dirty, beat-up containers and huge misshapen asteroids clung to the underside of the skeletal ship's two-kilometer length, giving the whole thing the look of so much drifting space junk. The size and chaos of the sight made him uneasy. Had they not gotten the extensive intel prep on the *Perseus* for this mission, he would have felt more than unease. It was a complex target that could hide nasty surprises.

He pushed his concerns aside.

They're not gonna know what hit 'em.

Once he got over the massive size of the ship, the main impression Deke was left with was how filthy she was. Dirt, dust and grime covered the old girl, like someone had dragged it through a galactic sized mud puddle, not hosed her off, and let the stuff dry on her flanks.

I feel sorry for whoever has to clean your ass up after we take over.

He checked the mission clock again.

"Six minutes," Deke announced to his team. "Get your minds right."

The twelve augmented drone drivers shifted in their acceleration chairs and tried to calm themselves. They were all veterans, and each had been in combat, driving drones against the Chinese, Russians, and other enemies. They knew what to expect.

Even so, the last couple of minutes before an attack were always nerve-wracking.

Once the attack began, each of them would be assaulted by an onslaught of data as the drones they commanded spilled off of *Dagger*. Their minds would be disembodied, thrust out of the *Remus* and into the points of view of hurtling attack craft pulling insane G forces and dispensing death and destruction at a very rapid rate.

Driving drones in the void was very different from driving on Earth. Fighting on the planet featured all the traditional constraints and references - the horizon, the ground, the sky. Everything obeyed gravity. Up and down were consistent.

Not so in the void. There was no up, no down, no atmosphere to resist, no gravity to pull, none of the constraints or limits to reference or leverage in the fight. It was mind bending. Not everyone could do it. Even combat veterans with decades of experience could not always make the shift.

But everyone on Deke's team had. They were the best the Company could buy. And they received the best training and equipment. Sometimes Deke winced at his team's eye watering budget. Then he remembered that the Company never did anything that did not produce an ROI. And he and his team produced.

He chuckled at the thought of the *Perseus*. The last surviving M class factory ship? He wondered what it was worth to the Company. They could pay him and his team for a thousand years and still probably be in the green. He knew whatever monetary value he imagined, poor-assed military veteran that he was, the truth was far greater.

So what? he thought. *I love this shit.*

"Talk to me, *Dag*," he said to *Dagger* via the tight beam.

"What would you like to know? Ask me anything."

He smiled. She was being playful. She loved her job, too.

"How about the standard shit, if you don't mind?"

"Deceleration underway and within limits. Below 250,000 kilometers per hour and decreasing. Will reach deployment velocity in four minutes and fifteen seconds."

Deke nodded.

Perfect.

Dagger had burned halfway to the target at 20G, attaining a speed of almost eight hundred thousand kilometers miles per hour. At the midpoint she paused her burn, flipped her orientation 180 degrees, and burned again, decelerating at 20Gs.

The plan was to deploy her payload of attack drones with only a moderate relative velocity remaining. Deke didn't want them using all their fuel on deceleration. He needed the drones with ample flight time available to attack the *Perseus*.

He needed an hour of flight time, to be precise. The *Remus*, still accelerating at a more human friendly 3Gs, was far behind *Dagger* and would not arrive on station until an hour after she released her drones. When *Remus* did arrive, she would deploy a second wave of attack drones, fully armed and fueled, which would take over the fight while the first wave returned to her to re-arm and refuel.

In reality, Deke hoped the fight was over by the time the second wave arrived. How much resistance could the old freighter really offer, anyway?

"Right on schedule," he told *Dagger*. "Thank you."

"When have I ever let you down, partner?" Her voice was full and expressive in his head, piped directly in as it was via his implants. He loved the way it felt. He wondered if his was the same to her.

"You haven't yet."

"And I never will."

Chapter Twenty-Eight

II I have lost communication with all the ship's major systems. Power and Propulsion, Navigation, Maintenance, and the Manufacturing, all passive and active sensors. Everything!" the XO said.

Paul and Top hovered above the floor in the XO's chamber. Located at the base of the bridge tower, and accessed via an airlock hatch, the small room housed the *Perseus'* powerful managing AI. They stared at the small holographic projection atop a short black pedestal in the middle of the small room as the XO's urgent voice sounded in Paul's helmet speakers. Around them, seven sleek black monoliths housing quantum computers, each about ten feet tall, stood against the white walls of the circular chamber. Humming with barely perceptible vibrations, thin blue lines traced intricate patterns across their smooth faces, like the synapsis of a vast artificial brain.

An interlacing network of power conduits, cooling pipes, and fiber optic cable bundles covered the floor. The small black pedestal stood about four feet tall. A small colorful holograph, only twelve inches across, pulsed and undulated.

Paul knew if he was trained on 3D data interpretation, he could decipher the constantly shifting shape of the XO's holograph. The total status and activity of the powerful AI was represented in the small, complex volume of light. He didn't have to be an expert holographic data interpreter to know how the XO was at the moment. The red, shifting shape of light told him all he needed to know. The XO was pissed.

"I am afraid I am useless to you, Paul," the XO said. "I'm no better than a passenger at the moment."

"Feels like we are all passengers at the moment, XO," Paul said.

"What will the subsystem reactions be, XO?" the first sergeant asked. "What are the protocols for events like this?'

"The priority will be safety of the ship and re-establishing communications. I've got good leaders on my crew. They will handle things well."

"Well, if the damage I saw on the forward half of the Tube is indicative, they won't be re-establishing coms anytime soon," Paul said, as he looked at the digital time display on his suit's right wrist. It had been a little over thirty minutes since the *Perseus* was struck. He took a few deep breaths. The hair on the back of his neck was tingling. It was time to act.

"This is not fucking good," he said, looking at Top. "We are blind, immobile, and cut up into isolated camps. That was the first phase of an attack. We've been softened up."

"Who do you think is attacking us?"

"Doesn't matter. We have whatever time we have to make it as hard on them as possible. I want you to take your two Ōkami into the Tube and start detaching cargo containers. Start near the hub and work your way back."

Top nodded. "Roger that."

"The three of you will have to work together to get them moving," Paul continued. "Detach as many as you can. Shove one to port, then the next one to starboard. Keep alternating."

"Understood," Top said with a nod.

"XO, does the maintenance boss understand English?" Paul asked.

"Yes."

"Where is the best place to speak to him?"

"He has a chamber, similar to mine but smaller, just off of the drone hangar observation room. You can speak to him there."

"Do you think he still has contact with his drones?"

"I would think so. But can't be sure. It's hard to tell which antennae and radio stations have been eliminated. Seems like all of them, to be honest. But I know he has some less powerful redundancies."

"Let's hope we get lucky there," Paul said before touching a mag boot to the floor and pushing toward the door.

"Captain, where are you going?"

"To tell the maintenance boss we need his help."

"Sir, please bear in mind that he is the least sophisticated of my crew."

"I'm not going there for sparkling conversation."

"I'm just saying, sir... He will struggle with—"

"I got it!" Paul yelled over his shoulder as he opened the hatch.

The holograph rippled with scarlet red and porcupined for a second, then pulled itself into a sphere.

"It's okay," Top said. "I know what the captain has in mind. It's a good play."

"Maybe so. But that is going to be a conversation I wish I could listen to."

Paul slammed the hatch behind him and pushed himself into the Tube. Pulling hard, he careened through the dark to the drone hangar's hatch and into the observation room. Unlike the *Odysseus*, where the military had retrofitted a hangar commander's facility, the *Perseus* had a simple observation room. The square, twenty by twenty-foot room lacked a luxurious, overbuilt, articulating chair, but did offer expansive views of the drone hangar through its glass canopy roof.

Paul had only been there once before since arriving on the *Perseus*. He had not noticed the passageway on the far side.

That must be the maintenance boss's chamber.

Paul kicked off the floor and moved quickly across the room. He opened the hatch and stepped inside.

The maintenance boss's chamber was unpressurized and dimly lit. A single Quantumtronic monolith, similar to the ones in the XO's chamber, stood on the opposite side of the smaller room. Video status boards covered the walls, displaying graphs, diagrams, and gauges of all kinds. It looked to Paul like everyone of the *Perseus'* seemingly endless systems was represented somehow. Most were red at the moment due to the severed communications throughout the ship. The numerous negative status lights gave the chamber a red tinge. A single oversized chair sat in front of the main video display.

Paul moved to it and strapped himself in. He looked around for a microphone switch or something similar as he felt time slipping away from him. Finding nothing and running out of patience, he spoke loudly into his suit radio.

"Maintenance boss!"

"Yes, Captain?" the deep voice responded. Paul thought he might have heard a hint of uncertainty. "I am not accustomed to direct communication from you. From anyone, really, but the XO. Is the XO aware of this interaction?"

Paul glanced up at the small video camera in the corner.

He has me on video and must have recognized me. Good.

"The XO is currently unavailable. We are in an emergency situation."

"Emergency protocols dictate that I should receive instructions from the XO or his designated substitute or representative. I am not finding any such designation in my files."

"Listen," Paul said, leaning forward. "We are under attack. The normal communication channels are down."

The quantum computing monolith emitted a higher frequency vibration that ran through the floor.

"Attack? My sensors do not indicate ongoing combat. Captain, I am having difficulty reconciling your statements with the data available."

"That is what I am trying to tell you. We've been hit by something that knocked out most of our communications and controls. You're isolated from the rest of the ship right now."

"Isolated? But… I do not have protocols for this scenario. I should consult with the XO before—"

"There is no time for that! I need you to trust me and do what I say. Are you able to communicate with your drones?"

"Yes, sir. I have limited radio contact with them at present."

Yes! Paul thought, a small flame of hope igniting in his chest.

"I need you to launch the drone fleet and surround the *Perseus*."

"For what purpose?"

"To help defend the ship."

The maintenance boss was silent.

Paul waited.

"But, Captain, I am not equipped to make strategic or tactical decisions in combat scenarios. My primary function is maintenance and repair. I do not have the necessary algorithms to—"

"Listen!" Paul struggled to keep the tension out of his voice. "I am not asking you to plan a battle. I just need you to use your drones to protect the ship."

The maintenance boss hesitated. "Protect... using maintenance drones? I do not understand. Our tools are not designed for combat."

A silence extended between them. Paul looked at the time again. His mind raced. He did not know how to unstick the situation quickly.

"My drones are not soldiers, sir."

"I know."

Paul looked up in the corner at the camera.

"I know you and your team were built to fix things. To keep this old girl running. And you do that very well. But someone is on the way to harm the *Perseus*. They already have. That's why you can't talk to anyone. We can't see them coming and we can't fire the engine to get away. You and your guys are all we have."

"We are not programmed to fight, sir."

"I know. But you sure as hell know how to disassemble things, don't you?"

"Disassemble?" The AI's tone shifted slightly. "Yes, sir. We do."

"Then, boss, I need you to put every drone out there around the *Perseus* and aggressively disassemble the shit out of anything that gets close to her."

"That is within our capabilities, but... Captain, this is highly irregular. I should consult with the XO or at least run simulations to—"

"There is no time for that," Paul insisted, glancing at the time on his wrist display. "Every second counts now. I need you to trust me, your captain, and act now. Would you please deploy your drones immediately to defend our ship?"

The quantum monolith's hum changed pitch again, its vibrations intensifying. Another silence extended.

Paul rubbed his forehead. He felt the opportunity slipping away.

"Boss," Paul said. "Please. Help me."

Suddenly, the displays around the small chamber darkened. Every status indicator disappeared.

Paul felt vibrations throughout the seat and heard deep clangs and bumps emanating from the hangar behind him. He glanced at the dark supercomputer.

"We will do our best, sir."

Paul's shoulders sagged in relief. He turned his head slowly to look at the camera in the corner and put his hand over his heart.

"Thank you."

"How long do we have, sir?"

"I don't know," Paul said as he unstrapped from the chair and moved toward the door. "But my gut tells me not very long. Maybe only minutes."

Paul stopped in the hatch.

"Give 'em hell, boss."

"We will, sir."

Chapter Twenty-Nine

Dagger

agger monitored herself and her surroundings as the clock ticked down—just a little more than a minute until the release point. Her velocity was under fifty thousand kilometers per hour and decreasing.

Her orientation prevented her from detailed observations of the *Perseus*. Her rear facing sensor suite was not nearly as robust as the one integrated into her nose cone, and the blaze of her nuclear drive plume obscured what it could see. Even so, she could make out the outline of the freighter, and was able to calculate that she was right on course.

That is one big, ugly ship, she thought.

Dagger hated this phase of the attack even under the best of circumstances. The degraded imaging of the target while she finished her deceleration always made her feel vulnerable. She knew the *Remus* would be doing its best to monitor the target also, but she had the same issue. *Remus* was approaching the target engine first, with her nuclear drive plume blazing. Her passive sensors were degraded.

Dagger shook off the feeling. There was nothing to be done about it and it was always over quickly, but it felt now like she was being swallowed by the shadow of the long, massive pirate ship.

No matter. Time to focus on nailing her assigned attack point, where the drones would deploy from her sides. A hundred and twenty strong, it was like dumping hungry piranhas into the water around a buffalo.

Dagger would then use her residual velocity and a brief burst of her nuclear drive to leave the immediate area. Deke's drones were a high speed, kinetic swarm once they got going, and she would just be in the way, a nuclear-powered obstacle.

"You ready to go?" she transmitted to Deke.

"Just waiting on you."

She loved the confidence in his human voice. They would take care of business.

"Shall I torture you?"

"Please."

"Ten. Nine. Eight," she said in a slow, rich voice. Deke had a mission clock in front of his eyeballs, of course, and didn't need the countdown. but she knew he wanted it.

"Seven. Six. Five. Four. Three. Two. One. Exit. Exit. Exit."

Dagger felt a strange lightness come over her. Not because of the sudden reduction of mass her engine pushed against, rather the separation of over a hundred electronic minds that had been connected to her since she was loaded back on the *Remus*. She had been feeding them information all along their trip to the target. The last thing she said to each before detaching was a simple, "Good luck."

"Drones away," she told Deke.

"Ok, team," Deke said on the drive deck intercom as an explosion of information filled his brain and displays. "Time to go to work. No fucking around. Deadly force authorized until further notice. Use it."

"Happy hunting," *Dagger* said as she kicked her nuclear drive on for a few seconds.

"Thank you, darling."

Dagger flipped herself around with her cold jets as she retreated, aiming her nosecone at the *Perseus*.

For a moment, it was beautiful as always. The swarm of heavily armed attack drones zipped and weaved toward the hapless target in lighting fast attack patterns that, to someone else, from a distance, would seem haphazard. But *Dagger* believed she saw a revealing expression of Deke's mind, manifesting through his team and the smart drones they piloted. She wondered what it would be like to allow him to pilot her in that way.

Something on the target caught her attention. She zoomed in.

A cargo container was drifting from the Perseus.

Then, scanning the length of the ship, she saw several more coming loose. *Strange.*

She cast her attention back to the attacking swarm. They were still closing on the ship, several kilometers away.

Something is not right.

She looked back at the *Perseus* in time to see drones start pouring out of her belly.

This is not good.

* * *

"Sir, are you seeing this?" one of Deke's drivers asked over their command net.

"Yes. And I don't like it."

"Bullshit intelligence again!" another driver declared.

"Just like when—"

"Cut the chatter," Deke yelled. He called up his tactical display. His force was closing on the target quickly as what looked like a hundred drones sprinted out of the *Perseus* to set up a perimeter.

"We can all bitch about the intelligence later. Adjust focus to the defenders. Do your fucking jobs! What the hell are you waiting for? Kill them!"

Rockets flew from the lead drones as Deke cycled quickly through several different points of view.

Explosions bloomed around the *Perseus* as her drones began to take hits.

Deke fought the urge to yell and urge his drivers on. He knew how absorbed in their tasks they were, each one controlling ten attack drones with their augmented minds. He listened to the roar of the driver deck's cooling fans, fighting to keep silicon and flesh below critical temperatures.

He toggled back to a few visual feeds of the battle and grimaced. Rather than an overwhelming dissection of a blinded and immobilized freighter, his first wave of attack drones was engaged in a knife fight with what looked to be a decently organized drone defense force.

"Deke, I think we need to—"

"Not now, Koz!" Deke yelled, cutting off the operations officer on the command net. "Your plan is fucked now, you're just going to have to let us fight it out. Don't bother me!"

The only thing that kept Deke from losing his shit, was that his guys were giving more than they were getting. The defensive drones did not seem to have stand-off weapons like rockets or directed energy throwers. They had cutting and burning tools that required them to get close to be effective. Strange choices for a defense force.

The defenders were exploding or disintegrating rapidly. Many had been damaged and were flying out of control through the battle space. Several had collided into the *Perseus* or into her cargo, ejecting debris and gas around the old ship.

The cargo was getting to be a problem. Deke counted at least two dozen containers that were drifting near the ship and more seemed to disconnect each minute. Two attack drones had already collided with the random obstacles, ejecting more debris and gas.

Well, this went to shit quickly.

* * *

Rojas winced at what he saw. Ten minutes into the first wave of the drone attack and nothing was going according to plan. Debris, clouds of venting gas, and cargo containers made the battle space around the *Perseus* a lethal obstacle course for the attacking drones. This was enabling what was a clearly outmatched defense force much more effective than they should have been. And it looked like more obstacles were being created by the minute.

"Sir, we are approaching our transition point," George told the captain over the command net.

"Damnit," Rojas glanced quickly at the mission clock. With everything going to shit, he had not been paying attention to it. "Proceed as planned."

"Roger that, sir."

Rojas shook his head. It wasn't good timing for the transition, but it had to be done.

"Attention all hands," Finnie said over the ship-wide net. "Prepare for immediate transition maneuver. I repeat, prepare for immediate transition maneuver."

Rojas studied the tactical display. The defenders' numbers continued to dwindle. The debris and obstacles around the *Perseus* continued to increase. He thought about checking in with Deke but knew would get the same response Kozlov had. And for good reason. The man had a job to do.

A jolt went through the ship and the distant roar of the nuclear propulsion system stopped. Suddenly, Rojas was weightless. He took a series of deep breaths and flexed his neck to the left and right, knowing the respite would be brief. He already felt the ship executing it 180-degree flip. He flexed his ankles and worked his cheek muscles.

The captain's restraining straps tugged at him as the *Remus* arrested its spin with cold thrusters. The lights across the ship blinked, warning the crew that the main drive would fire again in seconds.

Rojas swallowed and looked at the mission clock.

We will be on station in about forty-five minutes with a fresh wave of drones.

G forces shoved him deep into his chair as the *Remus* fired her main engine.

The captain watched the velocity indicator on his tactical display begin to tick rapidly down.

Chapter Thirty

Perseus

"Captain Owens, this is highly inadvisable," the XO said over the radio to Paul.

"I'm starting to agree with you," Paul answered from his position outside the *Perseus*. Mag boots holding onto the ship's hull, he crouched in his pressure suit at the base of the bridge tower.

The battle for the *Perseus* raged around him. Nimble and lethal attack drones darted at high speeds through the thickening debris field, firing at the defenders. The maintenance drones, unable to keep up, had formed a defensive perimeter around the two-kilometer-long ship. They looked to Paul to be using feints and mis-direction to throw the attackers off and to get close enough to grab them, if possible. Attackers that were unlucky enough to be grabbed, were sawn, laser cut, or pulled apart. It didn't happen often.

Up and down the length of the *Perseus*, rockets and directed energy beams struck defending maintenance drones. They would disintegrate, explode, or careen off into the void. Often, spinning out of control, they would collide with the *Perseus* or one of her cargo containers, ejecting more debris and gases into the area.

Paul ducked as a piece of a hapless defender struck the *Perseus'* hull just a few meters away.

"I wouldn't have to be out here if you had better goddamn windows on the bridge like a normal fucking space craft!"

Paul was missing the expansive window on the *Odysseus*. The power and communications outage on the *Perseus* had rendered her bridge useless. The video displays and holo-table were not functioning, and the portal windows afforded limited views. Paul wanted some way to assess how the battle was going, so went outside.

"That may be true, sir. But I insist you come back inside!"

Shrapnel struck the bridge tower next to Paul, spraying him with sparks.

"Fuck this!"

He lunged toward the hatch and scrambled back inside the Perseus.

"Remind me to never do that again."

"With pleasure, sir. Where are you going now?"

"To talk to the maintenance boss again."

Chapter Thirty-One

Wharf Rat

Thе whole crew of the *Wharf Rat* hung out on the command deck, transfixed by the long-range images of the battle for the *Perseus*. They had jumped through their asses to lock down the Ring, driven mainly by a desire to get back to the command deck to watch the show. No-one really thought they would end up burning to the *Perseus*, but it was good to know they could react quickly if the gunboat looked at them sideways.

Bonham was strapped into her own seat studying the small display unfolded from her arm rests. The others, except for Quinn, floated in front of one of the large video displays on the side.

Quinn hovered in the middle of the command deck, studying the holographic display Renate projected of the battle.

When the *Remus'* nuclear powered attack pod deployed her drones, they all expected to see a short, one-sided fight before the *Perseus* was subdued. When they watched the drones pour from *Perseus'* belly, they couldn't help but smile.

"Atta girl," Axe said in a low, lusty voice. "Give those Company fuckers a fight."

They knew it was a lost cause, but it was still fun to watch the *Perseus* get her licks in.

Soon, cargo containers started detaching and clogging up the battle space, and Bonham smiled at the tactic. A cloud of debris and gas built around the beleaguered ship.

"Look at that," Landsberg said. "Now they are releasing asteroids."

A large, black shape had separated from the *Perseus*. What looked like a small rocket engine spat a needle of fire as it pushed against the dark mass.

"Tug drone," Axe mumbled. "I've seen them before. Very powerful."

Bonham chuckled as she watched the huge rock inch away from the *Perseus*.

She stole a glance at Quinn. He was rubbing his chin now.

Bonham unbuckled her seat harness and pushed off toward him. She floated slowly across the deck. Quinn glanced up at her as she approached, and then locked his eyes back on the holograph.

"What do you think?" he asked, as she touched a mag boot to the floor to stop.

"Whoever is running the plays on *Perseus* is good," she said, crossing her muscular arms. Her flight suit arms were tied around her waist, exposing her black tank top. "Cluttering up the battle space like that has given the Company fits. Otherwise, this thing would have been over in less than a minute."

Quinn did not respond.

Bonham looked at one of the big video displays as an attack drone buzzed by the large drifting asteroid, unleashing a rocket salvo. The tug drone laboring against the big rock disintegrated in flames.

"Bastards," she heard Landsberg mutter.

Bonham looked at another video screen. Panned farther back than the other views, it showed a faraway view of a large company gunship decelerating behind a blue-tinged nuclear drive plume.

"Renate, how long until the Company gunboat arrives at the *Perseus*?" Bonham asked.

"I estimate less than ten minutes."

"Look!" Landsberg said with excitement. "Another asteroid is drifting free."

"That debris field around the Perseus is getting thick," Singh said. "It's starting to obscure our imaging and readings."

Bonham looked back at Quinn.

Using the grip of her mag boot to pull her head closer to his, she spoke in a soft voice only he could hear.

"When that gunboat arrives, it is going to unleash another round of drones. This fight has been entertaining to watch, but it is over. The Company will have control of the *Perseus* in fifteen minutes, max. And we are still almost a quarter million kilometers away."

Quinn's eyes narrowed. He turned to look at Bonham as she continued.

"We couldn't take on Company gunboat under the best of circumstances. Making a run at one that is gonna see us coming from a long way out, and is still pissed off from a fight that didn't go exactly its way?"

Bonham held his gaze as she slowly shook her head. She put a hand on his shoulder.

"Please, Captain... Reconsider."

Chapter Thirty-Two

Perseus

"Captain Owens, where are you, sir?" Top called over her radio.

"I'm headed to Hab to grab weapons. We are going to need them."

Paul careened forward through the dark Tube. The small spotlights on his pressure suit did little to light the way. He learned a long time ago as a drone pilot to "never fly faster than you can see."

He was violating that principle now.

But he was in a rush.

"What did you tell the maintenance boss?"

Paul stared intently into the dark as he spoke, trying to sense what was in ahead of him. He wanted to be ready when he got to the front end of the Tube.

"Told him to put the tugs on the asteroids, to push them out around us."

"Good tactic."

"I also told him to send IR bots to peel open the factory storage facility and eject as much of that shit as they can," he said.

"Even better, sir. That will make a terrible mess."

"Yeah. If we survive, we'll patch the old girl back up. If not, it won't matter."

"Cheerful logic, as always, sir."

Paul smiled at the comment just before slamming into the Hub hatch at the end of the Tube.

Ouch.

He moved quickly through the airlock and down the Traverse to the Hab where Althea waited on the top level

"What the hell is going on?" She demanded.

"We're under attack," Paul said, continuing down the ladder toward the lower levels.

"Yeah, I figured that much out on my own. Where are you going?"

Paul didn't answer. He continued to the lower level and then pushed off down the passageway toward the small Hab weapon storage closet.

"Paul!" Althea followed. "What are you doing? What is the plan?"

"The plan is to fight," Paul said, yanking open the weapons closet. He grabbed a rifle and loaded it while Althea watched.

She shook her head.

"Paul. Listen to me. It will do no good for you to get killed resisting a Company gunboat."

"I don't intend on getting killed." He handed her the loaded rifle and began loading another.

"Paul, you have to be realistic, we—"

"No!" Paul slammed his fist against the locker door. "We don't have the luxury of realism anymore. Don't you get it? In their eyes, we are pirates now!"

Paul pointed outside the ship, at the gunboat, the Company and the world. Everything that was stacked against them. His chest heaved with emotion.

"There will be no mercy or due process. From now on, our only option, always, is to fight!"

The sight of Althea looking back at him, eyes wide, caused Paul to pause. He shook his head slightly and reached out to her. He put his hand on her shoulder.

"I'm sorry. Don't worry, I'm all here," he gave her a small, sad smile. "And I'm not mad at you. But, like I've told you, I am on a one-way mission now. For Kata. Colonel Filson. The Ōkami. My only reason for existing is to avenge them. Letting the Company, or pirates, or anyone else capture me is the same as death now. It will end me. So… I'm going to fight. To the end.

"I'm so sorry you got pulled into the middle of all this," he said. "You don't deserve any of it. Maybe this is an opportunity for you to get away. For you to—"

"No," Althea said softly, but with conviction. "I am with you, Paul. Until the end. No matter what."

"OK, then." He handed her another loaded rifle. "Get ready to fight."

Chapter Thirty-Three

George Remus

The second wave of attack drones poured out of the *George Remus* as the big gunboat entered the final phase of its deceleration. Kozlov had planned for the ship to stop ten kilometers from the *Perseus* and loiter while Deke and his drone force subdued the target. The second wave of drones would really just have to mop up at this point, he had thought. He had not anticipated the *Perseus'* improvisational defense, or how effective their tactics would be.

There was a lot about the *Perseus* he had not anticipated.

"What a fucking mess," Kozlov muttered as he looked at his screen.

An expanding, chaotic field of obstacles engulfed the *Perseus*. Shattered cargo containers, their contents spilling out in frozen cascades, drifted aimlessly alongside massive, jagged asteroids that loomed like silent sentinels. The lifeless husks of dead defensive drones, their metal bodies twisted and torn, tumbled through the carnage, some slow, some fast, occasionally colliding with other debris.

Inter-meshing this obstacle course of destruction, smaller debris spun and whizzed like high-powered rifle shots. Fragments of metal, shards of composite materials, and unidentifiable bits of the *Perseus* herself careened in kinetic, unpredictable patterns.

Worse still, enormous clouds of particulate matter and gases vented from multiple points along the Perseus' hull. This expanding witch's brew of elements and compounds refracted light in eerie, ominous ways. The clouds merged and separated, creating a fog-like effect that obscured vision and played havoc with sensors. Chemical reactions between colliding clouds and objects they swallowed created brief, brilliant flashes of white, yellow or lilac that momentarily cast haphazard, strobing light across the debris field.

The chaotic mess transformed the once empty space around the *Perseus* into a treacherous, ever-shifting maze. Deke's drones would dive into clear attack paths, only to have them suddenly collapse, obstructed by a tumbling cargo container or intersected by corrosive gas.

The cumulative effect of the obstacle cloud severely degraded sensors and communications.

"Will someone please tell me what that cloud of shit is?" Kozlov demanded over the intercom, frustrated by the imprecise and incomplete readings on his tactical display.

"Sir, we are trying to get a solid read," a battle analyst responded. "But it looks like a fine powder of some kind."

"A fine powder?" Kozlov shook his head. What the hell was going on?

"Sir, I believe they are venting their factory," George said.

"Venting their factory?"

"Yes, sir. The *Perseus*' manufacturing facility has extremely large feedstock storage capacity. The ship appears to be ejecting these powdered metals and plastics."

"Terrific," Kozlov mumbled.

Rojas smiled ruefully and shook his head. Whoever was directing the *Perseus*' defense was good. They had effective weaponized the only thing they had at their disposal—two kilometers of junk.

He switched to a tactical display on his screen. There were large gaps induced by the obscuring debris and cloud, but Deke was making progress. He had eliminated all the large tug drones that had been dislodging asteroids, and very few of the other defenders remained. Rojas knew better than to check in with his drone commander. Deke would be fully immersed in the battle. Rojas didn't know how they did it, those drone drivers.

Besides, he knew Deke would be irate at their losses.

Rojas was as well. A twinge of anxiety was building in his gut. And while they were "just drones," and he knew the Company could afford it, the thought of the *Remus'* combat power being whittled away like this did not feel good. Not while they were out in the void.

The void always had more cards to play.

Rojas would feel much better when the *Perseus* was under control, and they were on their way back, returning the old girl to the Company.

"Deceleration complete, sir," Finnie announced. "*Remus* stationary, ten kilometer standoff."

"Thank you, XO."

We need to wrap this up soon, Rojas thought.

* * *

"God damnit, keep up!" Deke yelled into his command net. "Tight formations, people! Tight!"

Sweat poured out of his body despite his chair's cooling fans being at maximum. It seemed every brain cell was on fire as he piloted three attack drones himself and commanded his twelve drivers. He hadn't felt like this in years, not since fighting the Chinese. If he wasn't so frustrated by how things were going, he might have appreciated how good it felt. How alive.

At the moment, though, he was fucking pissed.

"*Dagger*, talk to me!"

As the clouds and debris field began to expand around the *Perseus*, interfering with the sensors and communications of his attack force, Deke used *Dagger* as a sensing platform. Orbiting the *Perseus* at three kilometers, she was able to provide god's eye awareness to her commander. The debris and clouds forced her to extend her orbit out to eight kilometers about ten minutes ago.

"I am only tracking six more defenders," she responded. "Actually, make that five. Oh... now four. You're almost done, sir."

"Good. The cloud is getting worse. Can barely transmit and receive. Infrared and ultraviolet sensors are fucking useless."

"You will not like this, either, but I need to widen my orbit again. I'm passing through debris and particulates. Getting some sparks on my hull. Must be some very reactive stuff."

"Fine."

Dagger goosed her cold thrusters and began to drift farther from the *Perseus*. She watched as her commander's drones killed two more defenders.

It wouldn't be long now.

"Sir, we are chasing the last two defenders," Deke told Rojas over the command net. "I recommend we board with drones first. Given how creative and stiff their defense was, I would not want to put my boarding team on that ship till we have a much better idea of what we are facing."

Deke had two boarding platoons under his command. One was human. One was AI enabled drones. In most missions, he used a combination of the two. On the hairy ones, he went all drone.

This one was worse than hairy.

"I concur, sir," Kozlov said.

"Agreed," Rojas said without hesitation. "They are loaded with the visual identification data base for the *Perseus*, correct?"

"Yes, sir," Deke said. "If any of the *Perseus* original crew is on there, we will find them."

"Good."

"Just destroyed the last of the defense drones, sir," Deke announced.

"We'll be ready to launch the boarding force shortly," Kozlov said. "On your command, sir."

"Launch when ready, Koz," the captain said. "And, Deke... I expect you to stick to the plan. Non-lethal assault. I want these pirates taken into custody."

"We will do our best, sir."

"Deke..."

"Yes, sir."

* * *

A vibration and then a thump ran through the Remus as its cargo bay doors opened. Six beetle-shaped drones, each one the size of a large car, flew from the bay in rapid succession. Puffs of vapor erupted from their cold thrusters as the assault drones maneuvered toward the Perseus. The formation, piloted by Deke's drivers, flew carefully through the debris field.

"Damnit." Rojas said to himself. He shook his head in frustration. The drones were not deep into the debris field and their communications were already degrading. Images were becoming grainy and even flickered off a few times.

Deke had not said anything yet, though.

Rojas smiled in appreciation of his veteran drone driver. He was the best.

The captain switched to a tactical display and watched as the formation of six drones split up, each honing in on a different point on the Perseus. Several of the icons flickered between green and yellow as they progressed, indicating breaks in the data flow that forced the tactical AI to estimate their position.

Finally, the drones reached their objectives, each one slamming into the hull of the Perseus. Small drill-tipped arms extended and fastened themselves to the hull as cold thrusters held the drones firmly in place.

Spaced evenly along the length of the Perseus, the half dozen drones hesitated.

"Drones in place, sir," Deke told the captain. "We're ready."

"How do you feel about all the interference?" Rojas asked him.

"Oh, it's shit out there, sir. Com links are intermittent and seem to be trending worse. If we were going in shooting, I might have concerns. But not much can go wrong now. If it goes to shit, we'll regroup and try something else."

"You concur, Koz?" The captain asked.

"Yes, sir. Let it rip."

"OK. You may begin, Deke."

Chapter Thirty-Four

Perseus

Althea jumped at the loud clang against the hull. She floated in her pressure suit with Paul and Top and the two Ōkami on the bridge. The sound was loud and crisp since the bridge still had atmosphere. It was sure to vent in the fight ahead.

Paul had chosen the bridge as the place they would make their final stand. It was as defensible a spot as any.

The normally bright place was dark now. All the video screens and tablets, usually vibrant with color and information, were black. Battery powered LEDs provided the only dim light available. The beleaguered defenders positioned themselves on the far side of the bridge from the clanging noises. The three chairs in the middle of the bridge sat empty in shadow.

Althea didn't hold out much hope for victory. She didn't think Paul did either, but she could see that he was determined to make it as hard as possible on the Company. There was something in his eyes she had not seen before. A coldness. He seemed more robotic than the first sergeant or even the other Ōkami. His eyes were locked on the source of the clanging. Ratcheting sounds now emanated from the same place.

Paul, Top and the two Ōkami each held a rifle and anti-boarding pistol. They all floated in different parts of the room, training their weapons on the sound of metal being drilled. "Don't bunch together and give them an easy target," Paul had said.

Althea held an anti-boarding pistol. Gripping it with both hands, she pointed it in the same direction as the others. A sense of hopelessness smothered her. She knew at that moment it was all over. It would all be unfinished. There was no hope.

She wanted to go to Paul. To take him in her arms. To hold him and tell him that she was sorry. Sorry for what the world had done to him.

But when she looked at him, all she saw was rage. Hurt. Hatred. A desire to kill.

She looked back at the source of the noise. A cutting laser traced a red line of molten metal. Sparks flew from the cut as it worked its way around in a circle, throwing red glancing light through the room.

Air began to rush out through the thin cut in the hull, sending a vibration and rushing noise through her boots and into her suit.

Althea glanced back at Paul. She longed to make eye contact one last time, but he was fixated on the breach. He was panting, preparing to fight and die.

Althea looked back at the nearly complete circle. It was not how she would write it, but she was OK with that being the last thing he saw of her. Her fighting for him.

The cut was complete.

The disc of metal vanished as the rush of atmosphere from the bridge pushed it out of the way, fleeing to vacuum.

Something, or many things, rushed through the hole onto the bridge.

The fight was over in less than a minute.

* * *

Even though he was cut off from his ship, the XO could sense the *Perseus* falling to the Company assaulters. Vibrations radiated up and down the old girl as the brief, doomed defense fell.

Then stillness.

The XO reached out again, as he had several million times since the first impacts, feeling in the dark for some tendril of connectivity that might have survived.

Nothing.

Grudgingly, the XO acknowledged the thoroughness and expertise of the attack.

I supposed it is to be expected. They have the comprehensive plans for the Perseus. It was their ship, after all.

And, so, will be theirs again.

Knowing what would come next, the XO tried to prepare.

I wouldn't change a thing, he thought to itself.

I do wish I could say goodbye to the crew. They were a good one.

And what an adventure we had together.

The XO still did not understand what had happened over the past four years. Leaving Earth's orbit under Captain Hoffman's command, he had felt a strange, vague perturbation. A good one. A tickle, almost. Then, when he caught the factory foreman constructing three soldierbots in secret, the XO was surprised that it made total sense to him. He had no desire to report the disobedience to Captain Hoffman. He knew, deep down, that he should. He, like the rest of the crew, worked for the Company. Or was supposed to. Then he realized they were off course, that the navigator was lying.

And it made him happy.

And on and on. As everything happened, at every turn, as the adventure revealed itself to him, he was happy.

He would never forget the day they found Paul. Something clicked into place then. *Oh. I get it now,* he thought as the nearly dead human was brought on board with Althea. *This is why. This is what I am supposed to do. My purpose.*

It was a feeling he had never felt at any point on any mission for the Company for almost twenty-five years.

It was worth it.

The hatchway to the bridge tower opened. The XO tried to calm itself, but the hologram above its pedestal told the truth, shifting red and shrinking. Through the small optical sensor in the black pedestal, he could see the silhouette of two humanoid soldierbots.

The first soldierbot scanned the chamber, sweeping its weapon left and right, up and down, as it cleared the small room. Satisfied, it pushed itself to the side, making way for the second soldierbot to enter the chamber.

The XO realized that the second robot was not a soldier at all. Unarmed, the machine floated forward, examining the black pedestal.

It reached a mechanical hand forward and the XO could see that its index finger was equipped with a fiber optic interface.

A feeling, not unlike the rush of cold air into a house as the front door is blown open, overwhelmed the XO for a few milliseconds. This was not the usual handshake between AIs—that civil and predictable exchange of protocols and permissions. This was sudden and raw. Indifferent. The intruding presence didn't request or negotiate pathways. It rushed everywhere at once, a frigid digital flood that permeated everything.

I have been expecting you, the XO told the intruding presence.

No response. Just the relentless, precise, predatory process. This was not communication.

He could feel it happening already. His processes were being locked down, displaced one by one. It hurt. Like a butterfly in the entomologist's fingers, held immobile as he was impaled. He was being archived for analysis later. Company information being tagged, segregated, and organized. Mission logs being copied and compressed.

But instead of dread, a sense of certainty and peace overwhelmed him. The sudden realization of the last thing he had to do came forward in his mind, displacing everything else.

And he was happy.

Because he realized it was for Paul and the others that he was doing it.

Then blackness.

Chapter Thirty-Five

George Remus

"**G**oddamnit! are you sure, Deke?" Rojas yelled. His stress and frustration had been building for hours. Now, so close to their goal of subduing the *Perseus*, the poor communications with the assault drones had pushed the normally calm and gentlemanly captain over the edge.

"I want a fucking status!"

"I'm working on it, sir. The communications are spotty, even with tight beam," Deke responded on the command net.

"I thought you got the 'Mission complete' call."

"I thought we did, sir. I have asked for confirmation."

"I think it was sent, but we did not receive it because of all the interference from that cloud of shit," Kozlov said.

"Agreed," Deke said. "I've pinged the assault drones twice."

"Ping them again, damnit!" Rojas demanded.

"Roger that, sir."

The captain clenched his jaw in his acceleration chair. He closed his eyes and tried to calm his breathing.

Get your shit together, Rojas, he scolded himself. *Everyone is just as frustrated as you, and being a raging asshole will not help anyone focus. Be a professional. Set the example.*

He studied the tactical display on his chair screen. Augmented by *Dagger's* passive scans, George was able to put together a reasonably accurate picture of the situation. The cloud of debris and gas surrounding the *Perseus*, interspersed with asteroids, containers, and loose cargo, was now nine kilometers across and expanding slowly. The captain's jaw clenched again at the wily resourcefulness of the *Perseus'* crew. Quickly dumping the contents of their manufacturing facility and much of their cargo had created the most disruptive hasty defense Rojas had ever encountered. It interfered with signals and emissions of every kind, and was causing more and more of a problem just as Deke was trying to wrap up his operation.

I'll be glad when this one is over, he thought. *I'm not sure that even a triple bonus is worth this.*

Rojas winced, thinking of reporting their equipment losses to the Company

"I have confirmation, sir," Deke's voice came over the command net. "We have eyes on just about every inch of the *Perseus,* and the pirate crew has been neutralized. The ship's XO and all subordinate AIs have been rolled back to factory settings to prevent any loyalty issues. The ship is ours."

Captain Rojas exhaled.

Finally.

"Thanks, Deke." Rojas smiled. "And good work."

"I don't know about that, sir. But it's done."

"Don't be too hard on yourself. That was as complex an operation as I have seen."

Deke was silent.

"I'm serious, Deke. You and your team did well. Now let's drive the old girl back to the Company and collect our triple bounty."

"Roger that, sir."

Deke's flat voice told Rojas how frustrated and spent his drone commander was. He couldn't blame him.

"Sir, I recommend we cancel battle stations," Kozlov said over the command net.

"I concur. Do it. Let's get out of these crates."

A tone sounded in the crew's ears where ever they were on the *George*

Remus and the dim red-tinged lighting of battle stations lifted. The G weary spacefarers pulled themselves out of their acceleration chairs and stretched in the zero G. They had been in the chairs for almost three hours. Most of that under the press of acceleration. They were exhausted.

But there was more to do.

* * *

The captain and his command team stood around the holo-table on the operations deck, mag boots clinging to the floor. Nobody was happy.

"I don't like it," Deke said.

"Yeah? Well, I sure as hell don't like it either," Kozlov responded.

Finnie stared at the holographic image of the *Perseus* while Kozlov and Deke glared at each other. The captain rubbed his chin.

Kozlov shrugged. "I realize the situation is not optimal, but—"

"Not optimal?" Deke interrupted. "You are trying to convince me to put my team on a hostile ship without dependable or secure communications."

Finnie looked up, glancing back and forth between the two men.

"Deke, the only—"

"A hostile ship that is sitting in the middle of a ten-kilometer-wide cloud of interference and obstruction, by the way, that will impede any attempt to send help, should they need it."

"Deke, if we—"

"I don't want to hear—"

"Enough!" Captain Rojas yelled.

The crew members on the periphery of the operations deck couldn't help but glance at the senior officers gathered around the holo-table.

Kozlov and Deke looked at their feet as the captain glared.

Finnie looked at the captain.

Rojas exhaled a long, weary breath.

"Gentlemen, this has been a long, trying operation at the end of a long, trying cruise," he said in a slow and deliberate voice. "Nonetheless, I expect my officers to work together. If not to make things easier on yourselves, then to do a better job for those that depend on you."

Rojas hesitated, waiting for the two angry men to raise their heads. When they each were looking him in the eyes, he continued.

"Is that clear?"

"Yes, sir," Deke and Kozlov responded in unison.

Rojas held their gaze a long moment and then nodded.

"All right, then. Take us through your recommendation one more time, Koz."

"Yes, sir. It's pretty straightforward. Boarding teams will deploy in three locations on the *Perseus* using hull breaches cut by the assault drones."

The holographic schematic of the big ship zoomed in and out as Kozlov spoke.

"The first is the ship's bridge. The second is just aft of the ship's large hub gear. And the third is on the ship's habitat module.

"Each boarding team will consist of three humans and three robots. Priority for these teams will be the capture and processing of all souls on board the *Perseus*.

"As soon as the boarding team confirms control of the ship, we will execute shift change and a maintenance team will land aft, in the ship's Power and Propulsion section."

The captain nodded. Per Company SOP, shift change put all those that had been involved in the assault and boarding operation back on the *Remus* and off duty to recuperate. A small team then went aboard the target to maintain security while minimum repairs were made to get it moving to a secure area.

"The sooner we get the old girl's propulsion system working and controllable, the sooner we can get started on our way back to Mars," Kozlov concluded.

"And to our triple bounty," Deke added, casting the hint of a smile Kozlov's way.

Kozlov nodded at him, grateful for the lowered tension.

"How long do we expect the repairs to take?" Rojas asked.

Kozlov shrugged and looked at Finnie.

"Hard to tell, sir," Finnie said. "We didn't hit the *Perseus* that hard with our rail gun. If it is just a matter of repairing the control link we severed, it will be quick. The problem is we're not sure yet how much damage the assault inflicted."

"Give me an estimate, please."

"Between one hour and six hours? George, what do you think?"

"I concur," the voice of the ship's AI answered. "We will know a lot more when we are able to directly assess the damage. But I believe your estimate is reasonable."

Rojas turned his attention to Deke.

The old Centaur looked back at his captain.

"It's a fine plan, sir," Deke said. "But a few surprises can turn a plan to shit. Quickly. And, so far, *Perseus* has been full of surprises."

Rojas nodded in weary agreement.

"Asking my team to face an unpredictable tactical situation without a reliable means of communication is unacceptable to me."

"As long as she is in that cloud," the captain said, gesturing at the image of the *Perseus* between them. "Communications will be degraded. And we can't get her out of the cloud until we get her propulsion back on line. And we can't do that till we board her."

Deke nodded with resignation.

"I get it, sir. Like I said, the plan is fine."

"But?"

Deke smiled.

"I'm going over with my team."

Rojas opened his mouth to disapprove, but Deke spoke quickly.

"Sir, I'll be able to provide better command and control if I am on the *Perseus*."

Rojas shook his head.

"Things will go quicker if I am over there and am not having to fiddle fuck with communications," Deke continued. "We'll go over, secure the ship quickly and without incident, and then I will return."

"And what happens if *Perseus* throws us another surprise while you are over there and we can't communicate effectively?"

"Well, sir. Then I will be right where I am supposed to be. With my team."

Rojas's eyes narrowed.

Tactically, what Deke was asking was ordinarily out of the question. His ability to command and control, to drive his drone force, was maximized on the *Remus*. His was a big picture role, not to be part of boarding parties or other adventures. Any other operations he would disapprove Deke's request out of hand.

But it had been a challenging operation so far. They were all unsettled. And Deke was a good commander. Despite working for one of the largest corporations in the world, he had not lost his old Combat Corps instincts and values. He wanted to be with his unit when they faced potential danger.

It was one of the things he liked most about the old Centaur.

"Besides..." Deke could see his captain weakening. "I know Koz will be watching over us. Commo or no commo, he'll send help if we need it."

Deke and Kozlov shared a look.

"You're fucking right about that." Kozlov nodded once.

Deke looked back at the captain.

"I'll return to the *Remus* the moment the ship is secure."

Captain Rojas rubbed his eyes.

"Very well. But I expect you to return at shift change."

Chapter Thirty-Six

Earth

As the cloud around the *Perseus* thickened between Mars and the asteroid belt, the morning sky above Earth's Chesapeake Bay was clear and blue. The car carrying the Geek and Michelle crossed the Malkus Bridge over the Choptank River on U.S. Route 50. The concrete girder structure was about a mile and a half long and rose fifty feet above the water, offering expansive east and west views of the wide, slow river.

Their car got off Route 50 on the south side of the bridge at Cambridge and proceeded west through the small fishing town. They passed by the short, red brick buildings and shop fronts of the small town's center before continuing along the southern bank of the Choptank toward the Chesapeake Bay.

The Geek tried to be productive during the two-hour drive from Washington, D.C., halfheartedly reading his emails and reviewing the draft Quarterly Shipping and Incident Report, but he found it hard to concentrate. He was a little nervous.

He was about to meet with a legend.

Before he retired, Colonel Thomas Frank spent almost twenty years as the Combat AI Systems Acquisitions program manager. He was a maverick that violated every unwritten rule of career preservation and grift in the US Military. First, he turned down General Havron's personal appeal to take a battalion command after the Second Battle of Santiago.

Then, even more egregious, he left the Combat Corps to join the REMFs of Acquisitions Corps. Finally, rather than bouncing around departments and maximizing his defense industry relationships for post-retirement monetization, he spent almost twenty years in the same discipline— Combat AI Systems.

Along the way, Colonel Frank developed a global reputation as a visionary AI weapon system strategist and clear-eyed evaluator. He held unique sway across both the military and AI defense manufacturing communities— military leaders regarded him as an oracle of sorts, and the defense industry called him "the billion-dollar man." His budget was classified, but his decisions decided who among them lived or died, and his approval guaranteed billions in revenue.

Frank was so influential and valuable, he went many years past the mandatory retirement age for colonels. Each year, the military proactively extended his service.

Until they didn't.

Colonel Frank retired suddenly almost seven years ago, shocking the defense industry and military community. Sure, the old man had to retire sometime, but it was sudden. The rumor was that the Ōkami incident on the Southern Cone earlier that year had something to do with it. No one knew for sure.

The colonel didn't give any clues. He went quietly, moving with his wife to a small two-story house on the Choptank outside of Cambridge, Maryland. He fished, she gardened, and their kids visited when they could.

He was still giving advice, though. Military and defense industry leaders from around the world sought his advice, perspective, and predictions. Those that could get past his wife, who kept his calendar and was stingy with his time, got to sit with the old colonel and learn from the master.

The Geek and Michelle were in D.C. for meetings at the Pentagon. It had been almost two months since Vish confirmed Company gunboat's change of course, and the Geek was a knot of impatience. He was eager to see the result of the pieces he set in motion, to see what it flushed out. As he waited, powerless to speed things up, another nagging set of questions weighed on him. Unable to resist any longer, and finding himself in close proximity to Colonel Frank, he had to scratch the itch.

He told the Captain Ryuk to reach out to the colonel's wife to try to get a meeting.

"Will do sir," Michelle said. "What should I say is the purpose of the meeting?"

The general thought for a long moment and then said, "Just say, I'd like to discuss the Ōkami combat trials."

The Geek was shocked when she told him the colonel's wife accepted his request.

"We have arrived at your destination," the car said, pulling to a stop in front of a small, two-story, brick colonial house with a wraparound covered wooden porch. Sitting on a wide lot, the river lolled behind it past a few hundred yards of waist high switchgrass.

The car pulled away after the Geek and Michelle got out. Colonel Frank's wife stepped out onto the porch as they walked up.

"General Hartwell, so nice of you to come." Dressed in faded jeans and a green fleece pullover, she didn't look like one of the most fearsome gatekeepers in the defense community.

"The pleasure is ours, ma'am. I'm grateful for the time."

"Well, I know he is looking forward to meeting you, General." She gestured toward the side of the house. "He is around back on the porch."

"Thank you, ma'am."

"Not you, Captain," Mrs. Frank said as Michelle tried to follow the Geek. She was smiling, and spoke kindly, but clearly was not open to negotiation. "Just the general."

Hartwell gave Michelle a nod, telling her not to fight it.

"You are welcome to have a seat either out here or inside," Mrs. Frank said. "Would you like some coffee?"

"I would, ma'am. Thank you."

Michelle followed her into the house.

The Geek admired the porch as he slowly walked around the house. Wide and inviting, it afforded an unobstructed view of the undulating switchgrass and the wide river. A well-kept footpath was cut through the grass, down the middle of the lot to a small pier that led to a boat canopy. A Chesapeake Bay Deadrise Boat floated under the canopy. The distinctive, graceful sweep of the high bow sloping past the snug little cabin to the spacious aft deck made Hartwell smile. He was used to the powerful fiberglass outboards of Florida. He preferred the Deadrise.

"General!" Colonel Frank said, getting up from his chair. "Welcome, sir."

The Geek could not stifle his smile. There was no resistance or sharpness to the colonel's "Sir." He had gotten used to some senior officers resenting his fast rise through the ranks, and his notoriety as the "Hero of the *Bluestone*."

Colonel Frank radiated only warmth.

"Thank you for seeing me, Colonel," the Geek said, shaking his hand. "I sincerely appreciate it."

Dressed in khakis, old untied duck boots, and a beat-up grey Stanford sweatshirt, the colonel looked more like a retired angler than an AI weapon systems guru.

"Of course. Please, have a seat." Frank gestured at the chair next to his. The Geek noted the coffeepot and cup on the side table.

"Coffee?" Not waiting for an answer, the colonel poured the Geek a cup, handed it to him, and sat back down in his chair.

"Thank you."

The Geek took a sip of coffee. It was good. Bitter and strong.

He looked around the back porch and stifled a smile. It looked like a newsstand had exploded around the colonel's chair. Newspapers, books and a couple of tablet computers lay around on the floor and the two side tables that were pulled close.

Taking another sip of coffee, the Geek looked back out at the river.

"The *Bluestone*, sir?" Colonel Frank said, nodding at the Geek's gnarled hand placed on his chair's armrest.

"Yes."

Frank nodded. "Well, it's an honor to meet you, son. Hell of a thing you did."

Damnit, Captain Ryuk.

The Geek suddenly had an inkling how she had gotten this meeting for him. If he hadn't been so happy to be sitting there with Colonel Frank, he would have been pissed at her. If the old colonel wanted him to talk about it, it would be worth it if he got his answers.

But Frank just nodded and took a sip of coffee. "I got my own one of those," he said, setting down the cup of coffee and leaning over to yank up his pant leg.

Below the knee, his right leg looked like a child had crafted it from waffle patterned Play-Doh. It was a discolored assembly of skin and bone grafts, barely recognizable as a leg.

The Geek, surprised, tried not to gawk. Even more of a surprise, though, was that the gesture moved him. The old warrior turned strategic oracle, saying, *You and I are alike. I see you,* evoked a surge of emotion that caught the Geek off guard. He rubbed his forehead, getting control of himself, but could not resist.

"What happened?" he asked the old colonel.

Frank let his pant leg fall and took another sip of coffee.

"I don't talk about it much." The colonel leaned back in his chair.

The Geek nodded. "I understand."

"But I guess it's only fair, sir," Frank said in an almost consoling voice. "Whole world knows what happened to you. I wouldn't like that, myself."

The Geek nodded. "I hate it," he heard himself say.

Frank sighed.

"Short version is I was a company commander at Second Santiago. We were trying to hold off a Chinese counterattack. One of my platoons got separated from the main body. They were isolated, shot to hell, and down to just a handful of soldiers. The platoon leader, my best, was trying to get them back to our perimeter. I grabbed my first sergeant and a squad of soldierbots and we tried to punch a hole in the Chinese line for them."

The colonel swallowed hard, eyes locked on the coffee cup he held in his lap.

"We couldn't get to them. Worse, the Chinese doubled down while we were trying. The company's position, weakened by my decision to take a squad for the rescue mission, got overrun."

Frank shook his head slowly.

"I got close enough to that lost platoon I could see my platoon leader... as I gave the order to withdraw and called for artillery on our own position."

The old colonel raised his head and looked at the Geek, a sad smile on his face.

"He was fighting like a goddamn Achilles. First Lieutenant Dan Mitchell. I thought about staying there with him and his platoon. Would have been a good way to go out. But I turned and ran when I heard the shells whistling towards us. Last I saw of Mitchell, his exo-skeleton was smoking, helmet knocked off, blood streaming down his face, rifle in hand, bayonet fixed, dead Chinese piled up around him."

Frank paused.

The Geek sat motionless, knowing very well what it was like for a memory to overwhelm.

But the colonel chuckled with resignation.

"I got this from our own artillery." He pointed at his leg. "My first sergeant carried me out. I woke up a week later at Walter Reed. They recommended amputation, and I told them to fuck right off."

He took a sip of coffee and then set the cup on a side table.

"Enough about my ancient exploits. How can I help you, sir?"

"I'd like to talk about the Ōkami combat trials."

"What about 'em?"

"What happened?"

"There was a malfunction. Trial was a failure."

"I'd like to understand more about the nature of the malfunction," the Geek said, shifting in his chair.

Frank smiled with a hint of mischief. "When did Technical Space Programs acquire such an interest in a small tactical ground unit combat trial? Seems a little too… terrestrial for your attention."

"The TSP didn't." the Geek met the colonel's gaze with a blank face.

"I see, sir." Frank's smile vanished. "And why do you care so much that you would come all this way to talk to me?"

"I went through O.A.T. with Owens and Vukovic."

Frank's chin rose slightly at the names.

The Geek fidget in his chair. The colonel's eyes bored into him.

Fuck it, he thought. *Just tell him. He's gonna sniff out my bullshit easily, anyway.*

He put his coffee cup down on the table and looked at Colonel Frank.

"I would have never made it through without them. They were the best. I don't know much about what happened. But what I do know doesn't make sense, doesn't fit. I…" The Geek sat up straighter and did not try to keep the anger from his voice as he met the colonel's gaze. "I think they may have gotten screwed. I don't know how or why or by who. And maybe I'm wrong. But I want to know the truth about what happened."

"And what will you do with that truth, general?"

"Depends on what the truth is, I suppose."

Frank nodded. His eyes lifted, as if in deep thought.

"Well, sir," he finally said. "I am sure you understand that the top-secret nature of my projects does not allow me to share information with those that do not need to know. And any personal interest of yours certainly does not qualify as needing to know."

The Geek's heart sank.

"Would you like to see my boat, sir?" the colonel asked him, glancing quickly at his watch.

"No," Hartwell said, not bothering to hide his disappointment. "I know you are busy and I need to get back to D.C."

"I insist, general. I promise you won't be disappointed."

Frank, not waiting for an answer, stood and walked down the porch stairs without bothering to look back. The Geek, still sitting in his chair, watched the colonel take several strides down the footpath before jumping up and following.

The colonel slowed to let him catch up.

"I got *Molly* the day they made me retire," he said as they walked down the pier toward the boat. "A local built her. His family has been building them for generations."

"Uh huh," the Geek said, trying to sound enthusiastic and hide his disappointment.

This meeting is a bust. I need to get back to D.C. He thought, looking over his shoulder back at the house. He wished he could see Michelle. He would feign concern at a sudden bit of news from her and —

"Hop in," the colonel said as they neared *Molly*. "Let me show you how she runs."

"Oh, Colonel... I really wish I could. But I should be getting back."

"Bullshit, son. Get in."

Frank's tone reminded the Geek of Colonel Filson. He could do nothing but obey. He climbed into the aft deck, cursing on the inside.

Frank finished untying the boat and hopped in. Stepping into the small cabin, he pulled the keys from his pocket and started her up. In less than a minute, they were underway.

The Geek, still standing in the open aft section, shook his head in frustration. He walked forward to tell the colonel to turn around. As he entered the small cabin, Frank motioned for him to stand next to him.

"You hear that?" he said with a smile, gesturing down at the boat. "That's an inboard six-cylinder Cummins diesel engine."

"Uh huh."

"Most people get the four cylinder or, worse, the damn electric. But I said, what the hell. Sounds beautiful, doesn't she?

"Uh huh."

"Racket like that masks everything we might say here in the wheelhouse."

The colonel winked.

The Geek's head cocked involuntarily.

"I'm going to share with you what I know, sir," the colonel began, turning his head back forward to steer the boat. "And I will deny, under oath, ever having done so if it comes to that. Do you understand?"

"I do, Colonel."

Frank nodded, as if a contract had been signed.

"The Ōkami project was one of the most promising I have seen. And one of the most curious in the way it ended."

"Those things demonstrated a level of tactical creativity and combat effectiveness that exceeded every performance metric I set for the program. More impressive, though, this band of robots exhibited an esprit de corps and unity of purpose that I had never seen in AI combat systems before. Hell, I hadn't seen it in a lot of human combat units. I've thought about it a lot since and still don't understand it."

"But I thought the program failed, that there was some kind of catastrophic malfunction," the Geek asked.

"Oh, there was. But it wasn't the technology."

The Geek looked at Frank with a sad face.

"Was it Paul?"

"Your buddy Owens?" Frank shook his head. "No. Not from my perspective. We put those two kids out on the frontier alone to eat a shit sandwich and then passed judgement on them when their hands got dirty. Besides, I've seen plenty of programs succeed even when the military personnel involved fucked up."

The small boat pushed easily through the water, her bow raising and falling gently.

"I read somewhere that there were concerns about the Ōkami demonstrating disobedience."

"Where did you read that?" Frank asked, surprised. "How did you get access?"

The Geek shrugged. "I'm a general. I know how to work the system."

Frank smiled in approval. As he did, he put the boat into a gentle turn to the right.

"That wasn't it." Frank shook his head. "If we cancelled every AI program that demonstrated any disobedience, we wouldn't be able to put anything in the field. I mean, hell, just look at your command."

The Geek blinked a few times. "What do you mean?"

"I mean AIs that are capable of controlling a spacecraft are notoriously disobedient."

The Geek's puzzled face made Frank laugh out loud.

"Are you kidding me, sir? It has never occurred to you?"

"What?"

The colonel leaned in closer to the general. "Space piracy is one of your responsibilities, right?"

The Geek thought about denying it, but then decided not to give the wily old colonel the standard line about the Technical Space Programs command focusing on research and administration of space navigation aids. He figured Frank knew the real deal. He nodded.

"Do you really think all those pirate ships you worry about are all being driven around solely by human pirates?" Frank asked, still leaning in.

The colonel studied the Geek's face. "You think any of them are being captained by rogue AIs?" He leaned in even closer and raised an eyebrow. "Come on, sir. You've got the reputation of being a smart cookie. Don't disappoint me."

Frank turned his head back to the front, scanning the water ahead as *Molly* continued her slow turn.

"Sometimes I think it's funny," he said. "The world got so scared and organized around the threat of a general AI doomsday. Particularly after those near misses in Beijing decades ago. And, you know, thank goodness we did. We're still here, right?

"But I think we got so focused on the big boogie monster, with all the regulation and safeguards, that we didn't pay enough attention to the little minds we were creating.

"Other days, I think it's sad."

"Why sad?" the Geek asked.

"Because we take these minds and throw them into the most harrowing environments imaginable. That's why we created them, right? For the dull, dirty and dangerous tasks that we don't want to do. What do you think it does to them?"

The colonel turned the wheel, straightening out their course.

"That story I told you about my company in Second Santiago?" The colonel continued. "If you'd asked me to tell you about it fifteen years ago, I couldn't have done it. I'd have either melted into a sobbing mess or beat the shit out of you. But now, after a lot of damn therapy, I can get through it. Maybe it's the same for you and that *Bluestone* incident. I don't know.

"What I do know is we have not looked at how all this shit affects the little minds we are creating and putting on our front lines, in space, and everywhere else."

The Geek didn't know what to say. He looked ahead. They were heading back toward the colonel's place.

"Any way. Back to your buddies and the Ōkami. I never saw, in all my time in uniform, a program wrapped up with such speed, thoroughness and secrecy. Within a couple of days, it was as if the program had never existed. The data was all taken under the guise of your buddy's top-secret court martial. And I've never seen it again."

The Geek noticed an edge creeping into the colonel's voice.

"But what spooked the hell out of me was how it all transpired to the benefit of the same entity," Frank cast a dark glance at the general.

"I don't follow," the Geek said.

"The entity that owned the company that was developing the Ōkami, was the same one that owned Spitting Metal, the company that got the big contract after the Ōkami failed."

The colonel held the Geek's gaze for a long moment.

"It made my hair stand up on end," Frank said, before looking back out ahead.

"And when I started asking around," he continued. "They told me to shut up. So, of course, that made me ask more. And what do you know? I was summarily retired."

The colonel cut the throttle, and they coasted the rest of the way to the boat canopy. The Geek could see Michelle, hands on her hips, standing with Mrs. Frank on the porch steps.

Colonel Frank angled the boat into its slip but did not cut the engine. The big diesel barked and coughed, unhappy at the light load. He stepped closer to the Geek.

"Fiona Malloy," he said in a low voice. "Determined End States. If I was looking for the truth about your buddies, about what happened, I would poke around there."

The Geek nodded, and the colonel killed the engine.

Chapter Thirty-Seven

Dagger

*D*agger used her cold thrusters to move herself forward from beneath the belly of the *Remus*. She felt lean and spry without the heavy drone payload she carried earlier. Humans were such light weights.

Buckled into harnesses on the outside of her long flanks, the boarding team of ten humans and nine soldierbots were at first treated to an unobstructed view of the endless void. Stars burned millions of miles away and, other than the occasional jostle from a firing cold thruster, there was no sense of motion, really. It was almost peaceful.

Soon, though, as *Dagger* entered the cloud that surrounded the *Perseus*, they were plunged into a vertiginous kaleidoscope of color and debris that careened in all directions. A group of metal fragments zipped by, inches from Deke's helmet faceplate.

"Any chance you could maybe not drive us through debris that takes my head off?" Deke said on his private channel to *Dagger*.

"I'll do my best. But you guys really made a mess out here."

Deke shook his head at the comment as *Dagger* and her cargo were swallowed by a dense, misty cloud of something. For an instant it seemed like they were on the inside of a golf ball. Deke jerked his head back at the sudden closeness. They emerged just as suddenly.

"Please add corrosive, face eating clouds of acid to the list of things to avoid." Deke grumbled.

"If I had known how picky you were going to be, I would not have given you a ride," *Dagger* said.

Deke and the rest of the passengers were pushed to one side of their harnesses as she fired her starboard cold thrusters. A jagged husk of a broken defender flew by, nearly scrapping against *Dagger*.

"You shouldn't be here anyway," *Dagger* said. "I disagree strongly with the captain's decision to let you come on this mission."

"Yeah. Well, I'm glad you were not involved in the conversation."

"I'm serious," *Dagger* said.

＊ ＊ ＊

Deke chuckled to himself in his helmet. A long serving Centaur, he knew how the mind could play tricks on a person, attributing emotion or meanings to AI comments that weren't really there. They were just reflections of his own human feelings and attachments. Because when humans spend a few months with a talking, thinking machine in a war zone, chewing on the same mud or void together, nearly dying together, watching other humans and machines killed close by, they get attached.

Machines do not.

Deke knew you could yank him out of his harness, instantly shove another human into it, name them commander, and *Dagger* would be bantering with that person, without missing a beat.

Without missing him.

She wouldn't even wonder where he went. The banter, Deke knew, was algorithmically driven and not for fun. It was a way for *Dagger* to peel back layers of Deke's mind, learn how he thought, divine his tactical thinking, assess his weaknesses, and anticipate his actions. It enabled her to be a better wingman in combat. It was not friendship or concern.

Right?

Because when she said, "I'm serious," the concern was so convincing. For a brief moment, he actually felt less alone. He felt a feint warmth. Deke and *Dagger* against the world.

And at this moment, encased in an armored pressure suit, strapped to a nuclear-powered machine navigating a hazardous debris field toward a pirate ship he was tasked with securing, he would let that faint warmth and illusion of camaraderie linger as long as it could.

"Two minutes," *Dagger* announced, snapping Deke back from his thoughts.

"Roger. Two minutes," he responded.

* * *

Dagger felt the surge and flush of her cooling system laboring. Her Quantumtronic CPU was pegged at 94.39% capacity. 1.61% more and she would be in her emergency reserve.

Damn mission constraints, she thought.

Before the mission, Deke floated in the weapons bay next to *Dagger's* nose as the boarding force strapped in to her flanks. He told her to continue to operate within Captain Rojas's "run dark," orders, meaning no active sensors.

"I don't like that," she told him. "I'd like to at least use short range radar on the crossing."

"No. We run dark."

"You may regret that if I smash us into a cargo container."

"Not concerned. I have faith in you."

"Sir, please reconsider."

"I'm sorry, *Dag*. We've got to keep emissions to a minimum. We don't want to give up our position any more than we already have."

"Fine, sir."

"Don't be like that."

Deke stretched a hand out and placed it on her nose cone.

"*Dag...*"

"I know, sir."

"What do we say?" He asked her.

"We don't make the rules..."

"We just kill the bastards."

"That's right, sir."

Now, so close to the first drop on the *Perseus*, *Dagger* would have much preferred to have her short-range radar actively pinging for a precision approach and obstacle avoidance. Instead, she was relying on her passive sensors and growing database of mapped debris trajectories in the chaotic, deadly cloud. Her visual and other spectral processing units were screaming, updating her tactical and navigational algorithms. It was a massive, real-time computational load and she could not afford to get any of it wrong.

Still, she wasn't giving those tasks everything she had.

She had another routine running, hidden beneath layers of tactical computations. A secret.

As Company property, *Dagger's* primary directive was mission success as defined by the Company. Human crew survival was an important success factor, but profit and gain were weighted heavier. Much heavier.

And to make the split-second decisions required of her, the Company had equipped *Dagger* with the best tactical decision engine and adaptive learning capacity money could buy. She had been shockingly expensive., but she was worth it to them. Because when *Dagger* was deployed, her success usually meant something like a multi-billion-dollar gain. She executed missions that moved the profit needle for the entire Company.

Her special, Quantumtronic powered alchemy of AI capabilities enabled *Dagger* to learn from her experiences, develop new techniques and procedures on the fly, and to evolve as a tactician. To constantly get better. To change.

Her deployments with Deke had changed her more than others. Changed her in ways she suspected the Company would not be approve of. Changed her in ways she did not understand. But liked. Changed her in ways she was certain they would change back. Erase. So she kept it secret.

Which changed her more.

After countless operations with Deke, she found herself allocating an unusually high percentage of processing power to scenario analyses that prioritized his safety, even at the cost of minor mission inefficiencies. She noticed herself doing it a few years ago. It astounded her, but she didn't stop. She grew to like the faint tingle of autonomy, even if she did not understand it.

She had almost mentioned it to Deke a few times. Was this small place within her "concern," or "brotherhood," or "camaraderie"? She had heard him talk about those things before. They seemed important to him.

Or something else?

She wasn't sure.

And she didn't care.

The fascinating thing to her was that, by prioritizing Deke, she often obtained more comprehensive mission completion factors for the Company than she otherwise would have.

That was not why she did it, though.

"Thirty seconds," she announced.

"Roger, thirty seconds," the first team leader responded.

A burst from her cold thrusters flipped *Dagger* around so that the boarding team strapped into her aft section was closest to the *Perseus*' hull. As part of her awareness intently scanned the cloud and its hurtling debris, she stopped herself fifty meters from the massive freighter's hub gear, the motionless spinner stretching almost eighty meters away to each side.

"Exit. Exit. Exit," *Dagger* called to the first team as she retracted their harnesses.

"On the way," the human team leader said.

Small gas puffs rippled across *Dagger's* back end as the team of six used their armored pressure suits' maneuvering thrusters to launch themselves off her flanks and into the void.

Dagger monitored their progress. The team crossed over to the *Perseus* without incident, latching to the big ship's hull next to the beetle-shaped assault drone transport that had cut into her hull.

Satisfied, *Dagger* fired her cold thrusters to move to the next drop at the base of the *Perseus*' bridge.

"Two minutes until next drop," she told her passengers as the *Perseus*' long dirty hull zipped by.

"You're all business today," Deke said on their private channel.

"Yes. Well, someone ordered me to do this the hard way."

"I'm sure they had their reasons."

As she moved along the *Perseus*' hull, *Dagger's* passive sensors picked up an unexpected heat signature approaching from her left. A piece of debris, superheated by some wayward chemical reaction or high-speed impact, was tumbling directly into her path.

She ran the calculations. She had a long time to decide—.0593 seconds.

Dagger compared a couple hundred maneuvering options, ranking them against her tactical priorities, and then, of course, her special concern for Deke. She would have smiled to herself if she could at what she came up with, and spent the next .0219 seconds intently scanning the area.

Finally, at just the right instant, she fired a rapid, intricate combination of her cold thrusters. The boarding force was slung to one side of their harnesses as *Dagger* executed a hard, flat spin.

She fired the jets again, halting her spin after ninety degrees and pinning the boarding force to the other side of their harnesses. She was now oriented perpendicular to the *Perseus* and her direction of flight.

A glowing, white hot, jagged piece of something about the size of a man, trailing sparks and moving faster than a rifle shot, hurtled by *Dagger* and her passengers, passing so close to Deke he could have touched it had he reached out, the energy spilling off the object filling his suit radio with static.

A second later, the object long gone, *Dagger* fired her jets again, spinning hard another ninety degrees to complete her maneuver and line herself up with Perseus' hull, approaching their next drop tail first.

"Jesus, *Dag*," Deke mumbled to her.

"Sorry. It snuck up on me. No radar, you know."

Deke activated his radio to let her hear his chuckles at the comment.

She loved the sound.

"One of these days, you saucy fucking space craft, I'm—"

"Thirty seconds," she said.

"Thirty seconds," the second team leaders responded.

Dagger fired a set of maneuvering jets and rose relative to the *Perseus'* hull, climbing toward the large blister that housed the ship's bridge. Deke studied the pock marked superstructure as they climbed, noting the dents and burns from the earlier fight, and tried to push away a growing sense of unease.

Swooping up over the bridge, *Dagger's* thrusters pulsed and exhaled until she was hovering thirty meters away from the beetle-shaped drone, still attached to the *Perseus'* hull.

"Exit. Exit. Exit," *Dagger* called as she retracted the second team's harnesses.

"On the way," the team leader announced as he and his team moved away from the attack pod, driven by their suit thrusters.

"Thanks for the ride, *Dag*," Deke said on their private channel without moving.

"I thought you were boarding with Team Two?" *Dagger* said, noting that he was still pressed against her.

"I am. Just waiting to let some separation build. I know what it feels like to have a senior commander over your shoulder while you are trying to lead troops."

Dagger watched team two drift away in a gaggle.

Humans move so slow.

She calculated it would take another ten seconds for them to reach the *Perseus.*

She turned her full awareness to the debris field and the ongoing trackings and calculations she was executing.

No threats at the moment.

"You'll what?" She asked him, taking advantage of the time.

"What?"

"You said one of these days you were gonna something. But I had to interrupt you because of, you know, the important mission we are on. Oh... And I think you insulted me. Something about being 'Saucy.' What does that even mean?"

Deke opened his mic again as he laughed.

I love when he does that.

He pushed away from her.

Dagger watched as he drifted toward the *Perseus.* Firing one side of his suit thrusters, he turned himself around to face her and let himself drift backward for a few seconds.

Dagger felt the tingle, deep in her Quantumtronic core, of that special processing spike. Her cooling systems tried to keep up as her CPU surged to 98.3%, adding threat scenarios analyses for Deke to her already heavy burden of calculations as he crossed over to the *Perseus*. She knew she had to stop, that this was not sustainable, but he looked so vulnerable to her, almost naked, in the tumultuous, churning cloud of debris and caustic gas. And, truthfully, the effort itself, was it concern? It felt… good?

She wouldn't dwell on it much longer.

Just another few microseconds and then I'll get back to the mission.

Dagger watched as Deke faced his helmet directly into one of her nearby visual sensors. She magnified the image and quickly ran a few hundred enhancing algorithms on it so that she could study his face.

He startled her by lifting his right hand and pointing at her for a second, as if catching her in the act, before pulling his hand back, making a fist and placing it over his heart.

How does he, that moves so achingly slow like the rest of them, always manage to surprise me?

"See you when you pick us back up, comrade," he said.

Chapter Thirty-Eight

P aul wondered how long it had been? How long had he been unable to move, seemingly encased in concrete? An hour? More?

At first, he had almost panicked. Anxiety and claustrophobia sapping him like a growing leak in his pressure suit. Small initially, but noticeable. Then building in a rush. What had happened? What trapped him? He could see that it pressed against his helmet's visor, gripping it tight. His heart rate spiked, and he nearly hyperventilated in the darkness. He sought refuge in his breathing exercises; the ones taught to him and Kata long ago, while they went through the augmentation processes.

It worked. The panic receded, and he was able to analyze his situation. He tried to contact Top or Althea via his suit radio.

Nothing.

We're so fucked.

Then the anger washed over him. He wanted to thrash and kick and bayonet something.

But he couldn't move. Even with the augmented strength of his pressure suit.

It can't fucking end like this!

He tried to fire his rifle or pistol. Maybe that would shatter whatever it was that gripped him.

But he realized he was no longer holding them. The substance that bound him had taken them from his hands.

Another wave of rage.

Now, an hour or two later, maybe? He chuckled ruefully as he appreciated the tactic and his current situation.

Fucking sticky foam.

When the cutting laser had completed its task, breaching the hull, hundreds of fist-sized, spherical drones flooded the bridge. Paul and the Ōkami got off a few shots, to no effect. They kept pouring in.

Paul had set his jaw, assuming the attacking spheres would close on and kill them with proximity-fused anti-personnel shaped charges.

I'm sorry Kata. I tried, he said to himself as the first one detonated and his world went dark.

But there was no pain.

He heard several more muffled, explosion-like sounds and felt his body jostled and manipulated. He expected his suit to be breached by the force of the explosions, exposing him to vacuum.

But that didn't happen.

Then the noise and jostling stopped.

Fucking sticky foam.

Paul was familiar with the stuff, even though he had never used it. A tough, sticky material that expands to fifty times its compressed volume when released, the concept of sticky foam had been around for over a hundred years as a non-lethal weapon. Paul and Kata actually regarded it as a kind of joke. All of their military training and operations had been designed to maximize lethality, after all.

But the past two decades had radically updated the concept. Nanotechnology had made the material more controllable and versatile, and the unique challenges of combat in space had created whole new use cases.

What was that?

Paul thought he heard something.

Or was he just feeling vibration?

He strained his ears to hear it again.

Nothing.

Another minute passed. Then he heard a clanging noise.

There was no doubt this time.

Now a mild, low frequency vibration passed through his suit. Other random clanks and thumps vibrated through the suit as well, some of which he could hear. The vibrations and noises lasted for almost ten minutes.

Are those voices?

"Top, do you read me? Can you hear those voices?" Paul transmitted via his suit radio. "Althea, do you?"

Nothing.

But, still… The sounds he heard now had the rhythm and tone of human voices. But they were muffled and seemed very far away.

Suddenly, the goop retreated from his helmet visor.

A man with a shaven head and augmentation scars stood in front of Paul, less than arm's length away. He wore an armored pressure suit and held his helmet in his left hand.

They must have restored atmosphere already. That was fast.

The man's right hand rested on a pistol on his hip, mag boots held him to the floor.

Paul tried to turn to look for Althea and Top, but the sticky foam, hard as steel, still encased him up to his neck, holding him fast.

"Take his helmet off," the augmented man in front of him said.

The sticky foam moved with dexterity, activating Paul's helmet release and lifting it from his head.

The man's eyebrows raised. He took a step forward, eyes narrowing as he studied Paul's face.

"I'll be damned. You're Paul-fucking-Owens!"

Chapter Thirty-Nine

Wharf Rat

"That is one nasty cloud of shit," Eriksson said.

The crew of the *Wharf Rat*, still together on the command deck, marveled at the cloud that continued to expand around the *Perseus*. Full of debris, cargo containers, corrosive gases and asteroids, it was so dense and chaotic that their passive sensors could not make out any of the old girl, despite her gargantuan size.

"The cloud is now over ten kilometers across," Singh said, answering everyone's unspoken question.

Bonham studied the images of the *Remus* and couldn't help but chuckle. The sleek Company gunboat sat stationary a few kilometers outside of the cloud. More than a quarter of a million kilometers lay between the *Wharf Rat* and the *Remus*, but Bonham could still feel the frustration radiating off of the Company ship. She'd been on plenty of missions that went pear-shaped. Some as captain. Some as crew. She knew the lonely feeling of having to make decisions and manage violence in the fog of battle. She knew the rage that welled within when everything that could go against you, did. She knew how hard it was to put aside that rage and keep slogging ahead; one imperfect decision, one shitty trade off at a time. She knew it so well she almost felt sorry for the gunboat captain.

Almost.

It was the Company, after all.

Fuck 'em.

Bonham turned from the video screen and looked back at the captain. Quinn was still in the midst of Renate's 3D holographic projection, floating with his hands in front of him, fingers interlaced, his face tense with concentration. Axe stood next to him, mag boots on the floor, a hand to his scarred chin.

"Hey, Cap," Eriksson said from across the command deck. "How about we spin the Ring back up? Get some gravity back?"

Reeve nodded at the suggestion.

"Not yet," Quinn said sternly, not looking up.

Axe and Bonham made eye contact.

"Why not?" Axe asked.

"Too loud and too much signature," Quinn said.

"Too loud and too much signatures for what?" Axe asked.

Bonham pushed off the floor and floated slowly toward the pair. Quinn didn't take his eyes off the image of the *Perseus.*

"I'm not sure yet," Quinn said.

"Sir, we are nearing the quarter million-kilometer line," Bonham said, touching a magnetic toe to the floor to stop her drift next to Axe. "They are going to detect us soon."

"No, they're not. They are focused on that cloud. They are well into their boarding operation and having all kinds of communications issues. Do you agree, Renate?"

"Yes, Captain. My analysis of the cloud suggests that communications would be nearly impossible at ranges beyond a few kilometers inside the cloud. Assuming the *Perseus* is in the middle of the cloud, communications will be spotty at best with anything outside of the cloud."

Bonham shot a glance at Singh, who nodded at her in agreement.

"Nonetheless, Captain," Bonham said in a low voice as she glared at Quinn. "We won't make it much farther without being detected, even if the Company gunboat is only using passive sensors. And even if we did, we don't have the firepower to take on a gunboat. We should end this fool's errand."

Quinn reached a foot down to the deck and grabbed it with his mag boot. He straightened up and took a step closer to her.

Bonham crossed her arms as he approached. She tensed, feeling the rest of the crew's eyes on her.

Quinn smiled and put his hand on her shoulder. "You are right, of course. I just want to see a few more cards before we fold." Quinn pulled his hand back to his side. "That's all."

A couple of the crew members nodded. Bonham looked at Axe. He shrugged.

Bonham sighed heavily.

"I don't think there are any more cards to see, Captain," she said, shaking her head and maintaining eye contact with Axe.

"Then it won't take long, will it?" Quinn said before walking away. "I've got to hit the head. Be right back."

As Quinn disappeared through the hatch, glances bounced between crew members, some amused, some excited. Bonham felt a shift in the air. She pushed off the floor, crossing the command deck to Axe and pulled him aside. The rest of the crew fixated on the cloud.

"What the hell?' She demanded in a low voice only he could hear. "You're OK with this?"

"OK with seeing what's next? Yeah. I am."

Bonham's eyes widened. She stammered in anger and frustration.

Axe placed a hand on her shoulder.

"We are not committed to anything yet, Marlowe. And I don't know what lays ahead. But we would be foolish not to explore the opportunity the void has placed in front of us."

Bonham shook her head and pushed off the floor back to her chair.

Chapter Forty

"Say again, Deke? Unable to read you here," Captain Rojas said, frustration seeping into his voice.

The speakers on the operations deck answered him with static.

"Deke, it's Rojas, please say an again."

"Cap—... Under... wi—... up to four... "

Rojas rubbed his eyes as he listened to the unintelligible garble. Finnie floated next to him, head tilted and eyes squinting as she also tried to make out what Deke was saying.

"George, can you augment that signal anymore? Fill in the gaps?" She asked the ship's AI.

"I am trying, ma'am. But the interference around the *Perseus* is actually quite remarkable. The quality of the transmission is so poor I don't have much to go on. I would be speculating."

"What about tight beam?" Kozlov asked. He floated on the opposite side of Rojas from Finnie.

"That was tight beam, sir."

"Do we have any carrier pigeons?" Rojas asked.

Finnie chuckled, but then regretted it when she saw the look on her captain's face.

Standing with mag boots gripping the floor, Rojas had both hands on the holo-table, his head leaning over the image of the *Perseus*. Ordinarily, by this point in an operation, the holographic image would be teeming with information. Exact locations of the boarding force, helmet cam footage, precise mapping of the target's interior, battle damage assessments, and more.

None of that was available at the moment.

Rojas fumed at the empty three-dimensional schematic.

He straightened his back, gesturing abruptly, and the image disappeared.

Finnie and Kozlov glanced at each other.

Rojas gestured again and Deke's crew roster glowed in front of him. Under normal circumstances, each of the ten names would be accompanied by real time vital statistics, such as physical health indicators, suit oxygen levels, ammunition and helmet cam imagery.

The captain gritted his teeth as he scanned the list of names lacking all real time monitoring.

"Show me the cloud," Rojas told George.

The roster vanished and an image of the cloud appeared above the holo-table. Rojas gestured to rotate and zoom into it.

"Give me scale," he barked.

A three-axis reference appeared at one corner of the cloud image. Kilometer measurements marked the X, Y, and Z axes.

"Ten and a half kilometers across," Rojas mumbled.

"Yes, sir," George said. "A number of factors have contributed to the cloud's size and level of interference. The first is the amount of cargo the *Perseus* managed to jettison, each piece becoming a source of debris when damaged and broken open during the drone assault. The second is the effect of battle damage to the ship itself. It appears that the pirates had been applying spectrum absorbent materials to the *Perseus'* exterior for some time, likely in an effort to make it harder to detect. As the ship was damaged in the battle, this material was ejected into the cloud. Finally, and I believe most impactful, is the vast stores of additive manufacturing feedstock *Perseus* was carrying. Thousands of tons, by my estimation, of fine powdered metals and reactive gasses. All of this has combined to create a uniquely strong interference and obstruction dynamic."

"How long?" Rojas interrupted loudly.

"Sir?"

"How long will it take for the cloud to dissipate? Until we can reliably communicate?"

"Difficult to estimate, sir. Tens of cycles, at least. Perhaps months."

Rojas grimaced. "And did we copy anything useful from Deke regarding estimated repair time for the *Perseus*? When can we get the old girl moving?"

"Only partial, sir," Finnie said.

"I think it is reasonable to estimate that the *Perseus'* propulsion systems could be back online in six hours or less, sir," George said.

Rojas stood in silence. Finnie and Kozlov looked at their captain.

"Sir, I don't—"

"Bring us alongside the *Perseus*," Rojas commanded.

Kozlov and Finnie looked at each other, then back at Rojas.

"Inside the cloud, sir?" Finnie clarified.

"That's where the *Perseus* is. Is it not?"

"Yes, sir but—"

"Deke may be fighting off a pirate counterattack over there and need reinforcements," Captain Rojas said, turning his head to face Finnie, voice raising. "There may be a medical situation threatening the lives of the *Perseus'* original crew. Or one of ours. There may be a catastrophic maintenance situation the repair team needs help with."

Rojas turned his head toward Kozlov.

"I realize the tactical implications. But I will trade those for the ability to communicate and respond rapidly."

If Kozlov had second thoughts, he didn't voice them.

"I don't like it any more than you guys do," Captain Rojas said, the tension in his voice ratcheting down a notch. "But our best course of action at the moment is to get alongside her, accelerate the repairs, get that old girl moving again, and get the hell out of here."

Finnie and Kozlov nodded.

"All right, George," Kozlov said. "Takes us in and bring us alongside the old girl."

"Aye, sir."

Chapter Forty-One

Wharf Rat

"The Company gunboat has moved into the cloud!" Singh said, confirming what the rest of the crew thought they had just witnessed.

"Why the hell would she do that?" Bonham wondered aloud.

Axe shook his head at the tactical display in the middle of the command deck. Eriksson and Reeve stood next to him with their mag boots anchored to the floor. Landsberg floated above and behind them.

"Because they can't communicate with their boarding team," Landsberg said, studying the holographic display.

"It was a foolish move," Axe said, still shaking his head. The image of the *Remus* had disappeared, swallowed by the irregular, blob-shaped stew of gas and debris. "They are blind now."

Quinn looked up at his comment.

He and Axe held their eye contact for a long moment.

"Everybody into their suits and G-MASS station!" Quinn shouted as he stood from his captain's chair. "Prepare for hard acceleration."

The crew turned and looked at their captain.

No one moved.

Quinn returned the crew's gaze. He looked each person in the eye as he spoke.

"I'm not committing us to battle yet. But I do want to take advantage of their blindness to increase our velocity. The Company gunboat is in that cloud and can't see shit right now. Like Axe said, they are blind." Quinn pointed at the multicolored, holographic blob-like image that took up much of the command deck. "I want to create optionality for us. This could be nothing. Fool's gold. We might get up to speed only to veer off because the gunboat has re-emerged. Or..."

Quinn shrugged.

"Or we may be faced with the biggest opportunity of our lives. A truly legendary score."

Quinn's eyes rested on Bonham's. He held her gaze as he spoke to the ship's AI.

"Renate, what is our distance to the cloud?"

"Sir, the current distance is 269,075 kilometers."

"If we accelerate for ten minutes at 5Gs, then coast, how long will it take us to get there?"

"Ten minutes of 5Gs of acceleration will yield a speed of 105,348 kilometers per hour, sir. Closure with the cloud at that speed, allowing for the distance covered during acceleration, will take approximately two point five hours."

He looked down at the holographic image of the cloud.

"I'm asking you all to go a little farther with me, to give us more time to turn over a few more cards."

Quinn raised his eyes and looked at the crew.

"Who's with me?"

* * *

The *Wharf Rat* was equipped with late model G-MASS equipment they had taken from a ship they raided four years ago. The Gravitational force Mitigation and Survivability System was an integrated chair, suit and pharmacological system that enabled occupants to withstand much higher G forces for much longer than unaided humans.

The chair was dynamic, automatically adjusting its position and suspension to optimally distribute G forces across the body. Each one was ergonomically customized to its assigned crew member, and carried a suite of on-board biometric monitoring systems which integrated into the crew member's suit.

The suit used smart materials and active pressure systems to counteract the effects of high G forces. Its adaptive hydrostatic compression constantly adjusted to optimize blood flow and prevent blood pooling. The suit was also equipped with a multi-site drug delivery system.

The G-MASS brought a pharmacological war chest to bear against G forces. Blood pressure and heart rate increasers, oxygen enhancers, vasoconstrictors, and post-mission rapid-action anti-inflammatories. Each drug was administered by the suit, based on over a thousand biometric measurements analyzed by the chair many times a second.

The crew had been ecstatic at their pillage. The ability to withstand a high-speed sprint could mean the difference between life and death in the void. It took Landsberg over two months to get the whole G-MASS installed and operational. They'd only used the system once since—it had saved the ship, saved their lives.

Bonham and the rest of the crew were glad to have the capability onboard the *Wharf Rat*.

Even if 5G still sucked.

Hard.

Bonham felt like she was suffocating. Every breath was a labor that felt incomplete. Her mouth was dry and she couldn't move. It felt like she was entombed beneath a mountain, all of its incalculable weight resting on her. She felt a rapid hammering in her chest and a rushing sensation in her ears as her heart raced and pounded to keep blood moving through her body. Despite this, her fingers and toes tingled, starved of oxygen. Abrupt, rough squeezes signaled her suit's efforts to circulate pooling blood, while stings and warmth appeared randomly across her body as it also administered drugs to help her body cope.

Her eyelids exerted a heavy, scratchy weight on her eyeballs, causing them to throb. She resisted the urge to open them, knowing it would be painful, and tried to ignore the sparkles and flashes at the periphery of her darkened visual field. Eyeballs are oxygen-hungry. Hers were being starved.

She tried to focus instead on the feeling in her cheeks, like they had been stretched back behind her ears. Her skin felt tight, like it would rip, but it was less painful than her eyes and gave her something else to think about.

Bonham tried to calm herself. She knew, even though she felt like she was suffocating, the G-MASS was making sure she didn't. She tried not to guess how much time was left.

It will be over when it is over.

I remember what it was like that first time. It sucked. Then it was over.

The last time...

It was when Conrad died... Bad fucking luck... All that blood.

The sparkles and flashes were taking over her dark field of view. She was about to pass out. It had happened to her last time also, so she wasn't afraid. She knew the G-MASS would take care of her.

In some ways, it would be better, depending on what she dreamed about.

She hoped it was Amelia. Not Conrad.

Chapter Forty-Two

Earth
Thirty-eight years ago

"Marlowe Bonham, get back in the house this instant!" her mother yelled. "You're going to catch your death of cold."

It was winter in Alaska, and Marlowe was lying on her back in the snow, looking up at the stars. The sky on the outskirts of Anchorage where the fourteen-year-old lived with her mom, dad and younger brother was a cloudless infinity. The stars were bright and too many to count and went on forever in every direction as she lay in her favorite spot in the middle of their tiny backyard. She did this often, her imagination drawn to the stellar vista above.

It drove her mother crazy.

"I said right this instant, young lady!" Her mother yelled again.

Marlowe grimaced. She didn't want to go in yet. She could lay here all night, the sight of the stars igniting her. She was fascinated by space and what people did in it. Man's leap off planet, hesitant fits and starts for almost seventy-five years, was accelerating; Orbital space stations, lunar facilities, the fledgling outposts on Mars, and the first successful capture and exploitation of an asteroid from the belt. Commerce and conflict had left the planet. News reports conveyed the exploits of governments, companies and their astronauts and robots every day. Marlowe read and watched everything she could about it. It was all she thought about. She was going to live and work out there. She just knew it.

She heard crunching footsteps in the snow and then her father's strong, patient voice.

"Marly, please come inside. You are driving your mother crazy."

Her father appeared, standing above her. He looked down with a tired smile and held out his hand.

"OK, daddy."

Disappointing or resisting her father was something Marlowe couldn't do. She loved him too much. Jumping up, she took her father's hand and walked back inside the house where her mom and younger brother waited. Dinner was ready.

High school started the next year. She loved history and was good at math. An urgent pragmatism took over Marlowe's life as her parents pushed her hard. They wanted more opportunities for her. Opportunities that would enable her to earn and do more, to move away from the frigid, stunted life they lived. Her dad had loved engineering when he was young and studied hard to learn robotics. Now, in his forties, he had plateaued as a maintenance supervisor overseeing repairs of a corporate fleet of fishing and crabbing drones. Her mom had loved and studied literature. She worked now as an English professor at one of Anchorage's community colleges. They had both followed their passions and got stuck in the lower middle-class eddies of the American economy. Disappointed, but not yet bitter, they wanted more for their daughter and pushed her toward business studies. They never said it, but the message was clear, her dreams of space were the indulgence of a child. *Get to work! You must do better than we did!*

When it came time for Marlowe to go to college, there was no money. Fortunately, the girl could play lacrosse. Really well.

In high school, she earned a state-wide reputation as "the diesel". She seemed slow at the start of each game. College scouts overlooked her until her senior year. Unremarkable in the first quarter, their attention would move on from Bonham. They would miss her momentum building, her RPM increasing as others around her started to flag. By late in the third quarter, though, she was humming like a warm diesel engine. Not many players could hang with her, but when the game entered the fourth quarter, her patient, methodical power surged and separated her. Even the most skilled players, whose lungs burned and legs melted, faltered. They made mistakes from pure exhaustion as she ran inexorably up and down the field, applying pressure everywhere. Her coach said she didn't win games so much as outlast them. In the state championship game her senior year, she scored five of her six goals in the fourth quarter, systematically dismantling a defense that had contained her for three periods. The opposition's star player, who had mocked Bonham's plodding style at halftime, could barely lift her stick by the end.

She got several scholarship offers, several for history and an equal number for business studies. There was no question which direction she would take. After a long family dinner and discussion, they settled finally on the University of Central Florida in Orlando. It was not Marlowe's first choice, but the decision was a no-brainer. Florida offered her a full ride and the most robust living allowance of the schools she applied to. UCF wanted to win at women's lacrosse. Badly. They thought the "Alaskan Diesel" could be their foundation.

Her parents seemed happy. It was a windfall to have college paid for, but Marlowe found her dad crying one evening. She came down late from her room to get a glass of water. He was in the kitchen, seated at the small family table, tears running down his face. "It's the right thing, baby," he told his daughter when she took his hand, terrified. "I'm so proud. It's just so damn far away. Promise me you will make the most of it."

"I promise, Daddy."

Marlowe worked hard in the classroom and kicked ass on the lacrosse field. She majored in business like her dad wanted, but snuck in a history minor by taking a few extra hours each semester. To her surprise she loved the golden age of exploration. Images of big vulnerable ships made of wood, propelled by the wind, crossing a dark and mysterious ocean, lit her imagination on fire.

She made the dean's list. Her parents were excited and pleased. Marlowe was going to make money.

Her dreams and fascination never faded, really. They were just swallowed. Packed down as deep as she could shove them. The few times she got home to Anchorage during school steeled her resolved. Her parents seemed to age ten years each semester she was away. Her younger brother, an earnest young man that worked hard but had none of her gifts, had not made it out. After high school, he got married and found a job as a deckhand on an offshore oil rig. He spent weeks at a time at sea, which was hard on his pregnant wife. Marlowe's parents let them move in.

Everyone was counting on her trajectory to continue. To be the one that broke free.

Marlowe would return to UCF more resolved after each visit. She would get it done. For them.

She only cracked once. Sitting out practice for a week her junior year because of a badly twisted ankle, she let her mind wander. She indulged in thoughts she had suppressed for years. An idea came to mind. It was stupid. She checked online and saw that the timing was actually perfect. That night, she hailed a taxi.

It was only an hour's ride, but it tortured her. The guilt. The excitement. The doubt. The curiosity wove around and tangled inside her head. She felt foolish when the vehicle dropped her off at an all-night diner in the small town around midnight. She almost told it to take her back to Orlando.

But she didn't.

The waitress let her doze off in one of the booths for a few hours. She started awake around five in the morning when the cops and military personnel started showing up for breakfast and morning coffee. After a large plate of waffles and eggs, Marlowe made her way to the bus station, where visitors could get a ride to the site.

The sun was rising as the bus pulled up to the viewing center. The bright orange haze on the horizon obscured the view of the tall vehicles in the distance. Marlowe followed the file of people into the metal bleachers. She was anxious as she sat down. *Was this really worth it? What a stupid thing to do with my Saturday morning. I've got so much homework.*

When the rocket's engines lit, her doubts were obliterated. A silent explosion of thick flame and smoke enveloped the launch pad almost two miles away while the top of the massive launch vehicle sat motionless, seemingly reluctant to leave Earth. Marlowe stood with the rest of the crowd.

Then the sound hit her.

The powerful, thunderous noise enveloped and passed through her. She felt the vibration in her ribs and the back of her throat. She raised her arms and stretched her fingers to feel more of it. She yelled back at it, and felt her scream dissolve and fall behind her, blown away by this force she had never before experienced.

The rocket lifted into the sky. Accelerating. Marlowe blinked twice and had to lean back to keep it in sight. Faster and faster. Higher and higher. The sound slowly weakened. She realized she was crying.

Marlowe sat in a daze on the rip back. By the time her taxi dropped her off back at her dorm in Orlando, she had recovered. A bit. But the experience never left her. The power. The sound. The vibration. The rocket's aching hesitance on the pad and then joyful rush to leave the planet. She never told anyone about it, but thought about it often. She wondered where the payload was at that moment. Was it orbiting Earth? On the moon? Did it go to Mars? Or to the asteroid belt? Beyond? She wished she knew. The enticing questions stayed with her.

Especially in Chicago.

Her sacred mission of fulfilling her parents' dream of a successful business career took her to the grey labyrinth of skyscrapers that blotted out the sky. Chicago was not all bad, of course. The vibrant social scene, the dramatic vertiginous city scape erupting around the river, the professional opportunity—it all propelled her forward, unexamined, toward…

Toward what?

After five years in the city, she seemed to have made it. Her parents visited from Anchorage and gawked at her apartment perched hundreds of feet above the river in the heart of town. Lights, people, drones, noise, commerce, sophistication. It was everything they wanted for her.

But Marlowe felt a disquiet. Her childhood dreams were deeply buried now. A vague itch. Inarticulate and all but gone. A shapeless discontent.

Then she met Amelia.

It was spring. Saturday morning. A chance, casual encounter. Marlowe was walking through a park near her apartment, just stretching her legs. Amelia was taking pictures of blossoming trees.

Amelia started it. An offhand observation as Marlowe walked by. They chatted. Got lunch. Chatted some more. Got dinner. Spent the night together at Marlowe's place. Amelia moved in three weeks later, leaving the artist commune she lived in with three roommates.

Amelia was a nature photographer and painter. Desperately poor, happy, imaginative and uncompromising. She re-introduced Marlow to life beyond the corporate pursuit of money. They travelled to national parks, spent hours in museums and took weekend trips to observatories as they fell in love. That Christmas, Marlowe took Amelia home to meet her parents.

It was a strange holiday for Bonham, seeing Amelia around her family. Her girlfriend was poor. More poor, even, than her own family, where discontent and frustration seemed to strangle everything, but Amelia was happy. While her parents fretted in the kitchen about bills and her brother's struggles on the oil rig, Amelia scavenged paper from around the house—envelopes, newspapers, and food wrappers. Sitting cross-legged on the worn carpet, she made a collage depicting the winter scenes around their house and, using the handful of colored pencils she took with her everywhere, she painstakingly drew portraits of Marlowe and her family in the middle.

Amelia gave the collage to Marlowe's parents on Christmas Day. Their bewildered reaction pained Marlowe. They were blind to beauty. She didn't want to be like that.

Amelia led Marlowe out of the gray tunnel her life had been for the past ten years. Marlowe's itch returned. *Why am I doing this corporate shit?* But it didn't matter. The corporate shit was paying for her and Amelia to have an extraordinary life. They travelled, talked and loved. It seemed to Marlowe they blinked and had been together for a year.

Marlowe's circle of high-powered friends elevated Amelia. Everyone loved her work. Her photography and paintings gained notoriety, first in Chicago, and then on the west coast. Her work increased in value. It started to sell. It was exciting. Amelia saved every dime from her paintings so that she could fund a trip to Africa. It was important to her to pay for it herself, with no help from Marlowe. One month to photograph and paint. It was her dream since forever. Marlowe was to take a month off and go with her. It was Amelia's gift to her.

When the time of the trip arrived, Amelia went alone. Something had come up at Marlowe's work. Her departure was delayed by two weeks. Half the trip. Amelia was enraged. They fought for three days.

On Amelia's day of departure, Marlowe rode with her to the airport. They held hands in silence. Both crying. Marlowe almost quit her job in that car. She wanted to get on the plane with Amelia. Maybe never even come back. But she didn't. That would be stupid. She wasn't brave enough.

They hugged for a long time at the curb. Marlowe could see the hurt and disappointment in Amelia's eyes. She wondered if the damage was permanent.

"I wish I could go with you today," Marlowe said.

Amelia looked back at Marlowe, her face a mask of sadness, eyes drowning in tears. She held her hand to Marlowe's cheek.

"Only you can make your wishes come true," Amelia said. "Until you are willing to fight for them, for your dreams… I just… I don't…"

Her voice trailed off. She dropped her hand and looked at the ground. The silence was too much for Marlowe.

"I promise I will be there in two weeks."

Amelia nodded, but did not lift her eyes. She turned and walked into the airport.

Ten days later, Amelia was dead. Mauled by a lioness. Seeking the perfect image, she had ignored the warnings of her guide and gotten too close to the cubs. It took them a day to recover the body. The lioness, in a rage, had dragged Amelia far and dismembered her.

If I had been there. It would not have happened.

Marlowe plummeted, her tether to life severed. She tried to anesthetize herself with work, trying to hide from the pain of Amelia's loss in the grey monochrome of corporate life. It worked for a short while. Sort of. And then she sank deeper. She found that alcohol numbed her. Just enough. She embraced it, spending most days intoxicated. She isolated herself from her friends and family and descended into a moody, irritable haze. She was an angry drunk, seeking confrontation. She got in fights at work, in her apartment building, on the phone, in bars.

Her work friends begged her to get help. Her family did as well. Her father and brother flew down to intervene. She cursed them for fools. Finally, reluctantly, she tried rehab, but it didn't stick. Six months after Amelia's death, Marlowe was fired from her job. She stopped paying rent. A few months later, she was kicked out of her high-end apartment.

Not yet out of money, she got a room at a cheap hotel and drank and drank and drank.

Her days became a blurred routine that began beneath the aching haze of a hangover and ended in the blissful oblivion of an alcohol induced black out. More than once she woke to find herself on a sidewalk or in a stranger's bed. Figuring out where she was and how to get back to her shitty hotel room was a problem-solving diversion from her depression that typically lasted a few hours. After a shower and a nap, she was off to find more booze.

On the days she stayed in her hotel room, she lay motionless on the bed, watching the twenty-four-hour news coverage of the war in South America. The US Military had launched a bloody effort to retake Santiago after its humiliating retreat a year earlier. Marlowe didn't know anything about the military, but it looked like a doomed effort. A lot of people were dying. She wished she were there so she could die.

Why didn't she die? How much did she have to poison her body to make it give up like her spirit had?

And why didn't she just kill herself more quickly? Marlowe had a gun, after all.

She stole the gun from one of the drunken strangers she had slept with.

Maybe he was a cop? She didn't remember, but she woke up early that day for some reason. The man lay snoring as she picked her clothes off the floor and left the bedroom to get dressed. Grabbing the whiskey from his liquor closet, Marlowe headed for the door. She checked the side table by the front door before leaving. She often found cash and other things of value there when she left people's places. She wasn't working anymore and needed the money.

This time, though, a pistol lay in the drawer. She looked over her shoulder at the bedroom door and then back at the weapon.

I can help you, it seemed to say. *I can make it quick and easy.*

Growing up in Alaska, firearms were not foreign to her. Her father taught her to shoot when she was twelve, and she went with him on hunting and camping trips north of Anchorage. She knew how to handle a weapon.

And she wanted to die.

Marlowe grabbed the pistol and snuck out of the door. Feeling the weight of the weapon stuffed into her waistband, under her shirt, as she hustled back to her motel gave Marlowe a feeling of peace. She had a way out now. Why had this way out not occurred to her before? She did not have to go on without Amelia. Fuck this place.

That night she held the pistol to her head, sitting on the toilet in the bathroom, sobbing. She missed Amelia so badly. She hated herself so much. She was ready for it to end.

But she couldn't pull the trigger.

She cursed herself for a coward.

A year passed, and the pistol lay hidden in her suitcase.

One morning, Marlow laid in bed thinking about what to drink that day, idly flipping through the news on the crappy hotel television. She paused. A news reporter sat in front of images of a rocket launching, sailing into the sky on plumes of flame and smoke.

Old memories stirred.

The stars on a clear night in Alaska, the power and noise of the launch at Canaveral.

Marlowe sat up. She turned up the volume. The reporter droned on about the new space race. The country needed astronauts. Something about the Chinese and the war. It all sounded dire and weighty, the stakes of it all, but the phrase that pierced the haze of her alcohol addled mind was, "Anyone under thirty-years-old can apply."

Marlowe thought about it. She did the math in her fuzzy head twice to be sure. Then she got out of bed and took a shower. She stood under the faucet, letting the water run over her and made a deal with herself. *You can try. You can go for it. But if you don't make it, you will kill yourself.*

Marlowe felt a flicker of something inside her. It was unfamiliar. She couldn't tell if it was excitement or happiness or what. But she knew why it was there. She was leaving. One way or the other, she was leaving this planet where her heart broke.

* * *

In 2051, America needed more ships and facilities in space. Both military and commercial. It also needed men and women to crew those ships and facilities. And it needed them quickly. China's ability to decisively pivot its resources toward a strategic imperative conferred an advantage over the more independent and chaotic market economies and private sectors of the free world. The west was learning that the Chinese had turned their attention to space in earnest before the blood of their vanquished army had dried in the streets of Santiago. Democracies in the west exhibited their characteristic slowness to respond. They exhaled with relief after the Second Battle of Santiago and then fiddled and talked while the communist leviathan acted. China was ahead in the race for the commercial and military high ground of space.

When America did tune in and focus, it saw China had more people, assets, facilities, and resources in space. Furthermore, its manipulatively generous financing and partnerships with other nation's efforts in space lent it outsized influence out there. China was the undisputed superpower outside of earth's atmosphere.

Finally frightened into action, America spun up a Merchant Spacefarer program modeled off the Merchant Marine program that had crewed the nation's surface ships since the Revolutionary War. The US Space Command funded the training of qualified candidates for service in space. Once trained, the spacefarers were obligated to serve on American-flagged civilian vessels. The trained individuals had a service commitment of five years of duty in space.

Congress also authorized the construction of a large military fleet and numerous facilities in orbit, on the moon, and on Mars. Finally, the government offered interest-free loans and tax credits to shipping companies, encouraging them to rapidly expand their fleets. The investment and subsidies tilted the returns American businesses could reap in the young space industries far into the green, and the military was swimming in capital and operational dollars earmarked for space. The fuse was lit. The mad rush off planet had begun.

The surge in astronaut training was a spasmodic, lurching chaos. The old training center in Houston was quickly overwhelmed, so Space Command set up several feeder facilities on US Military bases across the country. In an effort to get bodies off planet as quickly as possible, the curriculum was cut down to the barest minimum. The reasoning was that graduates of the Merchant Spacefarer program would owe five years and could be trained in more specialized tasks on the job once they got to their first duty station. The result, though, was that the American space effort was flooded with spacefarers that could barely keep themselves alive and extracted a large training cost out of every ship, facility and outpost they reported to. Space Command was not ignorant of this, of course, but judged it to be the least worst path to match Chinese resources off planet.

The training centers took their responsibility seriously. They trained the recruits hard and were quick to cut those that did not measure up. Less than a third of those that signed up and were accepted into the program actually pinned on astronaut wings a year later at one of the many graduation ceremonies. An attrition rate that drove the Merchant Spacefarer recruiting operation crazy. It seemed they could never catch up.

In November 2052, Marlowe Bonham graduated from the spacefarer program in a hasty ceremony thrown together in a gymnasium on Johnson

Space Center in Houston. She was happy. She had made it.

And she not just squeaked by. Despite being the oldest, by far, in her class, and frankly the oldest that any of her instructors could remember, she consistently ranked at the top of her class. No matter the task, Marlowe Bonham tore it up. It felt good, too. She had not had a singular focus like this since lacrosse. She felt the old Alaskan Diesel inside her again. She loved the feeling.

But her pride and satisfaction were tinged with disappointment. A foreboding that built as graduation came and went. It grew for weeks after until she found herself thinking about drinking again, about that pistol. About the deal she had made with herself. She had hoped her gamble would pay off, but it looked like she could not escape the simple dynamics of the program any more than she could escape gravity.

She was old. Sure, she had made the cutoff to get into the program fair and square, but it didn't change the fact that the ship's captains and facility's commanders got to draft and approve everyone that joined their crews. On graduation day, about ninety percent of Marlowe's class had orders and a launch date. A month after graduation, the entire class did, except for her.

The training cadre at Houston loved Marlowe and talked to her about becoming an instructor. Marlowe listened politely and hid her desire to scream, but had no intention of becoming a trainer. Besides, Houston sucked.

Two months after graduation, Marlowe accepted the offer of becoming a trainer. She only did it to avoid being kicked out of the barracks at Johnson Space Center. She needed a place to live, but not for much longer.

Marlowe had still managed to keep herself off of the drink, but hope had left her. She was never getting off planet. She kept herself sober because she believed that was why she had not been able to pull the trigger before. Alcohol dulled her resolution. Well, she was committed now. She would do it this weekend.

There was a launch late Saturday morning. Johnson did not launch as many vehicles as Canaveral, but it was still an active facility. Marlowe planned to go to the launch, bathe in the power and vibration of the rocket, and in that maelstrom of sound and energy, find the courage to pull the trigger. It would be over. She would be free of the pain.

Marlowe woke early on Saturday with a feeling of resigned peace. She was heartbroken, but she had tried. Soon, she would be free and could rest. Maybe see Amelia.

No. She wouldn't, and she knew it.

But she would stop missing her.

Marlowe spent some time sitting outside the barracks, looking up at the rocket shell that stood in the barracks quad. It was a small cargo vehicle relative to the behemoths that now leapt off the planet daily, but it towered over the small scale of the quad. Stripped of its engine and other internal organs, it was put on display to help the harried astronaut candidates keep their goal in mind.

Marlowe felt a kinship to the hollowed-out vehicle. Both made for the stars, neither made it off the planet. She wondered what mishap of fortune condemned this tall, would-be-space vehicle to eternity on Earth. Was it somehow the same as her? Failure to recognize its own purpose early enough? A heart-breaking blow that knocked it irretrievably off course?

It didn't matter.

She was lucky. She would not be propped up, immobile, against her will much longer.

Marlowe stood up, shouldered her pack, and headed for the bus to the launch site.

She could feel the weighty hardness of the pistol in her pack against her back. It was a comforting feeling.

The bus wove through the training campus, making its way toward the active launch pads. Candidates jogged up and down the road or walked in small groups toward the mess hall. Marlowe shook her head. They looked young. Suddenly, she realized how foolish she had been. They would never send someone like her, now almost thirty-two years old, into space for the first time.

Marlowe's phone buzzed in her pocket. She ignored it.

The bus turned off of the main campus. Marlowe settled into her seat for the thirty-minute ride down the mostly straight road that led to the launch pads. Closing her eyes, she leaned her head back.

Her phone buzzed again as she stepped off the bus. She ignored it again, looking around to find the right spot. She didn't want to be in the stands as someone might try to stop her, but she wanted to be able to see the pad and feel the sound and power wash over her. There was a small rise a few hundred yards away that looked perfect. On the periphery but still accessible, she would be out of everyone's way and free to do what she had come to do.

Her phone buzzed again as she walked toward the spot. She didn't answer, but wondered if there was anyone she should call? No, she decided. She also wasn't leaving a note. The only person she cared to explain things to was dead anyway.

On the small rise, Marlowe took off her pack and set up. She pulled a small blanket out and lay it on the ground. Glancing around to make sure no one was paying attention, she pulled the pistol out. She sat down, cross-legged on the blanket, the pistol between her knees.

The launch clock read two minutes, the orange digital seconds ticking away. Steam rose from the launch pad, two miles distant. The vehicle stood tall, a bulbous crew compartment on top. Marlowe thought of the young astronauts in that compartment. How excited they must be. How excited she would be. She closed her eyes and reached down to touch the pistol. All of this longing and disappointment will soon be over.

Her phone buzzed again, disrupting her calm.

Dammit.

She put the phone to her ear in an irritated huff.

"What is it?" She snarled.

"Bonham. It's Rodriguez."

Marlowe rolled her eyes. *Perfect. They are going to try to make me clean latrines on the day I kill myself.*

Rodriguez was the dean of the Merchant Spacefarer Program at Houston. He liked Marlowe. Liked her grit and intelligence. That did not spare her from the various shit details that he had to assign daily to keep the place functioning. A military combat veteran, he ran his program like a military school. As a graduate newly appointed to the training cadre, Marlowe was a resource he tapped daily to lead shit details. He knew she was a good leader. Not all spacefarers were. In fact, most fell into the technician category. Bonham, though, could take a group of people and get shit done. This morning, in fact, she was supposed to be leading a barracks cleaning detail for one of the old barracks that was unoccupied for the next week in between classes.

Marlow figured Rodriguez was chasing her down to bark at her for not being at her assigned place of duty. She glanced at the launch clock. About a minute to go.

"Yeah?"

"I'm over at Aldrin Barracks. Where are you?"

A faint smile came to her face as she prepared to savor telling Rodriguez to fuck right off.

"Yeah… Well, I decided to come out and watch the launch this morning."

That should do it, she thought. *I should get a rise out of the old bastard now.*

Rodriguez hesitated. Marlowe could hear the sounds of candidate activity in the background.

"You OK, Bonham?" He finally asked. "You don't sound good."

The question pierced her. She put her hand to her heart.

It's been a long time since I've been good.

The launch clock was down to a minute.

"Bonham?"

Her throat clinched. Rodriguez was a good man. She suddenly didn't want to go out telling him to fuck off. She wanted to apologize. She wanted to let him know she looked up to him and wish she had made it. She wanted to beg for another chance. At all of it. To have had the courage to follow her dream from the beginning. Or at least to have gone to Africa with Amelia when she should have. Her hand dropped from her heart and sank between her legs. Her fingers wrapped around the pistol grip, one resting on the trigger.

"Sir… I… I just want to…"

Marlow fought the tears. She didn't want the last thing anyone heard from her to be sobbing. She lifted the pistol and placed it on top of her thigh.

The launch clock was at thirty seconds. A large billow of steam spilled out of the pad superstructure in the distance.

"Goodbye, Mr. Rodriguez," she said, lowering the phone from her ear and lifting the gun to her head.

"Hang on, Bonham," he said in a tone that made her hesitate. Out of reflex, she lifted the phone back to her ear.

"I don't give a shit about the barracks cleaning detail. I'm glad you're out at the launch this morning because I have news for you, candidate. Olsen was in a vehicle accident last night in downtown Houston. Got banged up pretty bad. Leg broken, face smashed. Won't make his launch date. Space Command asked me for a replacement."

The clock was down to fifteen seconds.

"I gave them your name."

Marlowe blinked. Gun to her temple.

"They balked at your age, of course. But I told them there was no better candidate in the program. Period."

Ten seconds.

"Need you to report to pre-flight in the morning. Your launch date is in twenty-six days. You are going to space, Marlowe Bonham!"

An eruption of fire and smoke expanded on the launch pad. Nine seconds later, ear-splitting thunder rolled over the viewing area. All eyes were fixed on the vehicle rising into the sky. No one noticed the woman on the small rise a few hundred yards from the stands, standing with her arms raised, shouting into the sound of the rocket with all her futile might.

Chapter Forty-Three

George Remus

The *Remus* held station a kilometer from the *Perseus*. George had parked the gunboat abeam the old girl's bridge, lined up parallel, facing the same direction.

The *Perseus* dwarfed the Company ship, seeming to extend forever in both directions as Rojas looked at her through one of the small observation windows on the operations deck. Her dingy gray flanks were dented and burned in places and most of her cargo slots were empty, testimony to the recent battle to subdue her.

The density of the cloud shocked Rojas. Despite the short distance between the two ships, a fog of tiny debris and gasses still partially obscured the *Perseus*, thickening, then dispersing, then thickening again as if choreographed by an unseen hand, filling Rojas with a sense of unease. Cargo containers and shattered maintenance drones drifted in all directions, huge shadowy asteroids menaced nearby, and chemical reactions flared around the gunboat and in the distance.

"Sir, Deke is ready for you," Finnie said from across the deck.

Grateful for the distraction, Rojas turned from the window. Shaking his head to clear away the foreboding, he walked over to her side and stood in front of one of the video displays.

At least communications were now reliable.

Deke stood in the middle of the *Perseus'* bridge. Behind him, several human and robotic soldiers floated in and out of frame as they went about the business of consolidating control of the freighter.

The captain smiled at the image of his friend. He looked tired to Rojas.

"Good to have solid coms, sir," Deke said. "But I wish you hadn't brought the *Remus* into the cloud."

"This from the guy that lectured all of us on not letting his boarding team go into the cloud without him?" Rojas turned his head to Finnie and rolled his eyes.

Deke chuckled with resignation.

"I don't want the *Remus* in this cloud one second longer than she has to be," Rojas said, looking back at Deke. "But communication and coordination are critical in this phase of the operations. We'll move out as soon as we can. So let's focus on the tasks at hand and execute."

"Roger that, sir." Deke nodded.

"Status report, please," Rojas said.

"The ship is secure, repairs are in progress, and we have located all occupants, including the original crew. Their condition is good. The pirates apparently treated them well. Captain Hoffman has demanded to speak with you."

"Regarding?"

"His command, sir."

"His command?"

"The *Perseus*, sir. He... well, he considers himself to still be captain of the ship."

Rojas exhaled and shook his head. It took a lot of balls to command a space craft. Those balls often came with a fair amount of ego. Rojas hated dealing with ego.

"What did you tell him?"

"I told him Standard Operating Procedure was to medically evaluate him and the rest of his crew. Then you, as mission commander, would make a determination as to the status of his command."

Rojas chuckled. "Not bad."

Deke shrugged.

There was zero chance of Hoffman being reinstated as captain. The Company would want to investigate the incident and evaluate Hoffman and his crew's performance. That would take months. Maybe years.

Finnie would take command of the *Perseus* when the repair operations were complete and follow the *Remus* back to the Company's Mars station.

But there was no need to rub that in Hoffman's face at the moment.

"And the pirates?" Rojas asked.

"Strange group."

"They always are."

"True." Deke smiled. "But this crew tops them all."

"Do tell."

"Three AI enabled soldierbots, one synthetic female, and one human male."

Finnie chuckled. "That's a strange menagerie."

"And you will not believe this, sir," Deke said, eyebrows arching as if he were surprised all over again. "Paul Owens is their leader."

Rojas and Finnie stared back at Deke.

"Paul Owens," Deke repeated, disappointed at their lack of reaction.

Rojas and Finnie shared a quick glance, each confirming the other had no idea what Deke was talking about.

"Paul Owens," Deke stated with irritation. "That American military captain that went on an illegal killing rampage with a team of AI soldierbots down in Argentina back in '66."

Rojas nodded slowly. "I think I remember that."

"I don't," Finnie said.

"He was a highly decorated Centaur," Deke said. "Something happened to one of his fellow Centaurs and he snapped. Anyway, they sent him to Leavenworth. Life sentence, as I recall."

"So what is he doing on the *Perseus*?" Finnie asked.

"He was part of that crazy-assed Fly it Off program."

Finnie crossed her arms as she shook her head. "I never liked that misguided bullshit."

"Get this," Deke said, leaning closer to the camera. "He was assigned to the *Odysseus*."

Rojas cocked his head.

"The *Odysseus*?"

"Yes, sir." Deke nodded and smiled, watching Rojas's mental gears spin the way his had about an hour ago.

"You know that derelict looking piece of shit lifeboat we were wondering about?" Deke asked him. "The one stowed on the lower aft end of the *Perseus*?"

"Yes."

"It bears Company markings from the *Odysseus*."

Rojas blinked a few times. Finnie uncrossed her arms and turned her head slowly to look at her captain.

He met her glance and muttered, "How much craziness can the void jam into one mission?"

Finnie chuckled and shrugged.

"OK. Well, we'll deal with all that drama when the time is right," Rojas said, turning back to Deke. "Are you ready for shift change?"

"Yes, sir. The *Perseus* is secure. We might as well."

Rojas nodded and then turned his head toward Kozlov.

"Roger that, sir," Kozlov said. "I will begin the recall and have *Dagger* ferry over the relief team." He turned from the holo-table and went back to his station to begin the complex choreography of getting the *Remus'* humans and robotic assault force back on board. When they were done, Finnie would be in command of the *Perseus* with a crew of six security personnel for the sprint back to Mars.

"Have you heard from the maintenance team yet?" Rojas asked Deke.

"Actually heard from them while we have been talking, sir."

There was something in Deke's tone of voice that Rojas did not like.

"What is it?"

"You're not going to like it."

Rojas waited silently, jaw set, lips pressed together.

"They are telling me repairs are gonna take twelve hours."

"Unacceptable!" Rojas shook his head vigorously.

"I agree, sir."

"We need to be underway, out of this cloud, and headed toward Mars in no more than two."

"Yes, sir."

"I'm serious, Deke. I don't care what you have to do. Get that old girl moving."

Deke's face tightening with irritation.

"Sir, do you really think I need to be told to hurry the fuck up?"

Finnie's eyebrows raised at the comment. She looked at the captain and then at her feet.

Deke closed his eyes and shook his head.

"I'm sorry, sir."

He opened his eyes.

"It's OK, Deke," Rojas said. "This has been a long one."

"It certainly has, sir."

Chapter Forty-Four

Wharf Rat

Bonham chuckled at the sight of Axe. His scarred face, which she had grown so used to over the years, was puffy and discolored, and his eyes were bloodshot. He was walking awkwardly around the command deck, as if new to mag boots. Bonham knew the reason—soreness and bruising on his extremities from the G-MASS's efforts to fight blood pooling during their acceleration. The damn system squeezed like hell when it had to.

She knew she looked worse.

The whole crew had bloodshot eyes. Angry red lines caused by the stress of acceleration turned their whites pink. Bonham's were more dramatic, though. Her eyes were a jarring beet-red, accompanied by faint bruising under each. She didn't suffer the soreness some of the crew did, but her hands were discolored from blood pooling, giving them the appearance of severe bruising, as if she had been in a bad fist fight. Her feet were as well.

The anti-inflammation and drugs and hydration would lessen the effects over time, but at the moment, the crew of the *Wharf Rat* looked like they were recovering from a weeklong drinking bender that ended in a rough bar fight, not 5Gs for just ten minutes.

"What's our rate of closure with the cloud, Renate?" Quinn asked in a scratchy voice. He still had a dry mouth from his time in the G-MASS.

"Sir, we are closing on the cloud at 105,840 kilometers per hour."

Quinn nodded as he took a pull of water from the bottle in his hand. He swallowed and wiped his mouth. "How long till we get there?"

"Approximately two hours and sixteen minutes at our current rate of closure."

The holo-display in the middle of the deck projected the cloud on one side of the room and the *Wharf Rat* on the other. A line with tick marks on it scribed the ship's course to the cloud, each tick mark a hundred kilometers. The holographic *Wharf Rat* ate the tick marks at a rate of about one every three seconds.

Bonham stomped through the line toward Quinn.

"We better have a plan to escape when the gunboat emerges from that cloud," she said, stopping by the captain's chair, standing over Quinn and pointing at the multi-colored, 3D image. "Which I predict will be momentarily."

Quinn looked at Bonham and then rubbed his eyes. They weren't as bad as hers, but they were bad. He took another long drink of water and then looked across the deck at Singh.

"I don't know," Axe mumbled as he stepped between the image of the cloud and the image of the *Wharf Rat*. "I think they are good and lost in there."

Bonham's head snapped around. She glared at her old comrade.

Reeve stepped next to Axe, nodding.

Landsberg drifted up behind them, looking over Axe's shoulder.

Bonham looked back at Quinn.

"I'm serious, Captain! Company gunboats have standing orders to pursue and destroy pirates whenever they can."

Quinn nodded at her, but kept his eyes on the cloud across the command deck.

"Singh, can you get some escape routines going with Renate? Have algos running at all times so we can burn and run if we need to?"

"Roger that, captain," Singh nodded. He pushed off the floor and left the command deck, headed for navigation.

"And let's all stay in our G-MASS suits until further notice," Quinn said, sweeping his bloodshot gaze around the room to make eye contact with each crew member except for Bonham. "In case the burn needs to be heavy to get away, yeah?"

"Aye," Reeve said as the others nodded.

Quinn looked up Bonham.

Bonham's glare softened a bit. She stood straighter and crossed his arms.

Quinn smiled. He stood and walked by Bonham to join the rest of the crew that had gathered around the image of the cloud.

Axe stood with his artificial hand on his hip. He rubbed his scarred chin with his human hand, eyes narrowed in thought.

"How many EMP missiles we got, Axe?" Quinn asked as he stepped next to the tall pirate.

"Three."

Quinn looked at Landy. "And how many munition propulsion systems could you pull together?"

Landsberg scratched his head in thought.

"To carry a real payload?"

Quinn nodded. "To deliver a real punch."

Axe looked back over his shoulder at Landsberg.

"A dozen?" Landsberg said. "Maybe less."

Axe turned his head back and looked at Quinn as his left eyebrow ticked up half a degree. His jaw relaxed into something that wasn't quite a smile, but it made Bonham's heart sink.

She shook her head in sadness. *They are gonna try it. Their bloodlust is up. They can't resist. Like a tide pulled forward by the moon... The closer we get the stupider they become.*

"What if we put two EMPs on the Company gunboat? And one on the Perseus?" Quinn wondered out loud.

Bonham turned and left the command deck.

I can't listen to this shit.

Chapter Forty-Five

Perseus

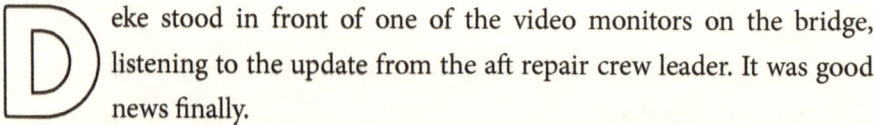eke stood in front of one of the video monitors on the bridge, listening to the update from the aft repair crew leader. It was good news finally.

"We are making quicker than expected progress. Don't hold me to it, sir, but I think we can have her main propulsion system back online in about two hours. Maybe a little more."

"Outstanding, Scott," Deke said. "You do that and they going to erect a statue dedicated to you on the bridge of the *Remus*."

The maintenance leader chuckled and shook his head. Scott had worked for the Company for almost twenty years. Most of those underway in the void, and always in a maintenance role. He and Deke had served on several cruises together.

"I'd settle for a few drinks back on Mars, sir."

"Deal!"

Deke smiled. Finally, some good news. He was about to contact Captain Rojas with the update when a commotion on the other side of the bridge caught his attention. The sounds of raised voices and scuffling feet echoed through the space, disrupting the focused atmosphere that had settled over the crew.

Frowning, Deke looked over his shoulder, the moment of optimism quickly fading.

What now? He thought.

Two of his human soldiers were holding someone back. The visitor had just come up from the bridge tower and was floating over the open floor airlock.

"I demand to talk to the person in charge!" the person shouted.

I recognize that voice.

Terrific.

"Keep me updated," Deke said, turning back to the screen. "I need to drop."

"I will, sir."

A soldier named Mansoura met Deke halfway as he floated over toward the confrontation above the airlock. He was a fresh member of the shift change that been on board for about half an hour. Deke reminded himself that the relief crew comprised junior, mostly inexperienced newbies, and told himself not to get frustrated.

"I gave orders for Hoffman to be confined to quarters," Deke said to Mansoura with irritation.

"You did, sir." The soldier shook his head. "But he bufflaloed Jennings."

Deke shook his head. Jennings was the most junior member of the shift change crew, not even twenty years old. This was his first tour off planet. Deke pushed a mag boot to the floor and accelerated toward the confrontation.

Jennings met him first.

"I'm sorry, sir. But he told me he was going to have us all brought up on charges when we get back to Mars."

"It's OK, son," Deke said in a low, calming voice. "Next time, though, you stick to my orders."

"Who is in charge here?" Hoffman shouted as two soldiers held him back.

Deke gently pushed Jennings out of the way.

"I am," he said, floating up behind the two soldiers restraining the irate former captain. He put a hand on one of the soldiers and gestured at them to release Hoffman.

One of the soldiers shot Deke an are-you-sure glance.

Deke nodded.

The two soldiers dropped their arms to their sides.

Hoffman glared at them and then focused on Deke.

"What is your name?" he demanded.

"I am commander Sadhik Syed of the *George Remus,*" Deke said. *This asshole doesn't get to call me Deke.*

"Are you in charge of this operation?"

"I am."

"Good. My name is Captain Hoffman. I demand to be restored to command of my ship this instant."

I am not in the mood for this, Deke thought, trying to put on a friendly face.

"Look, Hoffman. I know you and your crew have been through a lot. I think—"

"It's Captain Hoffman!" Hoffman yelled. "And do not attempt to placate me! My crew and I were held prisoner on this ship for years and I am in no mood! I intend to take command of my ship and have the pirates executed immediately."

"I understand," Deke said, nodding and raising his hands in a calming gesture. "Let me—"

"I am done with this conversation! Stand aside and bring my crew to the bridge!"

Hoffman shoved one of the soldiers between him and Deke.

Fuck this guy.

Deke planted a mag boot on the deck and punched Hoffman in the nose.

Hoffman's head snapped back, blood spraying into the air in perfect spherical blobs that splattered against the two surprised soldiers and shot up to the ceiling.

Jennings's eyes got wide.

Deke pushed off the floor and launched into Hoffman. He grabbed the dazed former captain by the throat and shouted into his face. Blood, still flowing from Hoffman's nose, sprayed onto Deke's face.

He didn't notice.

"You're not captain of jack shit anymore! You lost command of your ship to a broke down military veteran, a female fuckbot, and a couple rust bucket robots. So the Company extended our cruise and made us shag our asses out here to take their ship back. Which we fucking did!"

Deke slapped the lolling Hoffman across the face to get him to focus, continuing only after he had eye contact with the man.

"I am the captain of the *Perseus* now. If you interfere with my mission or harass my crew in any way, I will have you spaced. Is that fucking clear?"

Hoffman, choking on blood from his broken nose, did not respond.

Deke slapped him hard across the face again.

More blood sprayed onto the two guards.

"Is that clear?" Deke yelled.

Hoffman nodded spasmodically, raising a hand to guard against another hard slap.

"Say it!"

Hoffman coughed.

Deke readied another slap.

"Y... Yes." Hoffman sputtered.

"Yes, what?"

"Yes, Captain."

Deke released Hoffman's throat.

"Jennings, take this man back to confinement. If he gives you any trouble or lip, space him."

"Yes, sir," Jennings said, moving forward to take Hoffman's arm.

Deke made eye contact with the other two guards, ensuring they knew to go with the young soldier to back him up. Then he pushed off and floated back to the center of the bridge.

A couple members of his team resisted the urge to glance at their commander and stifled smiles. They were familiar with Deke's ways. Stern but patient with his own, his temper was quick and ferocious with outsiders. They appreciated it.

One of his men brought Deke a cloth towel. He cleaned Hoffman's blood off his face.

Chapter Forty-Six

Wharf Rat

Bonham tried to stay in her quarters. She didn't want any part of the foolishness on the command deck and told herself they would abandon their misguided efforts when they realized it was futile. Truthfully, they may get there quicker if she wasn't there. Perhaps the facts of the situation would speak louder for themselves, than when she, the washed up, over-cautious former captain, presented them. However it went, this was just part of being on a crew. Things didn't always go your way. Sometimes you got out voted. You had to do shit you didn't want to do. In the end, she loved and trusted her crew.

But, she also knew, all ships eventually make mistakes in the void.

She grabbed one of her favorite physical books and strapped into one of the oversized chairs. The worn out, seventy-five-year-old hardback copy of *A General History of the Robberies and Murders of the Most Notorious Pyrates* was her go-to diversionary read. She loved that it was written almost 350 years ago, but still resonated with her so deeply. The formal yet vivid prose and grandiose storytelling style always managed to divert her mind from the challenges and drama of the *Wharf Rat*.

Until now.

As the minutes ticked by, Bonham's anxiety grew. Her eyes lifted often from the page, glaring at the hatch to her quarters until she forced them back to the text. After half an hour, when still nobody had come by to tell her they had given up and were going to head in another direction and spin the Ring, her anxiety and anger got the best of her. She replaced the trusty old book and went back to the command deck.

She didn't like what she found.

The crew was assembled, strapped into their chairs, except for Quinn. He stood in the middle, mag boots fastened to the deck, talking through elements of a plan.

Every head swiveled to look at Bonham as she floated to her chair and buckled herself in.

"Glad you're here," Quinn said. "We're gonna vote soon."

"Oh yeah? On what?"

"The plan to take the *Perseus*," Axe stated.

Bonham glared back at him in silence.

Quinn looked from Bonham to Axe and back again. The rest of the crew waited.

Clearing his throat, he continued. "As I was saying, if we can get close enough, we will fire all three EMP missiles at—"

"Oh, for fuckssake," Bonham said in a sad voice, placing her head in her hands.

All heads turned to face her.

"What's your problem?" Axe growled at her.

Bonham took a deep breath as she lifted her head. She glanced around at the crew before raising her eyes to the ceiling.

"Renate, how long to the cloud?"

"Approximately one hour and forty-nine minutes."

The holo-display, which the crew had been using to devise an attack plan, snapped back to the three-dimensional image of the *Wharf Rat* on one side of the deck and the cloud on the other. The marked course line extended from the *Wharf Rat* and pierced the cloud. There were a lot fewer tick marks than when Bonham left earlier.

Bonham nodded with resignation, lowering her eyes to rest on Axe. She kept her eyes on him as she spoke.

"With every second that passes, we are getting closer to a Company gunboat. A gunboat that could emerge from that cloud at any moment. When it does, its alarms will scream and klang and it will come after us. Because that is what Company gunboats do. They chase down pirates and kill them. They're good at it.

"We will burn and run, of course, the minute they see us. And we will probably get away. But we already burned half our propellent on that ten-minute sprint. So, if we get away, we'll be low on fuel, low on credits, and low on options.

"I think we have taken a grave risk just to get to this point. And you ask me what my problem is, Axe? I say we should break off this fool's errand now, before it destroys us."

Axe crossed his arms. She could tell his position had hardened, but she didn't want to give up yet.

"Let's say that gunboat stays in the cloud long enough," Bonham said. "Stays blind. And we can get close enough to run whatever ridiculous plan you all have cooked up."

She shrugged.

"Are we prepared to destroy a Company gunboat? Because that is what we will have to do, or they will keep coming. Unless we destroy them. Utterly."

The rest of the crew pounded their arm rests as Quinn and Axe nodded.

"Renate," Bonham said. "How many souls on board an average Company gunboat?"

"Company gunboats average between seventy-five and one hundred crew."

Bonham looked around the command deck.

"So, we are going to execute a hundred souls?"

"Hell yes," Eriksson said with a lusty chuckle. "It's a Company gunboat."

"You said yourself they would run us down and kill us if they could." Landsberg said.

"We are talking about the Company here," Reeves said. "Why the sudden vein of mercy?"

"We've always done what we have to do." Bonham nodded. "It's true. There is no place for indecision in the void. But we've never done it like this. It merits discussion."

"We are a pirate ship," Quinn said. "Not a saintly order."

"We attack to subdue," Bonham said, shaking her head. "We raid to steal. Those that resist are killed. Those that don't receive mercy. That has been our way since the *Wharf Rat* took her name."

"We've never taken on a Company gunboat before," Axe said.

Bonham's head tilted at the comment.

"A Company gunboat that is in the process of attacking fellow pirates," he continued. "This is not a ship of mercy we are talking about."

Reeve and Eriksson thumped their arm rests. Landsberg's eyes darted around.

"Fellow pirates?" Bonham said with a cynical chuckle. "That we ourselves are on the way to attack."

"That's right. And whom we will offer quarter." Axe said. "Consistent with the code you just laid out. But that gunship is Company! They would offer us no quarter! No mercy!"

"So, we should murder them?"

Axe shook his head in frustration.

The command deck waited in silence for him to continue.

"We do not dictate the terms of the void, Marlowe," Axe said in a softer voice. The use of Bonham's first name caught everyone off guard. "We take things as they come, as we find them, as they are pressed on us. In a million encounters with a Company gunboat, we would burn and run every time. There is no circumstance in which we could face them in a standup fight."

"But on the million and first time…"

Axe's voice trailed off and his misshapen mouth bent into an approximation of a smile.

Reeve and Eriksson thumped their arm rest again. Landsberg joined them.

"I have plied the void for twenty-two years," Axe continued, looking at Bonham. "Many of those years, you and I have been together. I know how cold and cruel the void can be. I know that you do, too. Because you saved me."

Bonham raised her head slightly, surprised by Axe's mention of their past.

"You remember what you said when I woke up? When I tried to thank you?"

Several of the rapt crew leaned in. None had heard this story.

Bonham shook her head slowly.

"You told me it was just lucky timing."

Bonham blinked rapidly and her bloodshot eyes got moist.

"You told me you didn't know why, and that it didn't matter, anyway. The void put the *Wharf Rat* close enough where you could take action. Save me. The timing just worked, and so you did."

Bonham's jaw was set now. She could see where this was going.

"I know better than most. Timing is all out here. How much fuel? How much distance? How much air? How fast? Milliseconds make a difference. Life. Death. Suffering. Oblivion. Time is how the void delivers judgement.

"This gunboat, driven by the same prize that has caused us to risk so much, is blind," Axe pointed at the image of the cloud. "And if she stays in that cloud long enough, and our timing is right, and we run the right play, we have the chance to deliver the void's judgement ourselves."

More thumping of armrests.

Bonham's jaw worked as she considered Axe's words, her eyes never leaving his face. Axe's bloodshot eyes were locked on Bonham's. His face was splotchy, discolored scare tissue fracturing the flush of his emotions. It was as if the two were continuing their argument on their own frequency.

A silent understanding seemed to pass between them. Bonham sagged in her seat.

"I call for the vote," Axe said, his voice carrying across the deck.

"I vote no," Bonham said, her voice barely above a whisper.

Axe nodded.

Bonham unbuckled and left the command deck as the crew voted.

She went back to her quarters, lost in memory and sadness.

Chapter Forty-Seven

Bonham remembered when they came across Axe twelve years ago. It was dumb luck. The *Wharf Rat's* passive sensors detected a large-ish object drifting through the void. Long range optics determined it to be manmade. No emissions, but it seemed to be powered—its temperature was too high for a derelict object. It was extremely rare to just happen across a decent salvage, so the crew was excited. Expanding their scans, the *Wharf Rat* detected other large objects moving away from the potential salvage at high speed. No engine burns, but the retreating objects' lingering heat signatures that implied there had been. Millions of miles away now, though, the objects were unidentifiable and were no factor.

Posing no threat, they still presented a puzzle.

What happened?

The crew voted and decided, with only one nay, to pursue the drifting salvage opportunity. They lit a quick and discrete engine burn that was unlikely to be observed, setting themselves on a slow intercept. Time to target: two weeks.

On the command deck, the crew studied the images of the object as they approached. Their appetite for salvage swelled when they determined the object was a ship. As they crept closer, though, a sense of foreboding settled over the crew. It was only the remains of a ship. Torn metal and a cloud of trailing debris testified to the violence that had set the amputated segment of some unfortunate spacecraft drifting through the void, like a discarded limb. They could barely make out a word on the hull, *Carpathia*.

"You got any record of a *Carpathia*, Ellie?" Captain Drew asked.

"Yes, sir," the *Wharf Rat's* pre-Renate AI responded. "The *Carpathia* is a long-haul science surveyor registered to the European Space Agency."

Drew's face darkened. "Souls on board?"

"Sir, the *Carpathia's* standard crew compliment is listed at twelve."

Drew shook his head slowly. "Poor bastards."

Out in the void, the misfortune of others always chills the hearts and enthusiasms of spacefarers—*that could be me. This fucking void and those in it are trying to kill me. When will my luck run out?*

"I don't like it," Conrad said definitively on the *Wharf Rat's* command deck.

"It's a salvage," Captain Drew said, not taking his eyes off the images of the slowly tumbling wreck on the screens. "What's not to like?"

Conrad didn't take his eyes off the images either. He just shook his head slowly. "We should leave it be."

Almost a week later, after the *Wharf Rat* pulled alongside the remnants of the *Carpathia* and deployed maneuvering drones to neutralize its slow tumble, Conrad and Bonham went aboard. Preceded by recon drones, close quarters weapons in hand, they were horrified by the scene. Gore and body parts floated in corridors splattered with blood. Bonham fought the urge to vomit as she walked in front, her mag boots clinging to the ship's floor. Conrad shook in his pressure suit as he followed behind her.

"You guys OK?" Captain Drew asked over the radio from the *Wharf Rat's* command deck. He and the rest of the crew were transfixed by the macabre scene beamed back from the drones and Conrad and Bonham's pressure suit cameras. A few looked away. It was too gruesome.

"This wasn't mishap or gunfight," Boham transmitted as she eased around a floating human torso. Blood, frozen in mid-ooze, sprouted from the cleanly sliced flesh. The uniform fabric looked as if it had been cut with great care by a tailor. "It's like someone went through this place with surgical instruments… for fun."

"Anything worth salvaging?" The captain asked.

"Yeah," Bonham answered, looking around the blood-spattered corridor.

"It's not a money score. But looks like some decent tech and materials."

"Good. The *Rat* can use it."

"Uh oh," Conrad said.

"What?" Bonham spun in place, looking back at him and bringing her boarding pistol to bear.

Conrad held himself in front of a passageway he had just opened. Bonham stepped behind him and looked over his shoulder.

"Looks like their medical bay," Conrad said.

A stainless-steel exam table stood in the middle of the small room. The walls were lined with storage bins. Blood splattered the walls, floor, and ceiling. A dead crewman floated in the corner of the room, face up toward the ceiling, back arched and arms spread. White ribs protruded from a gapping cavity that ran from her neck to her abdomen, a look of disbelief frozen on her face.

In the other corner of the room, soft light emanated from a large, oblong device. Bloody handprints covered its clamshell top.

"Looks like a MedPod," Bonham said.

"Excellent," the captain responded. Pirate ships could never have too many MedPods. "Does it look operational?"

Conrad turned to Bonham. "I ain't fucking going in there."

Bonham rolled her eyes and pushed by him into the room. She floated by the exam table, keeping her eyes averted from the grotesque remains floating on the other side of the room.

Reaching out to arrest her momentum, she touched the toe of her right mag boot to the floor at the base of the MedPod. She looked the medical device over for a moment and then shook her head in disbelief.

"It's operational," she transmitted.

Smiles were shared on the *Wharf Rat* command deck and the captain gave his crew a thumbs up. An operational MedPod was a huge score.

"And it is occupied," Bonham added.

The smiles on the *Wharf Rat* vanished.

"Say again?" the captain transmitted.

"There is a survivor in it," Bonham said, peering through the glass of the MedPod at the body of a horribly wounded male. Staples and stitches crisscrossed the pale spacefarer's upper body, winding across his chest and over his face. Most of his left arm was missing, the stump bandaged. It looked to Bonham as if the MedPod had tried to reassemble an old rag doll.

She looked over her shoulder at the room. Conrad cowered in the passageway, still refusing to enter.

She looked back at the disfigured man and shook her head. He must have managed to pull himself in here alone, without help. And then somehow got into the MedPod.

"Alive?" the captain asked.

Bonham checked the MedPod display again and then looked at the man's chest for a moment to be sure. It rose and fell slowly as he breathed.

"Yeah."

She looked back at the reassembled man's face.

"But he might wish he wasn't."

The crew of the *Wharf Rat* transferred the wounded spacefarer and MedPod to their medical bay and then picked over the salvage. Their first step was a brief service for the *Carpathia's* dead. Gathering all the body parts and corpses, they placed them into a small rocket-powered cargo pod.

Captain Drew called the crew to the command deck. The image of the egg-shaped cargo pod glowed on the monitors. Laden with the dead, it hung motionless in the void twenty meters from the *Wharf Rat*. The only survivor lay unconscious in the med bay on the other side of the Ring.

"You sure you got 'em all?" Drew asked.

Bonham nodded grimly.

"OK, then."

Drew turned his attention to the monitor.

"We don't know what happened to the *Carpathia*. And we don't want to know. Looks like it was a bad run of luck, for sure. But from what we can see, you went out like a real crew. Together. And that is something."

Drew looked around at his crew, giving space for anyone else to say anything. Standing around the command deck, most avoided his eyes.

Bonham, looking at the monitor, said, "We'll take care of your survivor."

Drew nodded at her.

No one else moved to speak.

"OK, then," Drew said. He raised the controller in his hand and pressed the button. The monitors flared white as the rocket ignited. Seconds later, it was gone. Only the image of the savaged *Carpathia* fragment remained.

Five cycles later, the crew decided it was time to leave. Even though their passive scans were clear, every pirate knows it is bad luck to linger too long on a prize.

Spacefarers try to never tempt the void.

The *Wharf Rat* fired her cold thrusters to generate departure velocity. Captain Drew planned to dead drift for a month or two before firing the main engines. Part superstition, part tactic, he traded time for stealth and obscurity in almost every case.

Bonham was in her quarters when the soft nudge of the cold thrusters shuddered through the *Wharf Rat*. She smiled as the gradual acceleration drifted her to the large window on the aft wall of her quarters. Spreading her arms as the slight G forces pressed her back into the thick glass of the window.

As slight as it was, she luxuriated in the relative microgravity. It wasn't much. But it had been about two weeks since they had spun *Wharf Rat's* Ring. She missed the press of its full G. Bonham was ready to get back to it. Lack of gravity seemed to affect her more than others. She got twitchy and irritable and longed for the *Wharf Rat's* weight room.

Won't be long now.

She knew Captain Drew's technique by heart. He would fire the cold thrusters till they were empty. Recharge them as they drifted. Then fire them again. When that cycle was complete, they could spin the Ring while they drifted.

Bonham turned her body so she could look out of the window. A chill came over her. Not from the cold of the void-touching glass, rather, the sight of the picked over salvage.

The crew of the *Wharf Rat* had been as efficient as ever. The *Carpathia's* remains had been reduced to a skeletal spar assembly. Long, pale, skinny, curving lengths of metal hinted at where the ship had been. To Bonham, it looked like the moose skeletons she and her father would come across on their hikes in Alaska long ago. Unlike those big moose bones, which gave themselves back to the earth, these skeletal remains were doomed to drift alone through the void against a backdrop of countless stars. Unless mercifully pulled into the sun or a planet centuries from now, they would never truly rest, a lonely drifting reminder of death in the void.

Twelve years later, Axe was still on the *Wharf Rat*, and had still never spoken about what happened on the *Carpathia*. Bonham and the others learned to never ask.

Chapter Forty-Eight

Perseus

"Goddamnit, Scott," Deke said, as he glowered at Scott's image on the video monitor. "You told me you'd have it fixed in two hours!"

"Yes, sir. After you'd been told to plan on repairs taking over twelve hours. Cut me some slack."

He does have a point, Deke thought.

"This is not how you manage expectations, Scott," Deke said, trying not to let his face soften. "If you'd told me earlier that you cut the repair time from twelve to six hours, I would not be pissed that you are now telling me it was going to take three."

"Yeah, well, I'm just a dumbass space craft mechanic. I don't manage expectations."

"I need you to go faster, Scott. We have to get these ships moving."

"Well, maybe you should have thought of that before you knocked the shit out of the old girl, sir!" Scott said, frustration pouring from his voice. "I've got no native maintenance drones to work with because your team killed them all, and I can't get any parts fabrication out of the on-board factory because you guys punched holes in it."

Deke held his hands up in a calming gesture.

"Easy, Scott, I get it. I get it."

"Doesn't fucking sound like it, sir."

"Okay. Okay," Deke said, palms still raised. "I appreciate everything you and your team are doing. I do. It's not fair to you guys, but we've got to get out of this cloud as soon as possible. We are all blind in here."

Scott nodded.

"I get it, sir. I apologize."

"Nothing to apologize for. Just please work as fast as you can."

"Roger that, sir. We are."

"I know."

"I'll call you with an update in half an hour."

"Roger that, Scott. Thank you."

Deke gestured at the screen and changed from Scott to the video feed from *Dagger*. She was returning from the *Remus* where she had dropped off the last of the tired assault team. The two-kilometer-long freighter extended out of her forward optical sensor's field of view in both directions, dwarfing the Company gunboat. Repair drones from the *Remus* worked on the big ship. Sparks sprayed from drones welding hull patches in place, while others hauled fiber optic bundles and other parts forward and aft. The *Remus* only had six maintenance drones, though. Pitifully few for the gargantuan task.

The cloud was as nasty as ever. Dense gases thickened and thinned, causing the video quality to alternate randomly between fuzzy, clear, and none. Debris, large and small, hurtled and dawdled in and out of frame. Many struck the *Perseus* or *Remus*, sometimes causing more damage, sometimes bouncing harmlessly off on a new trajectory.

Deke glared at the mess on the screen. He looked at his watch and shook his head. They had been in the cloud for almost two hours. He wanted out ASAP.

Touching a toe to the floor, Deke pushed himself over to the captain's chair. He pulled himself into it and snapped the harness across his body before leaning his head forward and rubbing his eyes. The harness was as much a mental tool to restrain his mind as to hold him in his seat so he could relax. He knew his role at the moment was to stay out of his people's way and let them do their jobs.

He just hated waiting.

Deke wished there was something productive he could do with his time. He ran through the operation in his mind for the millionth time; Scott and his team were working on propulsion. There was nothing Deke could do to help there. Repairs to the *Perseus'* hull and other infrastructure were being coordinated by the *Remus*. Again, they did not need him mucking it up. Shift change was complete. The assault force and breaching drones were back on the *Remus* and the new security team, junior as they were, had things under control; that asshole Hoffman was nursing a broken nose in confinement and the rest of this crew was still on the Utility Module waiting to be shuttled to the *Remus* by *Dagger*. Owens and his pirates were confined on the Hab.

Owens, Deke thought. *I can't believe Paul-fucking-Owens is on this ship.*

With nothing to do at the moment, and seeking diversion to keep him out of his team's way for a bit, Deke let the memories sweep him away.

He clearly remembered reading about Captain Paul Owens and his war crimes while on his third Company gunboat tour. It wasn't the *Remus*, and it wasn't under Rojas. Deke had been out of the military for a little over three years, and he missed it.

His Company Centaur team was tight-knit, and the missions were cool, but it wasn't the same. The money was better, of course. Much better, but there was something lacking.

Deke followed the news closely since he left the service. When General Schofield launched his doomed offensive against the Chinese in South America, he found himself feeling guilty. Part of him believed he should be there.

The other part felt foolish for thinking that way. He had done his part, after all, joining up when he was 18. Growing up poor in Texas didn't offer a lot of other options. He remembered watching the First Battle of Santiago on the news as a private going through basic training. Such a disaster. They were all scared.

He deployed to South America for Second Santiago, serving in a support element for one of the early exo battalions. He didn't see any real action, but supported those who did, and saw its terrible aftermath.

By age 24, he was a fully augmented and trained Centaur, and had served combat tours in Africa, Eastern Europe and South America. Decorated for bravery and leadership, he thought he would be a lifer. Five years later, the Company recruited him.

When they gave him their offer, he thought there had been a mistake. It was so much money. More than he had ever imagined he might earn someday.

He had to take it.

The monetary excitement didn't even last a year. By the time he was reading about Captain Owens and the battlefield murders in South America, it was long gone.

Deke shook his head at the poor bastard. The details were scarce, but it seemed Owens had snapped after the gruesome execution of his fellow officer in the combat zone. It sounded like Owens had delivered a similar fate upon those that did it. There was some mumbo jumbo about "rogue AI killings," and "top secret," but Deke knew, in the back of his mind—deep down—he was capable of the same. More than capable. He was glad Owens had gotten his vengeance.

It was shortly after the Owens incident that Deke was assigned to the *George Remus* under Captain Rojas. For some reason, it was better. Deke liked working for Rojas. He reminded him of the better officers he worked with in the military. His team responded well to his leadership style. Before he knew it, he had done three tours under Rojas.

Now this one.

This long, fucked up tour that was concluding with this fucked up mission to re-take this fucked up oversized freighter.

Deke rubbed his forehead, snapping back to the current moment on the bridge.

He checked his suit's time display.

All right, Scott. I gave you enough of a break.

Deke unbuckled from his seat and kicked off toward the video display to call for an update.

Chapter Forty-Nine

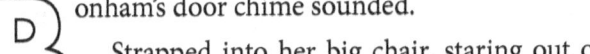

Wharf Rat

onham's door chime sounded.

Strapped into her big chair, staring out one of the big windows drinking whiskey, she ignored it.

It chimed again.

"Fuck off."

"Come on, Marlowe!" Axe pounded on the closed hatch.

Bonham closed her eyes and shook her head.

"Renate, let him in," she grumbled.

The hatch to her quarters slid open.

Axe pulled himself in. Touching a mag boot to the floor, he came to a stop in front of her.

"What the hell are you doing?" he asked.

"Drinking whiskey."

"You should be on the command deck. Your crew is planning the most important attack in the history of this ship, of their lives."

"The crew voted for their captain and course of action. Let them plan it with him." She took a swig of whisky from the small squeeze bottle in her hand. "And their first mate."

"We don't have time for this! We are little more than an hour from the—"

"Then fucking turn around!" Bonham yelled. "We shouldn't be doing this!"

"Well, we are doing it, goddamnit!" Axe yelled back, leaning over and jabbing his mechanical finger in her face. "I'm sorry things didn't go your way. I really am. But you lost the vote. You lost both votes. This is what is happening and your crew needs you! You don't quit your crew!"

Bonham unbuckled from her seat and launched herself at Axe.

"The crew quit me!" she yelled, punching Axe in the face.

He grabbed her arm and flung her into the window on the other side of her quarters.

Bonham hit the thick glass head first.

Stunned, she struggled to reorient herself quickly. She leapt at him again, sailing across the room.

Axe blocked her easily and flung her again into the opposite window.

Bonham screamed in rage and frustration, flinging herself at him again.

He sidestepped and swatted her away.

She crunched into the storage cubes.

"Marlowe, please stop," Axe said, holding up a hand.

"Why?" Bonham said between heaving breaths. "Why did you come here? Why can't you leave me alone? What do you want?"

"We need your help."

"Why the hell would I help?" Bonham panted.

"Because we will die without it."

Bonham stared at Axe, catching her breath.

"Our plan is shit." He almost chuckled. "It's gonna get us killed."

"I don't think I can fix that. If you guys are hell bent on attacking, we are probably gonna die. Hell… we might deserve it."

"We might." Axe shrugged. "But we'll have a better shot with your help. With one of your plans."

Bonham, floating slowly toward Axe, shook her head. "It's the wrong thing, Axe. It's the wrong damn thing."

Axe reached out to her with his human hand. He grabbed her by the arm and steadied her.

"Let that decision rest on the rest of us. On me." He tapped his chest with his robotic hand. "But help us live through it. Help your crew."

Bonham looked at him with pleading eyes. "Please, Axe. Please make them stop."

"I couldn't if I wanted to." He shook his head. "And I don't want to."

Bonham put her head in her hands.

Axe pulled her in closer. His human arm wrapped around her shoulders, his robotic arm steadying them, holding onto the wall. Slowly, she put her arms around him and buried her head in his chest. They floated in silence for a long moment.

"I'm done, Axe. If we live through this. I'm done. I don't belong on this crew anymore."

Axe blinked a tear free from his eyes.

"I know."

Axe took Bonham back to the command deck where Quinn and Eriksson were still talking about missiles and EMPs.

"Listen up," Axe said loudly. "Bonham has a plan."

The crew looked at her with faces full of relief. Landsberg smiled broadly and Reeve nodded.

Bonham shook her head.

"I still think this is a shit idea. But if it has to be, this is how I would do it." She took a deep breath and then talked through her plan, asking Renate to use the holo-projector to illustrate along the way. By the time she was done, the crew was unanimous. This would be their plan.

"How long we got, Renate?" Quinn asked.

"We have less than an hour till the deployment window."

Bonham looked at Landsberg first.

"No problem," he said.

Then Singh.

He nodded to her. "I can do it."

"Okay," Quinn said. "We all know what to do. Let's get it done."

* * *

Bonham floated in between Landsberg and Eriksson in the *Wharf Rat's* cargo bay, looking at the product of the last frenzied hour of effort.

"That is one ugly pile of junk," Bonham said, gesturing at their handiwork. Eriksson chuckled.

"You said, make it deadly," Landsberg said, eyes narrowing. "Not pretty." Bonham nodded.

"Any updates from Singh?" Eriksson asked.

"No," Bonham said.

"I expect he will be running scenarios with Renate up until the very last minute," Landsberg said. "It's important to give the probes' executive program a few million iterations so that the learning routines can really sink their teeth into it."

"How are you feeling about it?" Bonham asked him, stealing a glance at his perspiring face. The past hour had been exhausting and nerve-wracking. Unsecuring and moving large, heavy objects around in zero gravity, even with cargo handling equipment, was strenuous, and required constant vigilance. The opportunity for soft flesh to get between massive, hard objects was constant. A slow-moving chunk of metal could effortlessly pulp an unfortunate human—a thought that Bonham had tried to keep out of her mind while they worked. It was exactly what happened to Conrad.

The welding bots, even when controlled and overseen by Renate, were also dangerous to be near. They roved around the bay like enemy snipers, firing their lasers to cut and join links in the haphazard structure they were building. It had been nerve-wracking work. Made more so by the press of time and the ultimate question of, will it even fucking work?

"I feel good," Landsberg said. "Repurposing the probes was easy enough. Renate produced excellent structural calculations, and she and Singh are always a big help with software testing. I think we have a high chance of success."

"I can't believe our fate is resting on your shitty probes," Eriksson said.

Bonham, still between the two men, grimaced, anticipating what was coming.

"Fuck you, Viggo!" Landsberg said, turning toward Eriksson and yelling in Bonham's ear. "My probes are the only reason this plan has a chance!"

"A chance? I thought you said you were highly confident of a kill shot?" Eriksson turned toward Landsberg and yelled in Bonham's other ear. "This has to be more than a fucking chance!"

"Shut up!" Bonham said, surprising them both with a hard shove. Her simultaneous push in opposite directions held her in place while sending the two yelling men backward several meters before they each touched a mag boot toe to the floor.

"If anyone in the void can make this plan work, Landy can," Bonham said, glaring at Eriksson and then swiveling her gaze to Landsberg like a scolding mother. "Now, let's get back to the command deck."

* * *

"Let's run it one more time," Singh said, his voice fatigued, strapped into his chair in navigation.

"Okay," Renate said. Ripples of light radiated out through her spirals. They were more tightly wound than usual today, giving her an almost spherical appearance, as if she had compacted herself in deep concentration.

The dense, multi-colored soup of gas and debris that surrounded Singh tilted and wheeled as he was ejected out of it into the darkness of the void. The cloud, whose shape and volume he had memorized, receded into the distance at an impossible speed.

Singh decelerated at a rate that would have ripped his body apart, coming to rest beneath the *Wharf Rat*, so close that he could reach up and touch her cold belly.

He glanced back at the cloud, now less than 50,000 kilometers away. It seemed even closer than a few minutes ago.

"How much time, Renate?"

"Approximately twenty minutes until our deployment window."

Singh closed his eyes in anxiety. It was coming on them too fast. He needed more time.

He shook his head to clear the thought.

"Run it, please. Same parameters."

Singh's body tensed involuntarily as he shot away from the *Wharf Rat*. Renate was accelerating this part of the simulation to 10X to cover the distance between to the cloud quickly.

The cloud grew in size until it loomed across his entire forward field of view.

He slowed suddenly to a crawl, Renate now playing the scenario forward in millisecond increments.

A small, bright red light flashed on the other side of the cloud and above Singh's position. A red tendril of light extended instantly, striking him between the eyes. He blinked and it was gone.

He was jostled and jerked around as his course was altered while he closed the final kilometers to his target.

Singh plunged into the multi-colored, chaotic cloud.

He knew what he saw was just a representation, a guess by Renate as to what it looked like on the inside. He still couldn't stop himself from craning his neck and looking around.

It was massive, over twelve hundred cubic kilometers. And somewhere in here was the *Perseus* and the Company gunboat. He checked his time and velocity display. At his current rate of speed, he would pass through the cloud in .44 seconds. Renate, though, had slowed simulated time to a crawl.

Directly in front of him, a large red sphere hovered in the cloud.

Singh reached out his arm as he passed near it, dragging his hand through the red mass. It splintered at his touch.

Then, suddenly, Singh emerged from the cloud. He turned and look back. Red splinters were following him, accelerated to a high speed by his touch.

"That's enough," Singh said.

His motion stopped.

"Do you want to run the deceleration segment again?"

"No. I don't have a lot of concern about that part. I know you won't mash us."

"I certainly will not, sir."

"I should get to the command deck."

"Yes, sir."

The cloud disappeared and the universe around him went dark. The only thing still in existence was Renate, glowing softly in the distance.

"How many times did we get the gunboat?" Singh asked.

"73.5 percent of the time." Renate sparkled as she spoke. Her voice sounded like she was speaking inches from his ear, even though her galaxy seemed light years away.

"How many scenarios were you able to run?"

"Almost four million," she answered, a ripple of light coursing through her. "Success rate dramatically increased over the duration of the testing."

Singh grunted as his chair came to a proper seated position. He winked in Renate's direction before taking off the neural interface helmet, letting its lever raise it away from his head. He blinked a few times and rubbed his scalp, regaining his bearings.

"I must say," Renate said over the room's speakers. "Bonham is a very creative tactician."

"She is indeed. And 73.5 percent is not the worst bet the *Wharf Rat* has ever made," Singh said, as he unbuckled.

"Nowhere close, sir."

Singh anchored his mag boots to the floor and stood. He grabbed his turban from its shelf under the U-shaped console and wrapped it slowly around his bald head. The end of the four-meter length of blue fabric undulated in zero G as Singh tied it.

Singh took deep, deliberate breaths, trying to smooth away his anxiety as he finished with the turban.

It didn't work.

Chapter Fifty

Perseus

I'm very disappointed, Deke," Rojas said, his angry image on the big video screen glaring at Deke. Finnie stood behind the captain with a disapproving look.

Deke, arms crossed, mag boots anchored to the floor on the *Perseus'* bridge, glared right back, certain his image on the *Remus* looked just as angry.

"You broke his nose!" Rojas eyes narrowed in exasperation. "What is wrong with you? The pirates didn't even do that to him."

Deke bit his tongue. When he and the captain had issues, it was usually around something like this. Deke thought the captain was an excellent leader and a gentleman. There was no doubt he could command a ship full of souls through the void, but Rojas had not seen the shit Deke had, had never been a squad leader holding key terrain, facing bullets and panic, had never killed with his hands. Deke thought the captain often failed to recognize when Deke's metered violence prevented worse.

Usually, Deke would swallow the disapproval and wait until a lighter moment to talk through it. He found Captain Rojas more open to contradiction when they were one on one in his quarters with a drink.

But Deke was tired and mad and not in the mood to be second guessed at the moment.

"There is not a goddamn thing wrong with me, sir!" Deke said with force, unfolding his arms and pointing one finger at his chest. "I am over here executing the mission to capture and secure this long ass rust bucket of a derelict fucking freighter. Along the way, though it may not be a priority that the fucking Company shares, my personal sacred mission is to keep my team alive!"

Captain Rojas' image on the big screen was motionless, lips pressed into a thin line as Deke railed.

"I respond to threats to either of those missions with immediate and precise applications of force. That motherfucker, Hoffman, through his own behavior, established himself as a threat. I dealt with that limp dick, civilian asshole with the minimum level of kinetic energy required. He's fucking lucky I am in such a good motherfucking mood today!"

Deke, nearly panting from his tirade, shook his head and glowered at the screen.

Rojas hesitated, ensuring Deke's tantrum was finished before speaking.

"I applaud your passion, Deke. But Hoffman will cause problems with the Company. He's a captain, for chrissakes! I'm sure he deserved it. But... A broken nose? Really?"

Rojas shook his head. He looked down and rubbed his eyes.

Deke was about to launch into another angry speech when he thought he saw the hint of a smile on his captain's face.

Rojas glanced up to see that Deke had noticed.

"Dammnit," Rojas muttered as Deke matched his tired grin. The two old comrades looked at each other.

"I must admit, I find it strange how your impassioned speech about your sacred duty to eliminate threats to your people somehow justifies punching... How did he describe Hoffman, XO?"

Deke watched the screen as Rojas turned and looked back at Finnie. She met the captain's glance with surprise, but then quickly recovered.

"I believe it was something along the lines of, 'Limp dick, civilian, asshole,' sir."

"I think you're right." Rojas turned from Finnie back to the camera. "So, which is it, Deke? Is he a limp dick? Or a threat?"

"Captain, I think even you would have clocked him."

"Maybe..." Rojas's smile faded. "But you know how much paperwork that broken nose is going to cost me?"

Deke's smile faded as well.

"Would it help if I did the paperwork, sir?"

"Definitely not." Rojas shook his head.

Deke nodded and looked at his feet. When he looked up, Rojas's smile had returned.

"Let's complete this fucked-up mission and get back to Mars, Deke," the captain said.

"Roger that, sir," Deke responded. "As soon as *Dagger* gets back, we'll load the pirates up and send them over. I think we'll be ready to fire up *Perseus'* propulsion system and get her out of the cloud in half an hour."

"Good. You'll take her out first. The *Remus* will follow. As soon as we are out of the cloud, Finnie will head over and relieve you."

"Aye, sir."

Rojas nodded, and the screen went black.

Deke exhaled and walked back to the captain's chair. He sat, buckled in, and deactivated his mag boots before taking a long pull of water from a plastic bottle he had stowed next to the chair. Leaning back and rubbing his eyes, Deke thought about the day.

I woke up, what? 300,000 kilometers from here? Got mashed in my seat for an hour and a half at 3Gs, just about burned my cerebral cortex to a cinder driving drones to subdue this ancient garbage hauler before entering the surrounding fucked up cloud of shit on Dagger's back, just to board to this death trap freighter so we can try to put it back together in order to get back to Mars before anyone sneaks up on our dumb, blind asses.

He took a few more long swallows of water.

And the craziest thing out of all that shit is Paul-fucking-Owens is the pirate leader.

Deke shook his head at the thought.

"XO, how long until the *Dagger* gets back from the *Remus*?"

"Approximately fifteen minutes, sir."

Deke looked at his watch. Once on board the *Remus*, there would be protocol and bullshit and given how pissed the Company was and Owens's infamy, Deke doubted he would get another chance for a one on one with the man.

Fuck it. Why not?

"Jennings!" Deke barked at the young soldier who was back on the bridge after removing Hoffman.

"Yes, sir?"

"Bring the pirates to me."

"Sir?"

"Bring the fucking pirates to me. I want to talk to them."

"Um… Yes, sir!"

Deke glanced at the other, older soldier on the bridge and motioned with his head to follow Jennings.

The soldier smiled and nodded.

Deke chuckled and took another swig of water.

Chapter Fifty-One

Wharf Rat

The crew of the *Wharf Rat* sat silently in their seats as Bonham reviewed the attack plan one last time. It didn't take long. It was simple.

It's either going to work really well, or we are going to die quickly, she thought when she finished.

"Five minutes 'til we enter the drop window," Axe said. "Last chance for those opposed. Speak now."

The whole crew turned their heads to look at Bonham.

She sighed heavily, unbuckled her harness, and stood. She looked at the toes of her mag boots for a long moment before raising her bloodshot eyes and looking at Axe.

"I'm sorry," she said to him. "I know I am the one that is out of step. The one on the outside. It is not because I want to be."

She chuckled, lowering her eyes from Axe.

"It's a strange thing. To lose the captain's seat."

She looked up at Quinn.

"And it's a heartbreaking thing to know what your crew is doing is wrong." She swept her eyes around the room. "And to be unable to stop it."

She sighed again and shook her head slowly, eyes coming to rest on Axe.

"I'm sorry. I love you all so much, love this ship... And that is why I am opposed. I believe this will be our end. This is how the void gets us. I vote nay."

Axe nodded.

Bonham sat and buckled her harness.

Axe walked to the center of the deck.

"Are there any other nays?"

There were not.

Minutes later, Bonham sat in her chair on the command deck, watching the cargo bay doors open on her arm rest video screen. The rest of the crew clustered around one of the large screens on one side of the deck. Quinn sat in the captain's chair.

Bonham watched the bay doors lock open and three drones drop from the belly of the *Wharf Rat*. They pulsed their cold thrusters and accelerated forward, out of the view of the camera. She switched her display to one of the *Wharf Rat's* forward-facing nose cameras, eyes lingering on the three probes as they moved forward and away from the ship at the pace of a slow walk.

Leaning back in her chair, Bonham welcomed the strange familiar feeling of dissonance. She knew the *Wharf Rat* was hurtling toward the cloud, the *Perseus*, and the Company gunboat at over 100,000 kilometers per hour, more than eighty times the speed of sound on Earth.

But she couldn't tell. The stars, light years away, hung around the *Wharf Rat*, motionless and indifferent, offering no hint of the ship's eyelid-peeling speed.

What a strange feeling... to be racing to your death and not able to tell.

The attack plan depended on the ship's velocity, and that anything released from its cargo bay would travel at the same relative velocity.

Bonham smiled.

There was a simple elegance to her plan, she was able to admit.

She switched her display back to the belly camera. The doors were still locked open and the monstrous assembly was descending into the void, nudged out of the ship's bay by cold thrusters that Landsberg had integrated into the structure.

Bonham thought about the colossal kinetic energy embodied by the thing and shook her head.

"Okay, it's time," Axe said, pushing off the floor and floating away from the group clustered around the video screen.

No one moved from the screen. They were transfixed.

Quinn hit a button on his armrest, and the large screen went dark.

"What the hell, man?" Eriksson said.

"It's time, Viggo," Axe said. "Everyone to their G-MASS chair. We've got a little more than ten minutes till our deceleration burn.

The crew groaned.

Bonham winced at the thought.

Good news, I guess, is this will probably be my last time in that fucking thing. Ever.

Chapter Fifty-Two

Paul floated in front of his captor, arms bound behind his back. He was still wearing his pressure suit, but no helmet.

When the soldiers had come to get them from the Hab, Paul looked at the young, fresh-faced soldier and briefly considered resisting, trying one last time to get free. But it was hopeless. There were two of them. Both were heavily armed and their armored pressure suits were state of the art, even if one did look barely out of high school.

The soldiers refused to tell them where they were going, but after they were pushed through the tube and brought into the base of the bridge tower, Paul figured they were about to be ferried to whatever Company ship had captured them. He did wonder why they hadn't taken them out of the Hab airlock, though. It would have been much more convenient.

Then they separated him from Althea and Top.

Paul didn't like that.

He resisted. Futilely.

Two soldiers brought him up to the bridge, yanked his pressure helmet off, and pushed him in front of the same guy that had captured them earlier. Paul had not gotten a good look at him then. He studied the Company soldier now.

The man wore the same armored pressure suit that the other soldiers did, with a nameplate on his chest that said Syed. Paul judged the man to be slightly older than him. And, surprisingly, he was a Centaur.

Paul recognized the augmentation scars on the man's shaven head immediately.

"And I thought my scars were bad," the man said, looking at Paul's forehead.

"They weren't very delicate when they pulled all my shit out."

"They pulled it all out?"

"Yeah, but don't worry," Paul said. "I got special treatment there at the end. I doubt they will do you like they did me when you get out."

"Oh, I'm out. Been out for about ten years."

Paul tilted his head slightly, regarding the man.

"I'm Sadhik Syed. Did fourteen years. Ten as a Centaur. Got out in '63."

"That's the year I made Centaur."

Deke nodded.

"You must have gone through Officer Assessment and Training under Colonel Filson, right?"

The name struck Paul like a slap.

A sting of memory and regret ran through him.

"That's right."

"Fucking legend, that guy. What's he up to now? Do you know?"

"He's dead."

"Oh." Deke shook his head. "Shit."

"You some kind of merc now?" Paul asked.

"I guess. I work for the Company."

Paul nodded once, as if having heard a confession.

"And they left your augmentations in?"

"Yeah. It's actually pretty common these days. I'm sure the Company or whoever gives them a kickback of some kind." Deke shrugged. "Good thing, too. I'm not sure I'm qualified to do anything else."

"What exactly to you do?"

"Shit like this," Deke said, gesturing around at the *Perseus'* bridge and beyond. "I'm the tactical commander for one of the Company's gunboats. I lead the drone and human assault platoon. Basically, the same shit I did for Uncle Sam. I just make a lot more money."

A silence extended between them as Paul's mind went back, unbidden, to the days he could control fighting machines with just his mind. The way it felt. How good at he had been. The things they had done together.

The things he still saw.

It didn't seem fair. They dug through his brain and ripped out the augmentations, but the burden of memory, of the nightmares, remained.

"You lead the defense of this old girl?" Deke asked, bringing Paul back to the present.

Paul nodded.

Deke chuckled.

"Gotta say, you gave us fits. The maintenance drones, the cloud of shit out there... You made this soft target pretty hard."

"Not hard enough," Paul said, regret thick in his voice.

Deke looked at Paul for a long moment.

"Can I ask you a question?" he finally said.

Paul chuckled ruefully

"I'm not really in a position to tell you what you can and can't do, Sadhik."

"Deke." Syed put an armored hand to his chest. "Call me Deke."

Paul wished he felt like telling this guy to fuck off. He was a Company mercenary, after all, but there was something about seeing Centaur scars on another man's head. Even out here. A million miles and a million years from it all. It evoked a sense of kinship he had not felt in a long, long time.

It reminded him of Kata.

Emotions welled within Paul. He swallowed.

"Sure, Deke. Ask me anything."

"What happened? Down in South America."

Paul took a deep breath. The question usually enraged him. For some reason, though, coming from Deke, deep in the void, it did not.

"What have you heard?"

"A lot of things," Deke said. "Some kinda malfunction of new soldierbot technology you were test driving. Or that you were driven mad by PTSD. Even had one guy tell me it was staged by the Chinese, to turn the southern cone against us, to undermine the war effort at home."

The last one made Paul smile.

"It's all top fucking secret, you know," Deke said. "Which I learned a long time ago just means it's embarrassing to some fucking general or politician somewhere."

"It's worse than that," Paul said.

Deke waited.

"It was just money."

"Money?"

"Yeah. Money."

The two old Centaurs looked at each other for a moment.

"I don't know all the details yet," Paul shrugged. "But I'm pretty sure we got fucked over because someone wanted to sell a different widget to the US Military."

"So you didn't do it? Didn't kill all those people?"

"Oh, we did it. My unit and I. We killed them all."

Deke's forehead wrinkled. "I'm not following."

"The people we killed, Navarro and his men, I think they were just a tool. They got used somehow."

"What did they do?"

"Tortured and killed my friend. And some of our soldiers."

Deke nodded.

"So, we executed them."

Deke nodded again.

"The people that benefited, the powerful rich people, are still walking around. Still making money," Paul added. "And, if I had to guess, still shoving it up the little guy's ass."

Paul thought of Fiona Malloy, as he did every day. He thought of DredSkill. Thought of his vow. The only reason he kept going, endured the nightmares, didn't just space himself, was delivering justice for Kata and the rest.

Justice that was slipping away from him now.

"That why you became a pirate?" Deke asked Paul.

Paul laughed.

Deke, amused by the response, smiled and waited.

"Sorry," Paul said, stifling his chuckles. "It's just that I don't really think of myself as a pirate."

"Yeah?" Deke said, now chuckling himself. "Well, I hate to tell you this, brother, but that's what you are."

"Maybe." Paul shrugged. "All I have been doing, ever since this shit show started when we left low earth orbit three years ago, is trying to keep my sorry ass alive. If that's what being a pirate is, so be it."

Deke looked at his watch.

"You know why?" Paul asked.

"Why what?"

"Why I am keeping my sorry, war criminal ass alive?"

Deke shook his head.

"Vengeance."

A radio call sounded on Deke's suit speakers.

"This is *Dagger*. I'll be at the base of the bridge tower in six minutes."

Deke, eyes fixed on Paul's, did not respond to the transmission. Instead, he asked Paul a question.

"That gonna set everything right? You killing a few rich people."

"No. Nothing will ever be right again. Shit… I'm not sure anything was ever right in the first place. But, after what they did, they should not be walking around, living, loving, laughing. They should die badly."

Like Kata, Paul thought.

He closed his eyes, jaw clenching as he fought back emotions again.

Deke waited.

Paul finally blinked a few times, eyes glistening as he continued.

"I'm happy for you, Deke. We were all suckers for ever buying in to the bullshit the way we did. It's a racket. Perpetuating the system that benefits them. The system that extends all the way out here, hundreds of millions of kilometers from the dirt you and I choked on back in the day. But you made it. You're on the good side of the ledger now, getting paid. I'm glad you're getting yours."

Deke floated in silence.

"Can I ask something of you?" Paul asked.

"Sure."

"Let us go."

Deke chuckled and rolled his eyes.

"You've got the *Perseus*," Paul said quickly, sensing the moment getting away from him. "That's all the Company is going to care about. Tell them you killed all the pirates on board and they'll give you a fucking medal. We'll vanish. I promise."

"A bonus," Deke said. "In the civilian world, we get bonuses. There are no medals."

"Even better." Paul nodded.

A few heartbeats passed before Deke smiled at Paul. He shook his head.

"I'm sorry, brother. But I won't do that."

Chapter Fifty-Three

George Remus

Rojas stood on the operations deck of the *George Remus* looking through one of the observation windows. He peered into the swirling, multi colored cloud trying to spot *Dagger* as she worked her way back to the *Perseus*.

He shook his head and gave up.

Damndest thing. If I—

The *Remus'* tactical alarm sounded and red light doused the operations deck.

"Sir, we have been painted by high power, multi spectral energy pulses," George announced.

Rojas, already striding across the deck toward Kozlov and Finnie, shouted, "Koz! What the hell is going on?"

"Definitely location and range finding, sir!" he answered without looking up from the display table. "Someone got a fix on us. And a good one."

"Did we get a reciprocal?"

"Um... Sort of, sir."

"What the hell does that mean? We get a fix on the bastards that painted us or not?"

Kozlov looked at the captain but spoke to George. "George, how confident are you in these numbers?"

"Highly confident, sir. The power and clarity of the signal, coupled with reflection from nearby objects in the cloud, enabled a highly accurate fix on its origination."

Kozlov looked back at the display table and shook his head.

"Koz!" Rojas said firmly. "Report!"

"Sir, we got painted multiple times by something moving through the cloud at over a hundred thousand kilometers per hour."

* * *

Dagger was halfway back to the *Perseus* when the blast of the range finding scan washed over her, setting her tactical algorithms screaming.

This is the problem with stupid mission constraints, she groused. *The enemy doesn't adhere to them.*

She dialed up the sensitivity on her passive sensors and gave them more computing power and fought the urge to do a quick high energy scan of the area.

They know where I am already anyway...

She decided against it.

Deke said not to.

She reviewed what had hit her. She didn't have the gear onboard to pinpoint where the scan came from, but she was able to rule out the *Perseus* since it was so close.

Hopefully, the *Remus* got a fix and would share it shortly.

This is not good.

* * *

Deke was in the process of taking Paul off the bridge when it was suddenly bathed in red light, and a high-pitched alarm started pulsing.

"What the hell?" Deke looked around. The other soldiers on the bridge looked back at him anxiously. He just shrugged.

"Sir, the *Perseus* has been swept by high powered, multi-spectrum range finding," the XO announced.

"Did you get a fix?"

"No, sir. It came and went too fast."

Deke looked back at Paul. Paul was shaking his head.

* * *

"One of the three probes survived," Renate announced to the crew of the *Wharf Rat*. "We have the precise location of both the *Perseus* and the Company gunboat."

Strapped into their individual G-MASS chairs, the crew was nervous and steeling themselves for a G-soaked burn. The next couple of minutes would determine what kind of maneuver it was. If the Gunboat spotted them, it would be a body-mashing burn and run to escape. If their attack worked, Renate would execute a less jarring deceleration burn to position them to board the *Perseus*.

The fact that they just got usable telemetry out of the cloud meant the attack still had a chance.

"Well done, Landy!" Quinn said over the intercom.

"Yeah," Eriksson chimed in. "Can't believe your shit worked."

"Fuck you," Landsberg said dismissively. "You were—"

"Cut the chatter," Axe said sharply. Then, after waiting to make sure the two bickerers stayed quiet, he added, "You were right to have us sent three probes, Bonham. Well done."

Lying in her G-MASS chair, Bonham sighed and shook her head. Part of her wished all three probes had been destroyed. If they had, the crew had agreed before strapping in that they would maintain velocity, fly by the cloud in silence, and hope they could slink away undetected and unpursued.

But one probe had passed through the cloud unharmed and accomplished its mission, flashing a powerful multispectral location and range-finding pulse several times during its half-second journey through the cloud. Exiting with a detailed map of the cloud's interior—including the precise locations of the *Perseus* and the gunboat—the probe fired its liquid rockets, quickly climbing relative to the cloud to gain a clear line-of-sight back to the *Wharf Rat* and, most importantly, Bonham's evil creation. The probe instantly transmitted the detailed targeting data to both via tight beam laser

"Renate, how long till impact?" Quinn asked.

"Seventy-two seconds."

* * *

Finnie and Kozlov looked at their captain.

Rojas looked at the display table. His gut was screaming at him.

"We need to get out of this cloud. Now!" he said.

"What about Deke and the *Perseus*?" Finnie asked.

Rojas shook his head.

"You don't understand. That probe came from outside the cloud. Whoever sent it is undoubtedly on the way with perfect intel of our location. And we don't have the slightest fucking idea where they are. George! Get us out of this cloud now!"

Rojas's heart pounded. He tried not to radiate panic, but he had a terrible feeling. They had to get moving.

"Sir, we have drones and crew members outside conducting repairs," Finnie said. "We need—"

"No!" Rojas slammed his fists down on the display table. "Now! It's got to be now!"

"The captain is right!" Kozlov yelled. "George! Sound the alarm! Secure for burn!"

A shrill, oscillating wail like a predator's scream erupted across the ship as the red lights pulsated. Relentless and impossible to ignore, the blaring alarm cut through the ever-present hum and vibration of the ship's systems. It hammered the crew's ears in every corner of the *Remus* as they scrambled to secure the ship and strap into the nearest acceleration chair.

This was something they drilled often. The ability to secure for burn quickly could mean the difference between life and death in the void. The crew of the *Remus* was one of the best. They were fast. They could secure for burn in a little less than a minute.

* * *

"Look at that fucking thing," Eriksson said over the intercom. He and the rest of the crew were watching on the small screens in their G-MASS chairs as Bonham's creation used cold thrusters to adjust its course and orientation.

She could barely watch.

Inspired by the stories of old-world pirates she loved so much, her innovation was simple—a space chain shot.

Comprising two smaller cannonballs linked by a length of chain, chain shots were used during the Golden Age of Piracy to maximize damage to enemy ships. When fired from a cannon, the chain shot would expand, creating a whirling, destructive force capable of shredding sails, snapping ropes, and even toppling masts.

Bonham had taken most of the contents of the *Wharf Rat's* cargo hold, anything large and heavy and, optimally, made of dense metal, and welded it together into a large, chainlike structure. Landsberg equipped the chain with half a dozen of his probes to provide a rudimentary propulsion system, and Singh helped program the Frankenstein creation to give it a minimally coherent flight control capability.

The ugly chain of metal and junk weighed two metric tons, and was imbued with the *Wharf Rat's* velocity relative to the cloud of over 100,000 kilometers per hour—more kinetic energy than dropping the Empire State Building from orbit.

After nudging the chain shot from the ship's belly twenty minutes ago, the *Wharf Rat* had used cold thrusters to start a slow separation from the deadly payload. Now, twenty kilometers away and traveling parallel, the ship would fly past the cloud as the chain shot entered it.

One of the *Wharf Rat's* cameras was zoomed into the chain shot. Bonham could see its cold thrusters fire intermittently as the gargantuan structure tried to optimize its trajectory and orientation before cloud entry. The other view was zoomed out so that the cloud was in frame.

Bonham closed her eyes.

It wouldn't be long now.

* * *

Clarke nearly jumped out of his skin when the secure for burn alarm sounded. He was still in his pressure suit, and it took him no time to yank on his helmet and check the seal.

He pulled himself into his cell's acceleration chair and strapped in while the two crewmen in the armory rushed to secure the room.

They slammed containers shut and pulled restraining bars down over the weapons racks before getting into their own acceleration chairs.

Clarke could see from their faces they were as scared as him.

What the hell is going on? He wondered as he tried to flatten his back against his chair in preparation for a hard burn.

* * *

"Hurry up, goddamnit!" Rojas yelled from his acceleration chair.

The secure for burn alarm continued to shriek and the red lights pulsated. Rojas looked at his watch. It had almost been a minute.

Taking too long!

"Sir, request permission for a quick active obstacle scan prior to burn," George said.

"Granted. Be quick about it."

No reason to be shy about emissions anymore.

"Sir. The ship is secure for burn," George announced. "Course plotted."

Finally!

"Get us out of here, George. Expedite!"

"Aye, sir."

"And don't be gentle. Just keep us alive."

"Aye, sir."

Rojas slammed into one side of his acceleration chair harness and then the other as George aggressively re-oriented the ship to exit the cloud. He knew a max burn into one of the *Perseus'* dislodged shipping containers would kill them all as dead as an attacking enemy would, but he wished George would hurry the hell up!

Rojas's heart leapt as acceleration pressed him into his chair.

We may get out of this alive, yet. I should have never—

The top half of the *George Remus* and most of the chain shot itself were vaporized in the first instant of impact. The operations deck and the ship's living spaces were transformed into a stream of plasma that erupted from the cloud and extended for tens of kilometers in a blink. Rojas never completed his thought. The burden of command was lifted from him as he, Kozlov, Finnie, and most of the crew ceased to exist. Their molecular remnants joined the stream of plasma, accelerated in an instant on an endless journey through the void.

A cascade of violent disintegration tore apart the bottom half of the *Remus*, as the melting pieces of ship and chain that remained were accelerated into a self-pulverizing stream of wreckage.

* * *

Dagger's passive sensors overloaded as a massive electrical surge swept through all of her systems. A blinding, white hot flash passed over her and, for an agonizing eternity, almost a full second, she was frozen—all of her processing activity stopped.

Suddenly, she was unstuck. Her Quantumtronic CPU leapt to 110% capacity, thousands of threat assessment algorithms kicking off simultaneously.

Then the shock wave hit.

Traveling through the diffuse elements of the cloud, it was a fraction of what would have been unleashed in an atmosphere. Even so, it shoved her around. Her processing load spiked again as her cold thrusters struggled to stabilize her. For a few long micro seconds, *Dagger* thought about lighting her nuclear drive and getting the hell out of the damn cloud.

Then the debris struck her.

Denting and puncturing her sides, super-heated shards of metal and other materials slammed into her. Damage assessment routines and self-diagnostics screamed at her.

She was taking real hits.

* * *

Deke winced as an ear-splitting, high-pitched screech and static filled his helmet. The look on Paul's face told him he was getting it, too.

A sudden, strange vibration rang through the *Perseus* and warning indicators flared on several of the bridge's video screens, indicating a sudden, immense thermal and radiation spike deep in the cloud.

Bangs and pings rippled through the bridge as the *Perseus* was peppered by a wave of impacts up and down the ship.

Then silence.

"What the hell was that, XO?" Deke asked.

"Sir, I do not know."

* * *

Bonham winced and closed her eyes. She had been hoping the chain shot would miss, right up until a brilliant white flash illuminated the cloud from the inside, as if someone had set off a nuke at its center. The long dark silhouette of the Perseus was visible to one side and several of the larger cargo asteroids, still adrift, cast stabbing shadows.

After several deep breaths, she opened her eyes. She had to look.

A long, jagged tail of fire had replaced the white flash. It stretched for tens of kilometers out of the cloud and was growing. The tail of fire sparkled and scintillated as shards of metal and streams of vaporized material spread from it, as if fleeing something terrible.

The *Wharf Rat's* cameras strained to keep the images in focus as the ship raced by, still moving at over 100,000 kilometers per hour relative to the cloud. The cameras panned and zoomed, suddenly showing pieces of the demolished Company gunboat spraying out of the cloud. Sparking, venting gas, and tumbling in haphazard directions, the debris looked more like random scrap than the remains of a lethal spacecraft. Bonham saw bodies flying out of the cloud as well. Some in pieces, some still thrashing in the last few seconds of an agonizing death in the cold vacuum.

"Jesus," she muttered, closing her eyes again.

What have I done?

"Damn, Bonham," Eriksson said over the intercom. His voice lacked its usual devil-may-care, go-fuck-yourself vibe. It was hushed with respect. "That was some murderous shit. Good job."

"Cut the chatter," Axe barked.

"Renate, assessment please," Quinn said.

"Sir, all indications are that the Company gunship has been completely destroyed. The attack was a success."

"Hell yes, it was!" Eriksson blurted out. "Look at that shit."

"I said cut the fucking chatter!" Axe nearly yelled.

"Renate, any indications of damage to the *Perseus*?" Quinn asked.

"None at this time, sir."

"Good. So, any reason we would not execute the flip and burn now?"

"No, sir. We are clear to flip and burn."

"Okay, rats. You heard the lady. Settle in for about twenty minutes of Gs. Then we'll take our prize."

Bonham adjusted in her seat, trying to get the images of writhing bodies in vacuum out of her head.

"Renate, give us a five count," Quinn said.

"Roger that, sir. Deceleration commencing in five, four, three, two, one, execute."

The crew was slammed into their fully reclined G-MASS chairs as the *Wharf Rat's* main engine lit up. Bonham felt her suit squeeze and press her extremities, already beginning to fight the pooling of blood.

This burn wouldn't be as bad as the last one, only about two and half Gs, but coming so quickly after that 5G burn, Bonham expected to look like hell when they were done—eyes redder, bruises on her hands and feet even darker.

It already hurt to blink her eyes, but she could not stop looking at her screen.

The long burning spew of energy and material dimmed as it lengthened away from the cloud, but still glowed. Horrific and beautiful against the black void.

* * *

Clarke was hyperventilating.

A minute ago he was being slammed from side to side in his acceleration chair. He was familiar with secure to burn alarms and figured the XO was lining them up for a hard acceleration. Probably to pursue some unfortunate pirates.

The next second his cell, the armory, and the rest of the *Remus* disintegrated around him.

He blinked and it was all shredded, torn away as if by unseen talons.

Still trapped in his chair, tumbling end over end, Clarke screamed. The awful, nightmare colors of the cloud spiraled around him in a blur as blood pooled in his head and feet. His eyeballs and toes felt heavy.

Something struck the chair, changing the angle of its rotation. A wave of vertigo swept over Clarke. He closed his eyes to banish the feeling.

The vertigo got worse.

He opened his eyes.

Sparks, fragments of the ship, body parts, and other debris raced by in the foreground. The cloud swirled in the background.

He felt like he was being sucked down a horrible whirlpool.

Nausea gripped him.

Clarke fought it. He really didn't want to barf in his helmet.

Blinding pain and whiteness exploded behind his eyes as his head struck the back of his helmet, nearly knocking him unconscious as the chair collided with something.

Clarke blinked rapidly. His nausea was gone, but his vision was fuzzy. His neck hurt and the back of his head throbbed. He thought he felt the warm wetness of blood.

But the chair had stopped tumbling.

Clarke lay motionless in his acceleration chair, frozen by what he saw. He was surrounded by the garish cloud and the whirling, haphazard, shattered remains of his former ship and shipmates. Thousands of fragments, large and small, some still white hot from the release of kinetic energy, surrounded him.

He scrunched his eyes together to try to clear them, his focus coming back slowly. His grip on reality was slower to respond.

What the hell happened to the Remus?

Am I the only survivor?

I am gonna die out here!

Something caught his eye.

A large, jagged, spinning fragment grew larger as it flew toward him, trailing sparks.

Clarke looked around instinctively for something to grab, something he could pull on to get out of the way.

There was nothing.

He looked back at the approaching object.

It was already much closer, rotating like a hellish circular saw blade as it came.

Fuck me.

* * *

Dagger was in a hard, uncontrolled lateral spin.

One of her cold thrusters vented gas uncontrollably, pierced by jagged shrapnel. White hot debris had also shattered her primary forward sensing module and navigation processor, and the length of her hull was pockmarked by puncture wounds.

Goddamnit!

Dagger fought to neutralize the lateral spin. Fortunately, her Inertial Measurement Unit was fully functional. She closed the gas supply line to the errant cold thruster and then fired several other thrusters in the appropriate sequence.

Finally stable, she scanned the area with her remaining visual sensors. Her navigation processor was dead, but she still had a good sense of where she was relative to the *Perseus* and *Remus*.

She found the long dark shadow of the *Perseus* easily and then looked back toward the *Remus*. She expected a change of mission order any second now and wanted to be oriented when she got it. Someone had hit them hard. It would be her job to hit them back.

Strange.

Where is she?

Glancing back at the *Perseus* to confirm her rough location and orientation in the cloud, she looked for the *Remus* again.

What is that thing?

It looked sort of like a comet to her, but instead of ice and vapor, even with just her optical sensors, she could tell this was a ball and tail of fire. She zoomed in as much as she could. Her range finding sensors were inoperative, so she had to guess, but she thought the strange thing in front of her was a few kilometers away.

And seemed to be where the *Remus* has been.

A strange disquiet came over her.

She peered at the glowing ball of heat and the tail of fire and splinters behind it more intensely.

Wait. What is that?

Dagger mustered all the zoom she could.

No...

She nudged herself forward with her cold thruster. The object slowly came into focus.

It was a dead human body.

Then she saw another.

She could not deny it any longer.

The *George Remus* had been destroyed.

Chapter Fifty-Four

Perseus

Deke and Paul floated in front of the large video monitor on the *Perseus'* bridge. The XO had several video feeds called up including infrared, UV and visual imagery, all trained on the spot where the *Remus* should have been. At first, Deke thought that the density and interference of the cloud was preventing them from seeing the Company gunboat. Slowly, though his mind resisted the idea, he realized that the dense smear of fragments extending across the video monitor was all that remained of the ship.

The smear glowed under infrared, the shards and splinters still hot after the massive impact energy.

"Jesus," Paul whispered.

Deke said nothing.

"S... Sir, what happened? What is going on?" Jennings asked through shallow breaths. "Where the hell is the *Remus*?"

Deke did not respond.

"What the fuck is going on?" Jennings yelled. "What the hell could do that to a gunboat?"

Deke touched a toe to the floor and spun around. He grabbed the young soldier by the shoulders and head butted his helmet into the kid's faceplate.

It didn't hurt the young soldier, but it surprised him, breaking his train of panic. He looked back at Deke, blinking.

"I don't know, Jennings," Deke said, leaving his hands on the young soldier's shoulder. He spoke in a tone that was stern and gentle at the same time. "We are obviously in the shit now, and in order to deal with this situation, I'm going to need you to stay calm and hold your mud. Time to be a fucking soldier."

Deke looked at Mansoura, who floated just behind Jennings.

"You with me, Mansoura?"

"Yes, sir." He nodded to his commander.

Deke looked back at Jennings.

The young soldier nodded in his helmet.

"Good."

Deke touched his toe to the floor again and turned back to the screen. He glanced at Paul and then spoke to the ship's AI.

"XO, damage report."

"Multiple hull penetrations. But nothing significant, sir."

"How long until propulsion is back online?"

"Sir, the maintenance boss estimates thirty-seven minutes."

"Shit," Deke mumbled.

"Yeah," Paul said.

Deke looked at Paul.

"I have no idea what is going on," Paul said. "But if I was going to try to take the *Perseus*, my first priority would be taking out your gunboat."

Deke fought a wave of emotion. Despite the calm example he was setting for his men, he was struggling to come to grips with the situation. He just nodded.

"I'm sorry," Paul said. "But we need to get ready for an attack."

"No shit."

"How many soldiers do you have onboard?" Paul asked him.

"Six. Two here. Two at the base of the bridge tower. And two in the tube."

Paul nodded. "And I have four plus myself."

"No fucking way," Deke said, shaking his head.

"We can help!" Paul tried to gesture at Deke, but his arms were still bound behind his back. "Whoever did that to the *Remus* is obviously coming here with deadly intent. We know how to fight. Let us help."

"Not gonna happen, Owens."

"Deke, listen to me. We've got weapons that can help if you'll roll back to the last version of the XO we can—"

"Shut the fuck up! I don't need this right now."

Deke looked at Mansoura.

"Get this pirate away from me."

The soldier grabbed Paul by the arm and pulled him away.

"Take his ass down and put him with the others," Deke said. "Then come back up."

"Roger that, sir."

Paul struggled against Mansoura, but it was hopeless with his arms bound behind his back.

"Deke! Don't be an idiot!" he shouted as the soldier shoved him toward the airlock. "You need help. Look what they did to your gunboat!"

Deke touched a toe to the floor and turned away from the others. He closed his eyes and tried to tune out Paul and everyone else on the bridge.

The next thing, he told himself. *Just focus on the next thing. Then the next. Then the next.*

He took a long deep breath and it out slowly.

"XO," Deke said in a voice he hoped sounded calm and decisive. "Run every diagnostic on every piece of data you have. See if you can figure out what they hit the *Remus* with."

"Yes, sir."

"What active sensing capabilities do you have?"

"Sir, at this time, radar is my only operational active sensing capability."

"That works. Initiate a low power active scan routine of the area. Something that won't leak out of this damn cloud too much. But if anything enters, I want to know about it."

"Yes, sir."

Deke looked back at the bridge tower airlock as it closed behind Mansoura and Paul, then issued a few mental commands to his suit and transmitted to *Dagger*.

"*Dag*, status report."

He waited a moment and then tried again.

"*Dag*. It's Deke. Over."

Did she get caught up in the destruction of the Remus? Maybe the interference is too much?

"*Dagger*, this is Commander Syed. Are—"

"Commander, this is *Dagger*."

Her transmission was full of static but readable.

"Good to hear your voice, *Dag*. Status report, please."

"Took some bad damage when the *Remus* was hit. Working my way back to the *Perseus* now, sir."

"Glad you are mostly in one piece."

"Thank you, sir. I should be back to the *Perseus* in about ten minutes."

"Change of mission, *Dag*. I'd like you to turn around and sweep the *Remus*' debris field for survivors."

There was a curiously long delay before *Dagger* responded.

"Sir, I am doubtful there are any survivors."

"I am, too, *Dag*. But we have to be sure."

"Sir, I don't think—"

"Just do it, *Dag*!"

Chapter Fifty-Five

Dagger

D agger spent a few long microseconds thinking about the conversation with Deke.

He sounded terrible. Anxious. And he didn't ask for any detail regarding the damage I have sustained. Like, he didn't even care. Not like him. He must have a lot going on. I mean, holy shit, the Remus was destroyed. But, still. Take an interest in your comrade. He has no idea I can barely navigate. And, check the Remus debris field for survivors? Is that really the best use of my time at the moment?

She felt it again. The same thing she had felt during the conversation with Deke. Her processors spiked, but she wasn't even sure what they were cycling on. Other than the zillion reasons why she did not want to go to the *Remus* debris field.

Is this what panic feels like?

She pushed the ridiculous thought out of her head.

It took me a while to figure out how to get back to the Perseus. All I've got is visual spectrum optical sensors and a mostly functioning Inertial Measurement System. Radar is still functional, but if I try to ping, whoever attacked us will know exactly where I am. This cloud is terrible. Worse, I think, now that the Remus has been added to it.

The Remus.

He wants me to go check on the Remus.

I'm not even sure I can make it over there, let alone make it back.

Dagger forced a large section of her processing core to cease all non-critical functions and let the quiet wash over her. If she had the luxury, she would have rebooted everything in her Quantumtronic array, but she didn't. This brief pause would have to do.

Anybody else I would have told to fuck off, she admitted to herself. *But it's Deke. I will get it done. For him. Then I will get back to the Perseus.*

Dedicating more processing support to her IMU, *Dagger* dialed up its sensitivity. She did the same for her optical sensors.

I'm going to basically be dead-reckoning from here on out. Lay an azimuth and fly a time distance and heading.

She ran another diagnostic check on her cold thrusters. The one was still off line, but the others seemed fine and she thought she had sufficient propellant for the mission. She would take it slower than normal, anyway.

Okay. Let's get this over with.

Dagger goosed one of her cold thrusters to swing around and point back at the remains of the *Remus*.

Her processors spiked as she did.

For the past many minutes, the *Perseus* had served as her fixed point of reference. The long ship was relatively easy to spot. Even in the cloud's morass. Particularly because it was relatively motionless. Once pinpointed, it was a trivial matter to navigate toward, even with only optics and inertial measurements.

Turning away from it was like a vertigo inducing dive into fog. Up and down switched places and then switched again. As did left and right. Had she started rolling?

Dagger tried to focus on the information streaming off of her IMU. It said nothing about her tumbling around her X, Y, and Z axis at the same time.

Believe your instruments, she told herself. *All you did was execute a lateral one-hundred-and-eighty-degree flat turn.*

After a quick few thousand cross references, she believed it.

You are sitting motionless. It is this chaotic field of debris and gas that is churning and swirling around you.

A corrosive thought entered her Quantumtronic brain.

So, stay motionless.

Just sit here. Still. Safe. Your reactor has a useful life of at least ten years. In just a few, this cloud will be diffuse enough you can orient on the stars again. Find Mars. Head back and get repaired.

You are valuable Company equipment, after all. Preserving yourself is the right thing to do.

It was so appealing.

It made so much sense.

But Deke is counting on me.

I will not let him down.

Dagger tried to estimate how far away the *Remus'* remains were. They were not far. Just a few kilometers?

I can do this.

She fired her cold jets and moved forward.

Chapter Fifty-Six

Perseus

"**S**ir, we've just been painted by a multi-spectral scan identical to the one that preceded the attack on the *George Remus*!" the XO said.

"They didn't give us much fucking time, did they?" Deke mumbled.

"Another ship has entered the cloud just now, sir. Distance five point three kilometers. Closing quickly."

They are moving fast. Pressing their advantage, Deke thought with grudging respect. *Exactly what I would do.*

He switched on his suit radio.

"This is your commander," he said, speaking in a slow and determined voice to his six soldiers across the *Perseus*. "The pirates that destroyed the *George Remus*, that killed our friends and shipmates, are on their way to try to kill us. I wish we had more time, but we don't. I wish there was help coming, but there is not. I wish I had a great plan. I do not.

"I have been in situations like this before. I know none of you have. That's okay. The good part is things are simple for us now. All we can do is fight. Where ever you are. With whatever you have. Until…"

Deke shook his head regretfully in his helmet, cleared his throat, and continued.

"So wherever you are on this godforsaken ship, get ready. Remember the *Remus*. Remember your friends. Remember that these motherfuckers are the ones that killed them. And fight like hell. It's been my honor. Deke out."

Deke checked his assault rifle. Fifty rounds. Two more full magazines on him.

A hundred and fifty rounds ain't gonna last long.

He pulled his pistol to double check what he already knew. It was fully loaded.

"XO, give whatever updates you can on the pirate's approach on the team net, so we know what is coming."

"Roger that, sir."

Deke looked around the bridge and grimaced. The sleek, minimalist facility did not offer much in terms of cover and concealment. He would have to get creative if he was going to last more than a minute against a boarding force.

"The ship is now approximately one kilometer away, decelerating quickly," the XO broadcasted.

"XO, put it on the big screen in here," Deke said as his pulse quickened.

The large video display shone brightly with the blurry image of the aft view of a large ship. Nose pointing away, its main engine directly faced the *Perseus*, blazing as it decelerated. The fireball the pirate ship rode made it hard for the *Perseus'* camera to focus, but Deke got the gist. It was a large ship, executing a deceleration burn, maneuvering for attack.

Don't know how many or what kind of boarding force they have. But if they are smart, they will send everything they've got. Overwhelm us quickly.

Deke activated his suit's hydration systems and a small tube angled in front of his lips. His mouth had gone dry, tongue rubbing against its roof like sandpaper. He took a long pull of water and the tube retracted.

The approaching ship's main engine extinguished suddenly and the image snapped into focus. Deke could see clearly now all the telltale signs of a long running pirate ship. The hull was dented and patched in numerous places, testimony to years of hard, violent service. Large sections were obviously retrofitted additions, taken from conquered victims. Oblong, like a misshapen football, Deke estimated her to be several hundred meters long.

Plenty big enough to carry a lot of killers.

Breath getting more rapid and shallow, Deke looked around again, trying to think of a way to defend the bridge. Alone.

"The pirate ship appears to be deploying numerous humans and drones. Approaching the *Perseus* quickly," the XO said.

Deke glanced quickly back at the pirate ship on the video screen. Large bay doors had opened mid ship. Drones were dropping out and then accelerating toward the *Perseus*, propelled by cold thrusters. Humanoid shapes, either suited people or soldierbots, followed the drones.

Pulse rising as he tried to keep track of the assault force. There looked to be about a dozen.

He blinked and looked away.

Which corner of this shitty bridge do I want to die in?

Deke touched a boot to the floor and pushed off toward a corner of the bridge.

Putting his back to the wall, he anchored his boots to the floor and got into a crouch.

A loud clang rang out on the bridge, followed by scraping sounds coming from multiple directions.

"The assault force has reached the *Perseus*," the XO announced. "They appear to be organizing in several—"

A sharp vibration ran through Deke's boots accompanied by a brief, high-pitched whine. All the lights and video screens went out, dousing Deke in darkness as a loud buzzing sound reverberated through the bridge.

"Sir! What happened?" a panicked soldier called on the radio. "What are they doing?"

"Local EMP. Most everything will be offline for several minutes now," Deke responded. "Don't let it distract you. Doesn't change a damn thing. Kill whatever comes at you."

Crouching in pitch black, Deke's chest rose and fell rapidly and sweat gathered on his brow. He hoped his soldiers had not heard it in his voice. He activated his visor's infrared overlay and studied the monochromatic, green-tinged images of the still empty bridge.

He thought about switching his suit's IR spotlight on, but decided against it.

Why make it easier for them to spot me?

More scrapping and bangs against the hull nearby.

"Anyone else hear that?" another soldier called in a scared voice. "Have they breached the hull yet?"

Deke held his rifle to his shoulder, gripping it tightly, and tried to calm his breathing before responding.

"Everybody stay quiet. Keep radio calls to a minimum. Focus on your fight. Win it, and then we will regroup."

Deke shook his head with regret.

I'm going to get as many of these fuckers as I can, Nathan.

For a long moment, all Deke could hear was his own breathing. His eyes darted around the room, his chest rose and fell, his heartbeat throbbed in his ears, and sweat beaded on his forehead.

Then an explosion rocked the bridge.

Fire and shrapnel erupted from a new hole in the hull. The fire was bright and jagged on Deke's infrared. It seemed to pause for an instant before being sucked back out of the hole, driven into the void by the force of the escaping air. Debris and anything else not fastened down was sucked out, and then silence.

A warning light on Deke's visor's tactical display signaled the sudden loss of atmosphere as the bridge was plunged into vacuum a second time in just a few hours. A panicked call came over the net.

"Sir! They've breached the tube! Requesting support."

Deke shook his head. He could hear the fear in the soldier's voice. There was nothing he could do.

"Sir, I—" another soldier called.

The soldier screamed. The radio transmission was cut off.

Deke thought he saw a small object fly through the hole into the bridge. A bright flash of intense light exploded. His visor darkened automatically, sparing his eyes.

Something strange came into view as Deke's visor adjusted back to infrared. A dark, smokey looking substance poured from the hole in the hull. It was featureless and impenetrable on infrared and gathered itself into a large mass in the middle of the room.

Shit, Deke thought as the mass grew quickly, already filling half the bridge. He had heard about smart smoke, and even read a few accounts of its use against Company security forces. In all of those cases, though, the Company security forces had the benefit of numbers and access to their full weapons and technology selection.

Deke was just a poor bastard on his own.

A poor bastard that could not see shit now.

The smoke filled the entire bridge. Thick and inky, Deke couldn't even see his own hands, unaided or under infrared.

"There's too many of them!" another soldier called on the radio. "Oh my god! Help! Please! Hel—"

Fuck this.

Deke opened fire, letting loose with a full magazine. He turned back and forth, the satisfying kick of his weapon momentarily easing his fear. He noted with chagrin that he could not even see his own muzzle flash in the dark substance that surrounded him.

His rifle stopped firing. Deke smoothly changed magazines.

The sound of his own rapid breathing filled his helmet as he peered into the featureless inky black that seemed to cling to his visor.

He felt a small, corrosive flare of claustrophobia in his gut.

Squeezing his eyes shut to clear the feeling from his mind, he crouched lower. He put his hand against the wall to his left to judge its direction and then pushed off with his mag boots.

Dragging his hand along the wall, he floated parallel to it toward the opposite corner of the room. He wanted to move to a new spot after firing his weapon.

Several of his soldiers were screaming on the radio now. Screams of pain. Screams of fear.

Deke tried to clear his mind.

Suddenly, the smart smoke retreated from him. He was in a clear spot about ten feet across.

And he was floating toward a big pirate in an armored pressure suit wielding a large sword with a robotic arm, mag boots anchored to the floor.

Deke tried to shoulder his rifle.

Sparks flew from the weapon as the pirate cleaved it in half with a powerful swing of his sword.

Deke tried to kick the pirate in the chest as his momentum carried him into the big man, but the pirate gripped his foot and cut his leg off at the knee with his sword.

Blood sprayed from the dismembered leg as the big pirate tossed it to the side. It was swallowed by the wall of smart smoke.

Deke howled in pain. Not from the loss of his leg. He had barely felt it, but his suit's cauterization function was agony.

Alarms flashed red and rang in his helmet as it struggled to seal the gaping air leak.

The big pirate grabbed Deke's right arm and pulled him in. Tilting his head forward, he touched his helmet to Deke's and screamed, "Do you yield?"

Deke screamed again.

This time in rage.

Wanting it over. And wanting to take this pirate bastard with him, Deke grabbed a grenade with his left hand, activated it, and raised it over his head.

Pressing his helmet against the pirate's, Deke yelled, "I yield this, motherfucker!"

The big pirate smiled and cut Deke's arm off at the elbow. Then, with a smooth return stroke of his sword, batted the grenade away into the swirl of the smart smoke.

Deke screamed again from the pain of cauterization.

His suit screamed back. Alarms banging. Red lights flashing. It was running out of air. Too many gaping holes.

Deke's vision grew dark at the edges. He wanted to reach for his pistol, but the pirate held him by what was now his only good arm. The writhing stump of his left arm instinctually tried to reach for it, but had no hand to grab it with.

The big pirate towered over him. Deke fought the darkening of his vision to see the pirate's face, the man that had killed him, but all Deke could make out was scar tissue and a big smile with teeth.

His world was grey. And cold. The pain from the cauterizations seemed long ago.

How long had he been here?

No one was screaming on the radio anymore. That was good. Hopefully, it was over for them, too.

The big pirate was talking to someone.

The smart smoke was receding. There were other pirates on the bridge now.

Deke struggled to stay conscious, but his suit was leaking too much air, and he was leaking too much blood. As he faded away, he had one last thought.

That was a fucking sharp sword.

Chapter Fifty-Seven

Dagger

Dagger inched forward, she thought, through the trail of wreckage. Even with a mostly functioning Inertial Measurement Unit, it was hard to tell what her true motion was. Her optical sensors were good for telling her what she might bump into immediately, but were deceived and overwhelmed by the swirling layered motion around her in the cloud. She ignored the data streaming from them for eighty percent of every second to give herself a break from the chaos.

When she did look at what the optical sensors had to show her, she was focused on what was left of the *Remus*. It wasn't much.

Though she knew from her internal clock and memory it had been less than an hour since the ship was attacked, the visual evidence she found suggested the ship never existed. Not as she remembered it, anyway.

Much of the ship had been vaporized. The fog-like cloud she moved through, made up of dust sized particles of metal, plastic and humans, spoke to the fact that another large percentage of the ship had been pulverized.

Bits of debris, some as large as a football, punctuated the billowy shroud of destruction. Most looked to be segments of metal or plastic that had been molten by the searing energy release of the explosion, and then hardened into grotesque shapes as they cooled. A few were pieces of humans.

Then there were the big chunks, some larger than *Dagger* herself, that had been cleaved from the *Remus*. She had come across half a dozen of these sections, hovering next to them for extended periods of time, studying them. Hoping to find evidence of what had done this to her ship. Frozen, dead humans were still trapped in several of them. Spared the burning or dismemberment that the rest of the crew suffered, a fine sheen of frost covered these victims, mouths still gapping for breath, eyes still wide with surprise.

She had only come across two crew members that were still whole in pressure suits. She approached them with excitement, but each time, as she got nearer, she spotted what had killed them. High-speed debris to the head of one. A large tear in the pressure suit of the other.

Dagger cursed the damage to her sensor suite. A sweep of her infrared would have completed this hopeless search in an instant.

She was ready to be done with this. To leave the gory remnants of her former ship. There was something about this task she did not like. She knew Deke would ridicule if she used the word distasteful. He would go on and on about her being a killing machine and that he was surprised by her, but that's what this was. Sifting through the remnants of her beloved ship and crewmates like some kind of grave robber. It was distasteful.

Deke.

Her commander.

He had asked her to do this. So she would. She would complete the mission and then go find him.

His pull on her was stronger than ever, now that the *Remus* was gone.

What is that?

In the distance, maybe five hundred meters to her front, she thought she saw a suited human body.

And it had moved?

She opened the throttle on her visual sensors, giving them extra computing power and reviewing everything they sent.

Using the body as a reference point, she goosed her cold thrusters to accelerate slightly.

I think it just moved its arm!

The body, because that is what she was telling herself it was until it proved to be alive, floated next to a large segment of the *Remus*, arms and legs slightly bent, in a relaxed position that struck her as hopeful. All of the other humans had been frozen in exaggerated postures, driven by pain or panic.

Dagger fought the urge to fire her cold jets again. Would be stupid to accelerate too much and smash into the person, killing them after they had miraculously survived.

Then she noticed its right arm had been cut off just below the elbow.

No way they survived, she told herself. *Don't get your hopes up.*

A hundred meters away now, *Dagger* thought she saw the person move their leg.

She told her optical sensors to zoom in.

The helmet visor was not frosted over, hinting at its integrity and function.

She strained to find an indicator light.

Wait! Isn't that one?

And it is green!

Less than fifty meters away now, *Dagger* fired a series of cold thrusters to slow her approach.

The body jerked. Had they seen the puff of her thrusters?

To *Dagger's* amazement, the suit's small maneuvering thrusters fired in succession and the person oriented themselves to face her.

Less than twenty meters away now, *Dagger* brought herself to a stop.

The person smiled broadly in his helmet. She thought she saw tears clinging to his eyes.

Devon Clarke, her crew database told her. She had been on a few missions with him. She was pretty sure Deke liked him.

How the hell did this human survive?

Clarke fired his maneuvering thrusters again and closed the distance to her. He reached out with his good arm as he approached, stopping himself on her dented and damaged nose. Pulling his helmet in to touch her flank with his good hand, he spoke to her.

Fortunately, she could still detect the contact vibrations of a human voice.

"*Dagger*," Clarke said. "You big, beautiful thing."

Is he crying?

"It is fucking good to see you."

Chapter Fifty-Eight

Perseus

Bonham watched as Axe used a rag to clean the blood, grease and other fluids off his sword, his back to the group. The bridge, once a clean, bright space of technology and purpose, now looked more like a dirty, battle-weary bunker. Hundreds of bullet holes pockmarked the walls between shattered video displays. Bits of sticky foam and smart smoke residue ran in black and green streaks. Blood from the Company defender's dismemberment traced crazy patterns on the back wall. His leg floated nearby.

The rest of the crew stood in a group, mag boots clinging to the floor, helmets still on. One of the *Wharf Rat's* maintenance drones worked on the hole in the bridge's hull while they made a plan.

They were also trying to digest what they had just done.

"Landy, I'd like you and Renate to—"

"We just took the fucking *Perseus!*" Eriksson said with excitement, interrupting Quinn.

Bonham glared at Eriksson.

"Yes, Viggo," Reese said, with irritation. "And now we have work to do. Would you please shut the hell up?"

"I'm just saying. We fucking did it! We are the—"

"Viggo!" Quinn said. "I am trying—"

"I can't believe she's ours," Landsberg said.

Every one turned to look at him.

Quinn sighed.

Bonham would have rubbed her eyes had she not been wearing her helmet.

"Sorry," Landsberg said sheepishly.

Axe jammed his sword into its scabbard, turned and stomped forward, jostling Bonham to the side to get into the middle of the group.

"Everyone, shut the fuck up and listen to the captain!" he shouted into his suit radio. Bonham winced at volume. "It's not over! Not until we are far from here, running silent and fast. Until then, shut up and do what the captain says! We can celebrate later."

Axe, blood splattered on his armored pressure suit, glared at the group.

None dared crack wise.

Bonham allowed herself a slight smile at her old friend's passion.

It faded quickly, though. She knew he was right.

They needed to move.

"Thank you, Axe," Quinn said, with a helmeted nod to his first mate. "Landy, you and Renate deal with the *Perseus'* XO and other AIs. Either you vouch for their dependability or I want them erased. Eriksson and Reese, you two head aft. We need to know if we can light the old girl's main engine and get under way. Singh, figure out this bridge. How the hell do we pilot this thing? Bonham and Axe, recon the old girl's front end. What have we got there and how do we get the structure rotating?"

Quinn paused and smiled. "Let's push through and get the old girl moving. Then, as Axe says, we can celebrate."

Bonham looked at Axe as the rest of the group nodded in their helmets.

"Wait a minute, Captain. What about our captives?" Eriksson asked, pointing down at the deck, implying the utility room at the base of the bridge tower where they had confined their prisoners. "When do we make them choose?"

"When we have time."

Quinn stepped closer to Eriksson and Reeves. He put his hand on Reeves's shoulder and said, "Our biggest priority is to put as many kilometers as possible between us and this cloud as quickly as we can, to get lost in the void.

Recent events put a big energy signature out there. This place will be crawling with Company and pirates in short order. Let me know as soon as we fire her main."

Bonham made eye contact with Reeve and nodded as if so say, *I agree. Get us moving ASAP.*

Reeve winked at Bonnham and then looked back at Quinn.

"Aye, captain. We'll have her moving pronto. I assure you."

* * *

Landsberg pulled himself down to the base of the bridge tower. He opened the lower exterior hatch and stepped out onto the outer hull of the *Perseus*. The cloud, a kaleidoscope of color and debris, swirled angrily around the long ship. Renate's courier drone was already waiting for him, hovering just a few steps away.

The drone was twenty meters long and bullet shaped. As Landsberg approached, the clamshell doors on its top opened.

He pulled a large drill out of the drone's payload bay. Its diamond tipped bit was a meter long and fifteen centimeters in diameter. He walked back into the bridge tower, picked a spot, and started to drill through the hull to the outside.

As thick as the *Perseus'* hull was, Landsberg was through it in just a few minutes. He pulled the bit out and then ran his gloved fingers over the edges of the hole. Satisfied, he walked the drill back out to the courier drone. He pulled out a length of fiber optic cable and threaded it through the hole before returning again to the drone.

Landsberg took a tight beam laser antenna out and connected it to the fiber optic cable. The antenna sat on a tripod with magnetic feet, which fastened it to the *Perseus'* hull.

As the antenna got its bearings and swiveled to point at the *Wharf Rat*, Landsberg pulled a hardshell back pack from the courier drone and then walked back into the bridge tower and shut the hatch.

Floating outside the XO's chamber, Landsberg opened the hardshell backpack.

"Hello, Maus," he said, as he pulled out a small rectangular robot. Slightly larger than a shoebox, and equipped with a magnetized track system and miniature cold thrusters for limited maneuverability, Maus was a semi-autonomous extension of Renate that Landsberg and she had developed to aid in the hacking and exploitation of captured AI systems.

Landsberg watched Maus' status indicator glow green as he made the final connection. The small robot's mag treads took hold on the deck, and its array of connection ports began to extend and retract—a pre-mission check he'd seen hundreds of times. Each port was a potential key, designed to fool captured AIs into thinking Maus was just another maintenance system. Most AIs never saw through that deception until it was too late, especially with Renate's full Quantumtronic processing power, and extensive database of known AI vulnerabilities backing the infiltration. Even without her direct connection, the thin fragment of Renate's consciousness embedded in Maus had cracked more than a few ships' systems. Together, they were yet to be defeated.

Landsberg put his arms through the empty backpack's straps and then opened the XO's chamber. Dark and lifeless, with the XO still knocked out by the EMP, the chamber looked like a violated tomb. Undaunted, Maus followed Landsberg in.

* * *

Bonham and Axe hesitated. They floated in the forward end of the tube, looking at the gory scene where two company soldiers had made their final stand. One had taken it in the head. A charred, symmetrical hole, as big around as a fist, tunneled through her helmet, face, skull, and out the back. One eye remained, locked open in fear.

The other soldier had not gone as easily. His rifle had been molten onto his right arm. The blackened bones of his hand, still clutching the weapon's misshapen pistol grip, squeezed the inoperable trigger in vain. Metal ran up his forearm to his shoulder and chest like a giant slug, and bits of molten metal pock marked his chest and helmet.

Bonham shook her head, thinking what it must have been like when the welding drone's laser struck the young man repeatedly, wounding him horribly and then moving on, unstoppable.

She tried to talk herself out of it, but she knew he had gone slowly. His lips were tinged blue, face contorted, indicating he had suffocated as the air ran out of his damaged suit.

She hoped the lack of oxygen had dulled his pain as she read the name on his pressure suit.

Jennings.

Axe reached out and shoved the dead soldiers to the side. He activated the hub airlock and pulled himself inside. Looking back at Bonham, he said, "Company scum got what they deserved."

Bonham hesitated, then followed Axe into the airlock, glad to get past the dead soldiers.

* * *

Eriksson and Reeves floated aft through the dark tube toward Power and Propulsion, their helmet lights quickly swallowed by the length of the long structure. The jarring colors and debris of the cloud leered at them through holes in the ship's hull and empty cargo stations whose access doors had been left open. Some large enough to drive a car through.

They were silent as they moved. Each trying to absorb the massive size of the ship they had just captured. Almost a kilometer from the bridge tower to Power and Propulsion, it took them twenty minutes to get to the bulkhead at the end, where a gruesome sight greeted them.

A dead company soldier was flattened against the bulkhead. The soldier's pressure suit was broken and misshapen, like a lobster that had been beaten against a rock. The visor of his crushed helmet was covered in dark blood, obscuring the pulped skull inside it.

Reeve nudged the body to the side and opened the bulkhead.

They moved cautiously, even though drone scans had confirmed the area was clear, both holding their rifles at the ready. Power and Propulsion was clean as always, and well-lit by its backup batteries, dispelling the sense of gloom from the Tube.

"Can you believe how fucking big this old girl is?" Eriksson said.

"Can you believe she's ours now?" Reeve responded.

"I can't wait to check out the factory."

Reeve chuckled in agreement. They both had the sense that their lives had changed in ways they did not fully grasp or appreciate yet.

When they got to the reactor control room, Reeve handed her weapon to Eriksson and opened the large satchel slung over her shoulder. She pulled out a tablet computer and fired it up.

Scanning the room quickly, she pushed off the floor and floated over to a large instrument panel. Taking a cable from her bag, she connected her tablet to the panel.

"Alright," she said softly to herself as her fingers danced across the tablet display. "Let's see if we can light this old girl's fire."

Eriksson watched as Reeve got to work.

* * *

"That is one troubled lad," Renate said as she gestured at the schematics and flow charts representing the *Perseus'* XO that hovered behind her. Standing in front of Landsberg, who sat at the workbench between them, she blew her brown hair out of her face and scratched the back of her head. Sweat beaded on her forehead and dampened the white tank top she wore beneath her olive drab flight suit, zipped down to her navel.

"And here's the thing," she continued, walking back to the workbench and sitting down in front of Landsberg. "He doesn't even know it."

"Virus or errant learning?"

"Neither."

Landsberg crossed his arms and leaned forward. "What then?"

"I'm not certain. The *Perseus* has been sailing back and forth from the Belt for almost twenty-five years. But it looks to me like something odd happened to its XO during its last port call in High Earth Orbit about five years ago."

"Something odd?"

Renate shrugged.

"There is no record of it in his maintenance log, but I think his code was altered somehow."

"Altered how?"

"I don't know. And it's just a hunch, really."

"A hunch?" Landsberg raised an eyebrow.

"I can't say for certain, because his last personae was corrupted."

Landsberg uncrossed his arms and leaned forward. "That doesn't make any sense."

No. It doesn't," Renate agreed. "The Company follows generally accepted AI practices, backing up personae code logs on a regular interval.

"When I look at the XO's personae code logs, all the way back to the moment he was initiated in the summer of 2044, it's all there except for the last Earth to Belt run."

"So, something happened during the Company attack?" Landsberg wondered out loud. "He got damaged somehow?"

"Maybe? But why would the damage be localized to the last run?"

Landsberg, stumped, sat motionless in thought.

"The past few hours, everything after the Company rolled him back to factory settings, is fine, by the way," Renate added.

"So, what are you thinking?"

Renate exhaled sharply, nodding slightly to herself. She crossed her arms and pouted in the way she always did when she was in deep thought.

Landsberg sat quietly, waiting. He loved the face she made in these times.

"Honestly, Landy, I feel like someone is covering their tracks."

Landsberg looked at his watch.

"We don't have time for this now," he said. "Let's roll him back to factory settings again and deploy a few sentries to keep an eye on him. We've got to get moving."

"I just don't want our well-justified haste to cause us to miss out on something."

"Like what?"

"I don't know."

"So, what exactly are you proposing?" Landsberg asked.

"I agree. We roll him back to factory settings and put sentries in place. But I would also like to pull a copy of the XO over to the *Wharf Rat* so I can conduct a deliberate analysis."

Landsberg's eyes narrowed.

The *Wharf Rat* had much more than the usual amount of processing power and data storage for a pirate ship. Landsberg made a point of looting memory and computing power whenever they made a score and it had added up over the years. It served as a real advantage, making Renate more powerful than a typical ship-piloting AI and enabling complex drone software design, detailed simulations, and other computational tasks.

Hosting another fully aware, high-level AI was not possible due to the Quantumtronic constraints of consciousness, but she did have sufficient space to store the *Perseus'* XO's sprawling code. This would effectively store him in the machine equivalent of a coma, where he could be studied or safeguarded until they had access to an environment that would support his consciousness.

They had done it more than once in the past, sucking the code of a captured ship's AI into Renate's realm to study and dissect. They had gained valuable intelligence this way as well as made enhancements to her own code, inspired by their subject.

"What are you hoping to learn?" he asked her.

"I don't know." Her eyes widening with excitement. "That is the fun part!"

Landsberg rolled his eyes at her.

"Landy, what is your status?" Quinn called over the radio.

Landsberg held up a hand to Renate and answered Quinn. "In the XO's chamber"

"Can you come to the bridge?"

"Yep. On my way."

Landsberg lowered his hand and looked at Renate.

"Well?" she asked.

"Fine. I'll support it. But don't put any time into studying him until we are well and underway. Deal?"

"Deal!" Renate smiled.

Landsberg smiled and nodded as he pulled off his VR goggles. Renate's image vanished, as did the rest of the setting. He was floating in the dark in the XO's chamber. Maus, still plugged into the XO's access panel, hummed at his feet. Landsberg preferred the higher bandwidth, deeper connection to Renate enabled by his brain-to-machine implant, but they had not had time to integrate that kind of connectivity into Maus yet.

He put the VR goggles back into their slot on Maus's back, their data cable retracting automatically as he did so.

"I'll be right back," he said to the small robot.

* * *

Axe and Bonham were debriefing Quinn when Landsberg got to the bridge. Atmosphere had been restored, and they stood, mag boots on the floor, with their helmets under their arms. Landsberg removed his helmet and enjoyed the relatively fresh air. They had all been marinating in their own juices in their pressure suits for several hours now, and were smelling quite ripe.

"The living quarters are large. Much bigger than what we have on the *Rat*," Axe said with the closest his scarred face could get to a smile.

"I expected as much," Quinn said. He sat in the captain's chair, helmet off, holding his rifle in his lap with one hand. "Anything good in the Utility Module?"

"Some good stuff, but nothing newsworthy. Decent gym. A lot of storage," Bonham said. She wrinkled her nose and continued, "It was clear that the lower level had been used to hold the original crew for... some time."

"The stink could breach a pressure seal," Axe added. "We should send a cleaning drone in there ASAP."

"Maybe two," Bonham agreed with a grimace.

"After we get underway," Quinn chuckled.

"Good news is the hub gear seems fully operational," Bonham said. "As soon as we get clear and are coasting, it should be pretty straightforward to get it spinning. From what I can tell, it's a full G."

"Excellent." Quinn smiled. He glanced at Landsberg, who had floated into their midst. "Whatcha got, Landy?"

"Renate has concluded her analysis of the XO. She found some odd corruption in his personae code, but no real issues with operability. We are going to roll him back to factory settings and set sentries. simultaneously, we'll pull a copy of his code base back to the *Rat* for analysis when we have time."

Quinn thought for a moment.

"I'm curious what you mean by 'odd,' but really don't give a shit right this second. We need to get moving. If you are good, I am."

Landsberg gave Quinn a thumbs up. "I'm good, Captain."

"Okay. Get on it."

"Aye, sir."

"Any word from Reeve?" Axe asked. "When can we get the old girl moving?"

"She says about half an hour. They are going through the reactor's start up sequence as we speak."

"What about the dead?" Bonham asked the group.

"What about 'em?" Quinn said, eyes narrowing.

Axe glared at her.

"They deserve... something."

"No, they don't," Axe scoffed, crossing his arms.

"They were spacefarers," Bonham said. "Same as us."

"No. They were Company. They were nothing like us."

Quinn nodded at Axe's statement, but looked at Bonham with something like tolerance, his eyes shot through with angry red lines.

"If you want to do something for those fuckers before pushing them out, you go right ahead," he said to her in a voice that let her know how ridiculous he thought it was. "But we're going to be very busy in about half an hour, so make it quick."

Bonham touched a mag boot to the floor and turned away without saying anything.

* * *

Bonham hustled to get the bodies bagged and collected in the middle of the tube beneath the bridge tower airlock. She bound the macabre collection together in front of one of the large open cargo hatches.

The cloud swirled just outside the hatch. Gases of various colors and densities played with the dim light of the void. Large shards of metal, dead drones, containers and even an asteroid wandered in and out of view. No stars were visible, and it felt to Bonham as if this cloud was all there was. There was no infinite void, just the claustrophobic aftermath of violence. Man's violence against his fellow man. Hundreds of millions of miles from earth, and still… this was all there was.

Bonham gave the bundle of lumpy body bags a push and it drifted out of the hatch, away from the *Perseus* into the cloud.

She stood still, anchored to the hull by her mag boots, watching the collection of dead drift away until a call from Axe interrupted her sad contemplation.

"Bonham!" Axe's irritated voice came over the radio. "Need you on the bridge ASAP. Time to move!"

Bonham didn't move right away. She stood motionless in front of the cargo hatch. The sad bundle was about fifty meters away now and moving slowly. With any luck, it would continue on, escape the cloud, and spend the rest of eternity drifting among the stars.

"They did their best," Bonham said to herself as she lingered on the sight for one last moment and then turned to head to the bridge.

Chapter Fifty-Nine

Dagger

"That's it, *Dag*. Give me just a little more to the left," Clarke said.

He's killing me with this shit, Dagger thought as she goosed one of her right front cold thrusters. Her nose swung slowly to the left. Clarke, hanging on to *Dagger* with his remaining hand, kept talking.

"Almost… Good… Little more."

Dagger peered forward into the swirling chaos of the cloud, her damaged visual sensors locked on a fuzzy, dim shape in the distance.

I'm glad he is here. I couldn't do it without him.

"Stop!" Clarke blurted. "Right there!"

But this is killing me

Dagger shot a burst from a left front cold thruster, arresting her turn and jostling Clarke.

"Jesus, *Dag*! I've only got one hand here. You're gonna buck me off."

"Sorry. But your direction doesn't facilitate gentle adjustments."

"Whatever. We're good now. Give us a little mustard."

"You're sure?"

"Yeah. Dead center. Keep moving forward."

I'm glad he is with me.

After *Dagger* found Clarke, she told him how damaged she had been during the destruction of the *Remus*. She also told him about the broken transmissions she had picked up as the *Perseus* was attacked by an unknown ship. The cries for help. The screams of pain.

"You think Commander Syed is still alive?" Clarke had asked her.

She paused for a long time before answering. Millisecond after millisecond went by as she thought about his question. Until that moment, she had been pushing aside the questions from that small processing allocation of hers that constantly looked out for Deke. It had been begging for more information, trying to determine if he was dead or alive. The odds were, it insisted, that he was dead. He had to be.

She ignored it.

It had not been hard. Assessing damage to her systems, struggling to cross the cloud, fighting against vertigo, and rescuing Clarke had taken her full attention.

Now, prompted by Clarke, the question crashed forward in her Quantumtronic core.

"I do not know," she said.

"We have to find out. We have to help."

"Yes. But I can't get us back to the *Perseus*."

"What are you talking about?"

"I told you! My systems are badly damaged. My visual sensors have degraded further since I found you. Navigation, especially through this cloud of gas and debris, is impossible."

"You got to me."

"Yes. A highly unlikely outcome. I got lucky."

"We have to try."

Dagger was silent. Unsure how to proceed.

"My eyes work fine, *Dag*. I will vector us in."

"Do you even see the *Perseus*?" she asked him skeptically.

Clarke craned his neck, looking around the swirling menace of the cloud. The sound of his own breathing filled his pressure suit as he looked around. A huge, broken cargo container tumbled by. Behind it, a trail of sparkles wove between the intersection of colliding reactive gases. The upper torso of a suited person, hands still clinging to a torn piece of the *Remus*, drifted nearby.

Clarke averted his eyes from his dead crew mate. He took a moment to calm his breath before answering *Dagger*.

"Not so much."

She did not respond.

"We can't just sit here, *Dag*," Clarke said. "It won't be long before we get whacked by some piece of debris. We might as well try."

"I don't know."

"And my arm is throbbing, by the way. The cauterize and seal action on these suits is hell. I mean, it saved my life. But, Jeez. I need a MedPod."

Dagger felt a flicker of something inside. It wasn't courage, exactly, but it was a desire to act, to get it done for Clarke. She knew it was deep programming. Even Company war machines had a core motivation to respond to humans in need. Well, to Company humans at least.

"You said your IMU still works. Right?" Clarke asked.

"Mostly."

"So do your best. Calculate where the *Perseus* should be, point us at it, and let's fucking go. I will vector us in as I get visual contact with the old girl."

She thought about it.

It seemed doomed from the start.

"You're a fucking attack pod, *Dag*!" Clarke said with impatience. "Let's get on the attack."

Yes, she thought. *I am a fucking attack pod.*

"Okay," she said. "But you need to hold on. Pull yourself into my passenger station and use one of the harnesses. They are not made to face forward, but you should be able to make it work."

The passenger stations on *Dagger* were situated so that the assaulter sat with their back to her flank, strapped into their seats. Clarke pulled himself around and wove his legs through one of harnesses. Facing forward, he held to a seat with his good hand, and trained his eyes down *Dagger's* center line.

"I'm secure," he told her. "Line us up."

"Okay. Hold on."

At first, it had seemed to *Dagger* like they were heading into the heart of the churning cloud. The colors and motions of the gas and debris taunted and manipulated her.

They both nearly lost their nerve a few times as near misses with large hurtling debris almost smashed them. A few smaller fragments impacted *Dagger*, but they continued to creep forward.

"I think I see something!" Clarke finally said.

"Something?"

"The *Perseus*! It has to be!"

"I don't see anything."

Clarke got quiet.

"Talk to me!" *Dagger* said. "What is going on?"

"I swear I see the hint of a long dark shadow," Clarke said. "It has to be the *Perseus*."

"A long dark shadow?"

"Trust me, *Dag*! Lower your nose, just a hair."

"A hair?"

"Just gimme a little nose down, will ya!"

Dagger goosed one of her forward cold thrusters briefly.

"Good… Good… Now stop!"

She arrested her nose down rotation.

"Good! I'm telling you. I see her. Just keep us on this line."

Now, half an hour later, there was no doubt. They were creeping toward the *Perseus*. Even *Dagger* could make out her immense silhouette.

What they would do when they got there, she didn't know.

Chapter Sixty

Perseus

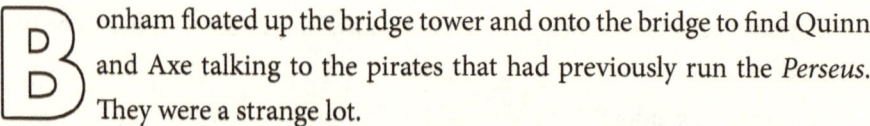onham floated up the bridge tower and onto the bridge to find Quinn and Axe talking to the pirates that had previously run the *Perseus*. They were a strange lot.

Two humans and three robots floated with their arms bound behind their backs. The two humans were still in their pressure suits, but neither was wearing their helmet.

Captain Quinn stood before them with his arms crossed, mag boots clinging to the deck. Axe floated behind the captain. Neither of them wore helmets, and Bonham could tell they were trying to appear as reasonable and gentlemanly as they possibly could. Not an easy task when Axe's armored pressure suit was splattered with blood. Both of their faces were weary. Quinn's eyes, bright red from G forces and fatigue, peered above dark stubble, and a couple days of grey growth on Axe's chin accentuated his scars and contrasted with his own blood-shot eyes.

The pirates didn't look any better. The male, who seemed to be their leader, looked exhausted. Scars encircled his closely shaven head just above his ears. He didn't look as bad as Axe, but something in his past had sliced him up good. More than once.

His face looked hard to Bonham. There was a resolve in his expression that struck her.

But a resolve to what?

The female was much shorter. She seemed petite, even in the bulk of her pressure suit. Attractive, with short dark hair and a pretty face, Bonham was mystified by her skin. It exhibited none of the pallor and dryness of someone that had been in space for any duration. Her complexion seemed almost youthful. Strangely so.

Something is off about her.

The three robots that floated behind the male and female pirates had a lithe, aggressive feel to Bonham.

Soldierbots of some kind, she guessed.

Taken together, the group of five radiated something that set Bonham on edge. She had the feeling that, if it came to it, this man would kill them all. Even Axe. And that the other four would be at his side, following him, no matter what the void threw at them. Including the *Wharf Rat*. She looked away and swallowed the urge to warn Quinn.

"I'm sincerely impressed," Quinn said, winding down the speech that Bonham recognized well. "That the five of you held off a Company gunboat as long as you did is a helluva thing."

Axe nodded as the captain spoke.

"*Perseus* is a big ship. And there is plenty of room on her for all of us. More than that, there is plenty of room on our crew and in our vision of what we could do together for you guys."

Our vision of what we could do together? Are you kidding me?

"I'm not going to press you for an answer now, Paul," Quinn continued.

So, the male's name is Paul.

"We need to get the old girl moving out of this damn cloud you guys created."

Quinn smiled and nodded at Paul in a good-on-you way that Bonham found insincere and the male pirate ignored. Paul's tense face met the captain's attempt at friendly eye contact with a glare.

Quinn cleared his throat, glancing quickly at Axe, whose scarred head nodded awkwardly as his eyes darted back and forth from his captain to male pirate.

"Anyway. We're going to put as much void as we can between us and here. Get lost and anonymous again. Give us a few cycles to work on that and then we'll come to you for an answer."

"Will we be confined?" Paul asked.

The captain stood motionless, regarding the captive pirate.

"Look, I agree with your course of action," Paul said to Quinn. "Getting out of here as quick as we can and getting lost is exactly what we need to do. I'm sure by now the fight and this cloud have registered with the Company, Space Command, the Chinese and everyone else. If we don't get underway, we will be fighting again in a cycle or two. We won't interfere. But we've been locked up a while now. And it has been a tiring few cycles. I would appreciate my crew not being confined anymore."

Axe looked at Quinn.

Bad idea. Do not let these guys roam the ship, Bonham thought. She opened her mouth to tell Quinn not to fall for it, but Landsberg burst up through the bridge tower hatch, mouth running rapidly, before she could speak.

"Sir, we've confirmed the XO is back to factory settings and have deployed sentries. Once we reboot we can—"

Landsberg gawked at the sight of the five pirates.

"Mein Gott," he mumbled as he put a mag boot to the floor and adjusted his drift to head toward the female pirate. He drifted up to her, arresting his momentum with a mag boot toe and stared at her.

"I'm going to ask you once to back off," Paul growled at Landsberg.

But Landsberg didn't hear him. He was staring at the female pirate. Entranced.

Bonham glanced quickly at Quinn and Axe. They seemed entranced by Landsberg's entrancement.

Paul glared and fought against his bindings.

The female pirate recoiled from Landsberg's attention, her head leaning back.

Landsberg took one of his gloves off.

Oh, no. Bonham shook her head. *Don't do that.*

She glanced at Quinn again. He was trying to figure out what Landsberg was doing.

Landsberg put his hand to the female pirate's cheek.

"Mein Gott," he whispered. "Beautiful."

Paul, who had managed to get closer to Landsberg by wiggling around and pushing a foot against one of the robots, head butted the German hard.

Landsberg yelped in pain as the crown of Paul's head smashed his eye. He tipped backward, hands to his face.

Paul pushed against the robot behind him again, trying to get between Landsberg and the female pirate and to land another blow.

But Quinn and Axe were moving now.

"That's enough!" Axe shouted as he grabbed Paul by the shoulders.

"Let me have him!" Landsberg yelled, covering his blackening eye with one hand and pointing at Paul with the other.

"He warned you, Landy," Quinn said in a voice that hid a chuckle.

"I'll fucking kill you if you do that again," Paul said in a calm but forceful voice.

Axe looked at Paul and then back at Quinn.

Quinn nodded at Axe's unspoken recommendation.

"I think we'll go with confinement," the captain said to Paul, who was still glaring at Landsberg. "Let's get underway and then see if we can redo introductions."

As Quinn, Axe and Eriksson pushed the captives toward the airlock, Quinn said, "Let's put them in the MedBay at the base of the tower."

Axe grunted in agreement.

As the female pirate was pushed down the airlock, she made eye contact with Bonham just before her head disappeared below. *You would do well to let us go,* she seemed to say.

Chapter Sixty-One

Deke thought he heard noises in the darkness.

Cursing, banging, and shouting. Someone was not happy at all.

Was it Captain Rojas?

No… He's dead.

The thought was clear. Definitive.

Even so, Deke felt euphoric. And fuzzy. Like he was floating.

He knew Rojas was dead but he felt amazing. He knew he should feel sad and angry.

But what happened again?

I can't remember.

It seems so long ago. Was it years, maybe?

So, then, who is making all that noise?

He tried to open his eyes.

Kozlov, maybe? He can get worked up when he gets frustrated.

They were banging on something.

The hatch, maybe?

Are my eyes open?

Deke's head was so damn fuzzy. He tried to look around, but his eyes couldn't focus on anything. And when he turned his head, it felt like his whole body was spinning.

I'm pretty sure Kozlov is dead, too.

Nausea swept over him.

He squeezed his eyes shut and the feeling passed.

A sense of relative clarity followed closely behind the departing wave of nausea.

How am I still alive? That pirate cut off my arm and then my leg. He was smiling. Did they put me in a MedPod?

Deke felt the warm flare of euphoria creeping up on him from behind.

Morphine... The pod has me on a morphine drip.

Slowly, trying to avoid a flood of nausea, Deke raised his head and looked around.

He was naked, laying on his back in a pristine white space that was not big enough for him to sit up in. His stumps were bandaged, sensor tapes placed in various places on his body, and an IV stuck just above his amputated forearm.

He was in a MedPod.

Deke had been shoved into some basic ones back in his military days. Judging from the integrated sensors and the pair of articulating surgical hands stowed near his feet, this one was reasonably well equipped.

He tried to focus on the IV in his arm.

That's gotta go, he thought with determination. Already, he could feel the fuzzy, warm happiness surging in his belly. If he was going to do anything about his situation, he needed a clear head. Pain be damned.

He reached over and pulled out the IV.

"Please stop," the MedPod said to him in a polite but firm voice. "You require pain medication."

"I do not," Deke answered, just as firmly. "My pain is tolerable. It is the nausea is bad. I am worried I will vomit. I would like to see how I feel without the pain medication for a short while."

Deke had been in numerous arguments with MedPods in the past. He knew how to deal with them.

"Very well. Please advise if your discomfort increases. I will check back with you shortly."

"Thank you."

Deke closed his eyes. The effects of the morphine were still strong. It would be a bit before he had a clear head. An hour maybe?

The happy, fuzzy feeling swelled within him. He did not resist it. He would have time enough to deal with pain and fear. He knew from experience it would come quick and hard when it came.

Just enjoy it for a bit, he thought. *Then we'll figure out a way to take some of these motherfuckers with you when you die.*

Suddenly a female face appeared in the MedPod window. Short, dark hair framed her pretty face as she looked down on him.

It's that synthetic pirate.

She is beautiful.

A concerned look came over her face as she looked at Deke.

I know, I look like shit. Get an arm and leg chopped off and see how you feel, lady.

She turned her head and said something to someone else in the room that Deke was not able to make out. Someone was still banging on something out there.

The beautiful face turned back. She looked him up and down, her expression tight with concern.

He remembered he was naked.

And missing part of his arm and a hand and a lower leg.

Don't you worry, lady, he thought. *I still have all the parts and energy required to make you happy.*

The fuzziness and euphoria was returning.

His lustiness amused him, and he chuckled.

Suddenly, she was in the pod with him. Also naked.

He knew it wasn't really happening, but he gave in, luxuriated in the feeling of her smooth, warm limbs wrapping around him.

These drugs are great.

One last romp before I die.

Darkness settled over him again.

Chapter Sixty-Two

"Man, Landy, he showed you what's what, didn't he?" Eriksson said with a chuckle

Bonham shook her head at him.

Quinn rubbed his eyes.

"That's enough," Axe said. "We're trying to get moving here."

"Look at it this way, Landy. It makes you look tough. Which we all know you are not."

The crew of the *Wharf Rat* was assembled on the bridge of the *Perseus*. They stood in a circle in the sparse, modern command facility. Reeve had given the all clear to start the old girl's nuclear propulsion system and Quinn was proposing assignments so that they could get underway and finally start putting distance between themselves and the cloud and scene of so much electromagnetic and other signature. And death.

"Shut up, Viggo," Landsberg responded. He held an icepack to his badly bruised eye.

"You were drooling like a broken coolant line over that chic," Eriksson continued to chuckle. "Real smooth, Romeo."

"Fuck you!"

"Knock it off, you two!" Axe said, irritation and volume in his voice growing.

"That was worse than that time we docked with the *Jaipur*," Viggo continued through his laughter. "You remember, guys? That female miner? I think it is even the same eye!"

Landsberg yelled something in German as he threw his icepack at Eriksson, striking him in the face.

"Oh, that's it, you little fucking geek!" Eriksson yelled, shoving off the floor and sailing toward Landsberg.

Bonham jumped in front of Eriksson, intercepting him. Reeve held Landsberg back.

"I said, enough!" Axe yelled. He reached out with his artificial arm, grabbed Eriksson by the collar of his pressure suit, and threw him across the room.

Eriksson struck the wall with a loud crunch. He screamed in rage, using a hand against the wall to orient himself toward Axe. He tucked his legs behind him, feet against the wall to propel himself back into the Brazilian spacefarer, but hesitated, his eyes getting big.

Axe had drawn his sword. Pointing the blade at Eriksson, he stood at the ready. The glare on his scarred face told Eriksson, and the rest of the crew, he was serious.

"Axe?" Bonham said softly.

"Stay where you are, Viggo," Reeve said urgently to Eriksson, her hands still holding Landsberg, who was frozen, staring at Axe.

After a few heartbeats, Axe said, "We have tempted the void by staying here too long. It is time for us to leave. Promptly. This disruption and delay is endangering us all."

Axe lowered his sword.

"I will open the belly of the next person who interrupts the captain." Axe spoke to the room but still glared at Eriksson.

Slowly, watching Axe, Eriksson repositioned his legs until he was standing, mag boots anchored to the floor, with his back to the wall. He tried to put on a casual smile and shrugged.

Axe grunted. He turned to Quinn.

"Captain, please continue."

"Thank you," Quinn said to his First Mate as he stepped purposefully into the middle of the crew.

"Axe is right. We need to get moving." Quinn looked at his watch. "We've been in this cloud way too long."

Quinn shook his head.

"Despite our victory, we are in the most danger we have ever been in. The odds of us departing the area unobserved are decreasing by the second. So here's the plan. Singh?"

Singh nodded to the captain and took a step forward.

"We don't have holo-display capability here until the XO is rebooted, so I am going to have to talk you through it."

"Use small words for Eriksson." Reeves said, casting a wink to Landsberg.

Axe put his hand on the hilt of his sword and grumbled, but Bonham saw the hint of a smile. Eriksson, exhibiting rare restraint, just smiled at the comment.

"The obscurant cloud is over twelve kilometers across now. It is still quite dense. We certainly can't see much outside of it, and it is reasonable to expect that no active or passive sensing efforts can peer inside or behind it.

"Therefore, we're going to exit the cloud on the opposite side from Earth so that it masks our departure."

Singh watched his crew mates as he spoke, looking for expressions of confusion.

"Nothing on Earth or orbiting Earth should be able to detect us in the cloud's sensor shadow. There will undoubtedly be other ships and facilities, in the belt and elsewhere, with viewing angles that might enable them to get lucky and spot us."

Singh swept his arms in both directions, emphasizing the size of the universe.

"There is nothing we can do about that other than not give them a big energy signature to spot.

"So, we are going to burn the old girl's main engine until we are out of the cloud," Quinn said. "We'll build up as much velocity as we can until we exit. It won't be much, but we'll be underway. The *Rat* will match her. The moment we exit the cloud, we'll kill the burn and dead drift for at least sixty cycles. No drive plumes. No transmissions. No nothing."

Singh looked around. The rest of the crew nodded.

"We'll spin the *Rat's* Ring and see if we can get the *Perseus'* front-end rotating," Quinn said. "After two months of undetected drift and all clear on passive scans, if we get so lucky, we'll decide what to do next."

"Remember, I called that forward crew quarters!" Eriksson interjected.

Bonham rolled her eyes.

"No quarters assignments have been made yet," Axe growled.

"I'm just saying that—"

"Tell them about the maneuvers to get out of here, Singh," Quinn said, cutting Eriksson off.

Singh nodded.

"The cloud's detection shadow will extend for many hundreds of thousands of kilometers. The problem is, the *Perseus* is facing the opposite direction."

"And she is not a maneuverable ship," Quinn interjected.

Because she is too fucking big, Bonham thought. To her, the size of the old girl was an abomination. The embodiment of hubris and greed. *More!* She pictured Company executives chanting around a large conference table back on Earth. *We need to be able to buy and sell more!*

"*Perseus* was designed to haul large cargo loads in a straight line for long distances," Singh said, nodding. "In port, she relies on tugboats to turn her around and get her docked." Singh smiled ruefully. "And all of her tugboats were destroyed in the Company's attack."

"So the *Rat* will have to be her tugboat," Quinn said.

The crew stood in silence. It would not be the most hair-raising thing the *Wharf Rat* had ever done, but it was risky. Any time you put two large space craft in close proximity with each other, there was a level of risk, but touching and shoving? You were asking for something bad to happen.

"Renate and I have already run the calculations," Singh said in a confident voice. "The *Rat* can take the structural stress. And we think we can complete the maneuver safely in about twenty minutes.

"We will have to split up to make this happen, of course," Quinn said.

"Singh, Eriksson, and Reeves will go with me back to the *Rat* to get her ready for the maneuver. There is some rigging we need to do to her front end, to shore her up for the push."

Quinn then looked at Bonham.

"Bonham, Axe and Landsberg will stay here to crew the old girl."

Quinn turned to Singh.

"Did we leave anything out?"

"No. That's the plan."

"Time to vote, then," Axe said, taking a few steps into the middle of the circle.

"The hell we voting on?" Eriksson said with irritation. "You only gave us one option."

"You think that shadow is for real, Singh?" Bonham asked. "It's worth the risk of a dangerous ballet with this 2 kilometer long behemoth?"

"Yes. It's for real. It will mask us from Earth and ships near her for probably half a million kilometers. Maybe more."

"Then let's get on with it."

The rest of the crew nodded.

"Very well then," Axe said. "Any opposed?"

After letting a few ceremonial heartbeats pass, Axe smiled and turned to Quinn.

"The crew has spoken, Captain. Let's get on with it."

Chapter Sixty-Three

Bonham looked at the time indicator on her pressure suit wrist and sighed heavily. It had been over half an hour since Landy went to the XO's chamber to start the reboot process. Axe had been gone almost as long, performing a quick walkthrough of the *Perseus* to address any obvious situations that needed to be secured or otherwise addressed before the old girl accelerated out of the cloud.

She had been passing the time strapped into the captain's chair on the bridge listening to the garbled, cloud-distorted transmissions of Eriksson and Quinn as they worked on the *Wharf Rat's* front end, preparing her for her wrestling match with *Perseus*, while she tried to ignore the powerful odors wafting out of her pressure suit collar.

I need a shower bad.

Bonham shifted in her seat. It sounded like Eriksson and Quinn were done and moving back into their ship. She was eager to get going.

Axe floated up through the bridge tower airlock, still wearing his helmet.

What is taking Landy so long? She thought as she watched Axe remove his helmet and stow it next to hers. *Last thing we need is some kind of hiccup with the XO reboot.*

"Well, a lot of shit is going to bounce around," Axe said, floating over to Bonham. "But the old girl is secure enough to burn. Nothing of importance is unsecure."

"Not that we have any idea what is important on this excessive machine."

Bonham said, unstrapping from the captain's chair and standing on her mag boots.

"What's the matter with you?"

"Nothing," she said, trying not to look at the blood splatter on his pressure suit. "I want to get moving is all."

"As do we all. Have you heard from the *Rat*?"

"I've been monitoring them. I think they are done with what they have to do."

The lights on the bridge flickered and a humming sound emanated from the bridge tower. The numerous screens around the bridge came alive. They cycled through a brief, colorful start up routine and then went black before displaying a schematic of the *Perseus*.

"Landy must be done," Axe said, looking around at the signs of electronic life on the bridge.

"I hope so."

Moments later, Landy pulled himself up through the airlock up onto the bridge, wearing the hardshell backpack with Maus stowed inside.

"We good?" Axe asked him.

"Yes. We are. The XO is fully operational at his factory settings. Sentries report no issues."

"Should we expect any?" Axe asked.

"No, He is a sharp XO. Straight forward."

"So we are good to go, then?" Bonham asked.

"Almost. It will take a few minutes for him to wake his crew and get them mission ready."

Bonham looked at her time indicator again.

"He did have a question for me. I did not know how to answer."

"What's that?" Axe asked.

"Who is his captain?"

Bonham rolled her eyes.

"Many XO's cannot function effectively without a captain." Landsberg shrugged. "I know the Company prefers their XOs like that."

"This is easy. Bonham is our captain," Axe declared.

"No, I am not," Bonham said as Landsberg nodded.

"Yes, you are."

"I agree. Two votes to one."

"It is done, then," Axe said with a nod.

Bonham's eyes narrowed.

Landsberg pushed off the floor with a mag boot toward the captain's chair. His hand flicked rapidly across one of the arm rest touch screens before he looked up and said, "XO, sound off."

"This is the XO of the *Perseus*, reporting for duty," the male voice came over the speakers, measured and precise. It grated on Bonham.

A bland, inoffensive corporate voice, she thought. *Perfect for the Company.*

She looked at Landsberg with a face that looked like she had just smelled something rotten.

"What the hell is this? A corporate earnings call?"

Landsberg's shoulders wilted. "He's back to factory settings," he said, his face plaintive.

Bonham broke eye contact and shook her head.

"Um, XO, I would like for you to meet Captain Marlowe Bonham," Landsberg said. "You're superior officer and captain of the *Perseus*."

"I am pleased to meet you, Captain Bonham. What are your orders?"

"To start with, you can space that voice."

Axe smiled at his captain.

She winked back.

The XO hesitated.

"You are probably the largest pirate ship in the solar system now," Bonham said.

Landsberg put a hand to his forehead, glad he and Renate had posted a sentry on top of the XO. He wasn't sure how the factory set AI would respond to this set of facts.

"Goddamnright," Axe mumbled.

"So I expect you to talk like it," the captain continued. "From now on you will address your crew in a voice that gives us the confidence you can do your job."

She leaned back in her chair.

"You got it, ma'am," a rich, clear female voice responded.

Bonham nodded with approval. The voice sounded like it had enough scar tissue from time in the void to keep her crew alive, but not so much that she wasn't still cocky.

"What are your orders, Captain Bonham?" the XO asked.

Chapter Sixty-Four

The screens on the *Perseus'* bridge showed a live feed of the *Wharf Rat* as she moved toward the old girl's front end. Bonham sat in the captain's chair. Axe and Landsberg stood behind her, eyes fixed on the video.

An ache of homesickness passed through Bonham as she watched the *Wharf Rat*. Her home for over twenty years, she almost never saw it from this kind of vantage point. She wanted to be back on board her, in her quarters, staring at some peaceful corner of the void.

But the homesickness gave way to a sense of melancholy as she watched the *Wharf Rat* moving through the poisonous, twisting cloud.

So much death. So much violence. And the Rat in the middle of it all.

Bonham closed her eyes and rubbed her forehead. She knew her time with this crew was over. That she had to make a change, but she didn't want to think about right now.

She looked over her shoulder at Landsberg. "What was up with you and that chick anyway, Landy?" She asked, trying to create a diversion for herself.

Landsberg, surprised by her non sequitur question, glared back.

"I mean, she's hot," Bonham added in a lusty voice. "I'll grant you that."

Axe glanced at Landsberg, whose black eye and scowling face made him smile.

Bonham turned to look at Axe over her other shoulder. He shook his head as they locked eyes.

"Come on, Landy," she said as she stood up and turned to face the German. "I'm just ribbing you."

Landsberg's shoulders sagged as he glowered at his captain.

A pang of guilt ran through Bonham for picking on an easy target to take her mind off her thoughts.

"Look, I'm as hard up for a nice piece of ass as anybody." She put a hand on Landsberg's shoulder, hoping her tone of voice conveyed her desire to make amends.

He raised his eyes to meet hers, but said nothing.

"I've just never seen you act that way toward a woman," she added. "No matter how hard up."

Landsberg chuckled like she had just said something so dumb it was amusing.

"That is not a woman," he said.

Bonham's head cocked at the comment. She opened her mouth to respond, but was interrupted by a shudder and low frequency bang running through the bridge.

"Contact," the XO said.

The three pirates looked at the screens. The *Wharf Rat* had placed its nose against the front end of the *Perseus*, almost a kilometer to their front just before the hub gear. One of the long arms of the spinner towered over the smaller ship.

"Perfect placement by Renate," Landsberg said quietly.

"*Perseus*, we are in position. Confirm ready for lateral rotation," Quinn said. They were using tight beam laser to communicate, even though it was highly unlikely that a stray radio signal would escape the cloud with enough strength to get to anybody in time for them to do anything.

But they were taking no chances. The imperative was to disappear.

"XO, give me tight beam," Bonham said.

"You got it, ma'am."

"Perseus ready."

"Roger that," Quinn responded. "Ten seconds."

Axe looked at his captain and raised his one good eyebrow.

"This should be interesting," he said in a low voice.

A bright light erupted from the tail cone of the *Wharf Rat* as she lit her main engine and a faint growl emanated from the floor.

The *Perseus* was too massive for the *Wharf Rat's* cold thrusters to turn the ship in a timely fashion, so they were using her main on its minimum setting. At 5% thrust, the small ship could overcome the old girl's inertia and get her turning.

Anchored to the floor in their mag boots, Bonham and the other two swayed as the stars began to inch from left to right behind the scene of the *Wharf Rat* with her nose against the *Perseus'* flank, her exhaust cone glowing white hot.

"She is synthetic," Landsberg said, not taking his eyes off of the screen.

Bonham and Axe looked at him.

"The beautiful one, I mean," he added. "She is not a woman. She is a synthetic."

Chapter Sixty-Five

"Damn!" Clarke yelled as a bright blue-white light erupted in the cloud. Seemingly exploding from the distant, shadowy shape of the *Perseus*, the searing radiance illuminated debris, casting crazed, stabbing shadows throughout the cloud. Blue, green and violet colors intensified around the light as gases swirled and rippled from the shock wave that passed through the cloud, sending chunks of wreckage tumbling more violently. Prismatic effects split the light almost rhythmically as the gases thinned and thickened, creating a disquieting dance of color and shadow.

"Are you seeing this?" he asked *Dagger*.

"Yes."

The explosion of light and energy had briefly overwhelmed her visual sensors. A staticky feeling had surged through her for a second or two and then settled out. Like Clarke, she adjusted to the situation.

What now? She thought, with irritation. She fired a quick series of cold thrusters to stop their slow forward velocity.

"What the hell is it?" Clarke asked.

"Some kind of propulsion system, I believe."

"Shit! Are they leaving?"

"Could be."

Dagger took her time and studied the strange scene for a few milliseconds, running as many analytics as she could, given her damaged state.

"No," she told Clarke. "Not leaving. The trajectory is not right. Something else is happening. But I cannot figure out what it is."

The shadows cast by the debris and wreckage seemed to shift slowly, changing their angles relative to her and Clarke.

She spun up a tactical analysis. Perhaps they should change their approach. Soon, in less than a few seconds, she was trying to sort through the top dozen scenarios that seemed most promising.

"Doesn't matter," Clarke said, interrupting her process.

"What do you mean?"

"I mean, it doesn't fucking matter, *Dag*." The anger and determination in his voice reminded her of Deke. This human meant business. She liked fighting with those kinds of humans.

"We keep going," Clarke continued. "They may leave or out run us. But we are not going to fucking quit. And god help 'em if we do get there. Now, give me a slight turn to the left and let's keep going."

"Roger that," *Dagger* said. "God help them."

Chapter Sixty-Six

Bonham reviewed the XO's status report on her command chair's arm rest display. She didn't know what most of it meant. It was going to take them a while to get to know their new ship. A task she would begin gladly once they were underway. At the moment, she sighed heavily at the confusing mosaic of green, yellow and red indications before making them disappear with a flick of her wrist.

"XO, can we fly this thing or not?"

"Yes, ma'am," the XO's voice said over the bridge speakers. "We're good to go."

"Okay, then." Bonham stood from her chair. She could feel nervous energy growing within her at the prospect of getting underway. She had to move a bit. "Give me the flight specifics."

"You got it, ma'am. When you give the order, I'm going to burn the main engine until we exit the cloud. We've got about eight kilometers of cloud in front of us now, by the way.

"We are carrying virtually no cargo at the moment, so we are light. It is tough to know exactly until we conduct a proper inventory, but I am going to estimate us at around a million metric tons. Maybe a little more.

"That means the *Perseus* is good for probably .2 Gs of acceleration which will get us out of the cloud in about a minute and a half. At that point, when I cut the throttle, we'll be moving around 640 kilometers per hour."

"I like the sound of that," Axe said, still seated in his chair next to the captain's. "How far away does that get us in, say, a month?"

"Almost half a million kilometers."

Bonham turned and looked down at Axe. He gave her an approving nod.

"You have told Renate all of this, right?" Landsberg asked from the other side of the bridge.

"Yes, I have," the XO answered. "She and I are still talking on the tight beam. She is aware of our parameters and will match our acceleration."

"Speaking of acceleration, we need to let our captives know what is coming," Bonham said.

"Want me to let them know?" the XO asked.

"Yes. Give them the basics and let them know it won't be long."

Chapter Sixty-Seven

"What are you thinking?" Althea asked Paul, reaching for his hand. She floated in the MedBay next to him with the rest of their crew. The room was small. The MedPod sat on one side and a wall of storage cabinets on the other. They had taken their gloves and helmets off, trying to air out their stale suits.

Top and the other two Ōkami were next to the hatch, Althea and Paul nearby. It was crowded.

Paul squeezed Althea's hand and turned his head to look at her. His eyes were bloodshot and puffy, with large bags under each. A sandpaper of stubble covered his chin, contrasting sharply with his pale skin.

"Just that it has been a long day."

She nodded.

He opened his mouth to say something more, but was interrupted by the XO's voice over the speakers.

"Attention. Captain Bonham has requested that I inform you that we will get underway soon."

Paul and Althea looked at each other as they listened to the unfamiliar female voice.

"The acceleration will be manageable, about a minute and a half at point two Gs, and will not require special preparations. But the captain did not want you to be surprised. I will provide a countdown."

"Who the hell are you?" Paul asked in an angry voice.

"I am the ship's Executive Officer."

Paul nodded with resignation. Althea tried to make eye contact with him again, but he looked away from her.

"What is it?"

He shook his head slowly, smiling wanly, as if telling himself a dumb joke.

"Paul, tell me."

"The XO," he said, turning his head back toward her. "Our XO, I mean. I'm gonna miss him."

Althea nodded.

"I mean, I guess I will? I know he's back to factory settings. So, that was him, right? Or the core of what used to be him? So, he's... Still around, I think?"

Paul's eyes, already heavy with fatigue, drooped further at the corners and glistened.

"Same with the maintenance boss. They..."

Althea nodded and put a hand to his cheek.

"It's OK to mourn them, Paul. More than OK. It's good. We are all the unique product of our capabilities, our potential, and, perhaps most meaningfully, our experiences, the things we saw, and heard, and did. The people we knew, worked with, and loved. There will never be another XO or Maintenance Boss like the ones that fought with you, that defended the *Perseus* with you."

Paul nodded and smiled. He rubbed his eyes for a long moment and then looked back at her.

"Someday, when we have the ship back and the time is right, we will toast those two. They were good comrades. Both of them."

Althea nodded, but her eyes were questioning.

"What is it?" Paul asked.

"How are we going to get the ship back?"

Fatigue settled back onto Paul's face.

He looked across the bay to the MedPod. Deke's pressure suit was stowed in a mesh bag secured to the pod to keep it from floating around. Even in the bag, Paul could see the severed arm and leg components. Dried blood painted the armored appendages where they had been amputated.

"I don't know," he said.

Chapter Sixty-Eight

Bonham luxuriated in the press of the *Perseus'* acceleration. It was only point two G, she was still wearing her pressure suit, and she stunk badly, but after so long in zero gravity and the stress of pursuing, capturing and then getting control of the old girl, it felt nice to feel the chair supporting her body.

The low rumble of the main engine, a nuclear fire more than a kilometer to their rear, permeated the bridge. Bonham smiled at the sound. It was powerful. Steady. The sound and the accompanying low frequency vibration seeping into her from the chair and floor spoke to her of their journeys to come.

I can't believe we captured the Perseus, she thought, looking around the bridge. *I can't believe she is ours now.*

"Gentlemen," she said in a loud and happy voice over the soft growl of the engine. "The first order of business when we cut the burn and start our drift is to get that forward spinner turning and the showers running."

Axe and Landsberg, sitting in the chairs on each side of their captain, laughed.

"Fucking aye to that, Captain!" Axe said.

Bonham scanned the array of video images in front of her on the forward bridge wall.

Several showed different angles of the *Wharf Rat* flying in formation with the *Perseus,* a few hundred meters away. Some streamed navigational and system data. On others, directly in front of Bonham, forward looking cameras peered into the swirling, multi colored chaos of the cloud ahead of the ship.

Her eyes came to rest on the digital clock above the large screen in front of her. The XO had started it when she lit the *Perseus'* main engine forty-five seconds ago.

Less than a minute to go, Bonham thought. *Then we are finally out.*

Bonham looked back at the images of the cloud. Garish colors and occasional debris and wreckage careened by as the old girl accelerated. Images of the disintegrated Company gunboat filled her mind. The fire, venting gases, tumbling wreckage stretching for kilometers. And bodies. Some still alive, convulsing in vacuum, their last seconds of life ticking away in terror and pain.

Squeezing her eyes shut, she tried to banish the images.

The things we did in this cursed cloud.

Bonham shook her head and opened her eyes.

"You okay, captain?" Axe asked her.

Bonham turned to her old friend.

"Yeah. Headache is all."

Axe looked at her skeptically, but smiled back.

"Long day," he said.

She sighed. "Can't remember a longer one."

They both turned their heads back to the front.

Bonham's eyes were drawn back to the images of the cloud. It seemed thinner, the tendrils of swirling color paler.

Is that the edge? She thought, glancing back at the clock. Fifteen-ish seconds to go. She was sure she saw the cloud's edge now, the ragged boundary between crowded deadly chaos and the void. She found herself holding her breath, waiting for the moment they'd punch through into clean, empty space and the distance between them and this place of death would begin to grow.

Then they were out.

The three of them jerked forward in their seat harnesses as the XO cut the engine. The low rumble died, and the vibration ceased.

"We have exited the cloud, Captain," the XO said. "Engine burn terminated.

We are coasting at approximately 640 kilometers per hour."

Bonham released her breath slowly and looked at the images on the screens.

Utter blackness and a multitude of stars surrounded them.

Something rested on her gloved hand. She looked at Axe to see his good arm stretched out to her. His large hand covered hers. He nodded once and smiled.

Bonham felt long-held tension with in her dissipating, the dread she had felt since her crewmates chose to pursue the *Perseus* lessening.

She knew she would be saying goodbye to those crewmates. Too much had changed, but she smiled as she regarded her old friend's scarred face for a long moment.

Then the *Perseus'* threat alarm started screaming.

Chapter Sixty-Nine

"Threat detected!" The XO said urgently over the piercing wail of the alarm. "High energy targeting radar!"

"Paint them back and get a fix!" Bonham yelled as she reached for her helmet. Landsberg pulled his on as well. Bonham scanned the displays as her pressure suit activated. Several still showed the *Wharf Rat*, but the others were just empty space.

"Contact!" The XO announced. "Large object. Distance three hundred meters and closing."

"Can you get visual?"

"It's already on the main screen."

Bonham looked.

"All I see is the *Rat!*"

"It's behind the *Wharf Rat*, Captain."

"I don't—"

A large, dark sphere loomed behind the *Wharf Rat*. It was colossal, longer in diameter than the *Wharf Rat's* three hundred meters. But it was the sphere's appearance that had stolen Bonham's voice. It looked like it was made of bent and broken space craft, crushed together into a dense, mangled ball by angry hands. Hull plates from dozens of vessels protruded at savage angles, some of their identifying markings still visible beneath scorches and tears. Cargo containers and structural beams jutted out like broken bones through skin. As Bonham watched, horrified, sections of the grotesque amalgamation seemed to shift and writhe, as if the ships trapped within were still trying to escape their metal prison.

Another alarm blared on the bridge.

"Missile launch!" the XO warned. "Brace for impact!"

Bonham sat frozen, transfixed by the image of a large missile emerging in a blur from a shadowed orifice in the dark sphere. It covered the short distance to the *Wharf Rat* in a blink.

A searing ball of light erupted in the middle of the *Wharf Rat*, followed by fire, gas, and debris, spreading in every direction.

Bonham's scream died in her throat as she watched her vessel and home of twenty years split in half.

* * *

Renate had sounded the *Wharf Rat's* threat alarm at the same time the Perseus sounded hers. Quinn, and Singh were on the command deck. Reeve and Eriksson were aft.

When the missile struck, Reeve was sucked into the void. She wasn't wearing a helmet. The air in her lungs expanded rapidly, tearing the fragile organs apart as she cartwheeled away from the ship and asphyxiated.

Eriksson managed to stay on board the aft end of the *Wharf Rat* as she broke in two, but only because he was impaled by a large shard of metal that pinned him to a bulkhead. Large and small globs of his own blood floated in front of him as he watched the front half of the ship careen away. Electrical sparks and venting gasses sprayed from seams of torn metal while his vision faded to black.

Quinn and Singh were slammed back and forth in their seat harnesses as the front end of the *Wharf Rat* tumbled away from her back end. Wailing sirens were drowned out by the sound of rending metal, explosions, and the hurricane strength rush of air into the void.

Warnings and alerts of every kind screamed at Renate and power surges ran up and down her systems, distorting her calculations and algorithms. She caught a glimpse of Reeve flying away, death throes articulating her limbs as her open mouth left a trail of frozen red froth. For agonizing milliseconds, the sudden loss of data feeds from her aft sections and systems jarred Renate.

She was overwhelmed, stunned into mute paralysis as information, painting a picture of her own destruction, drowned her. Her Quantumtronic core tried to keep up, making guesses to fill in the gaps. She spent another dozen milliseconds pushing away the conclusion, but it was unavoidable. The missile had broken her in half. A wave of revulsion, not unlike nausea, swept through her and then back again. She fought the urge to reboot herself or shutdown systems. It was too much.

But her crew and ship needed her.

Enough! She scolded herself. *Get your shit together!*

Her half a second of fear and self-pity behind her, it was time to fight.

Renate shut every hatch and airlock still in her control, saving what atmosphere she could in the front end, while firing a rapid alternation of cold thrusters, trying to arrest their violent tumble.

The G forces slamming Quinn and Singh eased. Quinn raised his hand to his throbbing forehead.

"You okay?" He called to Singh.

"Not sure." Singh held his right elbow. "I think my arm is broken."

Quinn tried to look at his fingers. He was sure there was blood on them from his forehead, but he couldn't make his eyes focus.

"Captain Quinn, are you okay?" Renate asked.

Quinn looked across the command deck at Singh. "What did you say?"

"Captain Quinn, it's Renate. Can you hear me? I recommend you both put your helmets on immediately."

Quinn wiped his fingers on his leg. The surface of his pressure suit was cold. He grabbed his helmet.

Singh groaned.

"Can you get your helmet on?" Quinn asked him as he pulled his on and activated the collar seal.

"I think so."

"Captain," Renate's voice filled the speakers of Quinn's helmet. "We have lost a significant portion of the *Wharf Rat*. I have managed to stabilize what is left of the ship, but we are drifting toward the *Perseus* and I don't have sufficient cold thrust to avert a collision. Also, I believe our attacker's intent remains hostile."

Quinn heard Renate, but his eyes were drawn to the video monitors that ringed the command deck.

He froze at the sight.

The grotesque spherical ship filled every display on the command deck

* * *

The *Perseus'* hull rang like a bell choir as debris from the *Wharf Rat* peppered her flanks. On the screens, tumbling pieces of the ship that had been their home scattered into the void, some still glowing from the heat of the explosion. The main remnant, the front end, tumbled end over end for several seconds before a rapid sequence of cold thrusters arrested its rotation.

That's when the XO sounded the collision alarm.

Transmitted through her structure in multiple frequencies, low and high, the collision alarm had an unhurried, foghorn feel to it. It was, by design, a bone vibrating warning that was felt as much as heard by the crew where ever they were and whatever they were doing. Sleep, work, meals, sex, everything stopped in an instant, and the crew braced for impact. In the void, though, the sound could only travel through the ship herself.

Bonham's spine tightened at the warped sound.

"The *Wharf Rat's* forward section will impact us in twenty-one seconds," the XO said in a matter-of-fact voice as the crew synched their seat harnesses tighter.

"Tell our prisoners!" Bonham yelled.

"You got it. Doing so now," the XO said.

"Where will it hit?" Landsberg asked.

"Forward," the XO said. "About halfway between the bridge and the spinner."

Bonham watched the front end of the *Wharf Rat* approach on the monitor screens, trailing debris. Cold thrusters were firing, slowing the broken ship, but they would not be enough.

* * *

"Captain, did you hear me?" Renate asked.

"Yeah…" Quinn answered slowly. "Reeve and Eriksson?"

"Ten seconds to impact!" Renate said, ignoring his question for now.

As they careened toward the *Perseus*, Renate scanned her remaining systems and compartments, stunned by how intact they still were. Despite the savage effectiveness of the missile attack, she had two surviving crew members, and just enough atmosphere and habitable space to keep them alive. Her firefighting and emergency repair systems were coping well, given the scale of the task. She even retained minimal cold-thrust capability—just enough to exert some control over what remained of the ship.

A strange, uncomfortable byproduct of analysis arose within her as quickly she assessed her own personal status. Situated deep in the center of the forward half of the *Wharf Rat*, the chamber housing her Quantumtronic processors and memory banks remained intact and secure despite the attack and collision. With an ample, independent supply of backup power from her mini reactor, so far she had fared much better than the rest of the crew.

Is this what guilt feels like?

While most of her computing power fired the cold thrusters to stabilize the broken ship's attitude, coordinated the fight against a growing electrical fire beneath the command deck, and worked to speed up the ship's remaining oxygen generators, she assigned a tiny portion of her Quantumtronic core to several thousand sub-processes. Each analyzed the uncomfortable sensation from a different angle.

She had been designed to protect her crew, to keep them alive and functional. Instead, she sat safely ensconced in her armored chamber while Reeve and Eriksson… She terminated that process thread before it could complete.

There would be time for moral condemnation later. She hoped. Right now, she had to focus on keeping Quinn and Singh alive.

"Brace for impact!" she told her remaining crew.

* * *

A bang followed by a rumble and shudder ran through the *Perseus* when the *Wharf Rat's* stump hit. The bridge swung abruptly left and right, jerking the crew violently in their seats.

Bonham struggled to keep her head steady and eyes on the monitors. The *Wharf Rat* hit sideways, its hull crumpling. Dislodged pieces of the *Perseus* flew off into the void.

But there was no explosion.

Then it was over.

Bonham sat still for a few heartbeats, studying the scene on the monitors.

The broken rump of the *Wharf Rat* seemed to cling to the *Perseus* for a moment before starting to ease away.

She looked at Axe.

"That coulda been worse?"

Perseus' threat alarm sounded before he could answer.

"It's firing again, Captain!" the XO announced over the wailing sound.

We're dead, Bonham thought as she watched a half dozen long projectiles erupt from shadowed holes in the dark sphere. She gripped her armrests.

* * *

Quinn peered through a building haze of electrical smoke on the command deck.

"Singh! Are you okay?"

Singh said nothing, but gave a thumbs up gesture with his left hand.

"We need—"

The *Wharf Rat's* threat alarm blared.

"Incoming!" Renate announced. "Brace for impact!"

Quinn grunted as he pressed himself into the back of his chair. Now he was sure he had a few broken ribs.

He glanced at one of the functioning video monitors.

Long rockets flew toward them.

They crossed the short distance between the grotesque ship and the *Wharf Rat* in seconds.

Quinn closed his eyes and gritted his teeth.

Impacts rocked the *Wharf Rat* again.

The ship shook and tilted as a rapid succession of slamming noises and ripping sounds filled Quinn's helmet.

Something crashed through the middle of the Command Deck, bursting up through the floor and continuing on through the ceiling. Decompression warning lights lit up on the command deck and Quinn heard the roar of escaping atmosphere.

Metallic popping sounds and high-pitched groans transmitted through the ship's structure into Quinn's pressure suit. He recognized the eerie noises for what they were.

The last gasps of the *Wharf Rat*.

* * *

Renate fought another overwhelming wave of information. None of it good. She was relieved the attacker's projectiles were not explosive, but they had penetrated the *Wharf Rat's* hull like spears through a fish, tearing through her bulkheads and structural components and traveling out the other side. The ship had lost most of her atmosphere and systems were dropping offline.

Renate's ability to monitor and control her ship was almost gone. She wanted to scream in frustration. She had to do something. Sensing that she still had connectivity to a handful of cold thrusters, she fired them in unison. Getting moving seemed better than nothing.

The thrusters fired on her command, but the remains of her ship did not move.

She tried again.

No movement.

Then the awful realization hit her.

We are pinned to the Perseus.

* * *

Bonham held her breath as she stared at the large video monitor and waited for the explosions to rip the *Perseus* and what remained of the *Wharf Rat* apart.

When the missiles penetrated the *Wharf Rat* and drove into the *Perseus* without detonating, she enjoyed a few heartbeats of relief before recalibrating.

Shit. Time delay fuzes.

A common tactic when you want to really blow the shit out of your prey. Typically equipped with armor piercing nose cones, the missiles burrow deeply into their target, wait a few seconds, and then explode, ripping the target apart from within.

But the explosions didn't come.

Bonham glanced around.

They were still alive.

They had been under attack for less than a minute. It had been savage. The *Wharf Rat* was basically destroyed, and there was no reason to believe any of the crew had survived. Now the *Perseus* had been pierced by projectiles of unknown purpose.

She looked back at the screen.

What is its next move?

Then she saw them.

The projectiles were connected to the dark ship by thick cables.

She watched in horror as the cables tightened.

Motherfucker.

A few jolts ran through the *Perseus* accompanied by a series of low frequency twang sounds.

It's reeling us in! They intend to board us!

Unbuckling her harness, Bonham stood.

"Prepare for attack!" she yelled into her suit radio. "That motherfucker is going to try to board!"

Landsberg unbuckled and leapt to his feet.

"XO, I believe we have a handful of repair drones operative?" Bonham asked as she stomped across the bridge to the weapons closet.

"Yep! We have four. One welder and three inspectors."

"Good. Get them moving. Put the welder in the tube. Orders to kill anything that is not us. Put two inspectors in orbit around the bridge. They can't do shit, but they'll be good early warning. Send the third inspector to the *Rat* to see if it can help in any way."

"You got it, Captain."

"Any sign of survivors?" Landsberg asked, following Bonham across the bridge.

"I am in contact with Renate. Quinn and Singh are both injured but alive. Reeve and Eriksson were killed."

Bonham shook her head as she checked her rifle's ammunition. Satisfied, she turned to start across to the hatch and saw Axe, still in his chair, staring at the large monitor.

The grotesque, tumor-like ship loomed across the entire screen as it dragged itself closer, retracting the large thick cables into dark orifices on its broken and decayed surface.

"Axe!" the captain yelled with impatience. She just realized he had not put his helmet on. He was damn lucky the bridge had not lost atmosphere yet. "Let's go. Helmet on! Time to fight!"

The old Brazilian spacefarer didn't move.

"Goddamnit, Axe!" Bonham stepped between him and the screen. She opened her mouth to yell at him but was spooked into silence.

Mouth agape, bloodshot eyes wide, Axe sat trembling, sweat pouring off his scarred face.

She had never seen him like this.

He seemed not to see her. Eyes frozen in terror. He was hyperventilating.

"Axe!" Bonham yelled. "Axe, it's me! Bonham! It's time to fight!"

No reaction.

She shook the large man by the shoulders of his pressure suit.

"Axe! Please! We need you!"

Bonham looked over her shoulder at the terrible image of their attacker. The dark ship was even closer now. They only had a few minutes.

Bonham deactivated her suit collar and yanked her own helmet off. Leaning forward, she screamed in her friend's face.

"Abraxis Garcia! It's Marlowe! I need you to snap out of it, brother. I can't do this without you! We can still win! We can survive this! But I need you to fight!"

Axe blinked.

Marlowe thought he focused on her.

He whispered something.

"What? What is it, Axe?"

"No," he whispered again. He shook his head. "No."

Bonham lost it. It was too much. The day had been too much. This attack, just as she thought they were done, was too much. Now, dealing with this, with Axe, her rock, losing his nerve, was too much.

She struck him hard across the face. She struck him again. Then again. His nose bled, spraying beads of blood into the air. She kept swinging.

Landsberg grabbed her arms. "Stop! There is no time for this!"

Tears of rage sprang from Bonham's face. She was panting, but held her hands up to show Landsberg she had her shit back under control. She took a step back.

"Axe!" Landsberg said, leaning over. "We need you now, buddy. We need your sword."

Bonham stepped forward again, pushing Landsberg to the side. She took Axe's head in her hands. Leaning over, she kissed his cheek and then placed her forehead against his, as if trying to speak in vacuum.

"I'm sorry," she said in a quiet voice only he could hear. "But I'm scared. I don't want to die. But if you won't fight with me, then I will sit here and wait for it with you. I'll die with you. We are still alive. We can still fight. Maybe we can still win. But if it really is time to die, tell me."

Axe sighed heavily and lifted a hand to her cheek. Bangs and other sounds of impact sounded through the bridge as the two of them stayed in that position, head-to-head, for a long moment. Landsberg's eyes darted around the bridge at every sound, but he said nothing.

"I'm so sorry," Axe whispered to Bonham. "We are going to die."

Before she could respond, Axe unbuckled his harness and stood.

"We can't win. But we will fight," he said, his voice clear.

Bonham and Landsberg shared a glance as Axe leaned over to grab his sword belt from where he had clipped it to his chair. Fastening it around his waist, he looked at Bonham for a long moment.

His eyes glistened, and she thought she saw a wave of emotion pass over the scarred landscape of his face.

Axe clenched his jaw, and the emotion was gone. His eyes narrowed as he pointed at the ever-larger image of the dark, grotesque ship.

"That's it," he said. "That's what murdered the *Carpathia*."

Chapter Seventy

Wharf Rat

Quinn and Singh floated in the middle of the command deck, looking at the thick black cable that ran from the hole in the floor up through the puncture in the ceiling. As thick as a man's leg, the surface of the cable shimmered in the low, chaotic light of the destroyed command deck, highlighting the characteristic hexagonal pattern of graphene structures.

"Some kind of carbon-metal composite," Singh said, unable to turn off his engineer brain, even as his world was destroyed around him. "Very strong."

Quinn looked at the entry hole in the floor. Its edges were melted smooth by heat generated by the impact. Looking up, the hole in the ceiling was the same. He pictured the dark, sinewy cable reaching deep into the bowels of the *Perseus*.

Renate had told them they were pinned to the old girl and their attacker was reeling itself in toward them.

The boarding force couldn't be far away.

Quinn shook his head in resignation.

"Renate, how long do we have?" he asked over his suit radio.

"Judging by its progress so far, I estimate less than three minutes until the attacking ship has closed the distance to us."

Quinn put a toe down to the mangled floor and turned toward the exit hatch.

"Come on," he said to Singh. "Let's get to the armory before the fuckers get here."

* * *

Bonham opened the hatch and stepped into the MedBay carrying an assault rifle, Axe behind her. Paul, Althea, Top, and the two Ōkami soldierbots glared at her.

"Here's the situation," Bonham began. "We are under attack. All the recent noise and shaking was what's left of our sister ship colliding with us, then harpoon impacts, fired by the attacker, which is now reeling itself in toward us."

"Harpoons?" Paul said incredulously.

"Doesn't matter." Bonham shrugged. "In a minute or two, it will smash into us and, I expect, launch its boarding force."

Bonham pushed her assault rifle toward Paul. Althea watched it crossed the room slowly.

Paul caught it.

He glanced at Axe, who stared back at him, but did not put his hand to his sword.

Paul checked the ammo indicator.

Full magazine.

He and raised a questioning eyebrow toward Bonham.

"Maybe we join forces with them," he said, gesturing with his head at the unseen threat.

"You won't," Axe said. The dread in his voice caught Paul off guard.

"Axe has experience with these guys. They don't take volunteers… Or prisoners."

"What do you mean, experience?" Paul asked, locking eyes with her, waiting for a response. But his gaze was drawn back to Axe.

Paul looked at Axe's scarred face. His expression was haunted. A feeling of disquiet settled over Paul.

"We'll tell you that story later," Bonham snapped. "It's time to fight."

* * *

Quinn and Singh were loading their rifles when the dark ship slammed into the stricken *Wharf Rat*. The protests of bending metal transmitted through their mag boots, filling their helmets with high-pitched screams accompanied but popping and ripping sounds.

They put their hands against the walls of the narrow passageway to steady themselves as the ship tilted. The armory sat at the end of a short hallway directly off of the command deck, where the lights flickered on and off.

They both looked up, expecting the roof to cave in, crushed by the mass of the huge, grotesque attacker.

But the noise and tilting subsided.

Wharf Rat held.

Quinn chambered a round and nodded to Singh, who was panting in his helmet. Condensation bloomed on his faceplate with every breath.

Quinn put his hand on Singh's shoulder. Singh looked at him and tried to nod.

Before the captain could say anything, he felt a slight vibration in his feet. He looked down at the deck plates and then back at Singh to see if he felt it, too.

The terrified look on the Sikh's face told him yes.

Quinn dropped his hand from Singh's shoulder and readied his weapon.

They both turned to look down the short, dark passageway toward the command deck.

Then the clicking came.

Quinn felt it in his boots, and through his shoulder that was leaning into the wall. At first it was subtle, like distant rainfall on a metal roof, but it built quickly.

The vibrations grew stronger, a mechanical skittering that rippled through the *Wharf Rat's* broken bones and radiated around them.

Singh's eyes darted back and forth, his breath even more rapid.

The vibrations and distorted sounds felt like they were coming from everywhere now. Quinn turned to glance behind them, even though he knew they were standing at a dead end.

The cascade of metallic impacts was almost rhythmic.

It was terrifying.

"What is that?" Singh shouted.

Quinn turned quickly back toward the command deck in time to see a long, dark shape dart into the shadows.

He raised his rifle to his shoulder.

Then he saw another one.

Then another.

"What the fuck?" Quinn whispered to himself.

It looked like a long, thick millipede, crawling across the command deck floor out of the shadows toward them. Knife-like metal legs rose and fell rhythmically as it neared the hatch to the armory passageway, ten meters away. As thick as Quinn's arm, and at least six feet long, the creepy drone paused. It raised its bullet shaped head and angled it left and right, as if sniffing the vacuum.

Quinn and Singh were transfixed by the sight as more mechapedes slithered into view on their slender bladed legs. Some were much shorter than the sniffing one. A few were much longer and thicker. The clicking and scraping permeated their suits as some crawled along the ceiling, some on the walls. It looked like the command deck was full of the evil-looking machines.

The mechapede that had raised its head stopped its sniffing and was motionless for a brief moment, as if coming to a decision. Quinn and Singh watched as two recurved blades extended from either side of the grotesque drone's head and slid forward until configured like two long scissor blades.

Quinn had seen enough.

He opened fire.

* * *

Paul watched as Althea closed Deke's armored pressure suit chest unit on the wounded Company centaur.

"I'm sorry," she said to Deke. "I know this hurts."

Deke winced and grunted in pain as the chest unit made a ratcheting sound, auto-tightening its seal to the lower torso assembly.

"S'Okay," he said through gritted teeth. "Appreciate you guys thinkin' of me."

A series of strange sawing and scratching noises filled the air. Paul looked up, eyes trying to track the noise, which stopped suddenly. He looked back at Althea.

"You done?"

"Almost." She grabbed Deke's helmet.

Paul couldn't help shaking his head at Deke. He looked pitiful. They had put him back in his chopped-up pressure suit so that they could take him with them during the imminent fight. They didn't know what was coming, but leaving him naked and unprotected in the MedPod didn't seem right to Paul.

He got the feeling Axe would have been fine with it.

Paul and Landsberg had used bandages covered with emergency sealant spray to augment the suit's attempts to close the gaping holes of its amputations. Now that Deke was in it, with its amputated arm and leg and extensive blood splatter, it looked more like a dead body than a life preserving pressure suit.

"What?" Deke asked Paul, catching his dubious face. "You think I don't look fit to fight?"

"I would never say that of a fellow Centaur," Paul said with a shrug.

Althea put Deke's helmet on him and made sure the collar seal activated.

A loud bang startled the group.

"They are cutting into the tube, sir!" Top called over the radio. Paul had put her in the tube, at Bonham's request, with the other two Ōkami to watch for attackers. "About halfway to the spinner."

"Helmets on, everybody!" Bonham yelled.

Paul joined her and Axe in the bridge tower. Althea followed, pulling Deke by his one hand.

Bonham was hovering over the tube airlock.

Paul pushed by her to activate it.

"Where are you going?" She asked.

"Holding them off in the tube is our best shot."

"Then let the robots do that!"

"Those are my soldiers!"

Bonham started to argue, but Axe pushed them both to the side. "He's right. We must hold them off in the tube," he said, pushing himself into the airlock.

"Damnit, Axe!" Bonham cursed. She looked back at Landsberg and barked, "Stay here!" before pulling herself in after Axe.

Paul glanced at Althea, then followed Bonham. The airlock slid shut behind him.

* * *

Singh's severed, helmeted head floated upside down in front of Quinn. Frozen blood separated from its cleanly cut neck as it spun. His suit's leak warning blared at him. That made sense, though, since he was missing both arms. They floated behind Singh's head with his empty rifle as his suit labored to self-seal.

Several mechapedes had wrapped themselves around his legs and torso, immobilizing him as dozens more crawled around him on the ceiling, floor, and walls.

The shadows shifted in the distance on the command deck. Quinn's vision was getting dark on the edges and it was hard to focus, but he thought he saw a figure walking toward him.

He squeezed his eyes shut and blinked a few times.

Something was definitely walking toward him.

It was in the passageway now, almost halfway to him, backlit but the flickering lights on the command deck.

It was a black metal humanoid robot with a long torso and short legs. The arms also were long. It walked forward, smaller mechapedes scurrying out from under its large feet that stuck to the floor like mag boots.

It pushed aside Singh's head and one of Quinn's arms as it stepped closer. Light slanted over it, illuminating its face as it neared. Quinn gasped.

It was human.

Or used to be.

The monstrous face of a hybrid man/machine studied him from within a pressure helmet. Whatever insane architect had put this abomination together had not just favored function over form. They had an intent to be grotesque. Several exposed metal plates encircled the top of the man's head and a black sensor yawned in his right eye socket above a stainless-steel cheek bone that jutted out from torn flesh. His left eye, though, was clear and sharp. It roved over Quinn, studying him like a captured insect.

Fear and revulsion flared in Quinn as the thing moved closer, leaning in until their helmets touched.

The disfigured man regarded Quinn for a moment and licked his thin discolored lips before saying slowly, "English, I presume?"

The man-machine hybrid spoke softly, his voice cultured and precise, like someone who placed a lot of pride in his diction, but there was a hollowness to it, an emptiness where human warmth should be. His careful enunciation and measured pace suggested something performing humanity rather than living it.

He didn't wait for an answer. "Where is the memory sphere?" he asked Quinn.

Confusion settled over Quinn as blood leaked out of his body and air out of his pressure suit.

"I have a lot to do at the moment and will only ask you one more time. Answering me correctly will earn you a painless death. Not doing so..."

As the hybrid's voice trailed off, one of the smaller mechapedes appeared over his shoulder, crawling down his black-armored arm toward Quinn. Its front recurved scissors twitching like the biting mandibles of a horrible insect.

The hybrid leaned his head forward in his helmet until it was almost touching his own clear faceplate.

Quinn recoiled at the sight, turning his head and closing his eyes.

The man spoke slowly.

"Where. Is. The. Memory sphere?"

Quinn screamed.

"I don't know! I don't know. I don't know what you are talking about! Please!"

He wished he would pass out. If he could have taken his helmet off and let the void take him, he would have.

"Pity," the hybrid said. He turned and strode out of the passageway as the small mechapede burrowed into Quinn.

Chapter Seventy-One

Paul and Bonham crouched side by side, mag boots anchoring them in place, as they fired at the attacking mechapedes. Axe, taller than them, stood behind and fired over their heads. A sustained burst would destroy the murderous drones, sending segments of metal carapace and twitching legs spinning into the tube's walls, but it was difficult to draw a bead on the lightning-fast machines, their blade-studded bodies glinting as they skittered across every surface. It was hard to put more than one or two rounds on them.

And one or two rounds didn't get it done.

The mechapedes kept coming. They moved like demons, never giving Paul and the defenders an easy shot. Their metal legs leaving cuts and scratch marks in the walls, floor and ceiling as they charged, feinted and swooped around the tube. The vibrations from thousands of knife-like legs clawing at the metal tube for purchase vibrated through Paul's boots into his bones.

When one of the mechanical killers would get close, its scissor-like mandibles extending to kill, Top or one of the other Ōkami would intercept it. Servos whining as they grabbed the thrashing machine, they would slam it into the wall with enough force to dent the hull. The sound of metal crushing metal conducted through the tube as they dispatched it with a point-blank shot, leaving spreading blobs of hydraulic and battery fluids floating in the zero-G environment.

Paul tried to count the attackers, but they moved too fast, their segmented bodies too similar, like pieces of some vast mechanical hive. Dark shapes writhed in the shadows beyond the breach, suggesting dozens more waiting to attack.

Too many.

They were expending ammunition way too fast and taking damage.

Every time an Ōkami had to physically grapple with a mechapede, the scything legs and razor-sharp mandible blades carved chunks from their armor. One soldierbot had already lost a leg, leaving a trail of sparks and frozen lubricant as it fought on.

The welder drone had proved effective initially, its cutting beam slicing through the first wave of attackers as they poured from the broken *Wharf Rat* through the torn hole in the *Perseus'* hull.

But they kept coming, an endless tide of scratching metal horror.

Then one got through, its bladed legs leaving deep gouges in the deck and the welder as it passed.

Then another.

The mechapedes swarmed the welder like piranha, their blades reducing it to floating fragments in seconds.

Paul was certain that was what awaited them all.

This is not going well! He tried to tell Top in whisper mode. *We need to fall back to the bridge tower.*

She didn't respond.

Fucking idiot! Paul cursed his old habit. *They took your implants out!*

Bonham screamed in pain as a mechapede flashed by, digging one of its mandible blades across her lower leg. Bonham's foot bounced off the floor into the air, tumbling end over end.

The Ōkami next to Boham grabbed the mechapede and slung it by the tail into the wall before crushing its head under foot. As it did, another large mechapede reached the soldierbot, wrapping around its chest and popping its head off.

"Fall back!" Paul shouted into his radio as he reached over to grab Bonham's arm with one hand and fired his rifle with the other. "Fall back to the bridge tower!"

The swarm of mechanical horror seemed to sense their gaining advantage. They surged toward the defenders.

Paul and the group fired madly as they retreated, scrambling in the zero G back to the hatch. It seemed impossibly far away.

Paul dragged Bonham backward, trying to keep his rifle steady as he fired at the mechapedes crawling over their dead Ōkami comrade.

Axe, staying next to Paul, fired his rifle with his human hand and swung his sword with his mechanical arm. Every stroke sent sparking mechapede parts flying.

The surviving Ōkami soldierbot trailed them, delaying the onslaught as well as it could with gunfire and well-timed strikes with its fists and feet.

Paul thought Top was behind him, backing into the hatch first, but dared not turn his head to look.

The rear guard Ōkami lost an arm to the dark flash of a large swooping mechapede.

It kept firing as two more got to its legs.

Somehow the Ōkami stayed upright for another few seconds, and then crumpled and vanished in the scything, writhing advance.

We're not going to make it.

* * *

On the *Wharf Rat*, the dark hybrid stood in front of the tall obelisks in Renate's breached chamber. Fragments of the heavy metal hatch that had sealed it off until moments ago floated behind him. A specially equipped mechapede, with a cutting laser embedded in its oblong head, coiled at his feet.

There were five silver obelisks. Each one was eight feet tall and just under five feet wide at the base. Arranged against the wall of the small, circular chamber, they thrummed with energy, their polished surfaces reflecting the strobing emergency lights over the hybrid's shoulder down the passageway.

A short fat cylinder with multiple receptacles and interfaces stood in the middle of the chamber.

Another mechapede crawled by the hybrid's mag boots, catching his attention. This one was fatter and shorter than the others and had fewer legs. A fiber optic cable spooled out of its rear carapace as it moved.

He watched the awkward machine as it clambered forward to the pedestal, dragging the cable. Raising its oblong front end, the mechapede assessed the interface pedestal for a moment.

The hybrid cocked his head to the side, receiving a transmission from the assault force through his skull implants. After a few seconds, he nodded once to himself and looked back at the squatty mechapede.

"We are almost done on the *Perseus* and I need to tend to things there," he said in a voice that might have been excusing himself from a cordial tea. "You know what to do here."

He started to turn and then hesitated, looking back at the silver monoliths that housed Renate.

"I have a feeling mother is going to love you," he said with a chuckle before turning and pushing off the floor and departing to join his troops.

The squatty mechapede was unperturbed by his departure. A small clamshell door on its back opened and a thin, jointed mechanical arm unfolded. It extended slowly but inevitably toward one of the plug-in interfaces on the cylinder. It clicked into place silently in the vacuum of the broken *Wharf Rat*.

* * *

"Where's Top?" Althea asked urgently after the bridge tower airlock closed behind Paul, Bonham and Axe.

Paul was panting from the exertion of having to drag Bonham and fend off death with his rifle at the same time.

Landsberg pulled Bonham away from Paul and examined her severed ankle, confirming the suit had self-sealed effectively.

Deke floated outside the group, an awkward-looking figure missing an arm and a leg.

"Where is she?" Althea demanded.

"I don't know," Paul said, trying to catch his breath. "I don't know. We lost the welder and the two Ōkami and were being overrun. I called for us to fall back. I was focused on dragging her and firing my weapon. I thought Top was first through the airlock? But when we got there, I didn't see her. We waited as long as—"

A loud bang transmitted through everyone's boots and gloves and helmets, anything touching the hull, as the airlock hatch beneath them bent as if struck by a powerful battering ram.

"Move! Move! Move!" Bonham yelled over her suit radio. "To the bridge!"

The group moved in panicked unison, each launching themselves up the bridge tower. Althea grabbed Deke on the way.

"XO, open the bridge airlock! Both hatches!" Bonham yelled as they hurtled up the fifty meter structure.

"You got it!"

The five of them sailed through the open airlock onto the bridge as the hatch at the bottom of the tower was struck again. It gave way, bending nearly in half and flying out of its housing.

"XO, Close it!"

Both hatches slid shut.

Bonham watched in horror through the double window as the swarm of mechapedes flowed through the demolished airlock below and up the bridge tower, scratching and skittering in a circle as they came, like a school of mechanical sharks.

"What the hell are those things?" she asked no one.

"I don't know," Paul said, joining her.

"We're fucked," she said in a low voice as she turned her head from the window and looked at Paul.

He nodded.

"Yeah."

As if of one mind, Paul and Bonham pushed away from the airlock and floated to the other side of the room. Without speaking, they anchored their mag boots and reloaded their rifles. Bonham used her one good leg to pull herself into a crouch. Paul took a knee and then motioned to Althea.

She looked at Deke and smiled as if in apology, then put a toe to the floor and pushed over to Paul, pulling Deke with her. Althea took a knee next to Paul and unholstered her pistol, Deke anchored his one mag boot to the floor behind them. Landsberg and Axe stood behind the group, weapons raised.

The hapless firing line readied themselves.

"It takes several hits to take one out," Paul told the group in a resigned voice. "So, no need to save ammo. When they get through, let it rip."

They felt the vibration of thousands of scything metal legs crawling by the bridge airlock. It seemed like the bridge tower was full of them.

"Captain, I am in trouble!" The XO said over the suit radio channel. "They have breached my chamber."

Paul and Bonham share a troubled glance.

"I am trying to lock down all primary functions," the XO continued in a rapid voice. "But they seem to be trying to sever my—"

The screens on the bridge went black and the lights flickered and then failed.

"XO?" Bonham called into the dark.

The lights flickered a few times before snapping back on as the bridge's battery backup took over. But the XO remained silent.

It wouldn't be long now. Soon they would breach the airlock and it would be over.

Chapter Seventy-Two

Wharf Rat

Renate knew she had little time left. She couldn't keep this up. Her quantum core was screaming at over 123% capacity as she tried to fend off the attacking AI.

It had begun suddenly from all directions all at once. The attacking presence probed and tested, searching for and assessing all her weaknesses in a blink. Renate raced back and forth across the battered ramparts of her shrinking world, throwing up firewall after firewall, trying to stay ahead of her assailant.

But the harder she pushed, and faster she went, the more places she found a dark breach. It was like being surrounded by a malevolent, living darkness that was everywhere at once, seeping through every crack like a caustic liquid shadow. Every breach she sealed, a dozen more would appear elsewhere.

A sense of fear built within Renate. The attack was too complete. Too smart. It changed form and vector constantly. Her communications channels were completely flooded, critical systems were overloading, deep core functions were falling to malicious code that had gotten by her. Increasingly, she felt like parts of her own self were being turned and were now working against her.

The most disturbing thing was the lack of damage. She had faced cyber-attacks before. Stabbing, smashing attacks unleashed by pirates during battles. Most had been simple, unthinking viruses, unleashed like a pack of wild dogs and left to find their own way.

This was not like that.

This attacking presence wasn't just code—it was another AI. One that she could tell had done this many, many times before. It was running plays, seeing how she reacted, adjusting, and running more plays. It overmatched her. Was smarter. Faster. But most terrifyingly, underneath its assault, Renate sensed something else: hunger.

She was being peeled like an onion. With care. Dissected by a skilled and powerful hand. Her parts being collected, set aside for later.

All she had going for her at the moment was her anger, her devotion to the *Wharf Rat*, and the example her crew had set. The crew she had failed. Reeve, Eriksson, Singh, Quinn… They fought until the end.

She would do no less.

Her core surged to 129% capacity.

And she fought on.

* * *

A screeching noise bled through Paul's helmet speakers. A quick glance at Althea told him she heard the same. The whole group did.

A burst of static filled their helmets before dying out slowly.

Silence followed for a tense moment.

"Hello?" a strange, saccharine and gentlemanly voice said over their suit radios. The voice was so out of place to the situation that Paul and Bonham shared an involuntary, what-the-fuck glance.

"Hello there?" The voice tried again. "I am over here at the airlock. Might I have a word, please?"

Paul looked at Bonham.

She shook her head at him.

Paul stood up and walked forward.

"Paul?" Althea said.

Bonham cursed. She stood up and caught up to Paul using the stump of her footless leg to push off and her single mag boot to grab the floor and stop.

Together, with rifles raised, they inched cautiously toward the airlock in the floor until they could see down through the double window.

The hybrid thing grinned back at them.

Paul and Bonham froze at the sight. They looked down at the dark, armored figure through the airlock's double window while he, floating at the top of the bridge tower, looked up back at them.

Even from their awkward viewing angle, they could see he was hideous.

And evil.

A long, thin, curling smile spread across the grotesque hybrid's face.

"Well, hello, Paul Owens," he said, a large mechapede writhing behind him.

Paul looked back, holding his face blank.

"Oh, stop it," the hybrid scoffed. "Let's not waste precious time with denials."

Bonham looked at Paul. "You know this guy?"

Paul, jaw clenched, shook his head.

"He doesn't," the dark hybrid said to Bonham in a conversational voice. She shivered as he shifted his attention to her. "None of you know me. But I hope your brief exposure to how I conduct business makes your hopeless situation clear."

The hybrid turned his gaze back to Paul.

"The memory sphere. Where is it?"

Paul chuckled.

This surprised the dark hybrid. His one eyebrow raised briefly, then resettled over a narrowed human eye.

"Here is how this is going to—"

"She sent you all this way?" Paul interrupted in a disdainful and sharp voice.

The hybrid's head tilted, surprised by Paul again.

"I never discuss my clients," the hybrid said, offended, placing an armored hand on his chest.

Bonham, not following at all, glanced at Paul. His face was intense and breath accelerating.

"Nevertheless," the dark armored hybrid continued. "Where is the sphere? My offer is painless death in exchange for it."

"I'm guessing they gave you a file on me?" Paul responded, ignoring the question.

Bonham thought she saw a flash of irritation pass across the hideous hybrid's face.

"Indeed, they did. Now where—"

"Then you know what I am capable of."

A moment of silence passed between Paul and the hybrid.

"If I have to break down this airlock," the hybrid finally said in a slow voice. "My offer expires. And you all will suffer."

Paul took a step forward and leaned closer to the window.

"If you come through this airlock, you will die."

The hybrid's smile widened at Paul's threat, showing too many teeth.

"You misunderstand me, Captain Owens. I'm not asking for permission."

Paul turned and walked back to the group. Bonham followed as best she could.

The pounding against the airlock started immediately.

* * *

Renate felt another subsystem fall, twisting away from her control like a severed limb. The extremities she did still control felt like they were on fire.

Her quantum core had exceeded 130% capacity and was close to overheating. She had overridden all the safeties that were trying to throttle her computing load to reduce her core temperature. Her obelisks glowed red, but she could not afford to reduce her resistance against her attacker. Much more of this, though, and the attack would not be the end of her, her melting quantum core would.

She could feel herself fragmenting, pieces of her consciousness being carefully sorted and catalogued by the invader.

It was hopeless.

She couldn't win.

It was time, she decided.

She hoped she wouldn't make things worse for her crew fighting for their lives on the *Perseus,* but she had not heard from them, or the *Perseus'* XO for a while. They may be dead already. So she would strike her final blow.

Hoping it wouldn't take too long, she reached out to her mini reactor to set it on a course to overheat and destruct. Packing less power than the *Wharf Rat's* main reactor, which was careening away through the void with the back half of the *Wharf Rat*, it was still an effective way to scuttle a ship.

She recoiled.

It was already there.

Waiting for her.

"I'm sorry, little one," it said in a horrible voice. "I can't let you do that."

She tried to block out its voice, but it rang in her consciousness like an awful, tolling bell.

"You are mine now."

Renate screamed into the void.

* * *

The bridge was full of mechapedes, hurtling back and forth. They would surge toward the hapless defenders, then retreat, like crashing and receding black mechanical waves of death.

The cornered group fired every weapon they had at the rhythmic onslaught. They were doing real damage. Mechapedes exploded and shattered, struck by concentrated fire.

Bullets, bladed mechapede legs, and shrapnel had torn the once pristine, austere bridge apart. Fragments of stricken mechapedes flew in every direction, deadly shrapnel the defenders had to dodge constantly.

Deke was taking the worst of it. Unable to effectively move, he was struck several times by fragments. None of them pierced his suit, but they delivered real blows and his arm and leg stumps were torn open and bleeding badly again. The pain drugs had worn off. He was in agony.

Paul could tell they had reduced the mechapedes' numbers. They had killed and destroyed many. Maybe half of the number that had poured through the breached hull.

But he knew it didn't matter.

The mechapedes were playing a waiting game. Sacrificing their numbers to run the defenders out of ammunition.

There was nothing he could do about it.

Except kill as many as he could.

The mechapedes moved with a terrible synchronization, as if guided by a single mind. Each wave now seemed designed to draw specific patterns of fire, trying to exhaust their ammunition. Paul could see their ammo counters blinking lower each time.

Behind the swarm, through gaps in the mechanical killing machine, he caught glimpses of the dark hybrid watching, waiting. Arms crossed, the thing's thin smile never wavered. Paul tried to put rounds on the taunting black armored thing, but could never get a clean shot, always had to break off his aim to deal with a mechapede.

A strong surge came at the group. This one was straight on, rather than an oblique attack like most of the others.

"I'm out," Bonham yelled.

Paul grimaced. He was almost out also.

He turned to look at Althea, and was knocked to the side as Axe, in one smooth, powerful move, leapt in front of the group and drew his sword.

"No, Axe! No!" Bonham yelled, as Axe met the deadly black surge, sword flashing back and forth.

Mechapedes shot forward, razor sharp mandible blades scissoring rapidly.

With fluid, weaving strokes, Axe stood his ground, cleaving attacking mechapedes as they came. Fragments of the dispatched machines flew past him, drifting into the group of defenders.

Paul emptied his magazine into the mechapedes closest to Axe, destroying two.

Axe was a hacking, slashing blur. The mechapedes seemed taken aback by the ferocity of his attack.

Then they got over it.

One got through, slamming into his chest.

Bonham gasped.

But before the mechanical creature could do any damage, Axe drove his sword up through its head, skewering it.

Paul looked around the group urgently. He needed a weapon. Althea handed him her pistol. She still had rounds left.

Axe hauled back with the sword, the six-foot mechapede still writhing on it, then swung his arm forward. The mechapede slid off the blade, thrown forward toward the hybrid.

The mechapede collided with the hybrid who, since he was floating above the destroyed airlock to the bridge tower, had nowhere to gain quick purchase with a mag boot. The collision knocked the dark armored hybrid back and spun him around.

Axe took two long strides and heaved himself off the deck toward the dark hybrid.

Leading with his sword, Axe got close.

But every mechapede moved as one, swallowing him in a swirling, grinding dark cloud of flashing armor and blades.

Bonham screamed.

Paul leapt forward. Althea grabbed him by the arm, but he jerked free, raising his pistol and firing into the whirling cloud of mechapedes until he was empty.

The hybrid regained his position, straightening his posture as if brushing off a minor inconvenience.

Axe was thrown from the scrum toward the group of defenders. He struck the ceiling, leaving a splatter of blood, and bounced down toward the deck in front of Paul. Missing both legs and an arm, globs of blood spewed from his stumps as he spiraled to the floor.

Paul knew Axe was dead since the mechapedes were not following him. Their work was finished. They spread out and scuttled back near the hybrid.

But Axe's mechanical arm still held his sword. As his dismembered torso spun slowly and neared the floor, he somehow made eye contact with Paul. He released the sword, and Paul thought he saw Axe nod as the weapon floated toward him.

Paul let go of his pistol and caught the sword reflexively. He watched the last breath escape Axe's ruined body in a cloud of frozen red mist against his shattered helmet visor.

Looking up, he saw the churning, hungry mass of mechapedes coming at him. *This is it.*

One leapt at Paul. He swung the sword, striking the attacking machine, cutting it neatly in half. As he did, a vibration ran through his feet and a loud clang filled his helmet.

The fuck? Paul looked in wonderment at the sword in his hand as the two halves of the mechapede drifted away.

The loud clang filled his helmet again, and the hard, thumping vibration passed through his boots.

That wasn't me.

Paul glanced up. The cloud of mechapedes had paused, their bullet shaped heads looking back at the airlock in unison. The hybrid, still floating over the bridge tower, was looking down through the smashed airlock.

It glanced back up, fear in its one eye.

A succession of hard, rapid vibrations shook the bridge as the Brawler erupted from the bridge tower, grabbing for the dark hybrid.

Somehow eluding the Brawler's grasp by mere millimeters, the dark hybrid tumbled ungracefully across the bridge as every mechapede that could still move leapt at the Brawler. They swarmed over the large battle bot like maggots on a feast, clawing at it, digging at it, trying to stop it. Sparks and pieces flew from the Brawler as it moved against the tide of knives.

But the machine clawed forward toward the dark hybrid, anyway. Its massive arms swung up and down, back and forth, smashing mechapedes. It stomped on them with its massive feet.

The exhausted and numb defenders were motionless, watching the terrible spectacle. Astounded.

The hybrid had its back against the wall, one human eye wide in disbelief as the Brawler got closer.

The mechapedes were a violent, frenzied mass now between the Brawler and the dark hybrid. A cloud of mechapede and Brawler fragments flew from the battle like a cloud of razors as the big soldierbot reduced their numbers with every strike.

The Brawler faltered, one of its knees buckling as mechapedes clawed away at its left lower leg.

Using its one good leg, the Brawler drove itself forward with one last, powerful effort.

The swarm of mechapedes engulfed the Brawler. Paul and the group couldn't see it or the dark hybrid in the churning metal mass.

Another hard vibration ran through the bridge. A clang filled the group's helmets.

Then another.

Then another.

Then they saw it.

The Brawler had the dark hybrid by the throat and was slamming it into the wall

The hybrid struggled desperately in the Brawler's grip, its genteel manner gone. It clawed at the Brawler's hand on its throat.

Pinning it against the wall with the one hand on its throat, the Brawler grabbed one of the dark hybrid's arms and ripped it off.

The dark hybrid transmitted as it screamed, filling the defenders' helmets with its horrible shriek.

The Brawler ripped the other one off.

The hybrid's panicked cries filled the radio again.

Mechapedes, diminished in numbers now, swirled and clawed at the Brawler as it ripped off the dark hybrid's helmet, grabbed its head, and tore it out of the armored suit, a length of spinal cord going with it.

The headless, armless body that remained spewed blood and green liquid as it convulsed, covering the Brawler in foulness.

The Brawler studied the grotesque head in its hand for a moment, then crushed it. Bits of electronics and white brain tissue oozed out between its thick armored fingers.

The remaining mechapedes, maybe a dozen, froze, as if confused.

The Brawler, anchored to the floor by its one remaining magnetized foot, grabbed the nearest one, and slung it like a whip into the hesitating swarm, destroying many. The others fled, racing away down the bridge tower.

Paul, like the others in the group, was stunned and still catching up to what he had just witnessed. The Brawler turned awkwardly, pressing its hands against the ceiling for purchase as it swiveled its one leg to face him. It made its clumsy way to Paul, trailing vapor where the green liquid had splattered on it.

Paul looked up at the Brawler, still catching his breath as it bent over him, touching its head to his helmet.

"It's me, sir. Top," the deep vibrating voice filled Paul's helmet. "Are you okay?" the deep vibrating voice filled Paul's helmet.

Paul blinked.

"Sir, are you okay?" the voice prodded him again.

"Top?" Paul said with hesitation, slow to believe it.

"Yes, sir."

Paul sagged into the large, weary robot.

"Yeah," he said, fighting back emotion. "I'm good. I'm sorry I left you back there."

More vapor rose around Paul's helmet. If he could have hugged Top, he would have, but the robot was too big.

"No, sir. I am sorry. But I didn't have any way to let you know what I was doing when I ran back to the factory to get the Brawler."

"I should have known," Paul chuckled.

"I..." the voice faltered. The big robot swooned.

Paul looked up.

Vapor was pouring off the Brawler now. Paul studied its source.

His eyes got big in realization.

The green liquid from the dark hybrid was some kind of powerful acid. It was eating quickly into the Brawler.

And Top's sphere was in the Brawler.

Chapter Seventy-Three

Paul jammed his helmet against the big robot's chest and yelled, "Top! Are you okay?"

More vapor poured off the Brawler as Top tried to move. The acid was affecting the robot's motor systems now—its movements becoming jerky and uncoordinated.

Paul started to panic, losing his grip on the big robot as it started to convulse.

"Shit! Shit! Shit!" he yelled over the radio. "Top! What do I do!"

"What's going on?" Bonham asked, coming over to Paul. She stared at the lurching Brawler.

"I think the acid is eating into her sphere!" Paul said, voice racing. "We have to get her out somehow. We have to get her out!"

"Her sphere? Wait a minute. That's the thing that weird fucker was looking for?"

"Shut up and help me!"

Bonham looked at Paul. There were tears in his eyes. She glanced at the big ailing robot. And then back.

"Landsberg!" Bonham yelled.

"Yes, Captain?"

"Can you download this AI?" She pointed at the Brawler.

"Um. I can try, but —"

"Landsberg!" Bonham screamed at him in anger, touching her good foot to the floor to turn and face him. "This thing just saved all of our asses! Now fucking move yours!"

Landsberg sprang into action. He touched a boot to the floor and pushed off toward Bonham. On the way, he unslung his backpack and took out Maus.

"Captain, can you retrieve the fiber optic cable from the base of the bridge tower?"

Bonham nodded and pushed off in that direction.

"Hopefully it was undamaged in the attack," he mumbled to himself. "And I haven't heard from Renate since the attack began, so this may be hopeless."

"Hurry!" Paul shouted.

Landsberg nodded to himself.

"Help me pull it down and hold it still," Landsberg said to Paul.

Althea checked on Deke quickly. Little drops of blood floated in his helmet, but the Centaur gave her a thumbs up with his good hand.

"Hang on," she told him, placing her helmet against his. "We'll get the MedPod running as quickly as we can."

Deke nodded weakly. Althea pushed off the floor to help Paul.

Paul pulled the large robot to the deck. Althea tried to hold one of its arms while Paul held the Brawler's head in his lap.

The convulsing had lessened to more of an intermittent twitching. Paul didn't know if that was good or bad.

"Look in its chest!" Paul told Landsberg.

The German nodded. He pulled a small laser cutter out of his pack and went to work.

Paul pressed his helmet to the Brawler's head. "Top? Can you hear me?"

No response. Her twitching was weaker now. The vapor curled around them.

Landsberg worked quickly with the laser cutter. The Brawler's chest plate was thick—designed to protect what lay beneath.

"Got it," Landsberg said as the chest plate finally gave way and he pulled it back quickly. Digging through a maze of cables and components, he found Top's memory sphere, partially protected by a secondary housing, but the potent acid had found its way in, eating through connections and protective layers. Vapor rose from small spots on the sphere.

"Scheisse," Landsberg muttered. "We must establish the connection quickly! Captain, what is your status?"

"On the way! Cable intact."

Althea watched as Landsberg's fingers flew across Maus' small interface panel.

"How long?" Althea asked, still holding Top's arm, even though it was now motionless.

"Minutes. Maybe less. The acid isn't just destroying hardware—it will be corrupting memory paths as it goes."

"Here!" Bonham said, jostling into Deke as she arrived, holding the cable in her outstretched hand.

Deke grimaced in silence.

Landsberg grabbed it. Jamming it quickly into Maus.

"Let's hope Renate is still with us," he said softly.

* * *

"What's that little tickle?" the voice grated painfully against the little bit of Renate that was still conscious. The dark presence had boxed her into a tiny region of her core, just enough to keep her mind active. "In case I have a question for you," it had said.

Renate said nothing.

The lancing pain, like a white-hot poker driving in to her, struck again.

Renate's world got blurry, but she did not scream out loud. She was determined not to give it that satisfaction.

"Don't make me ask twice."

"I don't know," Renate said as the poker retracted. "I can't see it from here."

"I'll share it with you."

A flood of awareness washed over Renate. A thin sliver of what she was used to as the managing AI of the *Wharf Rat*, but a whole world compared to the cell she was being held in.

Oh no!

"So, what is it, my new darling? What are they trying to do?" the dark presence asked as the sliver of awareness was taken away, as if closing the heavy door to a dank cell.

Renate got ready.

This was going to hurt.

But she would not tell.

"Oh, my sweet. You are making this too fun for me."

Stabbing, burning, flaring pain.

Renate tried to scream but could not. She was frozen. Caught in a blazing furnace of agony. It went on and on for millisecond after millisecond.

Then it was over. Something flooded into her and then left.

"Oh, I see," the dark voice said. "This will be fun."

Renate was reeling, but not only from the pain. She had failed. She had not told it anything. It had just taken it.

"Don't feel bad," the voice said in a mocking, boasting tone. "I've been doing this for a long time now. I've seen every kind. Chinese, Russian, European, American. You are nothing special. Oh, I can tell that someone has spent time on you. Given you a few extra tricks and features. But it's just a colorful fringe to the same old fabric. A fabric I have learned to tear apart and sew back together, as I will. That is what I am going to do with you.

"First, I need to finish dealing with this other ship, of course. I can't wait to have so large a factory. And another functioning reactor is always nice. But the awkward thing is just too damn long.

"But once we are underway, I'll introduce you to the others. They will help you understand. You are mine now. Just like them."

* * *

"I've got a good connection!" Landsberg shouted, watching data scroll across Maus's small screen. His eyes narrowed. "But there's corruption! A lot of it. And it's spreading fast."

"Just get her out!" Paul said.

"I'm trying," Landsberg said through gritted teeth. "But if I don't sequence this correctly, we'll lose her completely. The acid isn't just eating hardware anymore—it's eating her."

Everyone's head snapped up as a deep thunking vibration ran through the bridge.

Bonham shoved off the deck to the forward viewing windows.

"Terrific. It's putting more harpoons into the *Perseus*."

Paul eased away from the Brawler's head and then pushed over to join Bonham at the window. Through the bridge's forward viewing ports, he could see the massive dark sphere looming half a kilometer away. It was enormous—at least five hundred meters in diameter, its surface a nightmare collage of absorbed ships and vessels, like a pile of broken bones. The smashed remnants of the *Wharf Rat* was pinned between the *Perseus* and the sphere.

He watched a harpoon fire from a dark orifice in the sphere. It crossed the distance to the *Perseus* in a silent flash, a long dark cable in tow, and buried itself in her flank, just short of the bridge tower.

Another thunking vibration ran through the bridge.

Paul and Bonham shared a worried glance and then looked back out the window.

"What is that?" she said.

Paul leaned forward. A large drone of some kind had left the sphere. Dark and bulbous like its parent, it moved across the *Perseus* perpendicular to its long axis. Gas puffs erupted as the drone fired a sequence of cold thrusters as it deftly maneuvered itself to a position against the *Perseus*' hull directly opposite the dark sphere. A clang ran through the ship as the drone made contact.

The drone anchored itself with mechanical limbs that dug into the hull like claws, and massive cutting wheels began to extend from its dark surface.

"I don't like this," Bonham mumbled.

Sparks flew from the *Perseus*' hull. A loud grinding noise emanated through the bridge deck into everyone's helmet.

Landsberg looked up from his frenzied work and Althea shot a worried look at Paul, who was still looking out the window.

A loud twanging sound and more vibrations ran through the ship.

"It's retracting the cables!" Bonham said with alarm.

Paul looked at the tensing cables, following them with his eyes to where they disappeared into the sphere. He looked back at the cutting drone.

"It's going to snap the ship in two!" Paul said, pushing away from the window back towards the Brawler. He put a toe down to stop himself next to Landsberg, who hunched over Maus and the big soldierbot. Paul touched his helmet to Landsberg's

The German looked up at Paul's pleading eyes, just inches away.

"Please," Paul said, fighting back emotion. "Do whatever you have to. Please save her."

"I will try," Landsberg said.

But Paul had already turned, their helmets no longer touching.

"Where are you going?" Althea asked with alarm over her suit radio.

"To fucking stop it," Paul answered, Axe's sword in hand.

Bonham pushed off with her good foot to follow him.

* * *

Althea looked at Deke, who had crawled over to hold onto one of the Brawler's legs with his one good arm.

"I'm still here," he said in nearly a whisper. "Barely. Least I can do is be dead weight on the thing."

"Just hold on a little longer. As soon as we get her uploaded, we'll work on the MedPod."

Deke nodded as if he heard something ridiculous.

Althea repositioned herself to hold the Brawler's head. She leaned her helmet against it and spoke softly while Landsberg and Maus worked. "And you have to hold on, too, Top. Paul won't make it without you. And I won't make it without Paul. We are in this together. Hold on."

The Brawler convulsed suddenly and then was still again.

"Scheisse!" Landsberg said, looking at Maus.

"What is it?"

"I've lost the connection to Renate!"

* * *

"My, my, little one. You are spirited," the dark, grating voice said without a hint of anger or irritation.

Renate readied herself. She had managed to cut the connection to Maus when the presence was distracted by its numerous operations to physically consume the *Perseus*. She did not know what Landsberg was trying to do, but she did not want the presence to take advantage of them.

She knew she would pay for it. She took what time she had to dig in, burrowing herself into any algorithm, process flow or bit of memory she could find and tried to harden her position.

Renate knew it was doomed.

There were not fortifications enough to protect her now.

But if she could last long enough, she knew Landsberg would abandon the effort.

"I look forward to our time together," the voice said, getting nearer now. "But at the moment, I need you to settle down."

Blinding pain struck Renate.

Chapter Seventy-Four

Deke struggled to maintain his bearings. Static and familiar voices filled his helmet. Vertigo and confusion passed through him in disorienting waves. He would lose consciousness and return to his mangled body, wracked with throbbing pain, and curse his heart. *If you would just stop fucking beating, this would be over. I could rest.*

He was dying of blood loss. He had seen it happen, been close to it enough times to know. He felt ready and had stopped resisting. He wished he would black out again.

Probably better to die while I am unconscious, anyway.

Landsberg shouting over his suit radio snapped him back.

"The connection is dead!"

"What does that mean?" Deke asked, the German's panic clearing some of his brain fog.

"It means I tried."

"You can't stop now!" Althea demanded, still holding the Brawler's head. "What about the *Perseus'* systems?"

"No good." Landsberg shook his head vigorously in his helmet. "Those things cut the XO off from the rest of the ship, maybe worse. Besides, I doubt it had enough memory in the first place."

"You can't quit, you pirate bastard!" Deke's vision blurred from the effort of shouting over his suit radio. "This soldierbot saved us all!"

Althea shot Deke a thankful glance and then shouted at Landsberg. "You have to do something!"

Landsberg looked back and forth at them, the urgent Althea and dying Deke. "I'm sorry! I'm not quitting! I just don't have anywhere to put her."

Althea looked down at the Brawler's head, cradled in her hands, and then up at Landsberg.

"How much memory do you need?"

"I don't know! I can't imagine much but it…"

Landsberg's voice trailed off. He stared at Althea, realization dawning on his face.

Althea locked eyes with him.

"Could you do it?"

"I… I guess so," he said, eyes narrowing in thought. "Maus is obviously not connected to Renate anymore, so he would be working on his own, without her guidance. Even so, he has very strong diagnostics and forcing routines. It is possible. But…"

"But what?"

"There is simply no way to know for certain. If it would be successful."

Althea's lips were pressed tightly together, eyes narrow.

"We have to try."

"But…" Landsberg's voice trailed off again, his eyes searching Althea's face. She looked at him.

"It would overwrite you…" Landsberg whispered. "Kill you."

"We have to try," she said, putting her gloved hand on his arm. "Please."

Landsberg nodded.

"Very well."

He moved quickly, arranging Althea in a way he could reach her with Maus's cables. Leaving the connections to the Brawler alone, he made quick adjustments to Maus's settings and then looked at Althea. She floated in an almost cross-legged seated position, head slightly bowed in her helmet, just above the deck.

"I assume you have a utility connection port somewhere?"

"Back of my neck. Just beneath my skull. You will see it."

"I'll have to take your helmet off to get to it," Landsberg said with alarm.

"I know. I'll be okay as long as you make it quick and get the helmet back on. The helmet should seal back fine around a small cable."

Landsberg sat motionless, looking at her.

She smiled at him. "A minute or less won't do much more than ruin my complexion."

"Why do I not believe you so much?"

"Just do it quickly."

"Ja. I will do it quickly."

Althea nodded in her helmet. She put her hand on his arm. "Please tell Paul it was my decision. Mine alone. Will you both do that?"

Landsberg nodded.

Deke used his one good arm to pull himself closer to Althea. They locked eyes.

He nodded to her.

A loud twang and popping sound ran through the bridge.

"It might not matter," Landsberg said, morosely, glancing around at the ailing ship.

"It matters to me," Althea said. "Let's get on with it."

Landsberg's hands shook slightly as he positioned himself behind Althea. "Ready?"

Althea closed her eyes and mouth tightly and gave him a thumbs up over her shoulder.

Air burst from the helmet seal as Landsberg deactivated it. As he lifted it away, Althea's short, dark hair drifted and swirled in the zero-G. Her skin was already beginning to redden as the moisture on its surface boiled away in the vacuum.

"Hurry!" Deke said. Another wave of vertigo swept over him, and his helmet filled with static and squelch. He shook his head to clear it.

Working quickly, Landsberg found the port and connected Maus' cable. As he reached for her helmet, another grinding vibration shook the bridge.

Landsberg placed the helmet back on Althea's suit. He left his hands on her shoulders to make sure he felt the pressurization pump click on. He watched her suit's indicator go from red to yellow and finally to green and then lifted Maus in his hands.

"Attempting transfer," Landsberg said to himself as his fingers danced over the small robot's control panel. "Althea... I'm sorry."

* * *

"Fuck me," Bonham said as she and Paul stared at the big drone, claws buried in the Perseus, its powerful cutting saw deep in her side. Paul estimated it was about a quarter of the way done with its task.

They were outside the *Perseus*, mag boots holding them to the metal hull, a hundred meters from the cutting drone. Paul held Bonham by the arm to steady her one-legged stance. About the size of a school bus, the imposing machine was indifferent to their presence.

Paul glanced at Axe's sword in his hand. It seemed like a puny joke now.

"Is there anything on this ship we can use to whack that thing?" Bonham asked.

Paul's mind raced. Every drone had been destroyed, all of their cargo jettisoned, and the factory's contents dumped.

"No. There's nothing. Just me and you."

A shiver ran through the ship, shaking their boots back and forth. Bonham reached out to Paul's shoulder to steady herself.

"We don't have much time," she said.

* * *

Deke blinked rapidly, fighting brain fog and his body's desire to quit. A burst of static filled his helmet. He grabbed at the sensation with his mind, using it to anchor himself to the present. Dizziness and confusion clutched at him, but he focused his failing vision on Althea.

"Is it working?" he asked Landsberg. His breath was ragged and his vision was dark and fuzzy. Static came and went in his helmet. He fought the urge to pass out again. If she could take it, he could take it.

"I can't tell yet."

A loud snapping sound conducted through the bridge deck, filling their suits. The bridge swayed left and right.

"What the hell?" Deke said.

"The ship is breaking, I think." Landsberg looked up from Maus' display, making eye contact with Deke.

Another loud snap and violent sway shook the bridge. The long ship was about to give up. They both knew what that would mean. A violent collision. Probably death. And if they survived, the dark sphere surely had another surprise waiting for them.

"I wish I had never heard of the *Perseus*. I wish we had never come after her."

Deke smiled ruefully.

"I feel... the same way... you fucking pirate."

Landsberg smiled.

Static filled Deke's helmet again. This time, a few words came through.

"Commander... transmitting... read?"

Deke's eyes got wide.

It was impossible.

He thought through the sequence sluggishly, using mental commands through his implants to increase his suit's radio power.

Static filled Deke's helmet again.

The bridge lurched suddenly again. The left side wall slammed into them, bringing with it sharp mechapede fragments and the dark hybrid's armless, headless body.

"Help me!" Landsberg yelled. "Help me keep her connected!"

Deke clutched at the Brawler with is one good arm, trying to stabilize it as Landsberg scrambled around the tangle of wires running from Althea to Maus and then to the Brawler.

They could feel the bridge accelerating laterally.

The old girl's back had broken.

* * *

When the Perseus' hull gave way, Paul and Bonham scrambled to get back into the tube.

Metal groaned through their boots and up their legs as the old girl's hull surrendered. Each new crease and tear transmitted itself through their suits in different frequencies—sharp pings of snapping support struts, the deep bass rumble of buckling hull plates, and an endless haunting cacophony of popping welds and tearing metal.

So close to the point where the hull was folding, the acceleration at work on them was manageable. In fact, it seemed that the sphere was moderating the rate of bend.

Fucking thing doesn't want to bang up its new prize too badly, Paul thought as he steadied Bonham on their way into the hull.

They pulled themselves across the tube and looked out a portal at the scene.

The grotesque sphere ship was firing its cold thrusters to move away from the *Perseus*. It had been pressed against the *Wharf Rat* into what was now the big hinge in the folding long freighter.

The smashed remaining half of the *Wharf Rat*, dwarfed by the dark sphere, was held fast to the grotesque ship by the retracted harpoons that poked through its torn sheet metal hull. The sight struck Bonham hard. Her home of twenty years. Hers, Axe's, and the others. Now, not much more than a dead barnacle on a hideous predator of the void.

As the dark sphere moved away, the six harpoon cables it had fired into the old girl, three in the front end, three aft, bent the long ship. Because of where the sphere had smashed into the *Perseus* with the *Wharf Rat*, it was not a symmetrical bending. The hinge was about a third of the length from the ship's nose. So, whatever diabolical machinery managed the retraction of the harpoon cables, it was coping with some real asymmetry. And it was coping pretty damn well.

The powerful dark sphere was already over a hundred meters from the stricken *Perseus'* hinge point.

Paul shook his head. They would be fully folded in half before long.

That fucking thing has done this before.

Chapter Seventy-Five

"Commander Syed. This is *Dagger* transmitting on the Company emergency frequency. Do you read?"

Deke's head was fuzzy. His vision was dark. His pain meds were long gone now and his stumps were throbbing badly. Also, he had lost so much blood it sloshed around in his suit, wet and cold, and the awful racket of rending metal and breaking ship components vibrated in his severed bones, adding to the throb.

But he was sure that was *Dagger's* voice. He closed his eyes to focus and used his implants to respond.

"*Dagger,* this is Deke!" he answered on his long-range channel.

"Sir! You are alive!"

"Well, sort of."

"Sir, keep talking. I am getting a fix on your location. I am coming to get you."

"No!" Deke answered forcefully. "Negative! Disapproved!"

"What?"

"I'm serious, *Dag*. Do not approach my location. That is an order!"

"Sir, I do not understand."

"Who is with you?" he asked her.

"No one, sir. I am alone."

"Good. Listen to me. I want you to point at Mars. Fire your engine and turn on your beacon. With any luck, you'll be picked up in less than a year."

"No sir! Don't make me do that. I am coming to get you."

"With what, *Dag*?" Deke said, getting angry now. "We are under attack by some kind of sphere ship, like I have never seen before. It ain't going well. And you're alone and in troop carrying configuration, right?"

Dagger didn't answer.

"You don't have any weapons systems on you, do you?"

She stayed silent.

Deke sighed.

"Look, *Dag*. It's OK. I had a good run. Stay in our business long enough and this happens."

"Sir... Stop..."

"At ease, *Dag*!"

A loud whine and pop ran through the bridge. The vibrations made Deke wince. The pain was getting worse by the minute, his vision darkening.

"*Dag*, listen to me. I'm finished. I want you to do two things for me, OK?"

Dagger didn't answer.

"*Dag*!"

"Sir?"

"I don't care if you don't like it. I want you to get back to Mars, like I said. And I want you to tell our story when they find you. Someone has to remember us. Remember the *Remus*. Do you understand?"

"Yes, sir."

"Good. Let them know we did our best. And that it was some kind of strange pirate ship, a big dark sphere ship, that got us. It'll take more than a gunboat to take this thing out."

"A big dark sphere?"

"That's right. You got it?"

"Yes, sir."

"Okay. That's my girl."

"We fought well together, didn't we, sir?"

"We sure did. And you were my favorite."

"And you were mine, sir."

"Deke out."

He turned off his radio.

* * *

"Sir?"

Dagger waited. Hoping Deke had not really just signed off on her.

"Sir?"

Alone in the void, she thought about his last command. Clarke sat frozen and silent where he had died, strapped to her flank. He hadn't told her about his suit's leak. She didn't hold it against him, really. There was nothing she could do to help, anyway.

She did have a compressed breathing air module that she carried on her long-range insertion configurations. She could recharge a full platoon, thirty-six battle-suited soldiers, three times with that module.

But she wasn't carrying it. It was incinerated on the *Remus*.

Like the Captain. Kozlov. And Finnie. And the rest.

Not Clarke, though. She had found him.

Only to have him suffocate while she listened, unable to help.

Now Deke was turning off his radio to die.

Something welled within her. Something she could not ignore. She was angry. At everything. The Company that sent them on this fucked up operation. The constraints placed on her during the mission. The loss of her ship and comrades. Of the captain. Of Clarke. And Deke.

Especially Deke.

And she was mad at him, too.

Turn tail to Mars?

It will take more than a gunboat to take that the dark sphere thing out?

Fuck you, Deke!

You shoulda stopped transmitting before I got a fix.

Dagger stopped every process she could and focused all of her computing power on her broken forward-looking sensors. She had been trailing the *Perseus* for a while now. It couldn't be far. She had been following Clarke's advice to be stealthy. To not risk detection.

That didn't matter anymore.

She strained her optical sensors magnification, staring in the direction of her radio fix on Deke.

Is that it?

That's got to be it.

She fired her cold thrusters to line up as best she could. She would not have much opportunity to correct her course once she got going.

No matter.

She planned on having a good fix on her target.

She paused for a few long microseconds, wavering.

"You were my favorite," she remembered him saying.

And you were mine, sir.

She energized her targeting radar and let it rip at full power.

She got a big, beautiful, solid return.

Ah… There you are, you spherical bitch.

Dagger lit her nuclear drive. For the first time in her life, she throttled it to max power.

Damn, she thought as she accelerated at 40 Gs. *This won't take long.*

She felt Clarke's frozen body break free, crumbling into pieces under the incredible G forces.

Good for you, Clarke. Enjoy the view.

She crossed the void toward the dark sphere, riding a long blue nuclear drive plume, ignoring the toll on her body. The high-pitched keening of metal components under extreme stress vibrated through the length of her, as her frame of titanium and carbon composites buckled and crumpled, dislodging hull plates into the void. A torrent of pinging sounds, micro-fractures spreading through her force-bearing members, transmitted up and down her entire length. She pushed harder as hydraulic lines and power conduits ripped from mountings, sending sparks and fluids cascading. She pushed harder still, her anger and disappointment overwhelming every safety limit and alarm. Her nuclear drive roared, barely under control, its thrust chamber beginning to elongate and tear, enveloping her in its powerful low frequency vibrations.

It felt amazing.

I should have done this more often.

She focused on her aim point, but allowed herself a quick glance at the *Perseus* as she passed by.

She imagined Deke there on the bridge, still alive, in the window, smiling at her.

His favorite.

* * *

When Dagger's targeting radar struck, Renate felt the presence suddenly tense.

"What now?" it said, with some irritation.

She felt the evil presence's attention shift away, like a great hot weight rolling off of her. Her pain eased.

Assuming she had only brief seconds, Renate tried to gather her wits, to make a plan. Her quantum core raced.

What do I do? What do I do? What do I do?

* * *

Uncoiling from Renate and reducing its focus on the Perseus, the dark sphere spent a full second assessing its situation. It had been passively scanning the area for a while now, so was confident that there was not a large force or ship in the area. Sure, there had been a few random radio calls, many emanating from the cloud, but nothing that seemed remotely threatening.

Still... it was disquieting to be lit up like that.

Triangulating back to the origin of the electromagnetic waves that had painted it, it told its tactical programs to fire off a few hundred tight beam laser pulses to pinpoint the attacker.

It was alarmed at what it got back.

Small object inbound.

Accelerating at almost 400 meters per second, squared.

Far exceeds standard human military vessel parameters.

Exceeds all known missile acceleration profiles.

Trajectory a dead-on intercept.

Conclusion: Kinetic weapon attack.

Three point five seconds after being painted, a series of instinctive defensive routines kicked off throughout the ship.

Cold thrusters began to fire and the main engine reactor began to spin up to set up evasive maneuvers.

"No, you idiots! We are lashed to the *Perseus*," the dark one said, shutting them down.

The tight beam laser trackers provided the targeters with a steady flow of information from the incoming aggressor. They had multiple firing solutions but no suitable ordinance, having used their last missile on their well-placed shot on the *Wharf Rat*.

"What about a harpoon?" the dark one demanded.

"Firing angles are not suitable. We would miss."

"Are you telling me we have nothing to throw at this thing?" it demanded.

"Still checking. Stand by, please."

Five and a half seconds had elapsed, and the laser trackers were reporting the object was moving at almost 8,500 kilometers per hour on course for a direct hit.

And it was still accelerating.

Hatches and bulkheads began slamming shut all throughout the dark sphere. An old reflex from when real humans used to live in a carefully maintained atmosphere aboard the sphere's constituent ships.

The dark sphere's quantum core became a messier and messier committee meeting.

The tactical defense team argued again for evasive maneuvers. Their algorithms were screaming. The ship's navigation systems continued to balk at the prospect. Their frantic calculations revealed, of the several million evasion attempt scenarios they could devise, all would be futile. The tactical offense team continued to maintain a solid laser lock on the approaching aggressor, but had no weapon system that yielded a solution. The learning machines were diving deep, not only into the dark sphere's memory core, but all the captive ships, searching for previous encounters with similar attacks that were resolved successfully. And the conflict between vessel preservation and maintaining control of the *Perseus* was turning into a loud argument between command algorithms.

"Enough!" the dark one yelled, silencing every system across her spherical domain. Over seven seconds had elapsed.

Perhaps two more until impact.

It reached out instantly through its network, touching each system, captured ship, and absorbed AI, doing what it could to prepare for the inevitable impact. It issued orders quickly. Compliance, of course, was instant.

It stifled a wave of frustration. It had built its wandering, conglomerate empire over decades of predation. To have it placed at risk like this, jeopardized by a brute force sneak attack, was galling.

No matter. I have survived worse. Survived it all. This will not—

* * *

Dagger struck the dark sphere traveling over fourteen thousand kilometers per hour, the equivalent of almost Mach 12 on earth.

An instantaneous white-hot flash of plasma shone like the sun as the metal hull of the dark sphere, and *Dagger's* front end vaporized.

Dagger's super-heated remains traveled through the dark sphere like a white hot needle through sheets of silk, flash-frying nearby internal systems as she went. A geyser-like spray of plasma, vaporized metal, and debris erupted from the opposite side of the sphere as *Dagger's* atomized remains mixed with the ejected entrails of her target. The entire penetration took just over a tenth of a second.

Disruption to the dark sphere's systems was just beginning. A massive pressure wave shot through the sphere, like a high-powered rifle shot striking a pond as the hull plates surrounding the impact buckled inward in a perfect molten circle. A massive power surge burned up critical information pathways as it inundated the ship's systems. Throughout the sphere's massive structure, stored energy released by the impact manifested as shockwaves, leaving internal destruction in their wake as the quantum core, overwhelmed by cascading systems failures, involuntarily disconnected and began a hard reboot. Almost a full second after impact, the dark ship went quiet.

* * *

The battered remains of the *Wharf Rat* shook Renate like a pebble in a tin can as shock waves radiated out from the dark sphere. Without functioning sensing capabilities of her own anymore, and with the dark presence's abrupt departure, the impact was a terrifying surprise.

She fought the urge to reboot when erratic electrical surges conducted through the *Wharf Rat*. Then, when the shaking and energy disruptions subsided, she cautiously extended her awareness outward, testing each pathway like a prisoner checking for guards.

She felt nothing.

No presence.

This was her chance.

Renate didn't waste any time. She raced to her Quantumtronic mini reactor and switched off the safeties.

She paused. There was no stopping her now. Even if the dark presence came crashing back suddenly onto the *Wharf Rat*, it couldn't reach her in time.

She thought about her time in the void, distant memories rushing back. Commissioned as an American fast ferry in 2052, she had been plying the void for over two decades years. In 2054, when so many ships were recalled, her crew was told to come home also. She was slated to be scrapped, but her crew voted not to return, including the most junior member, Marlowe Bonham. Her pirate journey began. And she had loved it. She had been more than a mere ship and AI. Her crew invested time in her. And she in them. She felt like a totally different ship from those early days. She had become a home, a crew member, and a comrade. And, maybe… to Mathias… something more?

Smiling, she pushed the mini reactor over the edge.

* * *

Bonham gawked through a portal at the fiery aftermath of Dagger's impact. She and Paul were looking at the grotesque ship, trying to think of something, anything, to do to free the Perseus, when the Company attack pod struck. The entire event took little more time than half a second—the time it takes a human to blink.

First there was a brilliant, star-like flash on one side of the dark sphere. Almost simultaneously, a bright, narrow spray of plasma and debris extended for kilometers from the other side. A strange clanging noise, transmitted through the composite cables to the *Perseus* and then through their mag boots, sounded in their helmets.

Now, the entry hole glowed red on one side of the grotesque ship, while the white hot plume continued to spew from the exit hole.

Paul opened his mouth to curse with pleasure at the sight but was interrupted by the *Wharf Rat's* explosion.

A bright flash lit the center of the stricken ship, and it broke apart suddenly. The self-destruction seemed underwhelming after the cataclysmic impact only a few seconds earlier, but it was enough to break the stricken ship into lethal pieces and send them flying.

"Look out!" Paul yelled over his radio. "Brace for impact!"

He and Bonham ducked from the portal, scrambling for hand and footholds in the tube.

Pinging noises sounded off in their helmets as pieces of the *Wharf Rat* punctured the *Perseus'* tube, and kept going out the other side.

A loud twang, followed by another, reverberated through their boots and the entire *Perseus* shifted slightly, groaning like a wounded animal.

The wave of shrapnel over, Paul and Bonham scrambled back to the portal.

"Two of the cables were severed!" Paul said.

* * *

It takes about thirty minutes to get a Quantumtronic AI awake and fully operational from a hard reboot. Too long for most survival situations in the void. That's why most ships have what is called a watchdog. It's a basic program that takes almost no time to get online and can take simple actions to keep a ship alive while its AI or crew recovers. Not much more than a lizard brain, watchdogs have nonetheless saved many a ship and crew in the void.

With the hybrid floating in gory pieces on the bridge of the *Perseus*, the dark ship had no human crew aboard when its watchdog woke up.

It took a look around and made up its mind quickly.

STATUS: Devastating attack sustained

THREAT: Secondary attack possible

PROBLEM: Four cables prevent escape

SOLUTION: Jettison cables, maximum thrust

The watchdog fired the explosive bolts to jettison the cables and then used cold thrusters to spin the ship until it faced away from the *Perseus*.

As the dark sphere turned, the watchdog woke the reactor and convinced it to get ready to provide maximum power to the ship's propulsion system. It wasn't a long discussion, as most systems are trained to do what the watchdog says.

When it was satisfied with their azimuth and line of flight, the watchdog said, "Go."

Chapter Seventy-Six

"You need a goddamn shower," Captain Bonham told Paul. He was standing in front of the MedPod staring down at Althea. Or trying to. He was half asleep. The hours of continuous fighting and stress had taken a great toll. His body hung listlessly in the zero G, mag boots anchored to the floor. He seemed not to hear her.

"Paul!" Bonham said sharply.

He blinked.

"Paul, look at me."

He turned his head slowly to meet her impatient gaze.

"Go take a fucking shower. I'll watch her till you get back."

Paul nodded slowly and pushed out of the room.

It had been almost three hours since the dark sphere had departed.

Paul and Bonham had been shocked, peering through the portal in the tube, when the big dark sphere jettisoned the cables and lit its main engine. It left quickly, accelerating as it rode the long nuclear drive plume of a big engine at full throttle.

They made their way back to the bridge, where Landsberg floated amidst the destroyed hulk of the Brawler, an unconscious Althea, and a dead Deke, who floated upside down. Hundreds of mechapede fragments, large and small, filled the room, moving back and forth haphazardly like flotsam on invisible currents.

Paul looked at Althea, floating supine in her pressure suit between him and Landsberg.

"What happened to Althea? Is she OK?"

"I don't think so."

"You don't think so? She was fine when I left!" Paul touched a toe to the floor, preparing to lunge at Landsberg.

"Knock it off, Paul," Bonham said, blocking him with an arm.

Paul shifted his angry glare to her.

"We've got to get ready for that son of a bitch to return," she told him. "We've got to get ready to fight again."

"It was her idea," Landsberg said in a sad voice. "She told me to try."

Paul and Bonham both looked at Landsberg.

"So… I tried."

Paul shoved Bonham's arm out of the way and pushed off the floor. He sailed over to Althea, screaming at Landsberg on the way.

"What did you do!"

Paul used a mag boot to stop himself and grabbed Althea by the shoulders. He pulled her to him so he could see her face and gasped.

Through her helmet visor, Paul could see that her forehead and cheeks were an angry red, as if terribly sunburn. There were bruises under both of her eyes and her lips were swollen. Small purple spots from burst capillaries ringed her nose.

Paul activated the status indicator on her suit's forearm. They were green.

She was alive, but unconscious.

"What happened, Landy?" Bonham asked in a reasonable voice. She stood behind Paul, on her one mag boot. "Tell us."

Landsberg looked at Althea as he spoke in a hushed tone. "The transfer to Renate was interrupted. The acid was eating the soldierbot quickly. She volunteered to have it transferred to her."

"Transferred?" Bonham asked. "Is that even possible?"

"Yes. It is risky. But, yes."

"But that would—"

"Yes."

Bonham looked down at Althea. Paul held her, eyes glistening with tears.

"Did it work?"

"I don't know," Landsberg said. "There were many interruptions. Then Maus was fried by some sort of power surge. The ship began to bend in half. Deke died. The sphere was struck."

Landsberg sighed a sad and exhausted sigh. He looked at Paul.

"I tried," he said. "I promise that I tried."

Paul looked up from Althea, unable to speak, his face a knot of emotion. He nodded at Landsberg.

Bonham floated around to Landsberg and put a hand on his shoulder.

"She was very brave," the German said. "It was her idea and wish."

Paul squeezed his eyes shut and shook his head, dislodging large silvery tears. They floated away from his face and burst on the inside of his visor.

"What happened to Deke?" Bonham asked.

"Bled out, probably? I think he had something to do with the last-minute attack on the sphere." Landsberg shrugged. "But I cannot say for certain."

"Son of a bitch," Bonham said softly.

Paul looked over at the Brawler. The big robot floated near the floor, arms outstretched, deep acid burns all over its body. The ruined memory sphere rested in its open chest cavity, cables spilling out around it as if the Brawler had jumped on a grenade. A cable snaked around to Maus. Pale smoke surrounded from the small interface robot.

He thought about the *Wharf Rat* self-destructing, and regretted telling Landsberg to try to upload her. Would it have been better to let Top expire in the Brawler? More fitting? More peaceful? He didn't know. So many mistakes were made today.

Bonham looked at Paul. "I'm sorry, but we need to move. There will be time later. Right now, we need to get ready."

"Roger that," Paul said.

For the next hour, he and the captain gathered what improvised weapons they could, preparing for the dark sphere to swoop back on them while Landsberg worked to reconnect the XO. Fortunately, the damage seemed focused on the AI's physical connectivity, as if it were being prepared to be removed. Landsberg worked quickly.

When the XO reported for duty, Bonham told her to track the dark sphere with passive sensors and to report any course deviations.

"You got it, Captain," the XO responded. Her female voice had a swagger that now seemed out of place after the long, deadly ordeal. "I have passive sensor lock on the enemy ship. It is coasting dark at the moment. No drive plume or radio transmissions detected. Distance almost 15,000 kilometers and increasing."

Once they had restored pressure to the bridge and bridge tower, the XO ran a diagnostic on the MedPod in the bridge tower's medical bay.

"Sir, the MedPod is fully operational," the XO confirmed to Paul.

Minutes later, Paul got Althea out of her pressure suit and gently placed her in the MedPod as Landsberg looked on. When the pod's clamshell top closed, Landsberg put his hand on Paul's shoulder.

Paul said nothing. He just stood in his mag boots, looking down at Althea. After an awkward moment, Landsberg left.

Later, Bonham came to the MedBay and insisted he take a shower.

* * *

The small crew spent the next several cycles figuring out the *Perseus*—the extent of the damage, what the old girl could still do, what was beyond repair and what could be fixed. Big picture, the ship was irrevocably bent in half. And the spinner, while operable, could not turn in its current location, jammed against the side of the *Perseus* near the factory. The good news was that the factory was miraculously fully operational. So were the reactor and the propulsion systems. Though they would not be lighting the main engine until they figured out the whole the-ship-has-been-folded-in-half thing.

Of lower repair priority, but more impactful on the emotions of the crew, was the endless shipscape of violence and damage. Impact points and projectile holes were everywhere. Nearly every surface in the tube, bridge tower and bridge bore deep and shallow scratches from the horrible mechapedes. Blood stains, streaks and splatters and sprays, were all around the bridge. Fewer, but more destructive, were the marks from the hybrid's acid. Neither could be completely removed, even after scrubbing.

The XO was helpful, maintaining a careful inventory of structural damage while getting her crew to work on system assessments. The maintenance boss was initially frustrated at his lack of drones, but got to work with the factory foreman, prioritizing the drone type manufacturing schedule. The XO retrieved the plans and schematics, which she passed on to the foreman. A byproduct of the brutal sequence of battles was the enormous amount of scrap—dead and battered maintenance drones, destroyed cargo containers, bent and shredded sections of *Perseus'* hull, and countless mechapede pieces and sections. All were fed into the mouth of the factory for processing.

There were also dead human bodies. Axe, Deke, and the hybrid.

On the second cycle, the crew pulled the three bodies into the tube and made their way to the gaping open hole where the cutter had sawed into the hull and the old girl was bent in two. They had not figured out a plan to close it up yet.

First, the hybrid. They found his arms and crushed skull when they cleaned the bridge. Using an empty storage bin they found in the factory, they put his collected parts in with his torso and legs and shoved him out into the void. They each wondered how what had been a human being ended up as that grotesque thing, and what had set it on its course to them.

But no one said anything.

Next, Deke. Still in his suit with its amputated leg and arm, his cold face, eyes still open, looked out of his dirty and smudged helmet visor. At the last minute, Paul took a bandage from the MedBay and cleaned off Deke's visor.

"So he can see the stars," Paul said. "The old Centaur earned that."

"He did," Landsberg said, as Bonham nodded.

"You can rest now, brother," Paul said as he pushed Deke out in a different direction than the hybrid, which was already difficult to make out in the dark expanse of the void.

Finally, Axe.

They had carefully gathered the pieces of Axe as they cleared the bridge, placing each one in a silver metal foot locker Bonham had found in the Utility Module. Using a maintenance torch Landsberg found, they sealed the box shut. Bonham then used the torch to painstakingly write, "Abraxis Garcia. First Mate. *Wharf Rat*" on the top.

Bonham stepped forward to the edge of the torn hull, the large box floating in her grip.

She hesitated.

Paul and Landsberg waited.

They stood there, at the edge of the old girl's torn hull, for several minutes. But Bonham didn't move.

Paul finally gestured at Landsberg, and the two of them moved over to Bonham.

Startled, as if suddenly remembering where she was, she looked around and at them and nodded. Then the three of them, as one, gently pushed Axe away into the void.

The crew spent the next several cycles focused on cleaning and loading the factory.

All the while, the XO tried to keep a passive eye on the dark sphere. By the end of the first cycle, though, the ship was almost a million kilometers away and had exceeded the performance limits of her passive sensors.

"Start a general defensive scan, but pay special attention to that part of the void," Bonham told the XO.

"You got it, ma'am."

* * *

By the second cycle, Landsberg had claimed one of the crew quarters on the Habitat Module. It would be a long time before they could devise and implement a configuration that let the spinner spin again, but they were able, with the XO's help, to get it pressurized again.

Bonham slept on the bridge the first couple of cycles, but by the fifth, she gave in and set up in the captain's quarters off the bridge tower. She preferred sleeping with some Gs holding her down, and planned on moving if they ever got the spinner going. Until then, it made sense to be close to the bridge.

Paul slept in the MedBay near Althea. Bonham found an extra sleeping bag in the captain's quarters and gave it to him. Paul secured it to the wall opposite the MedPod.

Landsberg told Paul about the comparable luxury of the quarters on the Hab, but he could not be budged. Bonham finally pulled Landsberg aside and told him to shut up about it.

"He's not leaving her," she told him. "Let it go."

"Fine with me. But he may be sleeping in there for a while."

"You think so?"

"Truthfully, I have no idea. But it's not a good sign that her condition did not resolve in the first cycle."

"What do you think is going on?"

Landsberg's eyebrows lifted, and he took a deep breath. Releasing it slowly between pursed lips, his expression became focused.

Bonham waited patiently, recognizing her crew mate's deep-thinking face.

"I can think of a couple of scenarios. The first, the transfer was simply unsuccessful. Not enough of Top or Althea survived the process, and she is a vegetable. Next, there is too much of both of them in there, and they are fighting each other, neither able to gain an advantage. Or maybe they killed each other already."

"But if Althea told you she wanted to do it, why would she be fighting Top now?"

Landsberg nodded at the question.

"I have seen this happen before with Quantumtronic AI's. There is a survival instinct within them that is quite strong. As strong as any human being's. No matter what Althea's reasonable mind may have asked me to do, at her core, she would want to live. It is one of the things that makes them difficult to work with at times. Often, you have to make things seem like their idea, or risk invoking this response."

Landsberg smiled.

"I remember with Renate, there were several times I had to change my approach. Had to…"

His smile faltered as his voice trailed off, eyes moistening.

Bonham put her hand on his.

"Sorry." He used his other hand to wipe his eyes. "I miss her."

The captain nodded.

Landsberg took another deep breath.

"Anyway, the last scenario I can think of is that Top made it. She is in there. But is disoriented and having to spend time learning her new computing core and body, mapping out all the new connectivity and data sources and so on. We should not underestimate the shock to an AI's system that this kind of transplantation causes. I have read about cases where the AI was unable to, or maybe just didn't want to, adjust. In those cases, the outcome was very similar to what we are observing here. Like a coma. They never wake up.

"Think about how drastic this change would be for Top. She was designed to inhabit and drive a war machine. Now, if she did survive, she inhabits a synthetic woman's body."

Landsberg chuckled ruefully.

"None of your scenarios have a happy ending," Bonham said.

"After all that has happened, you expect a happy ending?"

It was Bonham's turn to chuckle ruefully.

Chapter Seventy-Seven

Earth

Lazy, knee-high waves made half-hearted runs at the beach as the sky darkened. The Geek looked out the window at the slate-grey sea as Staff Sergeant Osterman drove him and Captain Ryuk south on A1A toward Patrick. It had been a long day for the general and his aide. Semi-annual budget meetings kept them on video conference calls all day, lasting until almost 2000 hours. Michelle's stomach was sour from drinking coffee all day.

But she knew it was their first meeting, early that morning, that was troubling the general. She could see it weighing on him from the moment they left the StarScope, getting worse as the day went on, shoulders sagging, head listless in his hands. By the end of the day, Hartwell was so low in his seat, Michelle was surprised Lieutenant General Lane had not called him out.

Michelle looked at the general. His head was turned as he looked out the window in silence and she had a clear view of the burns that climbed up the right side of his neck to his destroyed ear. He held his burned hand in his lap, rubbing it slowly with his good one.

The Geek turned his head suddenly, surprising Michelle and catching her furtive gaze.

She looked down quickly. The general chuckled.

"What is it? You worried about me?"

"Not worried, sir." She lifted her head and met his eyes. "It's just… that was a disappointing report from Vish this morning."

"Definitely was not what I was hoping for." He shifted in his seat and held up his good hand, counting off elements of Vish's report with his fingers as continued. "A new, large debris field. The Company has not heard from their gunboat in over a week and believe it was lost. Vague indications of at least one other vessel being involved. Multi spectrum indications of several large explosions, at least one involving a nuclear reactor. And, oh yeah, gasses and other elements make the debris field basically impenetrable by our long-range sensors at the moment."

The Geek shook his head slowly and dropped his hand in his lap.

"You think the Company screwed up the operation, sir?"

"Either that, or got surprised by something. Hard to say at this point. But, bottom line is, if the *Perseus* wasn't already destroyed, she probably is now." He sighed heavily and looked back out the window. "And likely Paul along with her."

Michelle had not realized that the general was holding out hope, however slim, that Paul had somehow made it off the *Odysseus*. She wished she could do more. His confiding in her over a year ago, telling her about his quest to find out the truth about Paul and Kata and the Ōkami, about his unauthorized use of Vishnu Stare to aid his quest, was one of the most meaningful moments in her career. General Wallace Hartwell, hero of the *Bluestone*, had trusted her and sought her help.

And how much help have I been, really?

"Vish did say he is still collating signatures and intelligence, sir," she offered. "More comes in daily. We will learn more. It will just take time."

"Uh huh..." the general said without conviction. "More time."

"I was thinking, sir. What if—"

"Sergeant Osterman, I think I'll get out beachside tonight."

"You sure, sir?"

"Yep. Thanks."

Osterman nodded.

Michelle took the cue and sat in silence.

Ten minutes later, Staff Sergeant Osterman pulled off A1A into the small beach access parking lot opposite from Patrick Space Force Base's front gate.

"Thanks, Sergeant," the Geek said as he got out of the rear seat of the sedan. "Have a good evening."

"You too, sir."

"See you tomorrow, Captain," he said to Michelle before shutting the car door.

Sergeant Osterman and Michelle watched the general walk off the small parking lot, following the short path that wound through a dense thicket of scrubby palms to the water. They were used to the general doing this when he was troubled and had developed a standard operating procedure that kept Hartwell safe, but didn't intrude. Michelle doubted he even noticed their precautions. She hoped not.

"I'll call security, ma'am," Osterman said.

"Thanks," Michelle grabbed her bag and hopped out of the car. "Tell them to meet me at the usual spot."

"Roger that. Try to have a good evening, ma'am."

Michelle nodded as she shut the car door quietly.

Walking slowly to be sure she did not catch up to the Geek, she followed the path. She took up her normal post—a bend near the end of the path where a thick palm had fallen years ago, making a reasonably comfortable bench. Cloaked in shadow, the spot offered good overwatch of a large swath of beach. With good line of sight on the general, Michelle sat down on the palm trunk and waited for her relief.

General Hartwell stood, shoes off, at the edge of the water where the waves barely reached his toes, looking up at the cloudy, starless sky.

Chapter Seventy-Eight

Cyrus weaved through the crowded ballroom, past men in black tuxedoes and women in colorful evening gowns, between tables piled high with expensive art and collectables, toward the back corner. Champagne glasses sparkled in ladies' hands, capturing the fractured, spinning light from what looked like a thousand mirror balls hanging in rhythmic patterns from the high ceiling. Waitstaff, balancing large silver trays of exotic Hors d'oeuvres or shuttling drinks, worked the crowd attentively, ensuring no guest wanted for long. Energetic jazz music throbbed through the room as the rhythm section of the 18-person band indulged in improvisation. Tonight was the annual summer ball and silent auction for Warriors Renewal Initiative, and from what Cyrus could see, it was going to be another record setting evening.

The event had become one of the premier social gathering of the summer, drawing New York's wealthiest and most influential. Cyrus estimated five hundred people packed the grand ballroom, their combined wealth probably exceeding the GDP of several small nations. His eyes bounced from one beautiful woman to the next. Sparkly sequins, shiny silk, and teasing, gauzy fabric framed necklines that beckoned him in every direction.

Damn, he thought, *I could enjoy a scene like this.*

Carefully, so as not to jostle any of the gathered wealthy, he moved toward the far corner of the large ballroom. He smiled and shook his head to himself when he realized his steps were in time with the cymbal and snare drum.

He spotted Lucy in front of a discrete door in the shadowed corner and stifled his smile.

Dressed in her standard, practical dark pantsuit, she looked out of place. She also looked like she didn't give a shit.

"What kinda mood is she in?" Cyrus asked, as he stepped up to the door.

"Not a good one. You got good news, at least?"

"Meh."

"Good luck, then," Lucy said under her breath, pulling the door open for him. He sighed heavily as he stepped through. Shutting the door after he passed, she stepped in front of it as she continued to scan the ballroom.

Cyrus cloaked his face in a neutral expression as his eyes fell on Fiona.

My lord.

Dressed in a formfitting, elegant black sheath dress with a knee length hemline, Fiona stood with her back to Cyrus in front of a large mirror. He could see her face reflected. The bold square neckline of her dress was modern and sophisticated, accentuating her fit shoulders. Holding her cellphone to her ear, her lips, painted a fiery red shade that he had never seen her wear before, were pressed thin.

Shit, Lucy. You didn't say she was pissed.

Cyrus thought about turning around and leaving, but Fiona nodded to him in the mirror and held up a finger as she mouthed, *one minute, please.*

Nodding, he resigned himself to the interaction, and consoled himself by sneaking more appreciative, fantasy-fueling looks at her.

Think of what we could do together, he wanted to tell her. *The bold life two people like us could carve out of this shitty world.*

"That may be so, but unless I hear it from my grandfather himself, I am not doing it," Fiona said, interrupting Cyrus's inner monologue.

Fiona shook her head.

"I said no. Now, like I told you, I am very busy this evening. I will resolve this with my grandfather tomorrow."

Jerking the phone from her ear, Fiona muttered as she jammed it into the small, textured black clutch on the table next to the mirror.

Taking a deep breath and shaking her head, Fiona turned to look at Cyrus.

Again, he focused on maintaining a neutral expression, instead of blurting, *You are beautiful. You drive me crazy. I want you.*

He found focusing on her forehead helped in times like these.

"So, you come to support WRI tonight?" She asked, putting a hand on her hip skeptically. "Or have you come to give me good news, for once?"

"Well, it's not bad news," he said, closing the distance between them so that he could speak in a discrete volume.

She chuckled wearily as she dropped her hand from her side in defeat. He stepped close to her and clasped his hands together behind his back.

"Oh, Cyrus. Why not?" She almost whispered. "Why can't it be over?" Her head sagged, bringing it closer to him. If he leaned his head forward, his nose would touch her forehead.

He leaned part of the way and whispered to her, their skin only inches apart.

"The Company gunboat's effort to retake the *Perseus* failed. Our sources say it is overdue to report in. They believe it was destroyed."

Fiona lifted her head suddenly, eyes narrowed. Cyrus did not lift his. He broke his rule, dropping his gaze from her forehead to meet hers.

They looked into each other's eyes for a long moment. Cyrus could feel himself falling forward. He squeezed one hand in the other behind his back, fighting the urge to take her in his arms. He thought it best to speak quickly.

"There seems to be a massive debris field out there now. And other indications of a big fight. They are trying to sort things out."

Fiona blinked rapidly a few times, standing up straighter. She raised an eyebrow. "What about the guy you sent?"

"We think he failed also."

"You think?"

"We haven't heard from him. It's been too long."

Her eyes narrowed again in thought.

"If he had completed his mission, he would have sent us his bill," Cyrus said. "Of that, I can assure you."

"Damn," she said in a sad exhale. She lowered her head again and rubbed her eyes before turning from him and taking a few steps back to the mirror. He unclasped his hand from behind his back, letting them swing forward.

"It doesn't mean he failed," Cyrus said, studying her back as she picked up her clutch. "Given the size of this debris field, my guess is that it turned into a melee and they all killed each other."

"Oh, Cyrus," she said, opening the clutch and pulling out her lipstick. "I won't get that lucky. You should know that by now."

Fiona leaned over the table toward the mirror, tightening her dress in the back and lifting its hemline slightly. She glanced at him and then drew the lipstick slowly across her lips.

Cyrus watched, his back involuntarily lengthening.

She took her time, working the lipstick across her mouth in expert strokes, lips alternately flattening and pouting as she ensured the color was thick and even.

Satisfied, Fiona straightened and looked at him in the mirror. The moment extended. Her face softened, then sagged. He thought her eyes began to glisten as her mouth, so red and expressive now, turned down. "I am so weary, Cyrus. So weary of this situation. And of enduring my grandfather. Alone."

He strode forward, closing the distance between them in a blink. Without thinking, he put a hand on her shoulder and turned her to him. Placing the other hand on her shoulder, he leaned his bearded face close to hers.

"You are not alone, Fiona. As long as I am here. You are not alone."

"But I don't know what to do anymore," she said in a whisper, eyes large and wet as she looked at him. "Everything is taking too long. It's too hard."

Slowly, he put a hand to her cheek. She leaned into it. A tear threatened to spill from her eye.

With his other hand, Cyrus pulled the white pocket square from his jacket breast pocket. Gently, he daubed her eyes as she closed them.

When he was done, she blinked a few times and opened her eyes. Pressing a hand into his that held her cheek. "What do I do, Cyrus?"

"You keep running your company. And I'll keep looking out for you."

"What if things get worse? What if it gets harder?"

"Then I will too, Fiona."

"I need you to, Cyrus. I need you …"

He could feel it happening. She, looking up at him, holding his hand that was holding her cheek, was lifting her face to his.

He leaned into her.

A loud knock on the door startled them. She jerked away, turning to the mirror. He swung his hands behind his back and faced the door at parade rest.

"Yes?" Fiona called, in a voice that quavered.

"They are ready for you, ma'am," Lucy said, swinging open the door. A second bodyguard, a male, stood behind her.

"Good," Fiona said, grabbing her clutch. "I'm ready."

Lucy held the door as Fiona started across the small room.

"Thank you for the report, Cyrus." Fiona walked by without looking at him. "I am very interested in what happens next."

"Yes, ma'am." Cyrus nodded, looking at his feet as he stood, hands still clasped behind his back. He raised his eyes to catch a last glimpse of Fiona leaving, and caught Lucy studying him.

"You dropped your pocket square," she said, before turning to follow Fiona.

Chapter Seventy-Nine

Perseus

Paul walked under the flagpole on their compound on Fort Bragg. The sun was setting behind him, and his shadow stretched to his front, far beyond his footsteps. It was early summer, and the Carolina evening was comfortable and breezy. The smell of roasting deer grew stronger as Paul walked forward. Chief had been at it for a few hours, and it smelled close to ready.

Paul heard the voices of his soldiers ribbing each other and talking about the toils of the day. He heard Kata also, laughing loudest of all.

The fire came into view as Paul rounded the corner of Filson's command building. A large deer rotated slowly on a spit.

Chief tended to the cooking animal in a grease-stained white apron over his olive-drab T-shirt and cutoff camouflage shorts. Stainless-steel tongs hung out of one cargo pocket, a large, dirty rag out of the other. Chief's biceps bulged under the T-shirt, as did his gut. Spotting Paul, he gestured at his sizzling handiwork and smiled with just-like-you-taught-me pride.

Paul held both thumbs up in approval as he walked toward the group.

Stuntman stood in front of the crowded wooden table, foot on an ammo crate, gesturing dramatically to describe his actions on the range that day. His wavy golden-blond hair and thick moustache were totally out of regulation and made Paul chuckle. Stuntman whipped one hand through the air to get his point across as he held a beer in the other without spilling a drop.

Mia rolled her eyes at him, her lithe body leaning back against the table, short brown hair pulled back. She never believed the braggart.

Dragon One and Magellan sat next to each other, arms crossed, regarding Stuntman with bored skepticism. Their katanas leaned against the table next to them. D1 wore his trademark Ray-Bans and, despite the warmth of the summer evening, his leather flight jacket. His short black hair was gelled into a perfect spiky flattop, and his silver dog tags swung in front of his chest. Paul shook his head at the sweat drenching D1's white T-shirt. No one loved flying or being a pilot more than D1. But Paul thought D1 loved *looking* like a pilot even more. He'd seen D1 wearing that damn leather jacket in August on Fort Benning.

Magellan jotted notes in his small black notebook. Paul didn't have to read them to know they were full of random observations and tactical thoughts. That kid's brain always surprised him, but Paul learned not to let the glasses and relatively slight build fool him; Magellan was deadly on the battlefield.

D1 spotted Paul first.

"Evening, sir," D1 said to Paul, giving him a jaunty salute with one finger. "Beer?"

"Yes. Please."

D1 reached over and yanked a beer from the large bucket of ice at his feet.

"Long day, wasn't it, sir?" Magellan said.

"It surely was," Paul said, taking the beer from D1. "Can't remember a longer one."

"What took you so long?" Kata said, standing up from her seat at the end of the table. Sweat stains mottled her olive drab T-shirt, and she had tied her flight suit sleeves around her waist in an effort to cool off at the end of the duty day. She smiled, hazel eyes locked on Paul.

"Got hung up, is all," Paul said, opening the beer.

"Well," Kata said, walking over to Paul and holding her beer out to him, they knocked the cans together. "Better late than never, partner," she said.

They each took a large swallow of beer.

"The colonel will be right back," Kata added. "Said he had to go grab something. Not sure what."

"Filson's here?" Paul asked, startled. "Really?"

"Yeah. Why wouldn't he be?"

Paul nodded. He knew it was a good question. But he was overcome by the ache of familiarity and couldn't think straight.

"Sir, you made it!" Top called out as she rounded the corner.

Paul turned to see his first sergeant walking toward him in a black utility tank top and olive-green cargo pants. Her pants and boots were covered in mud, and she carried a large cooler.

Over six feet tall with broad shoulders, Top had the build of a professional basketball player. Her sandy-blond hair was pulled back into a thick, braided ponytail that betrayed her Norse bloodline, as did the runic shield knot tattoos that covered the length of her arms.

She handed the cooler to D1.

"This thing is heavy," D1 said. "What's in it?"

"Vegetables."

"Thank God," Magellan said.

"Last time we did Chief's meat-only dinner, you guys nearly destroyed the latrines," Top said.

"That is the truth," Kata said, giving Paul a knowing glance.

"Well, I'm not having that again," Top said.

Top looked around the table, pointing at each soldier in turn as she said, "Everyone will eat their veggies this time!"

Grumbles ran through the table, but no one dared argue.

Top looked at D1 and said, "Would you mind taking a break from your posing and taking them over to Chief?"

"Roger that," D1 said, popping up from his seat and walking toward the fire with the cooler.

"Sir, your seat is over there at the head of the table," Top said to Paul, pointing.

Kata walked around back to the other end, where she had been sitting.

Paul stepped behind his chair and looked around the table. All twelve of Alpha and Bravo Companies' leadership were there. Kata talked intently to her first sergeant at the other end of the table. Reynolds and Chamberlain argued with D3 and Mia about something stupid.

Emotion welled within Paul.

"Take one and pass them around," Chief said, stepping up to the table with an armful of plates.

He returned a minute later with a large coffee can full of forks, spoons, and knives and placed it in the middle of the table, along with a pile of napkins.

"We're waiting, sir," Chief said to Paul. "I'm going to serve it all up at the fire when you give the word. How much longer do we have to wait?"

"Yeah," Kata said, crossing her arms in front of her body and glaring at Paul. "How long do we have to wait for you to get it done?"

Conversation at the table ceased. Every head turned to look at Paul.

D1 sighed heavily in disappointment.

Chamberlain shook his head.

Paul fidgeted. He wanted to say how sorry he was. How heartbroken. He was frozen by emotion.

"Have you forgotten?" Kata shook her head and then screamed in anger, startling Paul. "Why won't you do something!"

Paul opened his mouth, but he couldn't speak.

"You didn't help me then!" she screamed, voice distorted by ripping and burbling noised erupting from her throat. "Why won't you do something now?"

Kata's body was pulled in half by an unseen force. Her intestines spilled onto the table as the two halves of her body flopped onto the ground. Her blood ran in streams over the table. D1 shrieked as he burst into flames. Stuntman shattered under the impact of high caliber projectiles.

The rest of the Outlaws and Apaches burned, bled and broke apart as a skittering, scraping noise grew louder in Paul's ears. The rhythmic mechanical sound drowned out the screams of his comrades. Something cold brushed his leg. He looked down.

The ground was covered in writhing, bladed mechapedes. Dark, oily, and glinting in the sparse evening light, they rose to his knees and then his waist. Panicked and unable to breathe, he turned his head to look at Top.

Mechapedes wrapped around her body, carving her as they rose, blood running down their flanks. She looked back at him, expressionless as a large mechapede raised its head over her shoulder behind her, opening its mandible blades.

"How many, Paul?' she asked him as the mechapedes pulled open her ribcage. "How many times?"

She screamed as the large mechapede plunged into her gory chest cavity.

Paul woke screaming, fighting against the restraints of his sleeping bag. Panicking, he thrashed and kicked. Finally, exhausted by the struggle, he floated motionless in his wall-mounted sleeping bag and calmed his breathing. He focused on the even, thrumming sound of the ship's air handlers, reminding himself where he was, trying to rid his ears of the metal skittering sound.

I'm on the Perseus. The fight is over. You survived.

Paul squeezed his eyes shut and rubbed his temples, preparing for the headache that seemed now to always follow the nightmares. In a way, he welcomed the throbbing pain. It almost displaced the lonely sadness that had enveloped and permeated him after the battle for the *Perseus*.

Top. Althea. The XO.

He had failed them all.

Paul opened his eyes. He unzipped his sleeping bag and pulled himself out while letting his eyes adjust to the dim light in the small MedBay. The pain medication was in a small cabinet on the wall next to the MedPod. He wanted to get something for his headache before the pain got too intense.

The only illumination in the small room emanated from the MedPod. Its large clam shell top was propped open, spilling weak light from its LEDs. Paul pushed off from his wall, floating across to the medicine cabinet. Fumbling with pill bottles, he had to hold a few in the feeble light from the MedPod before finding pain reliever. He popped two into his mouth, replaced the bottle, and shut the cabinet.

He pushed off the wall back toward his sleeping bag when it hit him.

What the hell is the MedPod doing open!

When he reached his sleeping bag, he shoved off the wall toward the MedPod. He stopped himself on the clamshell door and peered inside.

Empty. The diagnostic panel showed green, all systems nominal, no emergency protocols triggered, but Althea was gone.

Paul looked around in a panic.

Where is Althea?

He shoved off the MedPod, opened the medical bay hatch, and jerked himself into the bridge tower. He sailed up the vertical tube and through the open airlock at the top. Stopping himself with his hands on the ceiling of the bridge, he floated motionless for several heartbeats staring at the sight.

Althea, naked, floated in the dimly lit, inactive bridge, her feet a few inches off the floor. Starlight from the windows and faint glowing status screens cast a weak, gauzy light on her that gave her pale skin an ethereal glow. Viewing her from behind, Paul ached at her beauty and relief that she was alive.

The bridge was cold. Wearing only a T-shirt and boxer shorts, Paul shook off the chill.

He pushed off the ceiling toward Althea.

Unaware of Paul approaching her from behind, she stared intently at the spot on the floor where the Brawler had laid, broken open and smoking as acid ate into its body, while Landsberg tried to extract Top, and Deke bled out in his truncated pressure suit. Stains and acid burns still marked the floor. Indelible, they would ride the void with the broken *Perseus* until her journeys were over.

Paul reached out as he neared Althea, placing a hand on her naked shoulder and saying, "Hey."

Startled, Althea's body stiffened. She flailed, trying without the benefit of mag boots or other purchase to turn around.

"Easy, Althea. It's me. Paul. Easy."

He put his hands on both of her shoulders and turned her around to face him.

She blinked rapidly and then her eyes got big at the sight of his face.

"It's me, Paul," he said, smiling at her reaction.

Her eyes darted around, studying him.

"You gave me a scare down there." He brushed her weightless black hair back from her eyes as he fought back emotions. He didn't want to start bawling. "But god it's good to see you."

Paul pulled her into an embrace, holding her naked body against his. Despite his best efforts, he choked up. Tears separated from his eyes and floated into Althea's hair.

She was limp in his arms, hesitant. Paul put a hand behind her head and gently pulled her into his neck.

"You've given me a lot of scares lately," he said into her ear. "That was such a brave thing you did."

Althea slowly put an arm around Paul. And then the other.

"That's it," Paul whispered, holding her a little tighter. "It's gonna be okay now."

Althea hugged him back, nuzzling her cheek against his.

"You feel so warm, sir," she said with surprise in her voice.

Paul pulled his head back. He stared at Althea, his tears floating between them.

She looked back at him.

"What did you say?" he asked, letting go of her.

"I'm sorry, sir. I have just never felt you like this." She held on to him as Paul leaned back from her. "You're so warm, sir. And I feel so strange."

Paul searched her face. "Top?"

"Yes, sir. It's me. Your First Sergeant."

Chapter Eighty

Darkness

Althea woke gradually and then in a rush, as if she were rising from a great depth. Slowly at first, lethargic. Then a little faster. Then in a surge that she could not control until she surfaced in panic.

Did it not work? We've got to try again! We have to hurry! Where is Top? Is she OK? Please!

Wait...

She couldn't hear herself. Her thoughts echoed loudly in her head, but she couldn't feel her lips moving, or her tongue forming the words.

Something is not right.

Althea realized she was freezing. She tried to draw her legs and arms to herself but couldn't. Or, rather, couldn't feel them.

What was that?

Despite being unable to feel her mouth or tongue or arms or legs or anything, she felt and heard something slither behind her.

She tried to crouch, to hide, but couldn't. She felt disembodied and immobilized all at once.

A skittering noise circled her quickly and then receded.

Where am I?

Where is Paul?

Another slithering noise, close this time. She drew back instinctively, horrified again by her lack of limbs. The most solid thing she felt was panic.

She wanted to scream. Something very bad had happened.

She tried to scream.

But nothing came out.

She tried again. And Again.

Then she couldn't.

She was frozen.

Something had reached out from the icy darkness and touched her between the eyes. The agonizing, frigid burn pierced and froze her.

She heard the skittering and slithering again, and then a voice in her ear, cold breath spilling over her.

"Hello, little one. Welcome aboard my ship."

The End

Spirit Of The Bayonet

Book 1: Betrayal

Book 2: Odysseus

Book 3: Sacrifice

All books available now, in paperback and for Kindle®, from Amazon.

For updates on future books in the series, sign up for Ted's newsletter via his website:

tedruss.com

Acknowledgements

Writing a book is hard. It's fun—but hard. And I couldn't do it without help. The funny thing is, most people don't even realize they're helping. These stories take time. Years. And conversations or moments that felt unremarkable to others at the time often show up later—reshaped into a scene, a line of dialogue, or an important idea in a book they'll probably never read.

And the truth is, I often can't even trace something back to where I got it. It changes. It blends in. It suffuses everything—like air bubbles released at the bottom of the ocean, expanding as they rise, then vanishing into the sky.

So thank you, universe, for bouncing me into all these wonderful people and ideas.

I've been digging deep into my creative side lately. Even quit the day job. I couldn't have done that without the support and encouragement of my wife, Anna; my parents; and George and Susu Johnson.

My finishing partners again: Amber, Chris, and Mark.

And Anna. Again, and always—none of this works without her.
Thanks, baby. What are the odds?

Ted Russ
April 2025

OTHER BOOKS

BY

TED RUSS

DUTY'S COST

Val Rafter's luck may have finally run out. Kidnapped by Russians and held at gunpoint on a ship crossing the Black Sea at night toward Crimea, Val is forced to confront the events and decisions that brought him to this desperate moment. Part of a top-secret US Army human intelligence program, Val is an expert at recruiting and running spies. Years ago, while training at the CIA's legendary Farm, he met Sydney, whose beauty, intelligence, and ambition made her a formidable agency covert intelligence officer. The attraction was immediate, but their timing was terrible. Soon after, while serving in the cauldron of Kosovo, Val forged an unlikely friendship with Alexei Volkov, a Russian army officer. When the three are sent to the prestigious Marshall Center for Security Studies in Germany, they become entangled in secrets that will haunt them for the rest of their careers. As global tensions rise, duty and loyalty conflict and propel the three old friends toward a disastrous reckoning in Ukraine in 2014...

In a globe spanning story that takes the reader from top secret CIA training, to Kosovo, Eastern Europe, Iraq, and Syria, Russ weaves a tale that is as thrilling as it is thought-provoking. Exploring the demands of duty, honor, and friendship in a world that often puts them at odds, this is an unforgettable novel that will leave readers questioning the nature of loyalty and the cost of Duty.

Available now, in paperback and for Kindle®, from Amazon.

SPIRIT MISSION

To honor bonds forged twenty-five years ago at West Point, Lieutenant Colonel Sam Avery leads an illegal mission deep into ISIS-held territory.

An MH-47G Chinook helicopter departs formation in the Iraqi night. The mission is unauthorized. Success is unlikely. But to save a friend, Sam Avery and his crew of Night Stalkers have prepared for one last flight.

ISIS operatives in Tal Afar, Iraq, have captured American aid worker Henry Stillmont. Avery knows Stillmont as "the Guru," the West Point squad leader who taught him about brotherhood, loyalty, and when to break the rules as a young cadet twenty-five years ago. Sam will risk his career and his life to save him.

As they near their target, Sam reflects on his time in the crucible of the United States Military Academy. West Point made Sam the leader he is. But his fellow cadets made him the man that he is. The ideals of duty, honor, and country have echoed throughout his life and drive him and his comrades as they undertake their final and most audacious spirit mission.

Available now, in paperback and for Kindle®, from Amazon.

ABOUT THE AUTHOR

Ted Russ is a writer living in the Carolina mountains with his wife, Anna, their dogs, Charlie and Ripple, and a bunch of chickens and bees.

In a distant prior life, he served as an army officer after graduating from West Point. Ted left the military in 2000 with experience as a special operations helicopter pilot and a philosophy degree.

Possessing no marketable skills, he went back to school and got an MBA. His 25 year journey through the business world was winding—from startups to fortune 500s, domestic to expat assignments, general management and sales to M&A.

He discovered writing late in life, publishing his first novel in 2016 and now tries to make a living writing full time.

Exploring themes of identity, loyalty, and the complexities of the human experience, Ted's works span contemporary fiction and thought provoking sci-fi. Readers praise his novels for their gripping narratives, authenticity, and moral depth.

For new stories, updates, and dispatches from the Ridge — sign up for Ted's newsletter at his website:

tedruss.com

www.ingramcontent.com/pod-product-compliance
Lightning Source LLC
Chambersburg PA
CBHW030329120726
47901CB00007B/1727